VENOM & VENGEANCE

BOOK TWO

THE SHATTERED SOURCE SERIES

HANNAH DANIELLE

HD PUBLISHING LLC

Sensitivity read conducted by Jamecia Bellamy
Line edits by K.F. Starfell
Copy edits by Norma Gambini
Internal portrait art by @emmabovel
Cover design by Hannah Danielle and K.F. Starfell

HD Publishing
ISBN: 9798985751635, 9798985751642

CONTENT WARNINGS

Torture
Restrained against will
Grief after child loss
Substance abuse
Sexually explicit content
Violence
Fire
Genocide
Blood
Acting under duress
Mention of attempted self-harm
Explicit language
Themes of human trafficking (mentioned in a memory)
Panic attacks

CHAPTER 1
AURELIA

Thick ropes of dread coiled between my ribs and pulled taut, caging my lungs as I roiled against the familiar blackness. Just as every time I had been forced to endure this nightmare, this in-between space, I lay flat on my back, ropes of dark magic binding my limbs to a stone surface.

I must have drifted off. I had stopped hiking to rest my aching legs. I had only needed a moment. *Just a moment* to gather my exhaustion. I had done so well at avoiding sleep, fighting to remain conscious.

Until now.

A frigid kind of dread sluiced through my core as the weight of reality settled in. The pain of dredging through another endless forest was nothing compared to the agony I was about to endure. Bile rose in my throat as bitter terror coated my tongue. The stench of my own blood in this space still burned my nostrils from the last time I had fallen victim to this nightmarish dreamscape.

How was he doing it? How could he pull me into that space? Touch me, make me bleed while my body lay behind in that forest?

The soft pad of the false king's footsteps sounded in the distance, shaking my frantic train of thought and alerting me to his presence as he drew nearer. The last time, it hadn't just been Ragnor. He'd somehow brought Oberin with him, the soulless emissary to his courts and apparent torture master.

Much to my miserable surprise.

Not only could Ragnor taunt me here, but he had the ability to bring others. Use the will of them to break me.

Fuck that.

It would take more than knife wounds to shatter my resolve after what he'd done to make the realm suffer. After what Celvaria's citizens had had to endure because of his actions.

My carelessness.

That familiar pang of guilt threatened to choke me, but I swallowed it, focusing my thoughts on the dire circumstances at hand.

Surviving it was simply a matter of endurance, and I would need all my mental faculties to withstand this place. I could do nothing to defend myself here, as I was barely a whisper of my former power. My soul—torn from my body to hover here only until I blacked out from the pain. My consciousness—sent back to my reality with physical evidence of Oberin's wrath.

Somehow his blade had not only scarred my mind, but my flesh as well. The wicked magic of this source-damned place was not like any I'd ever seen. Oberin's vile form of torture was the precise reason I had done my best to evade sleep so desperately for the past weeks, trying to avoid any more hideous scars to remind me of the time I had spent in the dreamscape.

But I'd failed. I'd fallen asleep by that river with my back pressed up against a great oak tree. The sound of the wind through the leaves had lulled me into unconsciousness.

That was all it had taken for Ragnor to reach me again.

Only a few stiff moments passed before one set of footsteps turned to two separate beats echoing off the endless black walls of the dreamscape. I ground my teeth against icy panic as it flushed my neck. My eyes stretched wide, and my nostrils flared through quick and shallow breaths before I found the pair of gruesome males in the shadows.

"You've been hiding from me, Dove," Ragnor crooned. The cold slither of his voice moved over my skin like frigid water, raising gooseflesh along the way.

The false king's silhouette sharpened as a faint glowing light burning behind him illuminated the nightmare space enough to give me a clear view of the males. Oberin stood at his shoulder, digging at the grime under his fingernails with the tip of a blackened blade. The healing wound on my stomach from our last encounter twinged at the sight of the poisonous weapon, and I ground my teeth against the flutter of fear-twisted rage as its wings beat against my ribs.

"Not well enough, it seems," I hissed through gritted teeth, the resolve under my voice surprising considering the trembling beginning in my hands.

I clenched my fists against swelling panic, its ferocity moving through my veins at an alarming pace.

"No. Not well enough." Ragnor stopped near my head and trailed a cool finger along my cheek, his gaze predatory as it roamed the length of my body.

I shuddered at the contact, its intimacy causing a curl of nausea low in my core, and I fought the urge to flinch away as a crawl of disgust moved over my exposed skin. I could not refrain from jerking my chin away from his grasp, my breaths heaving through flared nostrils.

"You seem fatigued. Not sleeping well?" Ragnor taunted, a flare in his obsidian eyes.

Those eyes had once been so bright, an emerald to rival that of any other creation fae's.

"*Fuck off,*" I spat as Oberin rounded the table to stand on my other side.

A frenzy crept over my breastbone as the torture master drew closer, but the invisible bindings held firm. I could not move so much as an inch.

I kept my attention on Ragnor, refusing to allow my attention to fall on the dark blade Oberin twirled between his long fingers. The blackened weapon had been touched by corrupted source magic. I had felt it in every wound, every trail of the poisoned iron as it had severed my flesh.

I would know that cursed magic anywhere. It was not something I would have the privilege of forgetting in this life, as much as many of my other memories still evaded me.

The corner of Ragnor's full mouth twitched in amusement, the expression only flaring a vile kind of fury in my core. I blew a heated breath through my nostrils and ground my teeth further against the rage boiling in my blood.

The intensity of the false king's pitted gaze grew too heavy to bear, and I broke eye contact. My attention caught on the open neck Ragnor's tunic. This close, even in the dimly lit space, the darkened veins of deadly poison stood out against his pallid skin. Those spidery veins crawled along his pale chest, stretching just over the line of his collarbones like gnarled, twisting roots.

How prevalent had they been before? They seemed darker now. Were they getting worse? Was the source draining him faster somehow? Unless my memory was deceiving me, the veins stemming from the shard of source embedded in his chest seemed more severe.

My thoughts spun quickly as the small flicker of hope pulled my attention into an endless spiral of possibilities, a brief distraction before Ragnor's voice cracked the din of my imagination.

"Are you ready to deliver yourself to me, Dove?" Ragnor asked coolly, his voice centering me in this nightmare again.

The tainted pet name curled a fury within me I found impossible to ignore.

"I don't think you heard me clearly," I began as I bored my attention into his again, forcing venom through my tone. "*Fuck. Off.*"

"Pity," He sighed and brought his lazy gaze up to meet Oberin's eye. "Break her if you must."

The words fell from his lips as easily as his fingers fluttered through the air to deliver the command. My eyes stretched wide as a frenzy of horror spun my mind out of control. Without so much as a moment's hesitation, Oberin trailed the tip of his blade along the length of my arm, only applying enough pressure for me to feel the cool metal.

Teasing me. Toying with his prey.

"She can see you, you know. Your fated," Ragnor called flippantly, his voice an echo trailing through the dreamscape now, already on his way back to the comfort of his stolen palace.

Unfiltered panic gripped my entire being, and the dream world seemed leeched of oxygen as the ability to breathe left me.

"I know it's unlikely Oberin will be able to break *you*, but this will surely break *her*," his voice rattled off the distant walls. His taunt haunted me, coiling my fear into whorls of raging fire.

My heart thundered in my ears, and the edges of my vision sharpened as I whipped my head around to find Callista. The need to see her overwhelmed my senses, but she was nowhere I could see. Likely, she was with Ragnor, watching on the other side of a veil.

"You won't find her," he called, "but you can be sure she's watching every moment of our fun."

"*Callista.*" Her name cracked the air as I choked on my own voice. The tip of Oberin's blade hooked under the hem of my tunic to expose my already scarred stomach.

"Callista, *don't.*"

"She has no choice, witch," Oberin sneered, his voice a darkened gravel.

The sound of his snarl snapped my attention, an expression of burning fury twisting my features.

"I am no *witch.*" I lurched for him, straining against my magical bindings, but they held firm.

The torture master leaned in, the heat of his stale breath washing over my face. I recoiled as nausea rolled through my core.

"I don't care what you are as long as you scream."

He dug the edge of the blade into the sensitive flesh of my stomach without warning. I gritted my teeth against the wail of agony building in my throat for only a moment before the fire of poison released my voice. The edges of my vision darkened as pain thundered through my nerves. He took his time carving his lines, crisscrossing the already raised flesh.

As miserable as the source-dipped blade felt, I would not pray for relief. I would endure. It was the least I could do in the aftermath of all that I'd caused.

I closed my eyelids against the torture and allowed my mind to fall victim to my own endless screams of misery as he carved the same word into my abdomen he always had. I held on for as long as I could manage before my consciousness fell into the blackened void of release, relinquishing me from this twisted prison.

·· +) ☀ (+ ··

I AM ON MY KNEES. *A throbbing in my head makes it impossible to focus my thoughts. Or center my spinning vision. It's cold. I can't hear anything outside of a miserable ringing, a high-pitched squeal coming from deep within the recesses of my soul.*

I look down to see blackened skin stretched over quaking hands, veins of death stretching up to my elbows. My fingers are trembling, my heart is racing, and I don't think I have any oxygen in my lungs. I try to breathe, but my chest aches; a pressure there prevents me from finding relief.

The ground under my knees is damp but hard, and it's dark. Only a dim, blue-black glow illuminates the rocky earth.

I manage to focus my attention long enough to pick out jagged shards of black crystals in the darkness. Five of them are scattered on the ground in front of me. I move my sights higher and see Asteria, her small frame poured over Aeson's lifeless body, her chest heaving, her expression twisted into one of agony, her pale blue cheeks streaked with glistening tears.

I cannot hear her, but I know she's crying, screaming, wailing.

His eyes are open, staring up at the cove's ceiling, his blond hair muddied with damp earth.

I try to pull myself to my feet, but I am weak. My muscles cannot support my weight, and I topple over, landing hard on my hip, loose gravel scraping my elbow. The ringing in my ears only intensifies. My vision spins. The impact causes pain, but it is nothing in comparison to the torrent raging in my chest.

I try to say her name. Call for her attention. It is as though I am not here. She cannot see me. Her grief is a living beast flooding the space between us.

8

am not here. She cannot see me. Her grief is a living beast flooding the space between us.

CHAPTER 2
AURELIA

D*ove.*

The word carved into the soft skin of my abdomen reeked of Ragnor's obsession with claiming me as his own. My stomach turned over on itself at the thought. It had once been an endearing pet name given by a lover, but he'd twisted it into a reminder of my mistakes. For my inability to contain my own desires, to think about my actions.

I traced the jagged lines of the fresh wound with a gentle trail of my nail as I watched the water gurgle over the boulders in the stream ahead. They had already begun to scar over. My fae body's ability to heal aided in that process. But the scars would remain. The source magic within that blade made sure of that. They paired with the existing scar over my breastbone, a mirrored trauma.

Just as each time I had been made to suffer the horrors of that realm, I did my best to separate myself from reality. To tuck the visions of torture into the recesses of my mind to deal with another time.

With my back pressed to the trunk of a large oak tree, I

could almost lose my anxieties in the way the water flowed, turning over on itself at every obstacle, adapting to the rocky path ahead. A gentle breeze rustled the copper curls loose around my face, and a knot in my chest tightened as the memory of Oberin's blade in my flesh sent a shudder through me. It seemed I was never able to keep my thoughts from the pain for very long. The horror of his intentions were too severe.

Ragnor wanted me branded. Marked.

Who has marked you?

You are ruined.

His venomous words burned hot in my memory. I ground my teeth against the heated rage swelling in my chest and yanked the hem of my tunic back down over my stomach, pulling myself to my feet. My muscles creaked and ached at the sudden movement. With so little sleep, I was growing weak, but I needed to press on. There was no time to waste, and I had already blown through three months of travel with no success in regaining my strength enough to save Callista.

That was surely what the false king wanted. I could not allow that male to derail me from my journey to the remaining shards of source crystal, hopefully still hidden from Ragnor's grasp. Most of my memories from before were still foggy at best, a distant life I only had impressions of. What I could remember of the crystal shards told me they should have been hidden under the major trade cities acting as extra magic sources for travelers there.

The scattered pieces of source crystal were my only hope of bringing my near-dormant magic back from the pits of the underworld it had surely taken refuge in.

I shook out the drowsiness in my muscles and reached for the small leather pouch I'd kept tied to my hip, always full of dried viva berries. The small crimson fruit had been used by fae and witch alike for centuries to prevent sleep. It hadn't taken me long to find them, as they were common in the woods across most of the continent and most stayed clear for fear of the sometimes nightmarish aftereffects of their potency.

The berries were all I had to stave off slumber, to keep myself away from that horrific in-between realm. The risk of the aftereffects did not outweigh the possibility of falling victim to Ragnor's whims every night.

I brought the bag to my lips and tilted a few into my mouth. The shock of the sharp flavor barely fazed me as I ground the berries between my teeth. I'd grown used to the sting of tartness as it pinched the underside of my tongue. The effect was nearly instant. A newfound energy flushed through me only moments after I'd swallowed. My eyes stretched wide, and I released a steady breath as a vivid strength flooded my muscles. I stretched my arms over my head to displace any lingering stiffness and breathed a sigh of relief as the wave of exhaustion bled from my consciousness.

I needed to get a move on if I was ever going to have even a chance at getting to Callista. To be strong enough to get her back. Strong enough to save my sister from the fate of that obsidian collar around her neck.

Three months.

I had been traveling alone for *three months*. Desperately trying to find any way to tap into the rest of my seemingly dormant magic.

Shifting into the firebird the day Ragnor had stormed Safe Haven and taken Callista had drained me of nearly everything. It had taken me the better part of an entire month to be able to shift back into my fae body.

I had made the most of my time spent frozen as the historically feared firebird. I had spent the weeks terrorizing The Capital, circling the skies. Trying to find a way in. Desperate to swoop down and pluck Callista from his clutches with a nip of my talons. But the entire city had been sealed against me. No amount of flame would break the magical barrier around the palace and the surrounding city limits.

It infuriated me to no end. Ragnor had come to Safe Haven for me, killed innocents all to get to *me*. Why would he not want a fight? Why would he not want me as close to the palace as possible? I could not make much sense of it. The strongest conclusion I'd come to was his potential lack of strength. Those veins had been getting darker, the venom of the source magic likely taking its toll.

Good. He was suffering, at least. All I could hope for was his survival to last only long enough for me to tear his head from his shoulders myself. The need for vengeance after all he'd done was blinding. Thoughts of the thousands who had suffered in the past ten years plagued me constantly, let alone those who had fallen in Safe Haven.

It had been the only place the terrorized citizens of Celvaria could take refuge.

I had no way of knowing how many had perished that day. He'd made a mess of the town only to get to me. To get that collar around my neck. And when he'd failed, he'd left with my fated like the coward he was. A coward who was only strong enough to face me in my dreams.

That would have to do until I could figure out a way to reignite my magic. I had realized it had all but gone dormant after I'd managed to shift back into my fae form. I couldn't even so much as *ephemerate* a few feet. No amount of sunlight would replenish my stores of power for weeks on end. I couldn't go after Callista like this, but I had to do something. Setting off after a shard of the source to strengthen my stores of magic had seemed like my only option if I was to have any chance at all against Ragnor and Asteria.

If he hadn't already collected most of them.

That thought terrified me, but I had to push on; I had to do something.

After weeks of grueling effort, I was able to reach a small tendril of magic. I'd spent the last months allowing it to slowly replenish to some semblance of power. It worried me how difficult it was to wield even a small flicker of flame. I was afraid to use too much of it at a time and risk draining the well completely again.

The cycle was exhausting, and I ached for a rest, a reprieve. But I had no time to waste nor any ability to sleep in peace, so on I trekked.

Shaking off my fury-hazed daze, I stepped to the edge of the river and took a breath as the heat of the sun washed over my skin, chasing away the chill of the crisp morning air. I coiled a tendril of my weakened magic through my core and brought it to the surface, winding it through my veins until I could carefully wrap it around my fingertips. I focused the energy on the large boulders resting just below the clear surface of the running water. Sliding my magic under each one, I lifted them to the surface to create steppingstones all the way across to the other edge.

A pained sigh of relief deflated my lungs as the stones rose above the waterline one by one with ease. Knowing my magic was strong enough to at least perform simple tasks left me with a small sense of comfort. Testing my stores of power at least once a day had become customary. If only to make sure I still had some connection to what remained in my well.

I stepped out onto a slick stone, careful to balance on my toes, and hopped from surface to surface until I made it across. Relief settled over my strained senses as I released my hold on my magic, and the boulders sank back into the riverbed again. Double-checking the sun's position in the sky to ensure I was still traveling in the right direction before getting back out into the dense wood, I set off.

I trudged on for a while, careful not to leave a trail as I moved through the brush, listening to the sounds of the forest. Being so surrounded by the buzzing of wildlife provided by the wood always made my heart ache for Aeson, even all these centuries later. As children, we'd spent plenty of time in the forest so he could practice his creation magic. It had been the only place he'd ever truly felt comfortable, at home. The overwhelming grief at his memory nearly buckled my knees. Flashes of the nightmare of his death made a pit in my stomach ache.

I did not have the space to relive that. I needed to find shelter before night fell.

I swallowed my ancient grief and hiked until the sun began to droop in the sky. Eventually, I made it to a small clearing in the trees, where the brush pushed back to allow space for the mouth of a deep cave. A good spot to rest my aching legs for the evening, take cover from the chilled night air and any wandering, dangerous creatures that felt more comfortable under the cover of darkness.

I peered into the blackness beyond the mouth of the cave for just a moment before I made to move on, but my muscles froze as alarm echoed from the corner of my senses.

The chirping of the crickets and evening songs of the nearby toads I had been mindlessly tracking all evening seemed to cease, as though the creatures had never existed in the first place. The breeze, as it danced through the leaves above, became the only sound to fill my ears. My breath caught in my chest as the air stiffened around me, every fiber of my being alert. Something shifted out of place. Something dangerous, wild. It sharpened my intuition and caused the hairs along my arms to stand on end.

I pooled my fragile magic in my palms, heat buzzing beneath my skin as I prepared myself to face whatever lingered here. I hoped I was wrong, that paranoia from being alone for so long was getting to me. But when the scratch of what sounded like a claw against stone vibrated beyond the cove's entrance, rattling the evening air between me and the mouth of the deep cave, my anxieties were confirmed.

I had no time to retreat into the forest before a massive beast leapt from the darkness, bounding for me with a speed that would have left any other defenseless. Fear cracked my chest, the urgency of the beast's movements spurring action in my own leaden limbs. I whipped my hands up, throwing every ounce of strength I still possessed into holding the creature back, but I feared it would not be enough.

I screamed in agony as the last of my stores of magic broke free. The massive, triple head of the enormous, deadly reptile reached for me, its maws snapping, moving at a velocity I was not sure I would be able to break.

CHAPTER 3

AURELIA

The great beast froze in my grip for only a moment. Just long enough to allow me to take stock of what I had stumbled upon before its three reptilian heads broke free of my hold and writhed against my struggling magic. I swore as the name for the creature broke free of my memory.

A serpentine. A rare, territorial, and dangerous animal.

Of course.

Creatures like this had always been drawn to me. A never-ending test from the goddesses, if they even existed enough to mock my struggles. I would have rolled my eyes at my own damned luck if I'd had the space to focus on anything other than my fight to hold my weakened magic steady.

My arms shook as I frantically tried to maintain any amount of control long enough to come up with a plan. To call for my fire. To muster the strength to *ephemerate*. Anything. But my muscles strained, and the creature thrashed against me, jerking my arm viciously as I tried to hold firm.

Goddess damn it.

I managed to regain control, but only a few heartbeats

passed as I struggled to keep the beast frozen before searing pain ripped through my shoulder. I screamed as the slicing agony shattered my resolve. The strain in my arm tore a muscle. My focus split, but I couldn't let my magic falter. I dug my heels into the ground, and my voice shredded through my vocal cords as I pumped more power into my palms.

The serpentine roared as my focus slipped, and one of its three lizard-like heads whipped around the invisible hold I had on the beast. My right heel slid, and my torn shoulder gave out. My injured arm fell to my side, and I whipped my good hand in a frenzy, a frantic attempt to throw a solid, invisible wall up to block the reptile's blow, but I knew it wouldn't be strong enough. A head flew straight for me, its snapping maw open, jagged teeth moving closer. I prepared for the pain of its fangs in my flesh as I failed to wrangle any more energy from my core. Its rancid breath washed over my face as it passed through my piss-poor attempt at a shield.

Before it made contact, a blinding flash of silver soared overhead, slicing the air just above me. My attention had no time to focus on what it could have been before it hit the beast between the brow, stopping it a fraction of a beat before it could snap its teeth around my frame. The hilt of a silver sword protruded from its scaly brow, the entire blade of the weapon swallowed by the blackened flesh of the creature. The slain head fell to the ground feet from me, its tongue lolling to the side and its eyes hazy with the sudden wash of death. The stench of its breath rolled nausea through my stomach.

The serpentine's other two heads roared for its fallen sister and moved free from my grip for only a second as surprise shattered my attention. I threw up my uninjured arm to clamp them in my magic again, but I was weakening. I whipped my head around the moment I locked the remaining heads in my hold to find the source of the blade.

What greeted me sucked the air from my lungs. Dread mixed with elation coated my breastbone, and I wasn't sure which emotion was more pungent.

"What the *fuck?*" Atlas's voice bellowed through the air as he waived an arm boisterously at the scene in front of me, his gesture questioning the reality of my situation.

The lunar male's hair was longer and unruly, and he had silvery white stubble lining his strong jaw. He was dressed in close-fitting fighting leathers, a satchel discarded on the ground next to him. His feet were planted wide, and his expression twisted in disbelief and anger. Something wild warred with me in my chest. I hadn't seen him in months, having left him behind in Safe Haven after the battle with Ragnor, and I couldn't fathom how he'd managed to find me this deep in the continent.

But I could not deny the bubble of elation brimming in my core at the sight of him. The bright feeling was only eclipsed by sheer shock.

"What the fuck *me?*" I screamed, one arm dangling to the side, the other struggling to hold the roaring monster back. "What the fuck *you!* What are you doing here?"

I'd left him behind for a reason. I could not afford any distractions, and the reality of almost losing him in the battle had shaken my focus enough to lose Callista to Ragnor's capture. It had been a nightmare I'd been forced to relive every night out here on my own. I would not put anyone else at risk.

The torrent of anger, surprise, dread, and excitement was almost too much. Adrenaline spun my thoughts.

Atlas ignored me blatantly with thinned lips, an expression of irritation, and took off at a sprint, pumping his legs and arms, his brow pulled together in determination. He ran in a tight curve around me, and I screamed at him in protest, my arms trembling against the effort of maintaining my hold on the serpentine. Although, my words were not discernible through the swelling of my panic.

Atlas pulled his glinting sword from between the eyes of the fallen head and raced toward the one to its left. To my horror, it broke free of my grasp, only enough to snap at him, nearly catching him around the waist, but he twisted and managed to swing his blade to slice across its thick neck. With one strong strike, he severed the head. Blood poured from the wound, and he scaled the dead beast with impressive agility for his size. Atlas moved so quickly, I barely had time to react to the shift in my control before he was up high enough to face the third head.

I struggled to hold it back as it fought to snap at him, and my grip slipped enough for it to twist free. My heart seized, and another scream tore from my chest as the thing reared back with its vicious jaw open, ready to strike.

Atlas wasn't fast enough this time, and white-hot panic blinded me as I imagined its teeth leeching the life from him. A vicious cry of war rattled from my throat, and I whipped my hand forward, allowing a solid blade of fire to soar from my fingertips. It barreled for the creature, a promise of death in its wake, and as my weapon of flame made contact with its neck, it made a clean slice all the way across, decapitating the third and final head. The thing rolled with a few muted thunks across the grass to land near the already dead beast at my feet.

A hollow pang clattered through my well as exhaustion threatened to buckle my knees, the last of my magic drained.

I'd done it. The beast was dead. Another set of lifeless eyes stared up at me. It took me a few steadying breaths before I could clear my rage enough to look up to Atlas. It was an effort to remain upright as the overexertion of my power weakened my muscles, a dizzying spin to my vision making it difficult to focus on the silver male, but I managed to hold my attention firm.

His chest heaved, and he looked down at me with a beaming smile on his face, his expression alight with excitement. Blazing irritation flared under my skin at his carefree demeanor. He could have *died* and he was smiling as though he had just bested me in a sparring match, a complete disregard for the danger he'd just been in.

I shifted my weight to one foot, and a flare of pain lanced its way through my shoulder at the movement. I winced at the discomfort, but it was nothing in comparison to the rage burning through my core or the exhaustion pulling at the edges of my consciousness.

I thought I might vomit. It was too much. My fingers itched to reach for my bag of viva berries, but I refrained.

"Well, that was anticlimactic," Atlas mused, his tone playful.

I managed to keep my expression firm, but I would be lying if I said the sound of his voice didn't fill me with a bliss I had forgotten possible. It chased away some of the weighted exhaustion.

He sheathed his sword at his hip and hopped down from the dead animal, taking a few long strides toward me. His steps were light and casual, as though he hadn't appeared as if from nowhere from across the realm to risk his life. My rage simmered further.

Sweat stuck my loose hair to my neck, and I fumed, huffing an angry breath through my nose.

"Goddess *damn* you!" I shoved his chest with the heel of my good hand, pain throbbing through my shoulder again. "What in the infernal realm are you doing out here?"

My tone stuck somewhere between fury and panic, but I couldn't ignore the flutter of relief tucked behind my heart at knowing he was alive and well. When I'd left him with Mage, he had been nearly bleeding out from a knife wound to the side.

A day hadn't passed in the last three months where my every thought wasn't plagued by the image of that knife in his flesh, only to be followed by the searing memory of Callista's wounds just before Ragnor had Asteria take her away to goddesses only knew where.

"Looking for *your* sorry ass."

He waved at the beast behind him, taking another step closer to me again. I fought to keep my feet planted firm.

"And good fucking thing because look what would have happened if I hadn't shown up." His words were laced with anger.

He usually coated his tone in lightness and sarcasm, but the rage in his voice almost matched mine and I was glad for it. It gave my own frustration an excuse to bleed freely.

"*Bullshit,*" I snarled. "I had this under control. That thing almost killed you!"

"It almost killed *you!*" he shouted, closing the last step between us.

Atlas took my shoulders in his hands, and I groaned in pain, but before I could tell him to stop, he had his arms around me. The action shocked me. It was the last thing I'd expected to happen after his shouting, and I froze. He pressed my head into his chest with a firm hand and locked his other arm around me.

I stood there, tense and bewildered for a moment, until my rage simmered away. The feeling of his embrace provided me with a comfort I had been missing so desperately. I swallowed a mangled sob as it threatened to break my resolve. The swelling behind my heart overwhelmed me. My head spun.

His affection forced the cracks in my hollow heart back

together just enough for me to have to acknowledge the life still beating there.

"Don't you dare *ever* disappear like that again, you stupid idiot," he mumbled, his chest rumbling as he choked on mangled emotion of his own.

"Stupid idiot is redundant," I muttered into his chest.

A rumbled laugh rolled through him as he released me. I stepped away, the eagerness to be near someone again making it difficult for me to put distance between us. Mindlessly, my hand floated up to touch the prickling stubble on his cheek. He was usually so clean-shaven; travel had worn him.

Something in his glimmering eyes hardened, and he took a step back. My hand fell from his face. Atlas swallowed, and a corner of his mouth tilted as he plucked at my collar.

"What in the other realms are you wearing?" he asked with a raised brow.

I looked down at the too-big tunic and trousers held up with a rope tied around my waist with a frown. I'd been wearing these same clothes since I'd managed to shift back into my fae body.

"Well, they aren't mine."

"Clearly," he said through a laugh.

"I don't get to keep my clothes when I shift into the firebird."

His brow shot up, his features alight with amusement.

"You're telling me you nakedly stole those clothes from some poor, unassuming civilian?"

"That is what I'm telling you, yes," I replied flatly.

"Well"—he sighed—"it's a rather good thing I brought you something to change into."

I furrowed my brow and peered over his shoulder. He did not have anything with him other than his sword and that satchel he'd left behind on the ground. My thoughts raced, and

I quickly lost control of their direction. My adrenaline bled away, and the reality of the past few minutes settled in.

"What? Why? How did you find me?" I asked, my words spilling free in a frantic string of buzzing thoughts.

"You were an extremely large bird the last time I saw you. I didn't know what you'd need. And I have been tracking you since you left," he replied. "On that note, what in the holy mothers are you doing, and what is this thing?" He toed the serpentine's head with his boot.

"Don't deflect," I said, placing my good hand on my hip.

"Gengi had a spell." He grimaced.

I groaned. I did not want to have to deal with managing Atlas, let alone Atlas and an unknown companion through my travels.

"Who is Gengi? You need to go back. This isn't safe."

"I'm Gengi," a voice called from above. I turned my head to find a sandy-haired male with warm, golden-toned skin and bright golden irises perched on a branch of a nearby tree, a bow in hand.

I furrowed my brow at him. Confusion blended with irritation and settled over me.

"Where did you come from?" I muttered mostly to myself as surprise clouded my thoughts.

Usually, I was much more aware of my surroundings, but the effort it took to use my magic on the serpentine must have stretched me too thin to notice the male. Gengi slung the bow over his back before swinging his lithe body around and dropping to dangle from the branch. He let go and landed on his feet with grace. The dirt plumed around his boots, and he took a few strides to stand shoulder to shoulder with Atlas, a smile in his bright eyes. He was a few inches shorter than the lunar male and less broad. His ears were somewhere between rounded and pointed, much like Despina's.

Half fae.

"Nice to finally meet you. I actually feel like I already have. Atlas never shuts up." Gengi flashed a teasing smile, and Atlas scoffed as he rolled his eyes, but Gengi continued before the lunar fae could protest, "It's been quite a miserable time trying to track you across all ends of the realm."

I thinned my lips in irritation and turned my attention back to Atlas without a response.

"Go. Back," I demanded through gritted teeth.

"Absolutely not." A flash of anger flared Atlas's nostrils, and his expression hardened slightly around the edges. "I spent months trying to find you. If I am going back, you are coming with me."

"I can't."

I huffed and turned away from him, wincing at the pain in my shoulder as I began to stomp back into the forest. It would take much longer to heal without the proper stores of my magic, especially considering I had just expended what little I had left to take out the last of the serpentine heads.

"For fuck's sake," Atlas grumbled. "Where are you going?"

"I am going to keep traveling on my own," I called over my shoulder casually.

"Is she serious?" Gengi muttered to Atlas.

"She is, I'm afraid." Atlas sighed, and his footsteps fell in the brush behind me. "You will not. You're hurt, and you look like you haven't slept in weeks."

I tensed at that, and my hand instinctively fluttered near the pouch at my hip, a subconscious gesture to take stock of how many dried berries I still had. The bag was still at least half full. I wouldn't need to search for more for a few days.

"The nearest trade city is a few miles from here. We can't get there by nightfall, but you can *ephemerate* us and—"

I turned on my heel and stopped short to pin Atlas in my stare, interrupting his line of thought entirely.

"I will not be taking *us* anywhere," I said, a dangerous timbre to my voice.

"Alright." He huffed a dark chuckle and crossed his arms over his chest, a challenge in his expression as he cocked an eyebrow. "You have two choices. You stay with us or we stay with you. I'll give you a moment to decide."

I rolled my eyes, and a groan escaped my throat. The corner of his mouth twitched in amusement as he watched my resolve falter. The pain in my shoulder throbbed. The berries I'd taken had worn off, the thrill of the serpentine attack burning the borrowed energy right through my blood. I cocked my hip to the side and flashed him a glare, running my tongue over my teeth. The trade city was exactly where I'd planned to go next, where I'd been traveling to for weeks. But I had no intention of bringing the two of them with me.

"Right." He smiled brightly. "That's what I thought. Now, if you could just take us to the nearest inn, I would be largely appreciative."

He took a step nearer with his hand outstretched, reaching for mine, and I flinched away from his touch. Something wild and charged with fear fueled my muscles. Hurt flashed through his expression as he pulled his hand away. The flicker of emotion made something churn under my breastbone.

"I can't," I sputtered. He furrowed his brow at me.

"What do you mean, you can't?" Gengi asked. "It isn't far."

"No." I sighed. "I can't do it. My magic has been . . ." I hesitated and bit down on my bottom lip. "It's drained."

"What?" Atlas asked, gingerly stepping closer, his eyes searching me as though he were inspecting me for some kind of injury.

"I've had a hard time hanging on to any amount of power

for months, and the serpentine drained me. I haven't even *tried ephemerating* since Safe Haven."

Atlas's attention roamed my face once more before he loosed a short breath and nodded.

"Then we will find somewhere to make camp," he declared before setting off into the woods.

Gengi flashed me a kind smile and nodded after him.

"Shall we?" the solar male asked, waving a hand in front of him to indicate that I should follow Atlas.

After a moment's hesitation, one last flicker of time to try to figure out a way out of this, I gave in to the reality that I was too tired to put up much of a fight. I offered a curt nod and lugged my aching muscles along, trying desperately to ignore the wave of relief that settled around my heart knowing I wasn't going to have to suffer another night alone.

I WRUNG OUT MY HAIR, dripping from my wash in the river nearby, and emerged from the shadows of night to allow the warmth of the campfire to blanket my frigid skin. Atlas crouched over the fire, poking at the coals, while Gengi lay flat on his back with his arm over his brow. Atlas's face relaxed when his attention landed on me, and something in my chest loosened at the relief in his expression. I offered a soft tilt of my lips.

"I'll keep watch; you should try to rest," I said as I settled in to sit across the fire from him.

He furrowed his brow.

"No."

"No?" I scoffed.

"When was the last time you slept?"

My hand drifted to my stomach instinctively, my fingers brushing over the scars there, but I made an effort to keep my expression light.

"Last night," I replied with a shrug of one shoulder, breaking his gaze as I wrung my sopping hair out again.

"Why would you lie to me?" he asked, his tone stern and his expression hardening.

"Why would you think I'm lying?" I asked, though still pointedly avoiding the intensity of his stare.

He watched me for a moment, the air between us thick before he spoke again.

"Fine." He leaned back and sat with his legs crossed, tossing the stick he held into the fire. "If you're awake, then I'm awake."

"That isn't necessary," I protested, finally meeting his eye.

The intensity I found there in his bright violet stare caused a skip in the steady beating of my heart.

"Aurelia." Atlas's voice held a hint of scolding, but something in my core lurched at the sound of my given name on his lips.

I didn't think I had ever heard him use it before. There hadn't been time. The sound of it as it rolled through his tenor sent a shiver down my spine.

One that I very pointedly ignored, shaking the feeling off with a roll of my shoulders.

"Did you try to go after her?" I asked with heat in my words.

I needed a distraction from the sudden twist in my abdomen. What better than the pain of loss, of knowing I had caused so much pain to someone I cared so deeply about?

The image of Callista on the ground, bleeding from the wound to her stomach, tore through my mind's eye, trampling any previous line of thought. Atlas's expression fell, a gravity lining his features I rarely got to witness.

"Of course I did," he replied, his tone heavy with a hollow kind of sorrow. "You don't think I tried everything within my power to get her back? Did you? Or have you been traipsing out here for goddess knows what all this time?"

Anger brought faint heat to my fingertips at the accusation. The sensation surprised me—my stores of magic were still depleted—but I leaned into it, welcoming the warmth, urging it to chase away the pain brimming within the cavity of my chest.

"Why exactly do you think I've been *traipsing*'?" I replied, rage laced through my tone. I rose to my feet and dusted my hands off on my thighs. "I'll keep watch from a distance."

Atlas moved to follow and took a breath to speak, but I cut off any attempt to protest.

"Alone."

"Fine," he grumbled irritably and plopped back into a seat. "But I'm not falling asleep so I can wake up and find you've crossed the continent without me. Have fun sulking on your own."

I turned on my heel with a huff of frustration and found the cover of an oak tree to lean my back against. The spot was far enough away from the camp for the cover of darkness to provide me with relief, but not so far that I couldn't still hear the crackle of the fire as it twined with the serene sounds of the nighttime forest.

I sulked in the darkness for a while, allowing my anger to bleed through until exhaustion became too heavy to bear. I removed the pouch of berries from my hip and shook a few into my palm. Popping them into my mouth, I winced at the sharp flavor and let out a sigh of relief as their pungency immediately chased the fatigue from my consciousness.

A simmering panic I hadn't been aware of loosened as my awareness perked with the forged energy from the fruit.

I would not have to face Ragnor again this eve. Everything would be alright.

A painful pang in my chest hit me with sudden force, bringing tears to my eyes, and I squeezed them shut to will them away. I refused to allow them to release this feeling. I would not allow that monster to puncture my resolve any further than he already had.

Although, if I was being honest with myself, it wasn't just Ragnor's abuse I was trying to keep from my active thoughts. I wasn't sure what was more prevalent, though: the agony at knowing Callista still suffered alone or the relief of knowing Atlas was near again. Both thoughts racked me with guilt I could not bear. I swallowed them, tucking the tangle of emotion away in a corner of my heart in hopes of suffocating them entirely.

CHAPTER 4

BRENWYN

I had been tangled with the shadows for so long, I was sure it would only be a matter of time before I bled away from my physical existence. I'd been lurking at the edges of every room in that damned palace for months, trying to gather any amount of useful information. Anything that might help Callista and the firebird, but the rooms Ragnor spent his time in were heavily warded, the walls coated in magical barriers meant to prevent any kind of espionage.

It hadn't stopped me from trying, though. At least once a day, I would spill into the shadows of the war room, only to be thrown into an unending abyss of darkness, my mind and magic tangled in a sea of confusion. Each time, I knew it would be a useless effort, but I had to do something; I needed to be useful somehow.

Unfortunately, I turned out to be the most useless member of the resistance to date. Failure of this magnitude was not something I was used to, though I was getting comfortable with self-deprecation.

The first time I'd fallen victim to the tangled effects of the war room's warding spell, I'd been so shaken I'd needed more than a full day to recover. It had taken me hours to find my way back to my corporeal body. I had floated through the depths of the shadows, tumbling through the nothingness until I'd been able to gather enough of my bearings to figure out my location again.

The second time I'd tried, I'd been prepared enough to keep my mind, to hang onto my magic and find my way out of the shadows eventually.

It didn't seem like there was any kind of alarm set to alert anyone to my efforts. At least, no one had ever approached me about my attempts to breach the room. Which wasn't altogether surprising given how foreign my abilities were to this realm. Everyone thought I was still under Ragnor's control, so I doubted they had the minds to set up a trigger for my ability to travel through darkness.

This time, though, I spiraled through the shadows until they spilled me out into the darkened wood near the well just past the edge of the courtyard. I considered remaining one with the darkness, losing myself in the abyss and cool relief of the shadows, but the whirling black night made it difficult for me to regain my composure. My emotions quickly became one with the tangled web of twilight, hurdling through the realm at a rate that spurred an uncontrollable, crawling discomfort through the fiber of my being. It would be easier to ground myself if I could tether the emotions to my body.

I pulled at the edges of my physical being, willing the shadows to knit me together until my feet landed firmly on solid ground. It took another moment to center my spinning vision, but eventually, I gathered myself with a hand on the stone well to steady my balance.

Another failed attempt. Disappointing. I'd have to try again tomorrow.

Until someone grew suspicious, I would keep going, keep making an effort to break through the wards every day until someone had something better for me to do. Until I had any information to get back to Safe Haven. Any reason to stop pretending to be one of Ragnor's mindless puppets.

Although, no one had contacted me from Safe Haven. Not Atlas or Mage. Amaris, Mila. No one.

Even if I had any information to give, I would have nowhere to relay it. I'd tried sending messages through the veil of darkness, to get anything back to Haven, but each effort had been fruitless. Either the barrier around Safe Haven had been fortified enough to prevent communication or they had warded it against me.

It made sense. I had betrayed them. It was my fault Ragnor had found Haven. Even the thought of how many had suffered for my mistakes rolled a vile kind of nausea in my stomach. I'd let myself get too close to the false king, trusted him to keep to his word, to help me with my lifelong goal to get me closer to my past. I'd been too blinded by my own agenda to see his brand coming, the mark that kept me tethered to his every whim. He'd warped me into his puppet before I'd even had time to blink. I'd regret my own selfish motives for getting close to him until the day I took my last breath.

I could never make up for the horrors my actions had caused, but maybe I could play some hand in taking the bastard down. If anyone would give me the chance to reach out.

But I understood. I wouldn't trust me either.

For the time being, I would continue my nearly useless efforts from the palace. Watch over Callista, work to find any way to help from the inside. If it took everything in me, I would find a way.

To get Callista back to her fated.

To release Asteria from his grip.

I gritted my teeth against the gnarling feeling of disappointment that always threatened to choke the air from my lungs each time my thoughts got away from me and kicked the stone well in frustration.

This was useless. At this point, I was sure they hoped me to be dead, long gone at the very least.

Until I could find something worthwhile to prove myself to them—some way to redeem myself—I was stuck here trying to figure out any way to be more than a spineless, selfish coward of a being.

A heavy sigh passed over my lips, my shoulders curling in on themselves as I let the weight of the disappointment settle again. I spun the ring with my family crest on my right index finger with my thumb, a nervous habit of mine since I'd been a child, since before I had been ripped away from my family home, separated from my brother in the dead of the night all those years ago.

Another night had come and gone, and I would either have to resign myself to the shadows again or settle back into my role as slave to this wretched false king for another endless night. I shook my hand out at my side, took a deep breath to calm the writhing anxiety as it curled within me, and let my mind drift back to my room. I hadn't seen anyone from the guard all day, and there was a chance Oberin would want to check in with me to see if I had gathered any information on the firebird like I had been instructed to day after day.

I would much rather travel through the shadows straight to my chamber, but even those four walls felt like a weighted cage. Asteria hadn't been to visit me in weeks, and I was beginning to feel the familiar urge to duck and run again, leave all of this behind and become a part of the shadows permanently.

If I was being honest with myself, Asteria was the only

solid motivator to fight those instincts. I would never forgive myself if I took off without her.

I couldn't leave. I was sticking around for a reason. And it wasn't only Asteria that needed me. Callista had been trapped in her own cage for three months. As useless as I'd been, I wanted to be there for her, too. In whatever way I could.

I blew out the breath I'd taken to calm my itching muscles and allowed the shadows to curl around me, seep into my veins as though my blood were made of darkness and my soul attached to the night. The lines of my existence faded away, and I curled through the evening air, flying on wings of obsidian across the grounds of the palace. First through the rest of the wood, then along the creases and corners of the dimly lit corridors until I slithered under the crack of my door and pulled myself back together from nothing, my fae feet landing softly on the hardwood at the foot of my four-poster bed.

"Trying to break through the war room seal again?"

The sound of Asteria's flutelike voice nearly cracked my chest in two, and I whipped my attention around to find her perched on the edge of the large black-velvet settee in front of the fireplace. The fire there crackled with dying embers, no flame left, but it offered enough of a glow to illuminate the space. The warm light highlighted the deep indigo of her hair and cast a glow over the pale blue of her skin.

It had been so long since I'd heard her voice in anything but my dreams.

"Stair," I whispered, her name catching in my throat. "Where have you been?"

She pursed her lips and rose from her perch to float across the room, her feet gliding as the vision of her moved over the space. The lunar fae settled herself into a seat on my bed. As usual, her footsteps made no sound, and the plush grey comforter did not so much as crinkle as she let herself fall onto the mattress.

I would never get used to this particular brand of magic. One that allowed Asteria to be here with me in spirit alone. She seemed so real, so alive, so solid. But she was merely an image. A ghost of herself.

"That is not an answer to my question." She tilted her head and nodded to indicate that I should sit with her.

Without hesitation, I pulled myself up one knee at a time and sat cross-legged only inches from her, the urge to reach out and touch her overwhelming my senses. I had been so desperate to see her, talk to her. The urge to feel her skin under my fingertips seemed all-consuming.

But I knew I could not touch her. Not like this.

I had been through this so many times. Interacting with this phantom of Asteria. Her body stayed lifeless in her own chamber attached to Ragnor's rooms while she projected herself here, as she had so many times before. I swallowed a lump in my throat and took a short breath to steady my racing heart.

"Yes." I breathed an answer to her question.

"And?" Asteria asked with one raised brow.

I shook my head and bit down on my lip as the weight of disappointment threatened to choke me again. Her eyes softened, and she brought her hand up to her neck absently to rest her fingers on her collarbone as she often did in this form. This version of her didn't need to wear that infernal crystal collar, but her instinct to touch the stone was not left behind with her physical body. She'd been wearing it for over a decade. Even the image of the infernal device as it flashed through my mind cause rage to rise within me that proved difficult to temper. It bound her to him like some pet he could tote out when he needed something to scare everyone into submission again.

I hated it. She was not meant for this. Asteria was the gentlest soul I'd ever met. The most understanding, forgiving, but he had turned her into a monster. And every time she'd been wielded as a weapon in that way, I had been forced to watch a piece of her die. I wasn't sure how much more she could take before the light in her lilac eyes dimmed permanently.

The thought caused a roll of nausea, and a desperate kind of panic made me frantic.

"It'll kill you if you aren't careful," she warned, her tone heavy as her light eyes glimmered in the dim firelight.

"Let it," I snipped, my tone shorter than I intended it to be, but the roiling emotions threatened to crack my resolve. "It's been months, and I don't know what to do. I need to do *something*. And if we are being honest, my loss won't be worth much. The least I can do is try to get any amount of information first."

"Don't talk like that," she whispered, her bottom lip trembling.

"Like what? It's true."

"No, it isn't. You mustn't die fighting for a fruitless cause."

"Saving you is all that matters to me."

I lurched forward and reached out to touch her knee, but it fell through to the mattress as though nothing were there at all. My heart fissured as the reality of this gripped me again. I'd known that would happen. Of course, it would. I could not touch her. Not here. Only in my dreams, where she met me from time to time to make believe we could be something different. But that did nothing to stop the urge to reach out.

"Brenwyn." Her tone was stern and made me look up to meet her eye.

Her expression was hard, but the hurt that glimmered there was unmistakable.

"How many times must I tell you? I cannot be saved. I am not meant to be. What is important is saving the lunar female. Saving Aurelia."

"I will not have that," I shot through gritted teeth. "You know I don't give a *fuck* about your source-damned prophecy. Do not spew that bullshit to me."

The hurt that flashed through her eyes made me regret my tone, but she recovered quickly and responded with a level expression.

"I know," she whispered, something heavy in her voice, "but I have to. I watched both my brother and my sister die for this. I have killed so many myself, and I cannot allow it to mean nothing, be for nothing. The prophecy puts Aurelia in place to save the realm, and I *have* to believe she will. I do not have a choice."

She spoke with a fervor I so rarely saw in her, and my heart fissured at her pain.

"But what if you're wrong? What if *you* are the one meant to save everyone?"

She thinned her lips and shook her head, her eyes tilting sadly as she turned over my words. My own caught in my throat, trapped behind a wall of tears I refused to let free.

Before she could respond, her wide eyes snapped open, the blank look passing over her features unmistakable, and the crack in my heart only splintered more.

Our time was ending. She needed to go back to her body.

"No," I pled. "Not yet. Don't go, I have missed you so much."

She shrugged one shoulder, and a sliver of silver tears lined her light eyes as she met mine again, the sorrow I felt reflected in her gaze.

"I'm sorry," she whispered. "I'll come back tomorrow if I can."

"Stair," I croaked, leaning forward, desperate to keep her here however I could.

But before her name passed my lips, she was gone, her form disappearing in a blink, as though she had never been there in the first place. A mangled sob passed my lips, and the impact of her absence encouraged my fall the rest of the way to the mattress.

Curled over on my side with my arms crossed over my aching stomach, I pulled my knees to my chest. One solitary tear snuck free to curl over my cheek as the cavities of my ribs tried to cave in on themselves.

I wasn't sure I was capable of waiting out very many more tomorrows, but I would keep trying. If only to get more time with her than a fleeting few moments in the dead of the night.

CHAPTER 5
CALLISTA

I had never been so close to wishing for death than I had been in that place. That in-between realm. Forced to watch Oberin torture her, slice through her flesh with his source-damned blade.

This was a close second, though.

Pain lanced my consciousness as I strained against the leather straps binding my forearms and thighs, keeping me tied tightly to the iron chair in the middle of the witch's workspace. I gritted my teeth against a scream as the device he'd strapped to my chest sent another shock of electric energy through my every vein. It was a contraption made of metals with a chamber meant to contain the magic of whoever had the misfortune of wearing it. It seemed fashioned specifically for this painful experience. Its four metal straps spidered around my rib cage and over my collarbones, holding the thing tightly to my breastbone, connecting it to my soul, my well of magic.

The vile witch sneered at me, his eyes a putrid shade crossed somewhere between green and yellow, almost like a cat's. His thin lips curled over his teeth as he twisted the device, turning it like a dial on a clock as another wave of pain lanced me. This time, my fight was not enough. I tried to resist, but the magic bled from my well, every drop of it cyphoned into the device.

The pain was unbearable, but I met his eye, forced a viciousness into my stare I refused to break. If this witch was going to take from me, violate me in this way, I would make him watch what it did to me, force him to look me in the eye.

I would not give him the satisfaction of breaking me.

The witch's sickening smile turned up and he cranked the device thrice, releasing its hold on my chest. I sucked in a frigid breath as its pressure disappeared, all the muscles in my back relaxing as I slumped against the chair. Consciousness was fleeting. I wasn't sure how much longer I would be able to hold on.

He turned to Ragnor, who sat in a chair opposite me. I'd done my best to ignore him, to pretend he was not there. But he always was. This was for him.

The witch spoke but I could not hear the words, just the muffled sound of his voice as he used his dark magic to attach the device to Ragnor's chest, the chamber pouring my essence into the source crystal fused to his breastbone.

My vision blurred around the edges, the dark bliss of unconsciousness beginning to tug at my awareness.

I hung on long enough to watch the longest black veins of poison along Ragnor's bare chest retreat into the crystal. Somehow, my magic healed some of his affliction, strengthened him.

I snarled, baring my teeth, and tried to lurch for him, struggling against my bindings, but my energy was spent. My head lolled and the curtain of unconsciousness overtook my senses.

· · ◗ ☀ ◖ · ·

I DID NOT KNOW his name. The witch. Only that he was one of the few who did not seem to be branded by Ragnor's mark of mind control. Although, I was sure most of those branded would have done the false king's bidding anyway, the crescent moon over their breastbones merely marks of loyalty.

But not the witch. He acted of his own accord.

And he was not only a witch, but also a cyphin. I could not make much sense of it, having only known one in my life. I'd been under the impression that a cyphin had no roots in any magic, but he did.

Somehow, he was able to wield the ancient magic of the source, use conduits to funnel vile power, *and* drain others of their energy.

I would be fascinated by this unique ability if he hadn't used it to drive me to the edges of sanity every few weeks.

Used me to strengthen that monster.

The memory of every torturous session cycled through my mind's eye as the hours passed. The solitary confinement within the four walls of this prison chamber was maddening to me. The sessions always came after the nightmare realm. The place he could reach her, taunt her, torture her.

He made me watch every time. Trying to weaken my resolve, wear me down.

It was working. Every day I found myself further and further away from any desire to hang onto the good parts of myself, the parts that valued kindness, a gentle touch. Every day I descended further into a pit of despair I wasn't sure I would be able to bring myself out of.

I wouldn't allow him to see it, though.

Ironically, said prison chamber was not a prison chamber at all. It was a bedroom. It had been mine once before. The same drab four walls were in the guest wing, far enough away from the royal corridor that no one would pay any mind, but not so far away that we were out of sight of the king—the real king— my father.

That had been before Ragnor had staged his coup.

The bastard of a dark king had placed me here intention- ally, in my old sleeping chamber. He'd remembered existing in the palace at the same time as my brother and I just as well as we had. Except now, the room was stripped bare. Only a pallet on the floor and the bathing room, raided for all its soaps and salves. There was one window overlooking the old training courtyard, but it had been barred with deadstone, just like the door.

When I wasn't being used as a personal source of magic for that shit-face, I was made to wear manacles of the magic- barring deadstone around my wrists and ankles, with no hopes of wriggling free. A smart move considering I planned to tear their faces from their skulls the second I had the opportunity, and that particular goal was stunted without my magic.

In the first few weeks, I had tried to remove the manacles. After my first attempted escape, Ragnor made me watch Oberin torture her. Flay her skin in that nightmare in-between place.

I'd hoped it had been just that. A nightmare. But it had been real. I couldn't deny the way her screams had pierced my consciousness like iron stakes to the ears. The way the scent of her blood had filled the space, caused a dizziness, bringing me close to the blackness of unconsciousness.

I'd tried to break my own hands then, desperate to be free of the stone and use my magic to tear the monster responsible for her pain limb from limb. I'd tried snapping one hand between the heavy wooden bathing room door and its frame in an attempt to slide the cuffs off, desperate to use my magic to tear Oberin to shreds. To rip Ragnor's head from his shoulders. Rip that source crystal from where it sat in his chest and take his bleeding heart with it.

But no matter how I'd tried, I could not break my own bones. Much to my fucking surprise. The goddess-damned room had been spelled to prevent self-harm. I'd thrown myself against the walls, slammed the door over my fingers, anything to take control over this insanity-inducing situation. But I'd remained whole.

Only to be tortured in a different way every time he brought his dark witch with him to get his tendrils in my stores of magic.

As painful as the experience was, at least I got to look forward to the beating afterward. Not that I enjoyed having Oberin beat the shit out of me, but I looked forward to getting the chance to try to get under the king's skin. Every time, he'd wait for me to wake and allow his torture master to use his methods to try and get information out of me.

For once in my life, I was grateful for my mother's military training. I had been groomed to compartmentalize torture since before my magic had bloomed.

How lucky for me.

Despite Oberin's skill with implementing pain, I would give them nothing. Even if I had any information on where Elea was, they'd have to kill me before I broke under the pressure of pain.

The real torture was being forced to watch Oberin drain the life from her. *That* I was not sure I could bear another time.

Broken bones, lacerations, I could take. Elea's pain made

me feel as though my chest had been cleaved in two, like I would bleed out at the mere memory of her agony.

The last time Ragnor had told her I was there. I could not venture a guess at why that time, in particular, he had chosen to share my presence with her. I'd been there every time, watched Oberin shred her skin through every horrific attempt to break her. She had been so strong in the face of the pain. Until he'd threatened me. Her panic, screams, agony, and terror at the knowledge I was there made bile rise in my throat.

But I could do nothing but watch from the shadows.

Invisible. Useless. Broken.

Only to be taken to that witch's chamber, drained, and then forced to endure my own unending torture session.

I'd spent the time laughing at Oberin, taunting Ragnor for his inability to do anything right, to keep his talons in her. After all, he wouldn't need my magic to survive if he had been successful in his efforts in the first place, right?

It made me feel alive to rile them up. To take the pain and give them no satisfaction in causing it.

And when they'd dumped my broken body back into my chamber after hours of abuse to no avail, I'd spit on his feet, my bloodied hair hanging in my eyes.

Running my mind through the grim events from that morning grounded me as I imagined how viscerally I would tear all of them limb from limb the second I got out. How I yearned to feel the hilt of a dagger in my palm before sinking it between Oberin's eyes. The witch's.

The moment these shackles were off, I'd make sure they remembered every single action they'd taken that led them to their unsightly deaths at the hand of my blades.

I ran my tongue over my split lip and curled my knees into my chest, groaning at the pain the movement caused in my ribs. The fractures would likely take weeks to heal with the deadstone, but the pain kept me centered. Focused. I needed the motivation to keep the anger hot enough in my blood to follow through on all my gruesome fantasies.

"You should learn to keep your damned mouth shut," a familiar, crisp voice rang from the shadows, rattling my dismal train of thought.

A slight pressure lifted from my chest as I tried to narrow my eyes on the shadows cast by the glowing moonlight.

"Wouldn't do any good. They'd take their fun out on me either way," I said, my voice croaking from lack of use, and I winced at the pain in my ribs as I shifted in my seat.

Brenwyn pulled herself together from the darkness, her corporeal form taking shape in the blink of an eye, a scowl plastered to her sharp features.

"No, they wouldn't. You piss them off." She huffed irritably. "I think you're asking for it, honestly. Cut it the fuck out."

I rolled my eyes and let my head fall back against the wall as my gaze found the moon through the deadstone bars over my window.

"I brought a healer. They're waiting outside if you can cut the attitude long enough to let them fix you."

"I don't want help."

"Yeah, I knew you'd say that. You'll take it. You'll take weeks to heal this time, and you need your strength," the wraith said, her tone curt.

"For what," I snapped and pinned my attention to hers again. "This is useless. She's still out there, yeah. But what in the blistering underworld am I supposed to do from inside this goddess-forsaken room?"

"Well, sitting here with broken ribs isn't going to help anything, is it?" she said after a moment of meeting my intense stare in silence. "If your friends find a way to break you out, you need to make sure you aren't a pile of shattered bones. Think of the mess it would make if Atlas or the firebird or both were distracted because you're too sulky to take care of yourself."

I seethed at her with gritted teeth for a moment before I huffed in irritation.

"Fine," I said, my voice clipped.

"Fine," she replied, her tone lifting with pride at her small victory in time with one of her shoulders. She called for the healer. "Come on in, Laz."

The door creaked open, and a creation fae healer stepped through the threshold.

The moment their presence filled the room, I found myself lost in a strange sort of trance, captivated by their beauty. Their dark onyx skin seemed to soak up the moonlight in a way that made them appear more alive than most. Their emerald eyes shone brightly, standing out in contrast to their rich complexion. They did not shy their gaze away from me and my injuries, examining me with a quick glance as they kept their posture straight, and their lithe frame stood nearly a head taller than Brenwyn. They had a stern yet somehow kind expression fixed to their full features, their high cheekbones crested with golden flecks of freckles. Their black hair sat in twisted knots along the crown of their head, framing their heart-shaped face in an obsidian halo.

Their full lips tightened as their inspection ceased, and they nodded as though accepting the task handed to them.

"Lazuli will take care of you. I'll be back when I can," Brenwyn said before nodding to the healer and disappearing into the shadows without warning.

It took me a moment to gather my thoughts, as they had gotten lost at the mere sight of the creation fae. I had not expected another person to be capable of filling this bedchamber-turned-prison cell with so much life.

They met my eye with an intensity that made something

stretch tight over my chest, and I let my head fall back against the wall.

"You don't have the bidding of our gracious highness to do?" I asked, forcing a bite to my tone.

The corner of their lips tugged up at my words, and something flickered in their bright eyes.

"What happens under the cover of night is none of the king's business." They spoke with clarity, a tone of voice matching the strength of their appearance, their voice cracking the tension of the barren room.

They moved closer and folded their legs under them, sitting on their feet inches in front of me. This close, the gold flecks over their cheeks snagged in the moonlight. I traced the line of them with my eyes, a constellation splattered over their nose.

"We can either do this the quick way or the painless way," they said as they reached into a canvas bag slung over their shoulder. They pulled out a small vial full of a deep purple liquid: the essence of sleep. "Which would you prefer?"

"Quick," I said through gritted teeth.

I would not allow anyone to render me unconscious.

"It will hurt," they warned with a raised brow, replacing the tonic from where it came.

"No more than it did the first time. Let's get it done."

The creation fae nodded with a short breath, their gaze lingering on mine for a lengthened moment, as though they had been searching for something they surely would not find. The suspended fraction of time only lasted that long before they laid gentle fingers on my arm, moving with a featherlight touch to my ribs to begin their work to heal my many scars.

The wounds they could not touch would remain with me forever. Surely branded on my soul for lifetimes.

CHAPTER 6
ATLAS

Infuriating.

Aurelia was utterly, undeniably, absolutely *infuriating*.

That was nothing new, though. The months we'd spent together in Safe Haven had prepared me for that fact. All the times she'd ignored my instructions during training or had flashed me that expression of false aggravation that, admittedly, thrilled me to my core. The one that made her copper brow pinch and her full mouth pout in that way that was not at all as intimidating as she thought it was. It was the very same expression that usually cracked into a crooked smile with a twitch of the corner of her mouth as I said just the right thing to melt her icy façade.

It was the very same expression that made my heart flip in its cage as my untamed thoughts got lost in the gilded beauty of her wide eyes.

I did my best to tame the beast within my chest, rein in my thundering heart as I fumed over how difficult she had been the night before. How stubborn and unreasonable it had been for her to storm off on her own like that.

Three months we had been traipsing all over the goddess forsaken continent, only to find her half alive and fending off one of the most dangerous looking beasts I had ever seen.

And she'd tried to leave again. No *thanks for finding me,* or *oh, Atlas, I'm so glad you're finally here to help me in the quest to find your captive sister.* None of that. Just irritation and a demand to leave her be.

I had been stewing in my own irritation all night and well into the morning. She'd never fallen asleep, which was *also* irritating as all underworlds. A weighted exhaustion pulled at the corners of my mood, keeping a heaviness to my temperament.

That was all this was. I was simply quick to aggravation due to sleep deprivation. Not at all because my heart had fissured a little when she'd told me to leave. Not even a little bit because she looked to be half the weight she'd been before she'd taken off. And it wasn't that the gentle gesture of her touch across my cheek had both sent my heart soaring but also plummeting into a blackened abyss of despair at the same time.

Even now, as we made our way through trees at the borderline of Venridge, I couldn't help but lose my very pointed train of thought to the line of her jaw, the curl of her copper lashes, her bronzed skin as it shone in the light peeking through the leaves, the way her thoughts passed over her expression as though they moved freely, tangible behind her radiant eyes.

I was incapable of holding onto my weakening aggravation as the seconds passed.

Fucked. Absolutely *fucked* was what I was.

We made it to the market square in Venridge, and Gengi went off to check on some materials he'd need for a charm. Reia had pulled her hood up over her rust-colored curls the moment we set foot in town. She looked sallow under the shade of the fabric. Her usually warm bronze skin paled in comparison to what it had been in Safe Haven and her cheeks were hollowed out, surely from lack of sleep and food as she had journeyed on her own. The thought of her struggling so much, neglecting herself in this way made my stomach turn over on itself.

Gengi had glamoured me, as usual, bringing some color to my skin and hair and leaching it from my eyes, but Reia had refused. She'd claimed she wasn't sure her magic would allow her to hold onto the disguise for long, despite me insisting that it was necessary and Gengi showing her the amulets he'd charmed to help maintain a disguise. She'd stubbornly refused to take the one meant for her and had opted for concealing herself with the dense fabric of the cloak we'd brought her instead. The entire conversation had peeved me, as I was sure Ragnor's men would be looking for her and I couldn't understand her decision to hold onto her golden eyes and copper hair, but I could not sway her.

It seemed I would have to pick my battles, and I knew we'd surely have more to come.

On the way to the trade city, she had explained to mostly Gengi, as she'd seemed to not be on speaking terms with me in that moment, what she had been doing for the past three months. She'd been trying to get to the source, or a piece of it rather. She'd claimed her past life memories were still coming back to her in flashes, but she was sure that if she could get to the stone, it would replenish her stores of magic, which had remarkably gone missing since she'd shifted into the firebird.

I had to admit that we would need her at full strength if we ever had hopes of taking on Ragnor, or even making so much as an attempt at saving Callista from her imprisonment. But I hated the idea. The source was supposed to be corrupt, volatile, and I wanted her nowhere near the thing if it had the potential to destroy like the legends claimed. But she had brushed off my warnings and all but ignored me to engage in her conversation with Gengi.

Which had gone absolutely swimmingly. The two of them had gotten on just fine. Which I had expected, but it also proved to deepen my sour mood in light of my sleep-deprived state of mind.

Or maybe I had just been jealous that she'd wanted to talk to him and seemed so keen to ignore me after three months of the desperation I'd felt to be near her again. I was more inclined to ignore that little tidbit of pain in favor of blaming it on lack of sleep, though.

Gengi had told her of Emrys and Avery, who had been stranded on a scouting trip when Haven had been sacked. He'd explained that we'd need to be looking for them since we'd lost contact about a month ago, when their last message had come through to him, all the rest of ours going unanswered since.

Gengi and Emrys had been all but attached at the hip since he'd found her in Cresthollow five years ago. The lunar female had gone on a scouting trip with Avery for the first time, and naturally *that* had happened to be the worst opportunity to make a voyage like that. Or the best depending on how you viewed it. They had missed the ransack of Haven, keeping the two of them safer than the rest of us.

Gengi was worried about her, but my bets were on the pair being just fine. Emrys had the unique ability to cloak herself and others under a shield of invisibility. If anyone could make it after a sack on Safe Haven, it was Emrys.

Regardless, no one had heard from them since.

Reia had agreed to help our favorite young half-solar witch find our missing friends, and *he* had agreed to help her find a way to wield the source with minimal risk, after much protest to her plan on my part. Which she had not taken well until Gengi had reluctantly agreed with my stance that holding the literal source of all Celvaria's magic was a stupid and dangerous idea. But only when *Gengi* had suggested it had she agreed.

Typical.

And now the two of us stood together in the blacksmith's booth in the market, stewing in silence because Gengi had gone off to find the apothecary. Which was ridiculous because I was sure he'd brought enough stores of magical supplies in that enchanted bag of his to last an entire calendar year. But he'd left me alone to keep Reia company, nonetheless.

I could not stop my attention from flitting to the swell of her lips, which turned down in a frown, or the sharp line of her jaw as she turned over the weapon in her hands. The blacksmith herself was busy bartering with a group of men who were proving to be difficult. I kept one ear on them, but she had been handling herself just fine. The strong-willed blacksmith was taking no shit from the pretentious ramblings of men who thought themselves too good to pay full price for quality products.

"Are you going to pretend you don't like me all day?" I asked Reia, picking up a dagger to feign like I was interested in the design on the hilt. "Because I am getting *so* bored of this moody disposition. I would much prefer it if you would just yell at me and get it out of your system so we can get on with our regular banter."

The roll of her eyes was something I felt. I did not usually need to see it to know exactly how her expression changed at my words. She let out a short, frustrated breath and rolled her shoulders as if to dispel some tension, but she ignored me to step away and look at a sword on another stretch of the display. Irritation pricked at my chest, and I followed without hesitation.

"Really, I can take it. Tell me how much you loathe me and wish I had stayed behind. How you like to do things *alone* because you've always been alone," I drawled on. "Of course, I am paraphrasing, but I do think I am at least close. I would love to hear—"

"Goddess *damn it*, Atlas."

She set the blade down with a force that rattled the table and turned her furious gaze on me. Something about the way her expression set piqued my concern. She seemed tired, the bags under her eyes more prominent than I'd ever seen, and her shoulders sagged as though an invisible weight pulled at them.

Still, the contact of her golden eyes on mine sucked the air from my lungs, and it was a struggle to control the way my entire body responded to her sudden turn of attention. I managed to swallow the flutter in my chest and keep my expression light.

"There's a reaction!" I said, forcing a smile to my lips with a cocked brow. "Now, let me have it."

"I do not *loathe* you, for the sake of the bleeding underworld. And it is *because* I do not loathe you that I am absolutely *furious* with you. I almost lost you, Atlas. Ragnor almost killed you once already, and I cannot risk your safety like that again. He already has her. I *will not* risk your life, too. You should not have come."

The confession came out hot and fast, her words a rush as they tumbled over each other, and I could see the familiar rise of her anxiety as something wild swam behind her gilded eyes, a flush of color creeping up her neck. It took me a moment to completely catalogue each of her words in my mind, but the second I sensed her rise in panic, I relaxed my expression and forced a breath to calm the stirring within my core.

I can't lose you either.

The thought pressed against my resolve, but I could not allow myself the liberty of being so free with my emotions. Not with her. Not about this.

"Well, that's all well and good, but who is going to make sure you don't burn any cities to the ground just because you're pissed off enough, Feathers?"

She cocked a brow in question and seemed to still as she processed my words.

"Feathers?" she asked.

"Seems to suit you, I think. What, with being an enormous bird in your free time. Elea never fit you, anyway."

"'Reia' will do."

"No. Feathers, I think."

She rolled her eyes, but the corner of her mouth twitched in that way that made my pulse race, and I could not stop the smile as it stretched my expression.

"Besides, you'd be bored without me. And you won't convince me otherwise, so don't even try to argue," I said as I pretended to inspect another intricately carved hilt on a displayed dagger.

Callista would love this one.

The thought of my sister cracked pain in my chest. It centered my focus and reminded me of why I needed to keep my composure. I had never been separated from Cal for so long. I needed her back just as badly as the rest of the realm did.

Reia thought for a stiffened moment, examining me, and I could not deny the relief I felt as she relaxed her shoulders and released a tense breath.

"There is nothing I can say to make you go back to Safe Haven, is there?"

"Not in all the realms." I spun the blade in my palm and met her eye with all the seriousness I could muster. "That's my sister he's got. I will not sit idly by and hope someone else is going to be able to get her out. Not that I don't think you're trying. Of course you are. But you need my help. *Our* help. You can't do it on your own."

She bit down on the inside of her cheek in that way that meant she was wrestling with something, her thoughts flitting through her golden gaze as she processed them then finally gave a curt nod.

"Okay," she said.

"Okay?" I asked hesitantly.

"Okay. But you do exactly as I say at all times, and you will not so much as step a snarky toe out of line or I will cart your ass back to Safe Haven myself."

"No." I chuckled. "I will do as I please and you will deal with it and enjoy my company anyway."

She rolled her eyes again and let out a frustrated breath as she turned her face away, but I caught the twitch of her lip before it disappeared from view. Even the *prospect* of her amusement drove me wild, the need to see her smile incessant.

"I won't entertain any argument," I interjected before she could continue. "Tell me what our plan is from here."

After a pensive moment, she turned her attention back to me and crossed her arms over her chest as she propped her hip against the table.

"Well, ideally, we get my magic back and get in contact with Brenwyn somehow. I saw her in The Capital, which means—"

"*Brenwyn?*" I hissed the wraith's name as my mood soured, a fresh wave of anger washing over me, heating my blood. "You mean the traitor that double-crossed us and led that monster to our home?"

Reia furrowed her brow in confusion and tilted her chin as she took a moment to examine my expression, a tense kind of caution lining hers.

"Yes? Why are you acting like that's the short of it?"

"Is it not?" I asked, my tone still seething.

"No. I freed her before she fled. She was acting under Ragnor's will. Has she not contacted you?"

Before I could so much as sort one of the turning thoughts as they buzzed through my mind, the familiar pad of Gengi's light footsteps sounded over my shoulder and his voice rang out as he approached to stand at my side.

"So, good news and bad news. Good news is, I can get the things we need. Bad news is . . . Why do you look like that?" he asked as he caught sight of my furious expression. His attention moved between the two of us as he assessed our respective dispositions. "What happened?"

"Well, it appears as though everyone's least favorite wraith is not exactly what we expected her to be. Feathers, here, was just in the middle of explaining that we have spent the past three months *fucking off* for seemingly no reason whatsoever."

Gengi turned his pointed gaze to Reia.

"What is he rambling about?"

"Brenwyn was acting under Ragnor's control. I broke her bond, and she fled. In the time I spent flying over The Capitol, I saw her there, still in the palace. She's there but free. It's actually one of the only reasons I felt comfortable leaving to reconfigure my plan—because I knew Callista wasn't alone. But now I am learning that no one has contacted Brenwyn and you all were completely unaware of her current position."

"In case you didn't hear me the first time"—I heaved a great sigh—"we've spent the past three months fucking off."

"Great." Gengi groaned, and his shoulders sagged under the weight of this new development. "Well, that's worse than my bad news, so there's that at least."

"What is your bad news?" Reia asked.

"The vendor I need to see isn't available until the next half-moon, which is over a week from now."

"Right, then I suppose we find an inn," I said brightly as I clapped my hands together, thrilled to finally have the prospect of a bed in my future. Three months of camping had been, quite frankly, a goddess-damned nightmare.

I moved around Reia to the other side of the weapons display, where the blacksmith was still arguing with the same brutish men over the blade they wanted from her for a fraction of its valued price.

"I'll spare you any more grief and take this off your hands. It should probably only be handled by someone skilled enough to wield it, in any case."

I clapped a hand on one of the men's shoulders, plucked the dagger's hilt from his hand with a smile, and pulled double her asking price in coin from the pouch at my hip.

"You don't charge enough for your work; it's the finest I've seen on this side of the continent. I'll take these two."

I flashed her a smile and placed the coin on the table between us, enough for the blade I'd taken from the brute and the dagger for Callista. I'd save it as a rescue gift for when we broke her out.

The man puffed his chest in aggravation, but a smile titled with pride curled the vendor's lips and she crossed her arms over her chest as she raised her brow at the brute.

"Sorry, old boy." I patted him on the back and flashed him a wink before trotting back around the table.

Reia watched me with her arms crossed over her chest, a look of amused interest on her face. I offered a quirk of my lips and sheathed the blades at my hip.

"Let's go. If I don't get some sleep within the next hour, I am going to be less than pleasant company."

She huffed a laugh, and Gengi rolled his eyes, but they both followed me as I made my way to the nearest inn.

CHAPTER 7
AURELIA

It took Atlas no less than forty-five seconds to acquire us a room on sheer charm alone. We opted for an inn at the edge of town, farthest away from the bustling nightlife of the trade city, where I remembered the entrance to the source chamber to have been.

Just like most, those memories were foggy. I knew I'd lived them, but there was a haze over them. They were distant, on the other side of a veil placed the moment I'd plunged that dagger through my breastbone.

I remembered enough to know the entrance had been somewhere downtown, where the most travelers spent their time. That was largely due to the radiating power there. The citizens were none the wiser, but the very land was charged with source magic. People were drawn to it. Which proved for a significantly exciting nightlife.

I also had foggy memories of taking part in that particular sect of culture. Dancing the nights away, drunk on faerie wine, glamoured as someone else. Those memories might have been a blur for an entirely separate reason, though.

As enticing as losing myself to the relief of wine sounded, it was not the reason I tried to head straight for that side of town as opposed to spending more time fiddling around with goddess knew what. I had spent so much time trying to get to Venridge, and now, finally having arrived, I felt as though I had no more time to waste.

But Gengi and Atlas had other plans, and treating me like a misbehaving child entrusted to their care seemed to be at the top of their priority list.

I sat on one of the two beds in the room, flipping through some of the charm books Gengi had brought with him to try and occupy my time while Atlas freshened up in the bathing chamber below the inn. Gengi spent some time organizing the contents of his magically charmed, depthless satchel. I swear, he'd managed to store the entire inventory of an apothecary in that thing.

We had been sitting in silence for what must have been upwards of two hours, both too exhausted to entertain the other. I used the relief of quiet to gather my thoughts, sift through my memories, try to come up with anything useful to our goal at hand.

The door swung open, and Atlas's presence filled the room, an instant brightness undeniably piquing my interest as my senses flushed.

"Are you still pouting, or have we settled on trying to come up with a cohesive plan?" Atlas chimed as he rustled his towel through his magically darkened hair.

I flashed him a glare, but my attention snagged as the olive-toned color bled from his skin and his glamour faded to reveal the natural silver. The purple returned to his eyes, and the deep brown bled from his hair, leaving it a crisp white again. Atlas tossed the amulet he'd removed from his neck to the table near the door.

"I *had* a plan," I grumbled irritably.

"Traipsing around one of the busiest cities on the continent *unglamoured* and exhausted to find a magical entrance to a secret chamber of the most intense magical object in the realm is not at all a plan. It's a good way to get yourself killed."

"No one is going to kill me."

Ragnor needed me alive. *My* life was not in danger.

"You don't know that." Atlas's tone turned cold, deadly serious, and he moved to sit in the wooden chair across the room, leaning his elbows on his knees. "And I will not risk it. We do nothing without a solid, cohesive plan."

"Atlas is right. We've been scouting the continent for a decade, and as far as I know, you've done a lot of hiding. We likely know more about the current climate of trade cities than you at the moment." Gengi sighed as he stretched his arms over his head. "That, and I am exhausted and truly just want to rest in a bed for a night."

Gengi's words settled a sense of unease over me. He was right. I'd spent ten years without memories, hiding my magic and staying away from the eye of Ragnor's men. I had not so much as set foot in a trade city since before Ragnor's raid on The Capitol. Things had changed since then, and I had no way to measure that change myself. I did need them.

"It would be helpful if you could go over what you know about the source chamber and the source, and really anything that might be useful to us in gaining control of your magic again," Gengi continued as he settled himself into the blankets on the bed opposite me.

"I know your memories are hazy, but anything could help," the solar male went on when I did not speak.

Gengi's presence had been an instant comfort, and through the last bit of travel to the trade city, I'd had time to offer my perspective on just about everything that had happened in and before my time at Safe Haven. He'd had a secondhand account from Atlas, but I was able to make him more aware of my struggles with memory.

"I know the source is dangerous. We can't touch it for long. It could cause permanent damage," I offered.

"Which is why I plan to create a conduit, much like the one you would have used in the palace," Gengi recounted.

The amulet Ragnor had stolen. The one that had housed the shard of the source embedded in his breastbone.

"And that is going to take how long?" Atlas asked.

"Likely a week or two after that vendor is available. Work like that isn't quick."

Anxiety flushed me. I wasn't prepared to wait that long. Exhaustion washed over my resolve and my muscles filled with lead. The itch to reach for the berries at my hip overwhelmed me.

"So, we have time to gather our resources *and* search for any sign of Emrys and Avery," Atlas said. "Do you have any idea where the entrance to the source chamber is? What it looks like? What are we looking for?"

"I know it isn't a door. It was sealed with blood magic. Only Asteria and I could open it. Which is what I am still hoping for. I also know it isn't just a chamber. It's protected within a series of tunnels under the trade city that stretch into the surrounding forests."

"It is wildly unlikely that it is still hidden and protected like that," Atlas said, and I nodded, although the dread flushing my chest at the thought made my blood turn cold.

"Okay, so we need to watch for patterns in Ragnor's men. It's likely they have access to the underground tunnels. So, we can spend the next week watching for anything unusual. I can inquire with the checkpoint here for word about Emrys." Gengi nodded with a yawn, his eyelids already fluttering closed.

"It's a start," Atlas said with a sigh as he leaned back in his chair.

When I turned my attention to the lunar male, I found his eyes locked on me with an intensity that caused an electric crawl over my exposed skin, as though the air in the room had chilled. I swallowed a quickly forming lump in my throat and urged the flutter of my chest to quell.

The weight of the berries at my hip and the relief they offered me tugged at the edge of my awareness, pulling my thoughts away from the striking male.

"I think I am going to go wash up," I said as I rose to my feet.

Atlas rose too, his muscles stiff.

"Alone. I will be fine. I will be back. I am not going to leave this inn."

He assessed me cautiously for a long, tense moment before he conceded with a tight nod, reluctance in the gesture.

"If I find out you've gone against that word, I am going to brightly kick your ass," he warned, a hint of the playful tease I was used to lingering under his tone.

Gengi's soft snore from the corner of the room brought a gentle smile to my lips. He'd fallen asleep so quickly. Something deep within my core ached for that kind of relief.

I nodded to Atlas, my gaze trapped within the depths of his as I moved toward the door.

"Please take your amulet. You don't know who is going to be down there." He reached for the necklace on the table and offered it to me.

I met his eye for a moment. The air between us pulled taut as I considered. I did not want any outside magic interfering with my ability to harbor my own. It terrified me to know how unstable my connection to my well had become, but something in his gaze caused a catch behind my heart, and I nodded, a small concession to his honestly rather reasonable request.

I turned my back to Atlas and lifted the thick tresses of hair from my neck. After a tense moment lingered in the air for a fraction too long, I turned over my shoulder to peer at him. He took a quick breath, and his expression relaxed. The tension there bled away as he moved to drape the amulet over my collar, clasping the gold chain around my neck. The gentle brush of his knuckles over my sensitive skin sent a shiver along my spine, the sensation of cool glamour magic causing a blur around the edges of my vision.

Before I was able to assess the feeling, the flush of the glamour washed over me, chasing away any thoughts before they had time to take root. An inky black replaced the copper color of the waves over my shoulder. To my relief, the magic worked.

"I won't be long," I said softly as I moved for the door.

It took me the entire trek to the cavern below the inn to gather my thoughts and sort through my exhaustion enough to center myself again. Fear, dread, anxiety, and nerves all whirled through my core.

It was more difficult to suppress the horrors when I was alone, with no distractions to occupy my thoughts. Flashes of Callista's screams, the stench of my own blood, the sneer on Oberin's expression as he relished his torture plagued my peace.

I shook off the nightmarish memories, took a shaking breath to steady the piercing panic. Not much longer until I could be sure I was alone. I would be able to stave the horrors off then.

When I entered the dark cavern, a sense of familiarity greeted me. I had been here before. The vast, cave-like walls were raw, carved out of the earth, and they hollowed out to frame multiple hot spring pools. The entire space was lit with the glow of warm-toned fae light. Each pool was lined with every kind of salve and soap one could possibly hope for. Every fiber of my being yearned for the warmth and comfort those pools could offer me.

First, I needed to be rid of the exhaustion threatening to take my consciousness.

One glance around the cove told me I was alone. I removed the bag from my hip and popped a few berries into my mouth; the instant rush of relief sent a torrent of fatigue and weakness from the very hollow of my bones. I did not allow myself the liberty of guilt in my harbored secret as I relished in the energy the fruit provided.

CHAPTER 8

MAGE

Exhaustion weighed down every line of my posture as I struggled to wield my creation magic properly to repair yet another broken building in Safe Haven. Mila, Despina, and I had spent most of our free time exhausting our power, putting the broken pieces of our once beautiful home back together. Mila and I used the earth to help us. We curled vines and roots pulled up from the ground to lift stones too heavy for us to bear. Then we molded the clay itself to the cracks while Despina used her rare source-charmed ability to move any object with her mind. She brought water to the dry clay, where we left the repairs to dry in the sun for as long as they needed.

In the three months since Ragnor's siege, we had managed to clear a decent amount of the wreckage, starting with the damage done to the memorial temple and moving into the market square. But we still had so much to do. So much to atone for before we could allow Safe Haven's citizens to reside here again. I wasn't sure we could ever allow that, with Ragnor aware of the city's location. My hope had been to reinforce protection charms, but of course the most logical thing to do would be to wait for the war to be over, however long that took.

I wanted the city to be right for that day, whenever it would be. I wanted the people here to get to keep a part of their lives for once in this broken realm's existence. I wanted them to be able to call this place home.

From the moment Safe Haven had been attacked, I had been drowning in overwhelming task after overwhelming task. It had taken weeks to heal everyone who had been injured, and although that nightmare seemed like it would never end, the number of casualties could have been worse.

However, that fact did nothing to assuage the guilt and grief gnawing at me every day.

I was so tired. My efforts had been draining me for months, my magic spent at the end of every day. I wasn't sure how much longer I was going to be able to hold myself upright. But there was still so much to do. I had to find a way to keep going.

The efforts were paying off, at least. The buildings were beginning to resemble the life they had breathed before Ragnor's siege.

I tried to be grateful for our progress. Although it was difficult to be any shade of happy in the light of so much death.

Eleven.

Eleven fae had perished in the time it had taken me to gather everyone and get us back to Safe Haven the day of the attack. For the rest of my immortal existence, I would never forget any of their names. Their faces. The individuals who'd trusted me to keep them safe. People who hadn't wanted to fight because they'd given all the fight they'd had left already. I'd promised them sanctuary, a *Safe Haven*, for the goddess's sake.

And I had not delivered.

Kimani: A mortal woman who had fled her village after

being caught for making her home a safe hideaway for runaway solar and lunar fae.

Lumen: A kind, elven male who ran the only pub in Haven. His family had been killed in the raid ten years prior, protecting innocents.

Ricktor: A young solar fae, only twenty-seven, whose parents had been on the island training their skills with the armies.

Evany: A lunar female whose passion was to cook. She would bring the best pastries, a staple of her culture in the East, to the market to sell at the end of weekdays.

Remy: A quiet creation female who lived on her own, loved to read, and kept to herself, happy to spend her days in silence.

Cantis: A priestess of the triple goddesses from the south who had been with us since before the raid, helping us to get Safe Haven ready for the impending devastation.

Damien: A solar male who had only just been scouted from Cresthollow. His sister survived the siege, and it took me over an hour to get her to release her hold on her brother's body.

Gennie: A mortal who often helped Freya in the bookshop by cataloging her tomes.

Henriette: An elderly mortal woman who spent every evening reading to the faelings who had no parents to do so.

Bernard: The lunar blacksmith so fond of Callista and her lethal weapons.

Ava: A bright and shining soul, a solar fae who had been training her magic in the meadow every day in hopes of having the skill to protect herself if ever faced with Ragnor's wrath again.

She was not successful. But she shouldn't have had to be. I should have been there.

It gutted me to think of them, to list their names in my head, see their lifeless faces in my memory, so different from the glittering souls evident in their eyes only months prior. But I had to. I would not forget them. I would not allow their lives to be snuffed out in secret. Each and every one of them deserved better.

It had taken me some time to catalog my grief over the losses. After a few weeks of processing, Despina had helped me braid a bead into my hair for each of them. Each metallic charm represented the lost citizens in a way that forced me to remember. I would list their names to myself, reaching up to touch their beads in order like I could somehow stay connected to them.

Someone had to stay connected to them.

Every time I felt too tired to push on, too drained to do the work necessary to rebuild the homes of those who should have felt safe under my protection, I would remind myself of them and the homes they'd lost.

Safe Haven needed to be rebuilt. For them. For those of us left.

I gritted my teeth and heaved with all the strength I could muster, wrapping a great vine around a broken shard of stone and lifting it to place it in its spot on the wall of the broken pub. A groan shredding my throat turned Despina's attention to me, but I ignored her gaze and focused on the beads of sweat forming on my brow, pushing past the trembling in my muscles as I managed to complete my task.

As the stone settled into place, I released my grip on my magic, and a great breath feathered in exhaustion blew past my lips. I let my tired shoulders sag, and my long braids fell over my weakened arms; the heat of the sun on my skin subsided as the thick tresses shaded my neck.

"Mage." Despina's tone was scolding, but her expression tensed with concern as she approached me, one hand fluttering over my lower back as she pushed a few braids away from my neck to take a look at me.

I heaved a breath and rested a hand on her shoulder as I tried to will my expression to relax.

"That's enough for the day, Mila," she called over her shoulder to the small creation fae who worked with her vines on a building across the street.

"I'm almost done," Mila replied, a significant strain to her own tone.

I used Despina's frame to support my weight as I turned to focus my attention on Mila with concern, tensing my brow. The half-solar warrior was much shorter than I was but still sturdy and strong.

"Are you alright, Mila?" I asked as my eyes landed on the creation fae.

Before she could respond, a violent shriek left her throat and her outstretched arms buckled, causing the vine she willed to snap out in a vicious thrash. I sucked in a sharp breath and moved to help, my legs feeling as though they had been weighted down with lead. I made it not a full step before the vine whipped the stone it held down, sending it crashing to the ground only inches from where Mila stood, still struggling to control her magic.

The impact cracked the ground at her feet, and she screamed again as she was knocked off balance, falling into a heap, narrowly avoiding her wreckage.

"Goddess bless!" Despina shouted as she lunged to her aid.

We both trotted to kneel beside Mila as she rolled over her knees, her fingers to her temples. Her face twisted in a crumpled expression of pain.

"Mila, talk to me," I insisted with a crawl of panic over the skin stretched along my chest.

I knew how exhausted I had been, so I could only imagine

how far Mila had been pushed. We should have stopped sooner, should have taken more breaks.

"Goddess damn it." She groaned and rocked back on her heels, running her hand over her face as she took a few steadying breaths.

Her pale blond hair fell in whisps from the knot she kept it in at the base of her neck. The stray strands clung to her fair skin with sweat.

"I'm sorry." Mila breathed, disappointment pulling her pale brow together.

"No," Despina said. "None of that. Are you okay? What happened?"

Mila snapped her attention to mine, her light green eyes glimmering with worry, a silent plea in them.

"We're just spent," I told Despina, a hint of regret prickling my awareness.

It was mostly true. The part of it I had been keeping to myself was that Mila had been losing control of her magic. Every day, it seemed to be getting worse, and I would have told Despina; I told Despina everything, except I feared the same affliction had been affecting my power as well. And I wasn't quite ready to admit that to myself, let alone anyone else.

It terrified me. I always had control. Always had power greater than most around me. If Despina found out anything was wrong, she would spend all her energy trying to find a solution to fix it, to help. But I wasn't sure there was anything to be done about it at this time, especially not knowing where the slip stemmed from or if it was going to get worse. I would not allow Despina to worry until I was sure I knew what was going on myself first.

"I should have been paying closer attention, Mila. I'm sorry." I nodded and did my best to offer an expression that conveyed my unspoken thoughts.

She sighed and nodded, her lips in a tight line.

"It's time for a break anyway," Despina began. "Let's move to the shade and—"

Before the solar fae could finish her thought, a light crackling sound filled the space just before a bright spot of light broke the air in front of Despina's face. Only a fraction of a moment later, a piece of neatly folded parchment fluttered into existence, bouncing brightly, seemingly trying to get Despina's attention. The solar fae's golden brown cheeks flushed in surprise as she sucked in a breath.

We hadn't received a message from anyone in weeks.

Mila's eyes brightened and everything about the lines of her posture stiffened. Excitement flared in her eyes, hope. For good reason. Someone had sent us a courier message. Mila's brother, Emile, had been traveling to the blight for Goddess knew how long, and his line of communication had been quiet for quite some time. She had been waiting to hear from her brother. Although, I wasn't sure this message was from Emile.

"Gengi?" I asked.

The message bobbed and turned a folded corner to peck at Despina's chest, pestering to be opened, its magic urging the message to find its designated recipient.

She swatted at it a few times irritably before she managed to grab the parchment between her fingers. Despina made quick work of unfolding it, and I watched with anxious excitement freeing the breath in my chest as her bright eyes scanned the script written there for her.

"What is it?" I asked, unable to contain my curiosity.

"Well—" She lowered the note to her lap and met my eye with a whirl of emotion in hers. "They found her."

Elea. Aurelia. The firebird.

It was a message from Gengi.

"About bleeding time," Mila grumbled, plopping into a full seat on the ground.

The disappointment was a tangible thing as it weighed on her, and my heart called to her grief, her desperation to know where her brother was. A longing deep within my core rang out for her pain. I wished I could fix it for her.

"They're in Venridge for the next week or so," Despina continued, rustling the rose gold curls at the base of her neck and fanning off the skin there. The heat from the sun was unusual for this time of year, and we all needed to get some shade and water.

"What in the worlds for?" I asked in disbelief.

"It doesn't say. What it does say, however, is that we should make contact with Brenwyn."

"*What?*" Mila hissed, rage flaring in her pale eyes, her delicate face twisting into an expression of wrath.

My own chest flared with violent anger as I processed her words, but I managed to keep myself composed.

I pulled the note from her grip and read it quickly; sure enough, scrawled on the back was a scratched-out plea in Gengi's handwriting.

Contact Bren. She's with us.

Despina paced the room; the rust-colored silk nightgown she wore complemented her warm skin tone beautifully. I had just finished twisting her hair to protect it from slumber, and she moved to wrap her rose gold spun buns in her silk sleeping scarf. She had not stopped moving since she'd risen.

I allowed her to whittle herself into her spiral as I twisted my own braids into a knot on top of my head, wrapping the mound of hair in my silk scarf and lying down on the pillow, my head propped up on my elbow to watch her move.

Back and forth, she paced as she worried a nail between her teeth. It never did any good to try to break her out of one of these spirals. Even if I had tried to speak, she wouldn't hear me until she was ready. So, I waited. I watched her patiently, measuring her rising levels of anxiety until she stopped in her tracks and turned to face me.

"I think we should go to the blight," she said without warning.

"What?" I asked, pulling myself up to a seat with a furrowed brow.

The blight was dangerous. A blackened stretch of land on the other side of the mountain range in which everything had died, creatures had fled.

My thoughts raced as I tried to guess at her motives, but I truly could not think of a good reason to travel so far, leaving Safe Haven unprotected while the others were all still out and working to come up with a plan themselves.

"We haven't heard from Emile; the blight is on the way to The Capitol. I think Aurelia is going to need our help getting to Callista eventually. It's just—we need to go."

I took a deep breath and focused my eyes on hers, soaking in every word as I measured the golden glint there. Despina was blessed with a version of the sight—or cursed with it if she were to explain it herself. She couldn't see any version of the future for anyone, but she got these intuition feelings that always seemed to be for a reason. I had never known her to insist on something like this without good cause, without having something come from it.

But the thought of leaving Safe Haven, these people I had sworn to protect, sent me into my own spiral of anxiety.

"What about Safe Haven? We can't leave them here alone."

"We leave Amaris, Rupe, and Wren in charge. They are more than capable. We've trained them well," she explained.

"Mila?" I raise a brow at the significant exclusion of her fourth commander.

"She comes with us."

I opened my mouth to retort, but Despina beat me to the argument. As usual. Her tendency to sense things I couldn't did not usually irritate me, but I was so tired and already in distress about the prospect of leaving Haven, my lips thinned as she began to speak again.

"Her brother is out there. And having more than one creation fae can't hurt traveling the continent," Despina explained.

"Have you sent word to Gengi yet?" I asked.

"Just that we got their message."

"What about Brenwyn?"

"Not yet. But I will," she said with a nod.

I hesitated, worrying my hands together as I processed the possibility of traveling from Haven. Despina moved to the side of the bed, falling to her knees in front of me as she took my hands in hers. Something about the way her eyes flittered as she looked up at me made my heart lurch, and my breath caught in my chest. Her familiar, amber-dusted fragrance wafted over my nerves, instilling a familiar sense of calm under my resolve.

"I need you with me, Mage. I don't want to leave without you." Her tone was a plea, and all the buzzing of my thoughts stilled.

But she would. I didn't want her leaving on her own. It was

bad enough Atlas and Callista were already out there. I was sure I'd lose my mind if Despina left, too. I wouldn't be able to bear my own worry over it. And I was certain, with the way she was looking up at me, a plea in her expression, that there was nothing I could say to stop her from going either way.

"Alright." I sighed.

The light in her eyes at my acceptance made something in my chest soar. She brought my hands to her lips and curled herself up into the bed next to me, wrapping her strong arms around my waist. I huffed a light chuckle and swayed at the force of her embrace.

But something else pricked at the edges of my consciousness. Something I had been doing my very best to keep at bay, to ignore with every fiber of my being. I had not heard it in so long, and I was sure it had been the beginnings of a nightmare before.

But I couldn't ignore this. The way the hairs on my arms stood on end, the temperature of the air in the room as it dropped, making my stomach turn. I looked to the cracking fire to be sure it had not suddenly turned to ember, and it had not. The flame still flickered there; its dance strong.

A knot in my core twisted, and my awareness went on alert.

Despina said something else, but I did not hear it. Not over the rushing of blood between my ears as I tensed, listening, waiting for the sound.

Come to me, Mama.

The unmistakable timbre of Mariella's voice floated through the room like a ghost on an ancient, tyrannical wind.

CHAPTER 9

BRENWYN

The shadows resting in the corners of the corridor called to me, begging me to release myself from this fae body and bleed into the safety of the darkness again. I preferred to exist that way. The shadows always felt so much more comfortable, as though I belonged to *them* rather than within the confines of the miserable existence of this miserable fae realm. Too often my awareness focused on the prison of my skin, where the air met it, how the fabric of my tunic scratched against my flesh as I moved. I would much rather exist in the shadows.

But no. I had to play the part of a dutiful soldier or probably get both Callista and myself killed, not to mention the consequences Lazuli would suffer if anyone found out I was no longer tethered to the control of the bastard of a false king.

I had always preferred the shadows since before I could remember, before I had been condemned to a life shackled to the whims of those more powerful than me, as my kind always were. I remembered feeling freer as a child, less obligated to remain in this body for any amount of time. I used to spend hours, days at a time, moving through the shadows, making friends with their solemn whispers.

It had been simpler then.

Before I'd been separated from my family and sold to the assassin's guild in this world. Before I had been snatched from my home in the dead of the night and sold to the highest bidder. I had been eager to get control over my magic and learn to become one with the secrets between light and dark, the friends cast over spaces as the light skittered them into existence. I wish I'd known then what a curse my lineage would be.

A life of servitude. That was all my blood had gotten me. I would long for that time. A place where I had felt safe and cared for, loved like I wasn't some kind of monstrous creature only good for stalking the nights. That was, if I hadn't made it my life's mission to snuff that particular flickering flame of hope.

That was the reason I was in the palace, the reason I'd gotten myself tethered to Ragnor in the first place.

He'd promised me a way to find my brother, and after a lifetime of searching, hoping for any way to get to him across realms, I'd been foolish enough to believe the dark king. But the memories of my past were better left untouched. There was no use in tangling myself up over stupid mistakes. I had more pressing things to worry about.

Like getting this message to Callista.

I reached my hand into the deep pocket of my overcoat to grip the courier message tucked away safely in the depths of the fabric, my anxiety spiking as my fingers met the smooth material. I could not contain the flutter of my heart as I recounted the words scrawled in a hurried script over the parchment. It had been a message from Mage. The very one I had begged for, for what felt like every other minute of every day for the past months.

A found her. We know about your mark. D, M, and I will go to the blight to help E. We will send updates as we can. I'm sorry I thought the worst.

I know what side you're on.

It wasn't long, but it was enough to tell me that Atlas had found the firebird. Which was a relief. I'd been watching Ragnor use Asteria and his witch to make any attempt at tracking the firebird for months. Even knowing she wasn't out there dealing with Ragnor's abuse alone settled some kind of comfort, however small, deep within me.

The thick coil of emotion as it barbed through my throat had nothing to do with that flicker of relief. I swallowed past the thickened feeling as I wrestled with the hurt slicing through my chest.

The firebird had not bothered to tell my friends she'd freed me on her rather dramatic departure. I'd assumed they'd still thought I was a traitor, but assuming and being faced with the reality were two different things. It hurt to know my friends thought so little of me. Thought I would be working against them.

In fairness, my own selfishness had caused me to stray from our cause, but I never would have put them in danger if I could have avoided it.

I tried to quell the burning train of thought with self-soothing reassurance.

How could they have known if no one told them?

They know now.

I would never have hurt them on purpose.

They will trust that I'm here to help.

I wasn't sure any of the floating affirmations actually rang as true in my core, but I willed them to, nonetheless.

The message was relatively useless outside of those points. I hadn't expected much. With a courier message floating right into the palace grounds, risking the firebird's location was too dangerous. I understood, but that didn't make my lack of direction any less infuriating.

The only thing I had any control over was my ability to relay the message to Callista.

Maybe it would bring her enough hope to hang on to her strength.

They were coming for her. The message hadn't said as much, but I knew they were. I could feel it in my bones, and I intended to stick to my internal oath to reunite her with her fated, to play my part in saving the realm, however small it might be.

It was the least I could do after fucking everything up so much.

As I measured the thump of my heavy boots against the marble floor, I found myself wishing again to melt into the shadows, to bleed into the corners of the room they held Callista in. It would be much faster than this, and I wasn't sure I could hang on to patience any longer, but I needed someone to see me on the opposite end of the palace first. I could not afford for anyone to have any suspicions that my loyalty to that fuckface had been broken, and spending too much time in Callista's cell without reason would put a target on my back I needed to avoid.

As soon as I left my mark near the infirmary, I would whisk myself through the shadows to her cell. It would take me a matter of minutes to slither across the palace unseen. But before I could so much as think about that, I needed a damn body to mark me. And for some unholy reason, the corridors were uncharacteristically empty.

A grumble of frustration rolled from my throat, and I

worked the note between my thumb and forefinger in an attempt to stabilize my swelling aggravation. I had been walking in circles around this empty wing for what had to have been an hour. I'd hoped to find Laz but I'd had absolutely no luck, so I thought the palace creation healer must have been working in the libraries across the castle. I'd circled this wing three times with no sign of them.

I was just beginning to think myself into a reroute of the plan when the soft tread of multiple footsteps just around the corner perked in my ear.

Finally. Is everyone on bleeding holiday in this wing?

I rounded the corner, my shoulders back and my chin high, as I prepared to make myself known to whoever might be there. Perhaps it was Lazuli now.

My hope was short-lived, though, as the sight of what waited at the end of the hall froze the blood in my veins.

Asteria, Ragnor, and that wretched cyphin witch approached, moving at the end of the significantly vacant corridor. The false king's presence pulled the life out of the air around him. The sconces of faelight overhead seemed to dim with his every step, as though a cloud of poisoned dismay plumed from his shoulders. His sickly complexion stood out against his cinder hair, the points of his ears meeting the base of his crown of shattered glass. The pits of his blackened eyes found me, and his brow raised with interest.

My gaze spent a fleeting moment on Ragnor before I moved my attention to Asteria. I was met with the same image as always: a lifeless shell of a body, lilac eyes flat, expression neutral, stony. Her pale gaze met mine, but she stared right through me.

She was there, trapped in the prison of that underworld-cursed obsidian collar locked around her delicate blue neck.

The witch flanked Ragnor on his left, every inch of the vile male dipped in his own brand of poison. His expression turned into one of interest as he saw me, his feline eyes alight with a wicked kind of fire. His sickly, grey-tinged skin was stretched taut over the structure of his bones.

I set my expression and shook off the surprise threatening to crack my features at seeing the three of them in this wing of the palace. This was the healers corridor. What in the bleeding underworld could all three of them, a trio of nightmares, possibly be doing on this side of the palace?

Well, if anyone was going to mark me over here, I guess the bitch-king himself is the most reliable source.

I had to fight the roll of my eyes at the sting of the irony, but I managed to control my expression, keeping my features in the stony façade Ragnor would expect.

I had grown used to the practice of seeming tethered to his dark magic. I hated it, but it was necessary. However, the sight of that infernal crystal collar responsible for Asteria's lack of agency sent a flush of icy rage through my veins that I was not prepared for. It proved to make schooling my expression into one of neutrality a difficult task.

"Wraith." Ragnor's tone was light but held a hint of suspicion, a question lingering under his voice. "I haven't seen you in days, hopefully because you've been getting close to having anything useful to bring to me."

I managed to keep my eyes trained on the king and forced myself to bow at the waist before I responded, using the motion as a much-needed opportunity to take a steadying breath against my swelling rage.

Maybe I can will the shadows at his feet to slither down his throat and suffocate him where he stands.

"I am still gathering resources, Your Highness," I replied through slightly gritted teeth, my nose still pointed to the floor strictly because I did not quite have faith in my ability to play my role in this state of vivid emotion.

"You've been gathering resources for months," Ragnor continued, his tone cool. "It is beginning to seem like you are incapable of tracking down your mark."

"She has proven to be quite allusive."

I bowed deeper before returning to a stand, a look of false regret pulling my brows together. Ragnor assessed me, peering down his nose, and gestured for me to continue.

"It is also quite the hindrance to look for someone who could be in any corner of the realm from within the confines of the palace."

"Yes," the king replied with a pensive nod. "You've said that before. Perhaps we can discuss sending you deeper into the continent again."

My pulse spiked at the suggestion. He had been unwilling to let me out of his sight since my cover had been blown with the citizens of Safe Haven. Not once had he even considered letting me out of The Capital, and now with my communication with Mage restored, I needed to remain here to help Callista, help them get to her.

Why did everything always seem to line up in the most inconvenient series of events?

My thoughts raced as I tried to produce a way to rectify this development, but I fell short as Ragnor considered me.

"I was just headed into town to check my resources. Perhaps someone has caught word of her whereabouts since my last check-in."

"Do that, yes," Ragnor replied with a nod. "I expect a report first thing in the morning."

I lowered myself into another bow, my eyes catching on Asteria's on the way. They were devoid of emotion, dead stones of lightless purple, and my heart fissured at the sight of her like this, a shell of herself in this form.

Ragnor stepped around me and his cronies followed as they continued down the hall. Holding my breath until the sound of their footsteps faded entirely, I allowed my muscles to relax. Every line of my body ached, the tension of holding my rage and fear so closely to my core a struggle. I rolled my neck as I straightened my posture.

I ran my thumb over the ring on my index finger and took a steadying breath, the shadows beckoning to me, their call stronger than before, as though they could tell I needed them, needed to release myself from this misery and allow them to seep into my being. The darkness washed over me as I relaxed the lines of my body and focused my attention on Callista's cell to tumble into the relief the abyss offered me. The darkness whisked me away to that far-off corner of the palace without a second thought.

CHAPTER 10
CALLISTA

I had never seen Laz in the palace before my time in my prison room. I certainly would have remembered someone like them. With nothing to do in my solitary confinement but wait for Brenwyn to find it convenient to slither from the shadows to speak with me or for Ragnor's witch to retrieve me with another unholy session with that magic-draining contraption, I spent a decent amount of time trying to place them in my memories from before the raid.

I ultimately came up with nothing.

Nothing but a strange sense of comfort as the image of their gold-flecked cheeks passed over my mind's eye.

It had been a day or so since anyone had been to see me; not even the individual responsible for delivering my meals had come. I'd had plenty of time to process the note Brenwyn had received from Mage, turn over every possibility.

Atlas had found Elea. They were together. I couldn't help the slight pang of jealousy biting at me knowing as much, and I felt guilty for it. It felt so unfair to know that I had only just started opening up to her, connecting to her genuinely before

Ragnor had taken me away. It hurt to know she had been traveling alone for so long, and a very real part of me was relieved knowing Atlas was there. I had no right to feel jealous, but I was. I wanted to be the one there with her, helping her in whatever it was she planned to do.

But I knew he'd keep her safe. I could trust that much. As much as it pained me to know I might have missed my chance to know her, to help her, to be at her side, I could find some comfort in knowing my brother was there.

I had never seen him care for anyone quite the way he cared for Elea. Well, not since our sister, Julietta. Before Ragnor's attack.

Our beautiful, bright, ray-of-golden-sunshine sister. Heir to the throne, a relationship we'd had to keep secret, confined to the underground tunnels, secret rooms, and nighttime adventures.

Atlas had taken part in more of those adventures than I had. I had been too busy with Mother's training, but Julietta's loss was a fissure in my heart that would never heal, nonetheless.

I released a sigh, a meek attempt at relieving some of the uncomfortable pressure that had built in my chest in the passing hours. It was easy to feel sorry for myself, to wallow in the misery that greeted me within these four walls. I leaned my back against the wall and pulled my knees up to my chest, resting my chin on one to count the stars in the sky through the barred window for what had to have been the thousandth time, when a gentle knock on my door startled all my senses into alarm.

I jumped to my feet and balled my fists at my sides, ready to put up a fight if need be. I would not be taken to that room again so soon.

Although, the witch never knocked to announce himself.

Confusion tilted my chin as I waited for another knock. Perhaps I had imagined it.

I said nothing for a while, and nothing happened. I thought it must surely have been a trick of my mind. I had just relaxed my shoulders when the silver doorknob turned, and I forced my defenses back up.

The door slid open, and to my relief, it was not the witch, or Oberin, or even the false king. It was the healer from the other night, the one I'd spent most of the past few days thinking about, who stepped through the threshold. Again, I found myself enamored by their presence; the very sight of them in the drab room seemed to bring it to life.

They glanced over my frame quickly, as if assessing for any new damage. They held a tray full of food I had not seen in months. An array of breads, meats, fruits, and vegetables my body so desperately needed had been arranged nicely on the platter. The fragrance of all of it wafted through my nose and caused a wave of hunger so violent, it was almost crippling.

I glanced at the food and met their eye again, my fists still clenched at my sides, unsure of what to make of this new development.

"Hello." Laz nodded with a soft smile, gently lifting the tray. "I brought you something to eat."

"They have someone on schedule to do that already," I answered, my words cautious, hesitant.

"Yes, well, if you'd prefer your regularly scheduled serving of gruel and stale bread every other day, I'd understand," they said, their tone teasing. Their round eyes narrowed as they shrugged their lithe shoulders.

I could find no words. Why would this stranger, this creation fae, risk their position to be kind to me? How could they? Weren't most of them marked? Bound to Ragnor's will?

I glanced to the deep V of their tunic, the neckline plunging to reveal their breastbone, their chest flat enough to keep the fabric from revealing anything, but I found no crescent moon.

No mark.

I wasn't sure if that should have made me feel more comfortable or strike a stronger sense of unease within me.

My instincts settled into the latter.

"The mark does not work on those of original blood," they said, noting my turn of attention. "I only want to help. No one should have to suffer as you have."

"I would know you." My voice came out in a croak, nearly a whisper as I turned over my memory for the hundredth time. "If you are of original blood, why have we never met?"

"My family never registered with the solar and lunar court."

"And why are you here now?"

"So many questions for a little bit of bread," they said as they tipped their nose to the air, the gold flecks on their cheeks catching in the beams of moonlight, making them glimmer in stark contrast to their rich brown skin.

"Forgive me if I do not seem trusting of a creation fae healer from the bastard king's court," I said, my tone harsh.

"I am not asking you to trust me," they said, their tone light, almost amused, as though the bite in my words had not fazed them at all as they placed the tray on the ground. "I am asking you to *eat*. You need strength. I will leave this here for you, but I'll need to come back and get it within the hour. Your guards will be back by then, and they can't know you have this."

Laz nodded with a soft smile, their hand already on the door by the time they spoke. Their electric-green gaze met mine again for a lingering moment, and something alive buzzed through the air as the corner of their mouth ticked again. Before I could think to respond, they removed themselves from my line of sight, leaving me alone with my spinning thoughts and fresh, full meal.

CHAPTER II

BRENWYN

I leaned back, my elbows supporting my weight on the windowsill, as Callista moved across the room. Her pacing was slow and deliberate as she worked a nail between her teeth. A sense of relief settled into my core as I marked the improvement in her strength. Laz had been bringing her food, and I was pleased to see some life back in her face, a fullness there that had been missing.

I'd used my shadows to silence the room, blocking any sound of our voices from leaking into the hall, so she could speak freely to process the information I'd relayed to her about the message from Mage. It took everything in me to remain patient while she worked to find her words.

"If Elea is with Atlas and they are not going back to Haven, then they are coming here."

"Presumably." I nodded.

"And you've no idea what Ragnor is working on?"

I thinned my lips, a grumble of aggravation touching my resolve as I was reminded of my failed attempts to reach the war room.

"Still getting tossed from the ward like a ragdoll in a sandstorm."

I could see the thoughts as they passed over her face. She did so well at containing herself, keeping her mood suppressed under the façade of a stoic warrior. But I knew better. We had been so close for so long, Callista could hide almost nothing from me.

"What are you planning?"

"Nothing solid," she said, waving me off but still lost in her own internal torrent.

"Callista, if there is something you know that you have not told me, I suggest you spill it. Because there is only one of us, who is not trapped within the confines of a makeshift prison, with the ability to do anything about our current, rather unfortunate position."

"You said he takes me underground to drain my magic?" she said after a stretch of irritated silence.

"Yes."

I had told her as much the first time I'd slithered through the shadows, following them to the dungeon carved out of the earth to watch them torture her. A shiver racked over my spine at the thought and the slimy film of guilt at not having done anything to stop it.

Although, what could I have done? Any action would risk my position. Risk my ability to actually help her. Or Asteria.

"I have been wondering for some time if that choice of location has anything to do with the source chamber below the castle."

Surprise flushed me, and I pushed myself off the windowsill, my brow lifted with interest.

"The *what*?"

She looked to me with a coy expression.

"One of the shards of the shattered source has always been

kept in a chamber below the palace. If it's still there, if he hasn't done something to it, it could be useful to us in aiding Elea."

"Yes, a shard of the bleeding shattered source would be monumentally helpful with just about everything. Why have you waited until *now* to tell me about it?" I asked, anger laced through my tone.

I had spent how long uselessly tumbling through darkness to get to a goddess-blessed war room when I could have been trying to locate something actually useful? A desperate, exhausted kind of irritation clouded my mood at that thought. I could not think of a single spot in the palace I had not ventured, seeking out every inch of the shadows in my desperate attempt to find any way to help. I had come across no such chamber.

"Well, if I'm being completely honest, it took me a while to trust that you were actually on my side," Callista bit, her tone just as fierce as her expression hardened.

"And what, might I ask, convinced you?"

"Laz," she said, the lines of her posture softening at the mention of the creation fae. "You wouldn't risk your life to heal me if you were still bonded to Ragnor. And they told me of their ability to sense magical connections. They were very convincing."

Curiosity tipped my interest at that.

"I didn't realize they've been open to that kind of conversation."

"I can be a conversationalist. When I want."

"Huh," I pondered.

The mention of Laz stirred my already whirring thoughts. They had access to tomes, royal records, and the library, which meant they could provide me with maps of the palace. Perhaps there was some indication of the location of this chamber in a record somewhere.

"Speaking of, I'll need to pay them a visit. You'll be alright on your own for a while?"

"I'll have to be, won't I?" she said, her tone tinted with a kind of sadness. It pulled at the edges of my regret.

"I'll be back soon," I promised as I focused my energy on lifting the silencing shadows.

She nodded, and I pulled the darkness over me to whisk myself across the palace.

I needed to speak with Laz.

LAZ SAT at their mahogany desk, focused entirely on their small vials of tonics as I paced the room before them, spinning my ring around my finger, trying desperately to quell the anxiety tangled in my chest.

"You are going to wear a hole in my floor if you don't calm down," the healer said without breaking concentration on their task of pouring their freshly brewed tonic into its glass storing vials.

"Do you think the source is still down there?"

"Do you really think she was telling the truth?" Laz asked with a healthy weight of caution in their tone.

"I think Callista has no reason to lie about something like that."

Laz leaned back in their chair and set their vial down, taking a moment to look up at me from their workstation pensively.

"Then, no, I do not think the source still resides in a chamber beneath the palace."

I huffed irritably at that. They were probably right. It had likely been Ragnor's primary power source used to aid him in his takeover of The Capitol. Laz watched me patiently. They were always so patient, which was not something I was used to. Most people did not attach themselves well to me, but Laz had.

I'd never spent any time near the healer, never having any reason to spend much time in the infirmary. But when we'd returned from Safe Haven, each of us involved in the attack that day had been tended to, our wounds from the battle taken care of. Laz was a skilled healer, being of original creation blood, but I'd learned that day why they had been scouted for Ragnor's court.

Laz had the unique ability to sense magical influences.

And so, it had been their job to ensure that each of our magical bonds had been intact. I did everything I could to get out of the inspection but could not avoid it for long. I had resigned myself to being caught, sentenced to death, and had considered fleeing to avoid it. But when Laz had made their way to my corner of the infirmary, they'd met my eye, recognition passed over their face, and they'd reported my bond intact.

I'd taken the next opportunity to seek them out, only to find out they had no intentions of helping the false king and were looking for an ally themselves.

They had traveled to The Capital with the intention of getting close to the king's courts to find a cure for the blight, which had overtaken their home city, the magic there altered severely. They wanted the plague rectified.

"You're probably right. The crystal is likely goddess knows where by now."

"But that does not mean we cannot investigate for ourselves." Their tone lifted with the mischief I knew all too well placed there.

"I need the blueprints," I said, already planning the

mission, the halls of the palace opening up in my mind's eye as I tried to track my route through the shadows.

So quickly, the mindset of the assassin, the spy, washed away my awareness, replacing it with a calculated course of action.

"This could be it, Laz. A way to free her."

The healer looked at me, the intensity in their eyes a burning blaze of green as they considered. They knew I did not just mean Callista. Lazuli was well aware of my desire to free Asteria.

"I'll get them to you this evening." Laz nodded, a glimmer in their eye.

Hope. That was all the thundering of my heart needed to propel me onward.

"Now leave me be, you're a distraction and I need silence."

I huffed a chuckle and pulled the shadows close to me, blending my body into their fluid lines within a heartbeat as I nodded, flashing them a knowing smile.

BRENWYN

The wind rustles my hair in a way that makes me feel too real, too attached to this body, but something welling deep within my core illuminates the dread creeping up my chest at the realization. The bright spot is urged on by a sound that centers my mind, my awareness.

Her laugh. It echoes off the walls of darkness just loud enough for me to latch onto it, to follow it into the sunlight. And it isn't long before my consciousness is pulled into a scene of summer sun as it shines on my grey skin, my knuckles stretching a faint purple color as I grip a tree branch to haul my weight skyward, the rough bark scraping at the calluses on my palms.

I look up to see her bare blue feet as they scale the branches above me. My own laugh bellows from my chest as my heart flips in its chamber. She hangs from the branch, supporting her weight with one hand, dangling her legs over me. I squeal in surprise, anxiety flushing my skin as I note how high we have climbed and how far she would fall if she were to lose her grip.

But she is still laughing, her smile washing a warmth over

me I hadn't known I could experience, not the way the shadows claim me; the darkness seeps through my veins.

I know this place. I know that it is buried somewhere deep beneath my unconscious mind. A dream world she has crafted for us to exist within. Here, her delicate neck is not burdened with that ghastly black collar, her eyes are not sunken with dread, and her round, sky-blue cheeks are not hollowed out with the misery of being tethered to a monster for over a decade.

Here, she is free.

Even if it is only within the safety of my dreams.

"Catch up!" she calls brightly before swinging her weight to a nearby branch.

The gauzy grey dress she wears billows in the breeze as the green maple leaves rustle around her. The sun casts a glowing glimmer of shapes through the shadows of the foliage over her bare skin, the blue a radiant color in the sun of the warm season.

But it is not the warm season. It is nearly time for the frost to kill every sign of green, making way for a new cycle of life. It is not easy to smile and be free. My chest is not light; it feels like the weight of the world presses down on it, threatening to crack my ribs in two.

And I did not mean to fall asleep. I cannot afford to be asleep.

I SUCKED in a deep breath as I pulled myself from the clutches of slumber, its claws burrowed deep beneath my skin. Panic flushed me as my thoughts scrambled to make sense of my surroundings.

"You used to love that one." Asteria's voice rang out in the dark, a heaviness weighing at the edges of her tone.

I pulled myself up, propped my weight on my elbows, and snapped my attention to her. She sat in the chair opposite my bed, her spine rod straight, her navy hair falling in waves cascading along her thin arms.

"I didn't mean to fall asleep," I croaked, running a hand along my face.

I pulled myself to a seat and moved the dozens of open floorplans aside. I had been pouring over them, trying to memorize the interweaving halls of the palace, to find any place I had not yet visited. Even the possibility that there might be a way to disable that collar and free Asteria from the grip of Ragnor's control was enough to make me want to forgo sleep for the rest of my mortal life.

"What are you doing?" she asked.

A ping of anxiety pierced my core as her eyes darted to the parchment sprawled messily over my bed.

"They found the firebird," I answered, my tone weaker than I'd meant it to be.

"I know."

"And they'll come for Callista soon."

"As expected," she replied with curt words, a clipped tone.

"And we think there's a way to free you as well."

Her eyes softened around the edges, and her full lips puckered as she exhaled, her chest caving inward in apparent disappointment.

"Brenwyn, we have been over this."

"I'm well aware." My tone came out with more bite than I intended.

I pulled myself to my feet, and they took off on their own accord, sending me into a flurry of pacing the stretch of open floor between the lunar deity and the foot of my bed.

"Your priority cannot be me."

"The bleeding underworld it can't," I nearly snarled. "I am not leaving this castle without you."

"You know as well as I do that a day will come when you will have to. The prophecy—"

"Fuck the prophecy," I snapped, still walking in lines back and forth between Asteria and my bed. "I don't care what the goddesses said how many hundreds of years ago. I have no allegiance to the goddesses of this realm."

"Just because you hail from another world does not mean you are exempt from the wrath of the goddesses from this one."

I threw my hands up and opened my mouth to retort, but my words turned to a faint buzzing in my mind, whirling with the panic and dread that came with the possibility of her potential future. I snapped my mouth closed and looked to her with a clenched jaw, and the beginning of tears welled in my eyes, their sting difficult to ignore.

Asteria released a stiff breath and rose to her feet, gliding across the floor to stand in front of me. She reached up and her ghostlike fingers fluttered over my cheek as her glowing eyes searched my face, glittering with welling emotion.

Her touch did not land, but I could almost feel it. If I closed my eyes and imagined the way her skin would feel against mine, the way it had in my dreams . . . I could almost force the sensation of the delicate, tender brush of her fingertips to radiate through my senses. I took a shuddering breath and opened my eyes to meet hers again. Her hand fell to her side as she tilted her head.

"Sometimes I fear that loving me will hurt you too much to have been worth it. I can't give you anything," she confessed, her words a quiet tremble as her own eyes welled with tears.

I reached up to allow my fingertips to dance along the space above her phantom cheek; they shook with the desire to be able to offer her the kind of comfort I knew we both so desperately desired.

"Loving you is worth any atrocity this life could hand me. I would not trade it for anything. If whispers in the dark and fantasies in my dreams are all I get to have with you here, then that is enough. You are enough. What upsets me so is not whether you can give me anything. It is your freedom, your spirit, your life. You deserve those things."

Her bottom lip trembled as she processed my words.

Then her eyes hollowed out as she saw something in the distance I was not privy to. A pain in my chest cracked, as I knew our time was expiring so soon again.

"I love you, Brenwyn," she muttered, her voice beginning to take on the echo of a dream. She was already leaving.

I opened my mouth to speak, but she vanished before I could get the words out. My hand fell through the air as I tried to reach for her, instinct fueling a desperate need to keep her spirit close, but disappointment pulled at my mood as the effort failed.

"I love you, Asteria," I whispered to the empty room, nothing but the embers in the dying fireplace to hear my confession.

CHAPTER 13
ATLAS

Downtown Venridge was nothing like I thought it would be. Without the glittering night sky and glowing faelight, the cobblestone on the other side of the bridge bisecting the city seemed average, lacking life. The streets were not at all bustling and busy like I was used to, but then again, I had never had a reason to visit this side of town during the day. Not many did, as it was known by travelers to be the spot to lose oneself after the heat of the sun slipped away.

Any business we dealt with regarding scouting for Safe Haven was conducted on the west side of town near the market square, and my time traveling with the royal family as their escort and bodyguard for their occasional travels to the trade cities had been the same. I had, however, spent my fair share of evenings decompressing on a dance floor or two in my time. But the long stretch of pubs seemed almost ghostly without the bustling of busy patrons. Only a handful of still drunk fae and mortals alike trudged their way back toward the bridge, the occasional pub keeper out to clean up their storefronts.

This was . . . sad. The stone façades of the buildings were grey, and discarded bottles and glass were strewn about the edges of the walkway. I disliked it very much.

"This would be a much more pleasant task if we were taking part in the evening festivities, when this place puts on the mask of being welcoming and enjoyable," I grumbled as I kicked at a discarded wine bottle. It clattered along the path, and a strange, bright whirring sound caught my attention ahead.

I pulled my gaze up from my feet to find what seemed to be a sentient broom as it swept the walk ahead. It shuffled its yellowed bristles along the cobblestone, herding glass and debris along, leaving a perfectly pristine stone road in its wake. A magical cleanup crew.

"Oh, well, that's convenient," I said, stepping out of the way just in time for the charmed object to miss clipping my ankles.

"No, please, after you." I waved it on with a sarcastic twinge under my tone.

"It's early; they have measures in place to clean up after the travelers every night," Gengi said, nodding to a few more of the charmed brooms as they worked to clear an alley up ahead.

"I do forget sometimes that you've traveled more than I have in the past few years," I added.

Gengi had taken to scouting the moment he could and had spent most of his time in the major cities of Celvaria, scouting for solar and lunar fae to take to refuge in Safe Haven. He did so with Emrys as his partner most often.

"Speaking of your scouting career, what did the checkpoint say?" I asked.

Gengi had risen before dawn to check in with the owner of the bookstore, which was a mile or so from our inn. Reia and I had been awake, playing our regular stalemate game of sleep deprivation. Reia had returned from the bathing chamber the previous night with a significant amount of energy, much to my dismay. Something about it caused a tremor of worry within my core, though I could not quite place the cause.

Gengi had been in too sour of a mood when he'd returned from the checkpoint for the news he'd received to be good, so I'd left him be, allowing our walk over the bridge to remain silent while everyone had their chance to gather their bearings for the day.

Reia's attention piqued at my inquiry of the missing lunar fae, and she turned to face Gengi, interest in her stare as she tore her gaze away from the darkened alley across the way. She kept her cloak's hood up to cover her copper locks, having refused her amulet again this morning. Another fight I did not quite have the energy for.

"They were here up until we received our last message from them, but Vin has not seen either of them since. So, no new information."

"I'm sorry," Reia said, a heavy weight of regret in her tone. "What was their last message?"

"Emrys said the coverage of palace guards had increased, and they'd been keeping to themselves, but they were worried about an uptick in abductions. They'd been marking this area, actually. On this side of the bridge."

Something sallow sunk Reia's cheeks. The hollow expression matched the echo of pain in my chest at the recounting of information. I'd been worried for weeks that something had happened to our friends, but I had been successful in keeping the weight of that reality pushed to the back of my mind. The time for such luxuries seemed to be over.

I looked to the alley across the way to watch a pair of guards emerge from the darkness, dressed in palace black; they moved to join a few who had been patrolling the road ahead. It was common to find them roaming around aimlessly in any town, and these had been the only set we'd really seen all morning.

I shifted to conceal Reia, blocking her from view as I slung my arm around her shoulders.

"What are you doing?" she asked, her tone hushed but lifted with slight surprise.

"You still look like *you* and those guards are actively passing a poster about your bounty. I don't give them much credit for their ability to be observant, but I'd rather be safe than sorry, in any case."

Her shoulders relaxed as she released a breath and leaned her weight into me. I waited until the street was empty again, the guards paying us absolutely no mind. I wouldn't have been surprised if they had been recovering from a bout of drunken debauchery themselves.

Reia slipped out from under my arm and turned to get her sights on both of us again.

"I would like to mark now that I have not noticed anything particularly unusual in our morning stroll. Have either of you?" I asked, and they shook their heads. "I don't feel like there is an increase in number of palace guards, and no one really seems to be on edge. It does, however, seem strange to me that the vicinity in which you remember the entrance happens to be the same area Emrys and Avery were scouting. An area that is traditionally a relatively safe place for travelers on most days."

"I'm afraid they were arrested," Gengi said, his tone grave; it held a slight wobble, pain radiating in his eyes as the words left his lips.

"I am, too," I breathed, a tightness in my chest intensifying.

"If they were, where would they have been taken?" Reia asked.

"The cities have prison cells in the tunnels. *Those* we were already aware of. The connection to a chamber for the source of Celvaria was a surprise, but cells have been carved out under every city. They are most commonly used as dungeons before fae are taken to The Capitol," Gengi replied.

"So, we need to get to the tunnels either way. How do you get to them?" she prodded.

"*We* do not. In the trade cities in particular, we have never been able to get to the holding cells. Other, smaller cities, yes, but the trade cities are reinforced somehow. If we can't get someone out before they are arrested, we can't get them out," Gengi explained, his tone even, though I marked the sag of his shoulders and the weight in his expression as he spoke.

"Alright." Reia nodded. "A good start."

"We had a good start last night. We can only have so many of those. I was hoping to have progressed to the second phase by today," I teased.

When neither of them answered. I rolled a sigh from my lungs.

"I'll stay and watch the guards for a while if you two want to go find food. See if I can't gather any information."

"By yourself?" Reia asked, a hint of concern under her tone.

"Yes, Feathers. You're magicless and a beacon for trouble. And you need all the strength you can get. Go eat."

Gengi nodded in thanks and offered his arm. She took it, and they set off in the direction of the bridge, hopefully to get some rest and sustenance.

I turned to trot off after the guards. I would stay here, marking these black beaconed assholes for the entire week if I had to. If it meant finding our friends, saving my sister's life, and getting Aurelia her power, her strength back. Seeing her so drained and weak was wearing on my nerves. I needed her to be okay. I needed Gengi in his right mind. I needed my sister back. I would fix this for them.

CHAPTER 14
AURELIA

I waited until both Gengi and Atlas were breathing steady enough to be sure I could slip out of the room unnoticed. Atlas had not slept since they'd found me, sticking stubbornly to his promise to stay awake as long as I was. It had been starting to worry me, but I'd known he wouldn't be able to hold on long. Not without a little help. And sure enough, after the moon hit its highest point in the sky, sleep claimed him.

I slipped each boot on gingerly, careful not to make any noise as I strapped a dagger to my hip and draped my cloak over my shoulders. Slinking out of the room with featherlight feet, I took to the hall of the inn with nothing but the beams of moonlight to guide my way.

The moon sat high in the sky, leading me through the barren streets of the normally bustling square. The inn was located in a quieter part of town, much calmer than all the pubs on the other side of the bridge. It was late enough for even the drunk patrons to be close to passing out by now. The perfect time for me to steal away to the center of the city, to head for where I suspected the door to the source chamber to be.

If I was right, I didn't want Gengi and Atlas near enough to suffer any consequences of trying to breach the threshold. It would be dangerous, and getting my magic back was my burden to bear.

I popped a few viva berries in my mouth, their familiar flavor a comfort as it chased away the sluggishness in my limbs. My vision instantly sharpened as the weight of sleep lifted. My steps quickened and I found a strength in my resolve that had not been there moments prior.

There was something calming about the sound of my boots as they thrummed against cobblestone with no other noise to clutter my senses. I loved the way the cool night air settled into my clothes, keeping me aware of every exposed inch of skin. It felt open and free. A sleeping city with no expectations, no limits, no one to hide from.

I took a quick glance around to note that I was completely alone on my walk, and as the weightless feeling settled over me, I peeled my hood from my head, freeing my loose waves to fall around my shoulders. I tilted my face to the sky as I sucked in a breath of the crisp midnight air.

For just a moment, in that flicker of time, I was able to pretend I did not have quite so much responsibility weighing on me. That I was not stealing away in the dead of night to recover a shard of the shattered source on my own.

Almost.

I walked my way to the bridge over the iridescent, magically glittering river, glad for the time spent allowing my mind to wander through the quiet streets. I crossed with my head held high and quickly got lost in the magnificence of the enchanted waters and crystalline bridge. It looked so different under the cover of night. The faelight here along the prism bridge cast light through its glasslike surface into the water, encouraging more shards of beautiful rainbows to scatter over the waterfront. The refractions were absolutely enchanting.

Of the fragmented memories I had held onto, this had always been my favorite trade city. Most travelers felt the same, for good reason. This river provided the city with a life unique to only this land, its beauty honestly unmatched.

Little did the citizens know that beauty was largely due to the cavern housing a shard of the source of Celvaria, its magic responsible for the iridescent currents.

I stopped on the prism bridge to admire the stunning view for as long as I could before my good sense pricked at the edges of my awareness. It was so easy to get lost in the effortless feeling of a past life. An existence in which I could pretend to be whoever I wanted, glamour myself with any face to aid in my enjoyment of a reckless night on the strip of pubs and dance floors in a city like this.

The time for such had long since passed.

I released a breath, and the tightness in my chest reminded me of why I'd journeyed out on my own. I turned to make my way across the rest of the bridge, keeping to the shadows between faelight posts.

I did not make it one step before my feet caught on something solid. A significant pain jolted my ankle, a sharp force jerking hard, throwing me off balance. I could not stop the yelp of surprise from passing my lips as I lurched forward. I was too far away from the rail of the glass bridge to grip it to stop my fall. I curled my arms into my chest to break the coming impact with my forearms, but I went down at an angle, landing on my hip. The pain of the blow knocked the thought from my mind long enough to scramble my focus.

"If you have done anything other than sneak out in the middle of the night to admire the rainbows, I am going to be royally pissed off at you." Atlas's tone rolled through the air, and unfiltered irritation flushed me.

I rolled over to prop myself up on my elbows, the cold glass of the bridge biting at my skin even through the thick material of my cloak. The lunar male stood with his hip cocked, leaning against the railing with his arms crossed over his chest, his brow lifted, looking very unamused.

He was not glamoured; his silver hair and skin stood out in stark contrast against the black night sky. Anxiety flushed me at that. He was so diligent about the glamour amulets, so why had he not grabbed his? He was too easily identifiable as lunar without his glamour.

"*What the fuck are you doing?*" I hissed. My feet were bound together with a faintly glowing luminescent golden string.

Solar magic. Likely a bit he'd cyphoned from Gengi. The second the reality that I could not move my feet sunk in, a spidery crawl of panic settled under my breastbone as I tried to free my ankles. The binding was loose, but it tangled itself tighter the more I moved. My eyes stretched wide as frenzy did nothing to aid my efforts, the knots only getting worse with every passing moment.

Flashes of that nightmare realm overwhelmed my senses. The strain of my tired muscles against the bindings there, my magic useless. Oberin's hot breath over my cheek, his blade as it carved my flesh.

"*Atlas.*" My tone came out on a frantic breath as I looked up to him, the flush of anxious dread too hot as it crawled along my neck. "Atlas, let me go," I urged, my voice a plea as I reached down to fumble with the string, my fingers shaking and my breath coming in short bursts.

Atlas had already moved from his perch on the railing, concern pulling his features together in a tight-lined expression. He crossed the distance between us with graceful agility and dropped to his knees. The flutter of his fingers as they made an attempt to calm the panic in mine only barely pricked at my awareness.

"Hey," he said, his tone calm, soothing as he clasped both of my hands in his. He held them steady as his intense gaze searched my face. "It's okay. I'm sorry."

I heaved a few breaths, still trying to kick the binding free, and he pulled one of my hands to his chest, gently turning my wrist to press my palm over his steadily beating heart while his other hand made quick work of untangling the string. I used my free arm to prop up my weight and focused my eyes on the heat of his stare.

"You're okay. I've got it," he reassured. "Try to breathe with me."

The tight stretch of frantic energy in my chest made it difficult to oblige, but a sense of calm had already begun to bleed through my veins at his gentle touch. I took a few shaking breaths, attempting to match the timing of his, and before I could finish the third round of extended inhales and exhales, my ankles were free, the string faded to the silver sheen of lifeless metal as the magic drained from the weapon. He quickly curled it up and stowed the metal chain in his pocket, all while holding my hand to his chest and encouraging the steady stream of my breath.

I wasn't sure which cycle of deep inhale to forceful exhale began to quell the fear or when my vision began to clear, as though the haze that had overcome me had lifted, but before long, I was able to relax my muscles one by one. All while holding his gaze, using the sturdy concern in his vibrant eyes to center my mind again.

He waited for me to speak, patient, steady.

"You're not glamoured," I said after a long while of bated silence.

"No," he said, a weight to his tone, the seriousness still firm behind his violet eyes.

As I relaxed further, I became increasingly more aware of the contact of his skin against mine, the way his muscular chest moved under my palm as he released a sigh, the beating of his heart.

Something wild jumped within the cage of my ribs, sparking a kind of heat I was not prepared to process.

I pulled my hand into my lap and shifted my weight to adjust the cloak around my shoulders. He sat back on his heels and ran a hand through his tousled, silvery-white hair.

"Someone will see you."

"I don't care. Are you alright?" he asked.

"*I care*, put your hood up," I insisted.

"You put *your* hood up. You're the goddess-blessed firebird, and your face is plastered on every other wall in this bleeding city. I do not want to have to remind you of that again," he said, his tone fierce now. "Are. You. Alright?"

He emphasized each word of his question, an urgency under his voice, and that heat curled low in my core, sending my nerves spiraling through a confusing whirl of emotion.

"I'm fine," I bit, my tone harsher than I intended.

"*That* wasn't fine. You're not sleeping. You sneak out in the middle of the night for goddess knows what. That was *absolutely* a panic attack. Talk to me. What's going on, Reia?"

Reia.

The name on his lips felt familiar. Safe. It caused a flutter in my chest, urging on that spark near my heart.

"I thought you were sleeping."

"If you're awake, I'm awake, remember?" he said with a soft breath, one brow ticked.

"You don't need to do that. I'm fine. What I need you to do is go back to the inn with your hood up so the goddess-damned guards don't toss you in a cage and cart you to The Capitol." I nearly snarled.

"Okay, then let's go. Let's go back to the inn, you can get the sleep you have so desperately needed, and we can continue this discussion tomorrow. Unless my suspicions are correct, and you were *actually* out here to get to the source shard without us. In which case . . . well, you can just fuck off about that. You're not going near that thing alone."

Goddess damn him.

"You are so irritating," I bit.

The aggravation flushing through me caused a rush of heat I could not contain. I huffed and pulled myself to my feet, wiping my sweat-dampened palms on my leggings.

"I knew it." He rose after me, a hint of triumph in his expression. "Tell me why you think you need to do all of this alone. We're right here. *I'm* right here. Let me help you with this."

"I don't need your help," I said, my tone clipped as I pulled my hood up to conceal my copper locks. I moved past him, stomping off in the direction I'd come.

"The burning underworld, you don't," Atlas snapped, storming after me. "You are half the weight you were in Safe Haven; at this point, I am convinced you haven't slept in months. Something is severely troubling you, and you don't have access to even a lick of your magic. You—"

"Goddess *bless*," I hissed, turning on my heel to stop him short as we crossed the bridge into the shadows again, away from the glittering faelight to conceal his appearance. "Stop it. Just stop it. I don't want your help. I didn't ask for it."

"You are really starting to piss me off," he grumbled.

"Good."

"Listen to me." He leaned in, his tone low and dangerous. "Do not think that for one second, I am going to let you pretend like being a martyr for this realm is the right thing to do. You are stronger than that. Do not fool yourself into thinking that you do not want me here to help you. That you do not *need* me here."

The pause in his speech hit me in the chest harder than his words had. With a buzzing through my thoughts, I did my best to erase the reality of his claim, the weight of it. The pressure between us built on the tension of his gaze as he towered over me. This close, I had to crane my neck slightly to meet his eye. He leaned in so near, I could feel the heat of his flesh as it warmed the solid space between us.

"I have never needed anyone in my life," I said, forcing as much seriousness into my tone as I could manage.

"Somehow, I think that's a dirty lie," he replied, his eyes flaring as though I had presented some kind of challenge for him to overcome.

"And I think your overconfidence is going to get you killed." My retort reflected the same venom in his.

"That's my problem to worry about," he said, the corner of his mouth ticking, causing that maddening dimple to grace his expression, to falter my carefully crafted resolve.

Atlas leaned in ever so slightly and my breath hitched, that tight knot in my chest pulling at the strings of my core. I stumbled back a step; the sturdy composure I'd put so much effort into upholding cracked. Before I succeeded in putting any distance between us, he'd hooked his nimble fingers around the pouch at my hip, somehow untying it with just one flick of his wrist. He stepped back to dangle it between us.

A mixture of heated rage and frigid shock tangled through my ribs, and I gasped as I reached to snatch my berries from his grip, but he moved it out of reach as he opened the drawstring to pour a handful of the bright red fruit into his palm. His expression twisted with surprise as he shot me a heated stare.

"Viva berries?" The lifted shock in his tone was edged with a kind of anger I had not heard there before.

It startled me, and the slimy film of shame settled over my chest. It crept over my skin, and I did my best to conceal the feeling, to shrug it off, but it had already taken root. Shame itched over my breastbone, and I pulled my eyes from his, unable to face any potential judgment. The idea of that was almost worse than the potential consequences of not having them. I wasn't sure I could handle his opinions on this particular vice. I wasn't sure I was ready for his perspective of me to shift, as I was so certain it would.

"It's none of your business," I snapped and reached for the bag again; this time, I was fast enough to find success and turned to storm away, entirely disinterested in whatever scolding I was about to endure.

"Aurelia, stop." His tone was firm, but there was a plea there, a kind of concern under his voice that made that spot in my chest lurch.

Before I could make it more than three steps, his gentle touch found my wrist as he grabbed my hand. The contact halted my momentum, and I spun on my heel to face him. The warmth bloomed in my chest at his touch was entirely unwelcome. I wanted nothing to do with this. It was all too much, too overwhelming.

"No. *You* stop. How I manage my own sleeping habits is my problem to worry about."

"Right, but if you're too tired to manage your own overcharged ability to wield fire, to turn into an enormous fire-breathing bird, and you get my sister killed because you're too goddess-damned stubborn to accept anyone's help, then I swear to the shattered source that I will spend the rest of this lifetime reminding you of your own stupid mistakes."

The anger laced through his tone was so serious, it forced a hitch in my own frustration, my thoughts spreading out to the corners of my mind. Surprise at his ferocity wiped my resolve clean. I gaped at him, the mention of Callista a poisoned knife to my heart. The insinuation that I would do anything to compromise her safety was shocking.

"Those things could *kill* you. And then where would we be? What would he do to Callista if his leverage meant nothing?" Atlas's tone cracked as emotion rolled through his face, and he tossed his palms skyward as though at a loss for what to do.

"I don't know," I breathed. "It's why I wanted to get to the source—"

"Which will *also* likely kill you if you aren't careful. Fuck, Aurelia. Use your damned head. I am not following you around in the dead of the night to be a pain in the ass, as much as you'd like to believe that. If you die, then I am afraid I lose both of you. I can't do that. I won't survive it."

The weight of his words cracked my heart in two. He was right, of course. We'd been traveling for days, and I had been nothing but what he claimed me to be—stubborn and difficult, nothing more than someone with a bad attitude and a martyr complex. The realization hurt. It was a heavy stone as it sunk through my chest to settle deep within my core.

But I could not give up the berries. I could not fall asleep.

"I don't breathe fire," I managed to say on a heavy breath after a tense stretch of time, watching his labored breaths wrack his chest, the line of brimming tears in his eyes.

"What the fuck are you talking about?" he asked, exasperated.

"You said my bird form breathes fire. That's completely untrue."

"Oh, for the love of the holy mothers." He groaned and rolled his eyes, but a slight relief moved over my chest as I watched the lines of his tense shoulders relax slightly. "All that and that's what you have to say?"

"I need the berries," I said with a shrug of one shoulder.

"Why?" he asked with a narrowed eye.

"I—" I began, but the words got stuck, that same frantic crawl of panic itching at the skin over my breastbone as the edges of my vision began to blur. My breath hitched and I shook my head. "I just need them. I'm sorry. But I won't go to the source without help."

He examined me for a moment, searching my expression for a lie as I did my best to calm the raging memories of the dreamscape, to steady my breathing long enough to will the nightmare away.

"Good," he said as he pulled his hood up over his head and moved past me.

I turned to follow him, my eyes on the lines of his shoulders all the way back to the inn where Gengi slept soundly, not having moved so much as an inch from when we left him behind.

MAGE

Come to me, Mama.

Her voice was a ghost on the wind. A haunting presence always lingering in the back of my mind. Since the night I'd first heard her from the shadows, I had done my best to keep the hallucinations at bay, but they came nonetheless. Never her voice again, I'd been listening. But others. Scrambling words scurried through the shadows as we trekked through the forest. I could ignore them if I focused on Despina, on how desperately I wanted to get to the blight and get home, but if my mind wandered too far, if the stores of my magic got too low, the sounds of the dark spirits threatened to drive me insane.

It had to have been tied to the weakening of my magic. The idea urged on a constant crawl of anxiety, pulling at the edges of my frayed nerves relentlessly. It had been a while since I'd forced the last bout of terrors away, but that only left me worrying about when they would plague me next. I feared I would wear the tree emblem off the metal medallion around my neck as I worked it between my fingers over time, a pointless fidget to dispel some of my winding dread.

But it was of little comfort. If I wasn't obsessing over whether or not I had imagined my daughter's voice, if the spirits of the forest were trying to take me to the other realms, I was stuck in a loop of guilt, grief, fear, all revolving around those lost to this underground war.

"Should we set up camp here?" Mila's voice broke my daze.

I realized, not for the first time in our journey that I had not tracked time as we'd traveled through the dense forest. It proved difficult for me to keep track of our days as I worked to keep my resolve intact.

Despina wiped a line of sweat from her rose gold brow and turned her sights to the sky.

"We still have some daylight left; do you need to stop?" Des asked, taking a swig of water from her canteen.

I could see her fatigue clearly in the lines of her shoulders as well. We were all exhausted. If I could have *ephemerated* all of us to the blight, I would have, but taking two people through the pockets of the realm was not easy when my magic was at peak performance. Trying now would be irresponsible.

We needed to travel on foot in any case. We needed to follow the path Emile's group would have taken to try to find any sign of the missing fae along the way.

Mila looked at me, a flicker of dread behind her bright eyes before she schooled her expression into a neutral façade and slid her pack from her shoulders.

"Yes." She groaned. "I have blisters on my feet the size of lily pads, and if I don't eat something soon, I might die."

Despina released a laugh, the sound spreading warmth through my veins. It dispelled some of the tension in my own muscles.

Mila had been using her magic to move brush and clear a path for us, while I used mine to cover our tracks, and it was only a matter of time before her power would sputter out again.

I could feel mine fraying at the edges with every passing minute.

It was alarming how difficult it was to maintain our strength. Especially considering the forest was meant to replenish our stores, but the closer we grew to the blight, the harder it was to keep a firm grip on my magic.

"If we could *ephemerate,* we would," I said, my brow pulled together. "The risks are too high."

"Yes, yes, I know. Bandits in the woods and all, a strain on your magic, I get it. I am just burnt out for now and I want to have energy when we get to Emile."

Her brother still had not made contact, and it was growing difficult for me to hold onto hope that her messages were reaching their recipient. However, voicing those concerns would do nothing to help our current situation, so I offered a soft smile and nodded in agreement.

At this point, my motives for reaching the blight were more complicated than finding Mila's brother and the party he'd taken with him to investigate. I needed to know what was causing the strain in creation magic. I needed to see the blight for myself and find a way to stop its spread.

"I'll go get some firewood," the small creation fae said before turning off into the woods, her tone weighed down with the barest hint of grief after neither one of us managed to offer her any words of comfort.

"How are you doing?" Despina asked, crouching down to sit on her heels as she sifted through her pack for the provisions she'd brought with us.

"I've been better." I sighed and turned to wield my magic, spinning the green-tinged energy through the branches of the tree nearest me, urging them to create shelter for us. The branches bowed at my will despite the fatigue weighing on me over the excessive magic use.

Despina's arms were around my waist before I had a chance to sense her shift in energy. I jumped in start, and a laugh cracked free of my chest as she stretched on her tip toes to press a kiss to the nape of my neck. The sensation washed a warmth over my mood.

Despina chased away the darkness so easily. A ray of sunshine to break apart the dense shadows of my own weighted grief.

I turned to face her as I gave one final wave of my arm to solidify the structure and brushed the back of my knuckles over the apple of her cheek. She leaned into the touch and pressed a kiss to the heel of my hand.

"I'm okay, Des," I assured her, forcing a lightness into my tone.

"I am worried that you're lying to me. No, I am certain that you are; I just don't know why. *That* is what worries me. I know how important it is for you to be strong, but admitting a struggle is not a weakness."

Her words came out as a fervent plea as she gripped my hand, her brow furrowed and her posture lined with a tense worry.

"I—" I began to brush her concern off, but the words got stuck in my throat as the memory of Mariella's plea floated through my mind. I had not heard it since we'd left Safe Haven days ago, but it was not something I was capable of keeping from my tangled web of thoughts.

My throat closed around any ability to speak, and tears pricked my eyes.

It felt like a weakness. Something was wrong with my mind, and I wasn't sure how to cope with that.

"Something is going on, and I want to help," she insisted.

I nodded and forced myself to meet her eyes. Despina was shorter than me by nearly a head, and I had to look my nose down to get a full view of those luminous golden solar orbs, but she remained tucked into my arms, the contact a comfort to me as I pressed on.

"I think I'm losing my mind." My words came out on a nervous chuckle as I mustered the courage to admit it.

She furrowed her brow and stepped back slightly, so as not to crane her neck to meet my gaze, and waited for me to continue.

"It feels like my magic is slipping, and I—" The words got caught, and I choked on the desire to open up.

"What, Mage?"

"I am hearing things."

Despina nodded, but her expression did not falter. I would not have been surprised to learn that she had sensed as much. As I processed her lack of reaction, I realized how little telling Despina affected me.

If I were to be completely honest, it was the most difficult to admit potential weakness to myself. The idea of not being in control made my stomach turn; it sent a frantic kind of energy coursing through my veins.

"What kind of things?" she asked with a furrowed brow.

"I don't know how to explain it."

Despina opened her mouth to speak, her expression twisted with concern, but whatever she meant to say was interrupted by a violent torrent of wind. The destructive force of nature came on in a howl of horror capable of chilling the very hollow of my bones. Des jumped back, and her hands moved to the blades at her hips, the amber amulet at her throat glowing as her magic pulsed to life. Alarm stiffened my muscles, and I called what was left of the stores of my magic to the surface as well, my gaze whipping through the canopy of leaves.

A wicked howling ripped through the wood, causing a shiver visceral enough to keep me from maintaining any composure. The leaves above turned over on themselves, shrinking away from the violent wind, and the sky seemed to be cast over with a grey that had not been anywhere in sight only moments prior. A whistling sounded through the branches above, and the brush around our feet whipped at our ankles.

"What in the worlds?" Despina turned her attention to the wood, peering through the trees after Mila as she moved to follow the creation fae.

Before Des could take even one step, a bloodcurdling, soul-piercing scream split the air.

But it was not Mila. The voice that tore through my ears and cleaved my soul in two was not one I would have mistaken for any other.

It was the same sound that haunted my nightmares. The last thing I had heard of my daughter before being forced to move on through those tunnels under the palace without her. The last sound that had left her throat before she'd died that miserable day.

"*Mariella!*"

Her name left my lips in a panic, a wild and frantic hysteria coating my nerves as I shot into the forest after her.

Nothing could have stopped me. Not the branches of the trees above as they seemed to scoop down to block my way. Not the darkness of the cloud of black magic as it bled through the forest and tried to block my vision. Not Despina as she called for me from behind, tried to stop me from tumbling into this sudden terror with a grip on my wrist that I shook off with the determination of the goddesses.

Nothing in this mortal world would stop me from getting to my daughter.

Running through the forest was like moving through fear itself, as though the vile emotion had manifested somehow, turned to a substance meant to blind me, to suffocate me. It thickened the air, thieved my vision. It wasn't long before I could see nothing. Hear nothing but the wind. I had exhausted a decent amount of energy fighting through the living forest, moving the twisting branches from my path with my wild creation magic, and my chest heaved with labored breaths of overexertion. I spun on my heel, the cool presence of the black smoke on my skin only adding to the pressing feeling of loss. Isolation.

Then, her voice rattled my brain again.

"*Mama!*" The scream was a night terror, a howl on the wind as it whipped my braids free of the knot on top of my head.

A cry of my own broke my chest as my resolve cracked, the hysteria finally bubbling loose. I had no way of knowing which direction it had come from. I could not see the glow of Despina's amulet. Only dark. Only despair.

Just as panic gripped me, desperation buzzed through my already clouded mind—a faint green light glowed in the distance, a thin frame sitting on the ground, knees curled to chest in a tight ball.

I moved as quickly as I could, my feet carrying me on a flight of wind, desperate to reach my daughter. But when I fell to my knees, it was not the warm brown skin of Mariella's arms my hands fluttered over, but rather Mila's, pallid and drained of color.

She had her hands pressed to her ears, and she rocked back and forth, whimpering to herself. She did not seem to have any understanding of my presence, her awareness lost to this black void.

I flitted my attention around, desperate to find my child, but the deep haze was dense. And then Mila screamed. The same cry of despair I had heard before, the same shriek that had sent me into a panic, but with the timber of Mila's voice, not Mariella's.

What is happening to me?

Something was wrong, my nightmares coming to life before my eyes, but I had no choice but to compartmentalize that. No choice but to shove the hallucinations into the recesses of my mind.

I placed my hands on Mila's wrists, my chest still heaving with the lingering effects of hysteria. I said her name, but she did not hear me. She kept rocking. Kept crying.

I pulled as much of my energy to the surface as I could muster, pooling the healing magic in my palms. My vision swam, and the green glow over Mila's hands swirled in the blackness. I placed a palm on her back and one on her cheek before I pushed against whatever plagued her, desperate to force the healing magic through this poison. I had no way of knowing if it would work, as it wasn't a physical injury, but perhaps I had enough clean magic left to subdue her darkened power into submission.

Slowly but surely, I felt it: the darkness receding, peeling back from the intensity of my creation energy. It pulsed, pushed back, but I screamed against the effort, beads of sweat rolling along my temples, and finally the darkness broke. It skittered away as though deciding it was no match for my strength.

The wind ceased, and the cloud of blackness bled from the surrounding forest. I dropped my hands and Mila raised her head, blinking slowly as she met my eye. With confusion clouding her gaze, her expression twisted into one of unrecognition.

My own vision swam again, and my breaths came labored and slow, my muscles weighted with exhaustion.

"Mage?" Mila's voice was a whisper on her breath, and heavy footfalls sounded behind me.

"Mage!" Mila's cry of surprise was the last I heard before my head hit the soft earth, the weight of fatigue blanketing my consciousness.

CHAPTER 16
MAGE

As my consciousness lifted from the depths, a weight behind my brow pulsed a pain violent enough to cause a wave of nausea. My expression crumpled against the agony, and I rolled over on my side, pressing my fingers to my temples as life came back to my limbs.

"Goddess bless." Despina's voice rang out in my ear, but it sounded distant, distorted by a haze between realms.

I groaned against the pounding in my head. It stole my ability to think, to process my surroundings, to catalogue where I was, why I was on the ground, why I had been unconscious.

"Hold on." Mila's voice sounded closer, clearer as the haze lifted.

A cool hand pressed to my forehead, and another cradled the back of my neck just before the warm flush of healing magic bled through my skin. The soothing sensation chased away the pain behind my brow, and before too long, I was able to find my lungs again, my sense of sound, the ability to feel the brush of the forest beneath me.

I opened my eyes, and Mila removed her hands as she sat back, the glowing light of a fire illuminating her pale skin.

She looked like she'd been to the underworld and back. The dark circles under her eyes were like bruises, her pale hair was mussed up, and half of it had fallen from the knot at the base of her neck. Her cheeks were hollow, and she had sunken fear behind her green eyes. The kind of fear that only came from seeing the worst of your nightmares come to life.

"Are you alright?" Despina's voice rang out from behind me as I pulled myself to a seat.

My love sat on the ground between me and the campfire, which illuminated the entire dark space. The glowing light shone against her warm skin and rose curls. She stood out among the darkened forest, a hopeful light in the face of despair, a healing presence capable of breathing life back into anything.

Night had fallen. How long had I been unconscious?

"Yes, how long have we been here?"

"Half a day," Despina said, her tone hesitant.

She sat still, her breath frozen as she waited for me to speak.

The memories of what had happened flushed me in a rush. A crawl of anxiety flittered over the skin on my chest and my breathing turned shallow.

The black smoke, the wild, living forest, Mariella's screams, Mila curled in on herself.

"Mila thinks the black storm was a result of her lack of control," Despina said with a direct tone in the face of my hesitant silence.

I straightened my spine and did my best to still the wiry nerves coursing through my system.

"Something is wrong with her magic. Yours, too, she tells me. I am wondering why neither of you thought to include me in this development before we set out to travel across the continent."

An irritation pulled at her tone, her posture taut with frustration and worry.

"I'm sorry," Mila said, but Despina held up a hand to silence her, the solar fae's attention focused on me.

I met her eye with all the strength I could muster.

"I wanted to be sure I knew what was happening before I worried you," I explained, keeping my tone soft but steady.

Mila looked to her hands and worked the hem of her sleeve between her fingers.

"Worry me?" Despina said with the pain of betrayal laced through her tone. "Mage, I am your partner. I want you to trust me to be able to handle something so important. I want you to be able to lean on me. I want to be there to help you when you need it. Have I done something to make you feel like you can't?"

I kept my eyes on Despina's, forcing myself to face the consequences of my decisions, despite the way her words pulled pain from my core, how my heart cracked knowing I'd made her think anything of the sort. I relaxed my shoulders and reached out for her hand, lacing my fingers with hers and giving it a gentle squeeze. A longing in my core begged for her forgiveness, and worry tangled through me knowing that might take time.

"No." I shook my head and swallowed a lump forming in my throat, "This is my fault. I was scared."

"Scared of what?"

"I was trying to tell you. Just before the storm. I have been hearing voices. I feel like I'm losing my mind. My magic has been draining more and more every day. I feel like my very connection to my well is slipping. And I am scared."

"I feel the same. Voices, nightmares, strange magic. And I

am so *tired*," Mila said, her words clipped and rushed as though to avoid the pain I knew lingered there.

Despina took a moment to assess us both, her expression tense as she considered, but she did not release my hand, offering me a slight comfort to quell the stirring of emotion within me.

"You both need rest. We'll travel slower tomorrow so you don't need to use magic. I'll keep the fire going and try to contact Gengi and Wren about all of this. For now, sleep."

I looked to Mila, and she nodded with tears in her eyes. The sight of her pain caused a pang of dread behind my heart. I had never seen the female so quiet, so shattered. I wanted to take it away, lift the burden from her shoulders.

Despina offered my hand a squeeze before she rose from her seat and moved around the fire to hike off into the shadows of the trees. I watched her in the darkness as she broke off dry branches for more firewood, her posture still rigid as she worked both her muscles and her thoughts.

It took me a while to concede that she was not coming back right away, likely needing space to process what she'd learned. What I had kept from her.

Mila lay down and turned away from me, covering her head with her arm. I rolled over on my side and watched the flame crackle with a heavy, sinking kind of guilt settling in my core.

I should have told her sooner.

I should have been able to admit to a need for help.

And as the embers in the fire lulled me to sleep, coaxed my eyelids closed, I could do nothing but think of the way Mariella's voice had called out to me. My dreams had been no more than twisted nightmares as of late, but perhaps she would visit me there. Perhaps instead of fearing it, resisting the whispers, I needed to listen.

CHAPTER 17
CALLISTA

It was remarkable how time seemed to circle in on itself when left alone with nothing but your own thoughts. The existential dread from watching the sun rise and set every day made me want to crawl out of my own skin. Although it wasn't all bad. At least not as bad as it could have been. A family of silk-string weevils had taken root in the corner above my window, busying themselves with their business of weaving their impossibly strong silk webs through shards of moonlight. We had honestly had the loveliest conversations in the dead of the night.

In addition to my new weevil friends, it had been some time since the witch had come to collect me. I'd admit the anxiety of anticipation was tiresome, as I never knew when my next session in the chamber would be, but I counted every moment without the beast of a bastard king in my presence an unusual blessing.

I was slowly descending into madness, though. Laz had not been back to visit me. Neither had Brenwyn, and the worry of not knowing anything about the outside world, my brother, Mage, Elea . . . it was enough to drive me absolutely insane.

"I see you've managed to build your web up nicely after that mishap with the rain the other night," I mused to the weevil as it worked to rebuild its bioluminescent web over the window. The moonlight cast a lovely glow through the forged sanctuary. It made me ache for home, the safety of the forest. The tiny, multilegged thing stopped, and I swore it turned to look at me with its glowing silvery eyes.

"Well, yes, I would have been disappointed, too. You worked very hard on it."

"Who are you talking to?" The voice echoing through the room was not one I recognized, and a violent jolt of alarm shot through me at the sound. I was on my feet in a blink, every muscle at the ready.

I had not heard the door open, and when my eyes landed on the ornate wooden frame, I found it still very much closed and bolted. I tilted my chin, and that buzz of alarm sharpened.

"Sorry." The unfamiliar voice sounded again, the tone bright as the blue fae, Asteria, phased into existence in the center of the room.

"Goddess, *fuck*," I exclaimed, breathless as I brought a hand to my chest, the anxiety of sudden fear still bleeding through my breastbone. "You scared the *shit* out of me."

"I had no way to warn you, now did I?" she replied, her tone curt, but a smile curled the corner of her full lips.

As the tension in my shoulders relaxed, my vision focused on the fae. She was no threat to me, I'd been well informed of her relationship with Brenwyn over the past months, but she had never been to visit me. In fact, I was under the impression that astral projecting like this was quite difficult for her to achieve and her visits to Brenwyn had been few and far between recently.

"Well, I can't expect a visit from you in the dead of the night means good news." I sighed, rolling my shoulders.

"Unfortunately, no," the lunar fae said with a tilt of her head, her posture remaining rigid, her shoulders back.

Her lavender eyes shone in the moonlight, standing out against the shimmering blue of her skin.

She was beautiful. I could see Elea in the slope of her nose, the curve of her cheek. It caused a pang of agony behind my heart. But there was something eerie about the ancient lunar fae. Something felt off, like the darkness tethering her to Ragnor clung to the very fabric of her soul. It set my nerves on edge.

"They're coming for you tonight."

Her words caused a spike of hysteria so visceral, I had trouble maintaining my composure. The flare of my eyes as I faltered a step back pulled a look of regret from the fae.

"I'm sorry."

"Why warn me?"

"I need you to survive."

"Why? Does he finally have the stones to kill me?"

"No, he wants you to lure her here, but too many encounters with the source will kill you anyway. He is . . . reckless."

The mention of Elea pulled at the fracture near my heart, the hollow ache of our bond I could not feel with the deadstone on my wrists. I knew as much, it was only a matter of time before she came close enough for him to attempt a strike at her, but there had been so many questions circling my mind these past months. I needed to get some answers before Asteria withdrew herself again.

"How does he manage to survive it? He's got the source crystal in his chest. What does that collar do and what does he want her for?"

"That is a lot to go over in our limited amount of time."

"Please." My plea came out on a desperate breath as I took a step forward. "Give me anything. Anything I can use to help her."

"Ragnor is a tortured man, and he's acted on the darkest corners of his soul. The source is weakening him. He needs her magic to complete the power of three."

"Three?"

Her eyes widened and her expression went blank, as though something in another realm had caught her attention.

"I must go soon."

"No, wait."

"I will be back when it is time to help her. Keep this with you," she said as she gave a wave of her hand, and a small stone appeared in the center of the room.

It floated closer to me on an eerie flush of invisible energy, and I reached out to pluck it from the air. A cool tingle bled from my flesh at the contact.

"I've charmed it to keep you alive. They won't find it on you. He is reckless. But keep this close and it will harbor your strength.

"They are coming. I am sorry," she offered, her tone weighted with the heaviest kind of regret before her spirit disappeared into the fabric of the realm, back to the cage of her mind.

I sighed and looked to the stone in my palm, doing my best to cage the beast of dread coiling within my core before I slid it into my pocket. The fear was only slightly eclipsed by the hope of any ability to help Elea.

I will be back when it is time to help her.

Asteria seemed to have a plan, and if enduring a little bit of physical pain was all I had to do to see that plan through, I would manage.

The witch did not knock as he entered, but I would not

flinch in the face of the terror that awaited me in the chamber below the palace.

*S*EE, *I didn't give them nearly as much sass and that asshole still tore my back to shreds.* The thought echoed through my mind, and it was entirely directed at Brenwyn, wherever the wraith was.

I lay on my side, my bloodied back to the door as I did my best to compartmentalize the searing pain there. I coiled my thoughts through the chambers of darkness they took to keep the weight of my circumstances at bay.

This time, I was certain Oberin had meant to take his frustrations out on me. I had barely spoken, and he'd found an excuse to string me up and peel the skin from my back with a vile weapon, a whip poisoned just like everything else in his arsenal. How delightful for me.

A knock on the door stirred my consciousness, and I allowed my mind to float back to the land of the living just in time to hear the heavy slide of the wood against the floor as it opened. I did not have time to catalogue who might be with me before a soothing presence met me on the floor.

"Fucking underworld." Laz's voice pulled me the rest of the way through the darkness, and I lifted a head to peer at them over my shoulder.

They sat on their knees, their hands fluttering over the shredded flesh of my back.

"Where have you been?" I asked as I tried to sit up, but they placed a hand on my shoulder and gently stopped my ascent.

"Don't move," they said, their tone serious.

"Don't be silly. It's not that bad."

"Shit all, it's not," they spat. "I said *don't. Move.*"

The dominance under their tone surprised me, and I would have been lying if I said it did not cause a curl of heat low in my core. I huffed a breath through my nose and propped my head up on my arm, staring at the wall again, trying my best to keep the whir of my thoughts under control.

"Thank you. Now be still, it's going to take me some time to fix it."

"Why? Just let it scar," I said, my tone laced with miserable irritation.

"For what reason? So you can wallow here in your own misery for weeks while it heals?"

"Yes."

"No. Do you want the sleeping tonic?" they asked, curt.

"No."

"Moody tonight." This time their tone curled playfully, and I turned over my shoulder to catch the lift of a brow over their depthless eyes.

"Wouldn't *you* be if you'd been left alone here for weeks on end?"

"Are you saying you missed me, Moonlight?"

"No," I snapped, irritation lacing my tone.

Although, that was a lie, and they knew it. They'd visited me regularly for a stretch of time and then nothing, no sign they had ever existed until now. As much as I hated to admit it, any amount of interaction was a relief in this prison, and going without it did turn my mood sour.

"Right," they said, entirely disbelieving.

Moonlight.

"Did you give me a nickname?"

I received no response before pain lanced its way through

my muscles as they began their work. I had to stifle a scream as they began the grueling effort of knitting my skin together.

"I told you it would hurt."

"Just get it done," I hissed through gritted teeth.

They did. It took them what seemed like hours, and the pain nearly blacked me out, but I refused to fall into submission, relishing every lancing slice of heat. Until finally they breathed a sigh, and the warm glow of healing magic bled into my muscles to soothe the pain as they finished their work.

A long beat of silence stretched through the room as I pulled myself to a seat and spun on my tailbone to face them.

A line of sweat beaded over their brow and dark circles shadowed their eyes, a weight in their expression I had not seen there before. The green of their irises seemed to have less light, their skin void of some of the glow I remembered there. The golden freckles I had grown accustomed to counting strewn across their cheeks seemed to have lost some of their sheen.

"Are you alright?" I asked, concern pulling at the corners of my awareness.

"Not at all," they said, their tone clipped and final. I waited for them to continue, but it was apparent they had no intention of elaborating.

"If healing me like that is too much for you, then don't do it. I am well versed in pain."

"Don't be ridiculous." They wiped the damp line of their brow with the back of their sleeve as they settled into a more comfortable seat. "I am the best healer in Celvaria."

"That is entirely untrue. I know the best healer in Celvaria, and she would run you in circles," I teased playfully.

Although it was true. Mage had more power in her well of magic than most. It would be difficult to match her strength.

"I wouldn't be so sure," they said with a soft smile.

"What is it then? You look worn down, like someone has drained your magic."

I would know what that felt like—the sessions with Ragnor were as much that as anything else. An attempted drain of my magic, my connection to Elea. He needed her magic to survive, and I was his only tether.

Their lips thinned and they did not respond, the lack of a reaction piquing my interest.

"I thought you couldn't be marked," I whispered, my eyes flitting to the spot on their chest, the only explanation for any drain of magic being a potential tether to Ragnor.

They pulled the line of their collar down, revealing the plane of their breastbone and no mark.

"I cannot," they said, "but something has been happening to creation magic. Something has poisoned it."

"Not something, someone," I nearly snarled. "The blight, creation magic. He will destroy the entire realm if he is not stopped."

"I know." They nodded. "I am on your side."

"I am sick and tired of everyone coming in here and telling me they are working on things. That they want things to be different. And by everyone I expressly mean Brenwyn, who also has not shown her face in weeks. I want something to happen. I want out of this goddess-forsaken room. I want to kill him with my bare fucking hands. That will fix your damned magic. I am sure of it."

"I know you're frustrated. And hurt. I am doing my best to keep you safe. Brenwyn is too."

"Right," I scoffed.

Their shoulders sagged and their eyes glittered with a kind of pity. It turned my stomach. Pity was the last thing I wanted from them. From anyone.

"I can't stay much longer."

I peeled my eyes from theirs and turned my attention to the weevil, who seemed to be watching us as though we were some source of entertainment.

"I'll be back with food in a few hours." They sighed after I offered no response.

It was only a few sweeping moments before I was alone again in the room.

"It's a good thing I have you," I mused to the bug. "We'll stick together, little buddy. We'll make it through this."

The weevil seemed to acknowledge, beginning to weave their glittering web in peace, giving me something to focus on outside of the realm of my darkened thoughts.

CHAPTER 18
AURELIA

"I find it significantly difficult to believe you are going to find anything you need in this hodgepodge of a market," I mused to Gengi as I lifted a jar of luminescent mushrooms to inspect.

The solar fae sifted through a basket full of various trinkets, looking for goddesses knew what, and flashed a glance up at me before digging for a few more moments and giving up his search. I put the jar down and adjusted my hood, ensuring it still concealed my hair, which I'd kept braided down my back so it would be easier to hide.

"You'd be surprised what you'd find at a secondhand market like this one," he said, moving along to another booth in a row of similar makeshift storefronts.

The market only popped up at the edge of town every half-moon, and it had been what we'd been waiting for. Gengi insisted he was almost done with the contraption he'd spent the past few days building for me to wield the source with, that he just needed one more thing to finish it up, and he had been waiting for the vendor he needed to become available.

I'd asked him to explain his extensive plans to me a few times, but each try had gotten me more frustrated. The parchment drawings and scrawled handwriting of his notes had been nearly indecipherable. I wanted to understand the magic the male used, and the infuriating part was I *felt* like I did. At least I should have. I had before, when my memories had been completely intact. But each time Gengi had tried to walk through the design and the intricacies of the solar witch magic he'd used, my thoughts had tumbled over one another, the memories I should have been able to recall without any effort had been clouded, blurred in the mess of my black spots in time.

"What is it that is going to bring your device to working order again?"

Despite my inability to understand what he'd planned, I'd been around my fair share of witches in my time, and I had enough memory to pull from to work with. I knew I was generally familiar with the ways of their magic.

Unlike Gengi, most witches were not descended of the triple goddesses. Elven and mortals normally found ways to tap into the magic of the source using other means, conduits and charms. Some solar, lunar, or creation dabbled in the art, usually half mortals like Gengi or Despina. It was a way to strengthen their ties to their magic. Something full-blooded fae did not need.

I had learned in the short time I'd spent with Gengi that he devoted most of his skill to creating gadgets, innovative ways to utilize both solar and witch magic. Like the whip Atlas had used on the prism bridge. Gengi loved experimenting with magical charms and using his skill to tie magic to mundane objects. He used conduits, sealing them within the devices he created. He'd been working on a number of things, the device he intended me to use to wield the source without allowing it to consume me entirely being only one of them.

"I need a conduit strong enough to filter the energy. I have everything prepped, but I need a gemstone or a precious metal clean of any other influence, so the spell on the device will funnel your magic as well as the source magic safely."

"Ah." I crossed my hands behind my back and nodded, tipping my chin into the air as I hopped my step to land near the male as he turned over a large brass gear displayed on this stretch of trinkets for sale. "So, a marketplace full of used objects people are selling to declutter their homes is the *perfect* place to find something like that. Got it," I poked, my tone teasing.

"Listen to me." Gengi huffed, but his lips stretched into a smile as he rolled his honey-gold eyes and turned to look at me. "Traveling with the two of you is surely going to be the death of me. Just trust that I know what I'm doing and take your sass elsewhere. The vendor should be here past noon, and it doesn't hurt to browse."

I smiled playfully and turned my eyes to Atlas, who stood a few booths away, the mention of the lunar male immediately turning all my thoughts to his attention.

Atlas had lowered himself to the ground, crouched and sitting on his heels with his elbows propped on his knees as he held a finger out to a rather large feline for a domestic animal. The creature's fur was black, flecked with scattered splotches of an equal amount of white. It curled up on its hind legs and nuzzled Atlas's outstretched fingers. A bright smile stretched over his face, and he opened his arms, giving the feline an opportunity to jump into his lap and stroke the top of its head along his stubbled chin.

Something warm bloomed in my chest at the sight of Atlas's smile, the unusually relaxed line of his shoulders. I hadn't known I'd been staring at the male, lost in my own bliss-tinted thoughts, until Gengi's voice pierced my trance again.

"He's worried about you, you know." Gengi's low tone pulled my distracted attention back to his, the effort to peel my eyes away from Atlas feeling as though I had hauled my gaze through a slowed spot in time.

"Yes, well." I sighed and rolled my shoulders. "I am worried about me, too, if I'm being honest. What are those?" I asked, glancing down to the hilts Gengi held in either hand. They were made of a distressed looking gold metal, and they held no blades.

"I don't know what they were, but I know what I can turn them into, if you think they'd be useful to you."

I raised a brow in question.

"Blades of flame?"

"Oh!" I nearly gasped and took the hilts from him, my eyes wide with interest.

"I'll take that as a yes." He chuckled and motioned to the keeper of the booth, who had been out of earshot, to pay for them.

The bladeless weapons already had circlets to hook them through a loop on my belt. They felt like they were meant to be there, their weight a comfort I hadn't expected.

"I can get them hooked up with conduits pretty easily. You are going to need them if getting to the source chamber is going to be anything like I think it will be."

"How fucked do you think we are, exactly?"

In the past days Atlas had spent a decent amount of time patrolling the city to gather information. He'd come back late the previous night claiming to have seen the king's men emerge from a wall. A portal door concealed with a charm to be invisible. A door I was entirely familiar with as the entrance to the source chamber. I knew it had been compromised, but having it confirmed sunk dread in my core that was difficult to reconcile.

"A one hundred percent chance, I'd say." Gengi sighed, stressing his hand over the back of his neck. "But we'll make it because we have to."

I huffed a dark laugh at that, one of skepticism and disbelief. We certainly did not have to make it. In fact, in my experience, most did not make it out of situations quite so bleak. It was precisely what terrified me so much about these two males clinging so closely.

"*I* will," I insisted. "Ragnor wouldn't have *me* killed. But you and Atlas?"

"We are grown males," Gengi insisted. "We can handle ourselves. Better than you give us credit for, I think. And honestly, if you don't let up on the worrying, it might be precisely what gets someone hurt."

His words snapped my focus, and a flush of irritation heated my chest at the accusation. But I could not argue the fact. Nor did I want to agree. So, I settled with stewing in my own angst with another huff of frustration.

"What has you so grumped out, Feathers?"

Atlas's voice startled me out of my irritated haze. I had not heard him approach, and Gengi had moved on to the next booth over. Still within earshot but far enough away to indicate that he had given up on our conversation at my silence.

"Nothing." I sighed and turned to look at him, surprised to see the cat still cuddled in his arms, its tail swinging happily as it slowly blinked its yellow eyes at me.

"What is that?"

"Archer."

"You can't name that thing. It can't come with us," Gengi called over, not looking up from the objects on the table.

"Why not?" Atlas insisted, a false sense of shock and irritation in his tone.

"Because I have a difficult enough time keeping the two of you alive. I will not be responsible for a cat in the middle of the forest."

"Well, it's a good thing it isn't your decision then," Atlas chimed and turned back to me.

"What are you going to do with a cat in the middle of the forest?" I asked, unable to stop the smile as it creeped over my moody disposition.

"Whatever we normally do. It's a cat. If he follows us, it's meant to be, otherwise he is free to do as he pleases."

"You're ridiculous." I laughed.

"And incredibly charming, irresistible, hilarious, undeniably the best lunar fae warrior in the realm," he mused as he scratched between the cat's ears. "Am I missing anything?"

"Utterly infuriating and a huge pain in my ass," I replied, but the lift in my tone was measurable, a kind of bliss chasing away the darkness previously clouding my thoughts.

"Always." He flashed me a wink, a smile of his own cocking his mouth in that maddening way that flashed his dimple.

"I am glad to see you're in a decent mood. It makes what I am about to say much less irritating," he said.

"Oh goddess, what?"

"We aren't going to be able to get near the source chamber for another few days. It's been sealed and the next cycle to get through the door isn't scheduled until midweek."

"How do you know that?" I asked.

"Like I said before, I am incredibly charming. Which means I can get just about any amount of information from anyone."

I cocked a brow at him in question.

"Okay, I overheard one of the idiots in a palace uniform talking about it." He rolled his eyes.

"That's fine. I'll need a few days to settle the gemstone into her conduit," Gengi said mindlessly as he sifted through more random objects.

"So then, a few more nights of waiting." I sighed.

I did my best to keep the weight of disappointment from my tone. I knew Gengi would need more time, but I was so desperate to have my magic back, to sleep, to get any amount of reprieve from the nightmare that had become of this existence.

"You'll be alright," Atlas offered, his tone gentle and it pulled my attention to his.

All I could manage was a soft smile and a nod as I moved to help Gengi sort through his baubles.

CHAPTER 19
AURELIA

The wind as it weaves its way through my feathers reminds me of why I love this form so much. With my wings outstretched and the sun in the sky above me, I truly feel free. I can almost pretend this is it for me. No shattered source to manage, no responsibility to shoulder, no disapproving sister to judge every selfish decision I have the urge to make for myself.

It's just me and the sky.

I release a cry to the clouds, my shriek splitting the air, and I send a rush of solar energy through my veins, relishing in the heat as the sunrays charge my flush of magic. Flame dances from the feathers of my wings, trails behind me as it flutters from my tail, and I tip my head to dive straight down, spinning in a tunnel of fire as I let my energy flow free.

MY SENSES ARE OVERWHELMED *with frantic energy. A darkness threatens to creep through my bones. It sours my mood, taints my disposition. I know the feeling well. The poison of the corrupt source magic is near.*

The forest around me is dark, the trees dense. Woven through them is a thick web of briars, the vines of thorns all as wide as one of my legs. I am alone, the feeling of dread and guilt overwhelming. I look to my hands, and the soil at my feet is over-turned and my palms are streaked with fresh blood.

THE WAR ROOM IS FULL, *every seat at the table occupied with the king and queen's advisors. The general of their army is standing and speaking vehemently, greyish white skin flushed almost blue with heated emotion. I can't make out what she's saying, but she speaks to the queen, who looks back at her with a hatred I would not wish on my worst enemy.*

I am standing by the door, watching over the room with Asteria by my side. She is glamoured as the high priestess, and I can see my own glamoured dark hair as it spills over my shoulder.

Something draws my attention, and I find my gaze locked with a pair of bright green eyes. Ragnor's raven hair falls over his brow and he looks over the heads of the other advisors at me with a heat in his stare that curls my stomach. A smile breaks my expression, and I can't help but nod, a confirmation of our connection. A response to his silent request to see me afterwards.

I AM in the source chamber under the palace and something twisting is winding through the cavity of my chest. Some better instinct is pulling at me, begging me to turn back, but I do not. I turn over my shoulder and find Ragnor just as he scoops me off my feet, his strong arms wrapped around my waist as his warm lips crash into mine.

ASTERIA IS FURIOUS. Screaming at me. I have never seen her so angry. She's right. Only the two of us should have ever had access to the source chambers. And now we need to relocate the source shard. But it must remain in The Capitol.

I hang my head and do as she asks, pooling my magic with hers to place the source shard in the amulet. When the deed is done, she snatches it from me to keep it safe.

I know it will weaken her. It should be me to wear it, keep it close.

But she does not trust me.

I've broken something I am not sure I am capable of repairing.

AN ICY BREATH stretched my lungs to the point of discomfort and my spine went rod straight, sitting me upright in bed. Panic gripped me, my breaths coming in short, frantic heaves as I scrambled to assess my surroundings. I brought my hands to my chest, grappling at the stretching pain there as the room around me focused. I was in our room in the inn.

I had fallen asleep. It had all been a dream.

Although, it hadn't been. They'd been memories. Fragments of time once lost, the consequences of fulfilling my leg of the source-damned prophecy.

The images swam through my mind as I tried to piece them together, make sense of them, fill in the dark spots. But it was no use. The broken moments in time came to me so infrequently. It was one of the most frustrating things I had ever experienced. I knew who I was, what I was, but I was missing the detail. Centuries of time wiped clean, lost to the abyss of amnesia.

Once the adrenaline washed through me, the realization settled in that I had not been subjected to that nightmare dreamscape. Panic pierced me at that. How could I have been so careless?

I was not sure why I had been spared the torture, and the idea of narrowly escaping for whatever reason flushed me with frigid dread. I could not allow that to happen again.

What had I been doing? What had lulled me into sleep?

Atlas. I had been watching him sharpen his blade. He'd been sitting at the table across the room and the monotony of the repetitive sound must have pulled me into unconsciousness. But where was he?

I scanned the room, a new flush of worry settling over me, and I found Gengi asleep in the bed opposite me surrounded by various pieces of metal, unfinished gadgets, and parchment covered in the scratch-like handwriting of his designs. The droning sound of his soft snoring floated through the still night air, but Atlas was nowhere.

I pulled myself to my feet and shuffled to Gengi's bedside. With the inside of my cheek between my teeth, I considered whether or not I should disturb his slumber. He had been working so hard on his magical devices, and it pained me to have to disturb whatever dream made his eyelids flutter, kept that sleepy smile on his lips. But the flush of fear at not knowing where Atlas was pinched at me in a way that made it impossible to ignore.

I placed a hand on his shoulder and shook him as gently as I could.

"Gengi," I whispered.

"I'll fetch the goats in the morning," he muttered and batted my hand away, sleepily rolling over and rustling his parchment.

I sighed and rolled my eyes.

"Gengi, wake up." I poked at his arm, and he groaned.

"Atlas is gone," I urged, anxiety fluttering under my words.

"He went to scout prism bridge," he muttered sleepily, his back to me.

"By himself?" I asked with a roll of my eyes at my own words.

Of course, by himself. Who else would have gone with him?

A room shattering snore answered my question, releasing another sigh of frustration from my lungs. Gengi did not so much as move another muscle before his breathing settled back into the steady rhythm of sleep.

I made my way to the door and swept my cloak around my shoulders, hesitating with a hand on the doorknob before I stepped out into the hall. Gengi's glamour charm hung on the hook, meant to aid me in maintaining a long-term disguise as I roamed the city. I had all but refused to use it thus far, but Atlas was right. The more time we spent here, the more fliers requesting my delivery to The Capital seemed to become prevalent. It was irresponsible for me to walk amongst the citizens of Celvaria undisguised. Especially in the bustling downtown strip under the cover of night.

I grabbed the necklace from its hook and slung the amulet around my neck. The amulet called on the small stores of magic I had to wash color over my hair and eyes. The cool flush of glamor magic left a tingling sensation over my skin, and I ran my hands through my raven colored hair before I stepped out into the night.

I slunk through the dark streets with my hood down, basking in the feeling of brisk air through my tousled hair. The locks bounced around my shoulders, shining their oil slick black color.

It was freeing to walk through town with the weight of my burden a little lighter on my shoulders. As much as I had tried to blame my reasoning for resisting the glamour on my unstable magic, I knew there had been another motive. One I had kept at bay, unwilling to process within the recesses of my tangled mind.

I had so desperately wanted to wear my own appearance, be done hiding for once in this miserable existence. But with my solar magic concealed, I could almost pretend I was someone else again. Someone insignificant with no responsibility to save anyone and no significant amount of power.

No fated mate relying on me to balance a connection. My heart cracked at the thought.

The feeling of false freedom was familiar. It was the reason I'd taken so fondly to existing as the firebird in the first place. That body disconnected me from this source-damned realm.

The thought of Callista sent my eyes to the moon with a

poison-tipped dagger in my heart. The familiar lurch in my core stole the breath from my lungs and I reached through the bond on sheer instinct, hurdling my consciousness into the abyss between us in hopes of finding her there on the other end. I often did so as I waited for night to give way to day. I spent the hours trying over and over again to reach her through the bond.

But for the thousandth time, I was met with an icy wall of nothing. My attempt to find her on the other end of our connection was cut short by whatever cage he held her in.

It took no time at all for my feet to carry me to the prism bridge. The path was familiar enough. But when I made it to the iridescent glass structure, I found no sign of Atlas anywhere. I cursed myself for not getting more information from Gengi before I'd set out on this seemingly pointless task.

I wandered across the bridge toward the sound of the bustling nightlife. The businesses rang familiar in my mind. Flashes of heated bodies, dark rooms, and pulse-pounding music swirled in the blur of my memory over the years. I knew the escape of a good dance floor was something I had indulged in often in my past, and the vibrating energy from within the depths of the city called to the recesses of my still slumbering soul.

I moved through the thickening crowd for a few paces before I had half a mind to turn around. I had no way of knowing where Atlas was. Searching the few establishments surrounding the hidden door to the source chamber, I found nothing. He was either inside one of the pubs or he had found a way to conceal himself under the guise of night somewhere along the strip.

Either way, he could handle himself, but I could not stop the itch of anxiety from closing off the steady stream of air to my lungs.

"Dark hair looks good on you, Feathers." Atlas's voice

pulled my attention to the building to my right, the timber of his unique baritone cutting through the din of the crowd around me.

I found him leaned against the wall, one boot propped up on the stone with his hands in his pockets. His coloring had been glamoured, his own charmed amulet around his neck turning his hair deep brown to match his dark eyes, his skin a rich olive tone. Something loosened in my chest, and I released a breath, shaking out my nervous hands at my sides.

"Were you worried about me? I thought you'd finally found some sleep," he said, his tone light and teasing as he cocked one brow.

"I had, but when I woke, you were gone," I said, moving toward him, keeping my body language relaxed so as not to draw any attention to us from the business of the drunk passersby. "Why aren't you sleeping?"

"Why do you *think* I am not sleeping?" he asked with a cocked brow and a crooked tilt of his lips.

"It looks like it's to spend your time irresponsibly taking part in the infamy of nightlife in Venridge."

"Why do you sound so disgusted with that idea?" he asked.

"Because we have shit to do, Atlas. We don't have time for this."

"What shit? Watch Gengi fiddle with his baubles and gizmos? Or are you referring to the countless hours I've been made to endure your sulking?" he droned on.

I narrowed my gaze at him and shot a glare.

"Oh, bite it," I grumbled and turned away, meaning to stalk off in the direction of the bridge, but his hand caught my wrist before I could make it two steps.

He spun me gently to face him again, and the smile on his expression sent a flush of tangled emotion through me. Even glamoured, his beauty was striking. My instinct was to hang on to irritation, to keep the disgruntled expression plastered to my face, but I could not ignore the confusion of excitement bubbling in my chest as he brought himself closer to me.

"Stop it," he mused and turned me to lean against the wall next to him, draping his arm over my shoulders. The heat of his body washed over me, his lavender and bergamot scent instilling a sense of calm through my wired nerves. "Just relax for a fraction of a moment. Look there."

He nodded across the bustling road, and his fingers mussed with the loose strands of hair over my shoulder. The sensation sent a shiver along my spine and my breath caught in my chest, seized behind the pressure building between us, but I managed to focus my attention on his direction.

From this spot, we had a view of the alley on the other side of the bridge. There was nothing there but a few waste bins, some shadows, and cobwebs. I stiffened and opened my mouth to speak after a few moments of staring at nothing before the air over the brick wall seemed to shimmer as the surface of a body of water would if disturbed. I would have missed it if it had not been so wildly familiar to me.

A rush of memory flooded my senses, and it spun my focus, but I furrowed my brow, determined to hold onto the evidence in front of me. Only moments later did two males dressed in palace black appear as if from nowhere, pulling dark hoods down over their heads just before they stepped out into the light.

Before I could categorize what I'd witnessed, sort through the flush of my past life as it hit me squarely in the chest, Atlas shifted from the wall and turned swiftly to face me, his forearms on either side of my head to box me in. The movement was quicker than I had expected, and a sharp breath stretched my lungs as he leaned in. The look in his eye as he met mine curled a wild heat low in my core.

"What are you doing?" The question left my lips on a whisper of a breath as my heart hammered against the walls of my chest.

"We can't very well be caught staring at them, now, can we?" he muttered with a twitch of his lips, his tone low.

I could do nothing but gape at him, his nose only inches from mine, his deep eyes searching for something. Every one of my muscles stiffened, and I found the sudden urge to lean into his frame overwhelming. The comfort of him this close washed over me in a way that nearly buckled my knees.

Too close. He was getting too close. His presence affected me too much. Everyone who had ever been this close to the thundering of my heart had been hurt, most killed. Callista had been hurt. Goddess bless, Callista had been hurt *so much* and it was all my fault. I could not let the same fate befall him. I knew deep within my soul I wouldn't survive it if I lost one of them, let alone both.

But goddess damn it, I could not think straight when he looked at me like that.

"I don't like your eyes like that." Atlas's words surprised me after the unusual amount of time I'd spent turning over my tortured thoughts in silence.

"Like what?"

"Dark. It's not you."

"Well, isn't that the point?"

He said nothing but made no effort to move away from me.

I need you to move away from me.

"I used to come here. Looking a lot like this. Like someone else. To be someone else."

The words out of my mouth were absolutely not the *get away from me now before I ruin your life* I had intended them to be. I sighed and nearly rolled my eyes at my own inability to function.

It wasn't that I was afraid of breaking his heart. *That* I knew for certain. In my time in this realm, I had loved many, often multiple at a time. It was natural for me to open my heart to more than one kind of connection.

But that was the problem, wasn't it? The connection to me in the first place was what proved to be dangerous for those I loved over and over again.

"To the prism bridge?" he asked.

"Yes. To pretend," I replied with a release of breath, the action doing nothing to quell the whirring within my soul.

"Pretend?"

"That I wasn't me. That I had the liberty of being an average fae. Getting drunk on fae wine and tumbling whoever suited my fancy on any given night. It only ever lasted an evening or so before Asteria would call me home. But when home got to be too much, here I was."

"You've had an incredible weight on your shoulders for far too long."

All I could do was nod, the tightness in my throat threatening to suffocate me.

"It's too much." He leaned back, and I expected relief to wash over me at the space between us, but the cold was depressingly unwelcome. "Let's leave it behind for the night."

Atlas offered his arm, nodding for me to take it.

"We can't do that," I said, shaking my head.

"And why not?"

"Because—" But I could not bring a decent answer to my lips. Gengi was asleep, we were both glamoured, and Atlas had gathered crucial information on how to access the source chamber on his own. We only had to wait for Gengi to finish his device and try to get to the source chamber.

And I so desperately wanted to. With every fiber of my

being, I wanted to leave it all behind and be free with him for just a moment.

"We can't go anywhere until we get to the source shard. Your magic will be useless until then. You don't need to be the guardian right now. Just be you," he insisted, his tone gentle but almost pleading.

An undeniable wave of anxiety flushed my veins as I considered. I should have said no. I should have gone back. I should have left this where it was and shoved this feeling back into the box I had been doing a decent job of ignoring until this moment.

"'Just me' ruins most good things," I said finally.

"Well, if that has any truth to it, I know what that feels like." He sighed but did not lower his arm. "Then let's pretend. Let's be other people. Regular people. We will have a drink and dance, and tomorrow you can go back to sulking."

I bit down on the inside of my cheek and met his eye, the urge to take his offer coated in desperation. I wanted to lean in. My toes were on the edge of this cliff, my weight teetering on either side, waiting for my heels to either land safely on the ground behind me or fall forward, hurdling through time and space toward the bright fields of wildflowers below. It took everything in me not to fall, not to ask him to go with me, to take me back to the ocean like that day in Safe Haven.

I could not make sense of it. I could not sort my thoughts enough to make a decision. The buzz of the crowd, the warmth in my chest, the desire to stay near him, to leave everything here in this spot and indulge in the weightlessness I knew would come with his offer was so tempting.

"Please, Reia."

His tone was low, another plea, and it cracked the last fracture of my resolve. I hooked my arm through his and met his side, looking up to meet his eye.

I would fall. Headfirst over the cliff it was.

"Who will we be?" I asked, forcing a lightness into my tone as I released a breath of tension.

"I don't care." He shrugged, a smile stretching his face as he moved toward the pub. "As long as you allow yourself to have a little *fun*."

CHAPTER 20
ATLAS

Exquisite.

There were no other words to describe how she soaked up the life in the room. The very second she had permission to leave it all behind, I watched the weight leave her shoulders, the perk of her brow, the way the rhythm of her breath seemed to come more naturally.

I nearly had a heart attack waiting for her decision, but I could not begin to describe the bliss coursing through my veins at her willingness to trust me.

Aurelia moved to the music with her arms above her head, her dark, glamoured hair tangled in the heat around her. Her cloak had been long discarded at our seats near the bar and she'd rolled the sleeves of her tunic up. It had taken a glass of faerie wine and the better part of an hour to get her to loosen up enough to dance, but once her disposition had cracked, once she'd allowed herself to breathe, it had been as though there was no turning back.

She scrunched her nose as she jumped to the beat and took my hands in hers before spinning to the music, her hair twirling around her as I held firm to stabilize her movements. I laughed and did my best to commit this moment to memory. I wanted it carved out in time, a golden moment to hide away for the darkest days. The curve of her full lips, the line of her jaw as the cool-toned faelight caught it with her head tipped back, the timber of her laugh, the sparkle in her eye as she relaxed further and further into this. Into us.

In that moment, nothing else mattered. I was more than happy to pretend with her. Pretend she could be free. Pretend she could love me in the way I so desperately yearned for. Pretend I was enough to earn that right.

But I wasn't. Try as I might the thought pecked at the back of my mind, reminded me with every crack of her smile, every sway of her hips, that she was not destined to be with me. I would never be enough.

But that wasn't a new development, now was it?

I heaved a sigh as the sting of it all pierced my chest and ran my hand through my hair as I tipped my head to the bar. She stopped dancing and furrowed her brow, but I turned on my heel before my expression had the chance to crack under the weight of my looming disappointment.

"Something wrong?" Aurelia's voice chimed over my shoulder, worry laced through her tone.

I forced my expression to relax and plopped into a seat as I scooped up her cloak.

"Not at all," I breathed. "Well, only that the sun will rise within the hour and if Gengi finds us both missing again, we will be in a time-out."

"Oh, done pretending, are we?" She raised a brow and perched her hip on the stool opposite me.

"Who, exactly, are we pretending to be? Because I think I'd like to have all the information before I make my decision."

She tapped her finger on her chin and feigned thought for a moment, but her lips curled into a soft smile before she spoke.

Goddess, what a gorgeous creature.

Even with hair and eyes that did not belong to her, she stood out. Nothing could conceal how remarkable she was.

"I think I would like to be Enora. A simple elven woman who has plenty of time to read and tend to her goats and chickens."

I wasn't sure if it was the wine that left her so bright and open, but I was going to savor every moment of this mood of hers.

"Enora?" I pondered, "Well, would Enora have the time a day for a fisherman from the east? Of course, his values might be a little rigid, dealing with trade from The Capitol and all. But he could be worn down over time."

"A fisherman?" She laughed. "Have you ever even held a fish?"

"Of course not, they are slimy and smelly. I don't know why anyone would go near the creatures. But Kier, the fisherman, he is very skilled with handling such things."

"Keir?" She raised a brow, and I nodded with a slight bow at the hips from my seat "It's a pleasure to meet you. I do hope you find time to meet me again in the future. I have had a truly wonderful evening."

"Well, Enora, I would be honored to escort you again, the next time you need a reprieve from the tedious work of goat milking."

The smile as it stretched her expression was worth every moment of pain it caused me to be near her and not be able to express my emotions, not let the cage of my heart open to show her how desperately I wished for her happiness every given moment of every day.

How desperately I wished to be the one to give it to her.

I held her cloak out to her and she took it with a ginger touch, some of the light leaving her eyes as reality sunk in.

"We can be whoever you want us to be until the moment we get back to the room, if that will keep that frown from your lips."

She met my eye with a sadness in hers, the lines of exhaustion evident again, but she nodded.

"Thank you," she breathed as she secured the clasp of her cloak around her neck.

I tilted my head in acknowledgement and stood, offering my arm again.

She took it, and I led her from the pub back to the now nearly empty street. The sun pressed against the weight of the night sky on the horizon, the deep indigo fading into the lavender crest of dawn. We made our way back to the inn on the other side of the prism bridge, talking only of mundane things as Enora and Keir. She told me of her dreams to live in the forest on her own and learn witchcraft to sustain herself. And I told her of my wild siblings, all tales of my real family, but she need not know the details.

Better if she thought it was truly pretend. It would be easier to fool myself into thinking I could handle my own heart that way.

THE BREATH that stretched my lungs as I was thrust into consciousness filled my chest with icy daggers. The same frigid blades cut through the skin of my face as I sat straight up. It took me a dizzying moment to adjust my fear to perspective, but I managed to focus my sleep weighted thoughts on Gengi, who stood over my bed with a wet bucket in his hands, a look of livid rage on his face.

I was drenched in the ice water that presumably had been in that bucket.

"What the fuck?" I hissed, rage lancing through my core.

He tossed the empty bucket to the ground, and it clattered, echoing his own anger.

"You tell me? Why in the goddesses' names did you think it would be a good idea to go out until the ass crack of dawn *drinking* days before we are supposed to perform the most dangerous mission of our lives to date?"

"Are you angry about not being invited? I understand feeling left out, but an ice bath seems uncalled for." I kept my tone light as I curled my legs over the side of the bed, pulling my sopping shirt off over my head.

It took a quick scan of the room to note that Reia wasn't with us. My muscles tensed and worry threaded through my veins. I hadn't meant to fall asleep.

"She's in the bathing chambers." Gengi sighed, noting my turn of attention.

I relaxed slightly, but a line of tension still stiffened my shoulders. She could encounter anyone there on her own.

"I'm serious, Atlas. What were you thinking? You're both exhausted. I am frightened for our ability to make it to the end of all of this alive, if I am being honest."

"I was marking the entrance, and she came after me. She's so stressed all the time, I just thought a little fun might loosen her up. It is just as dangerous to go into a mission scared and stressed."

"I think you're getting too close," he warned.

I rose to my feet and pushed past him to my rucksack to find dry clothes, entirely ignoring his plight. I knew full well what he meant, and the seize of my heart would betray my feelings on the matter if I spoke on it now.

Gengi followed me, crossing his arms over his chest.

"Don't ignore me. You told me to keep you focused. And I can see you slipping. I know how you feel about her, but you have to—"

"I have to what?" I snapped, turning on him as I pulled my tunic over my head. "Ignore her? Be cold? Jeopardize our chances of getting close to anything useful in this mess? Of getting to Emrys and Avery?"

"Watch yourself. You know the risks." His tone turned deadly.

"I do. But it's just—"

"It's what?" he snapped.

"I cannot begin to describe to you what even being in her presence does to me. She looks at me and I feel alive. I haven't felt that way in *years*. And I would be lying to you if I said I didn't think that kind of vibrancy wouldn't motivate me to fight harder, push myself to be stronger. I feel like *living*, Gengi. She makes me feel alive. And I think there is a possibility she could feel the same way."

Gengi's brow softened, and he met my gaze with an emotion bordering on pity. It made me break the connection, turning my eyes to the ceiling as I ran a hand over my jaw, my heart pounding against the cage of my chest.

"I'll be honest, I think you're right."

I snapped my focus to his again, a blistering kind of hope swelling behind my heart.

"I see the way she is around you. I can feel it. I think she probably does feel similarly. But Atlas, does it matter? Is it worth it? Are you willing to risk the entire realm for the chance?"

I ground my teeth together and released a breath through

my nose as I contemplated. I knew what the answer should have been. No. Nothing should have been worth the chance to release the realm from Ragnor's dark grip. Nothing should be worth risking the fated bond, the balance of magic.

Risking my sister's life.

Goddesses, even the thought of it caused a pain so visceral it made my bones ache. I could not bear the guilt of knowing my desires could risk Callista's safety, her life.

But my answer was not what it should have been. In my core, I knew that. And that fact made me feel ill.

Before I could take a breath to respond, I was spared the strife of having to place my next words carefully as Reia opened the chamber door, rustling her long, raven-colored hair with a towel. She removed the glamour amulet from her neck and tossed it to the table as she glided into the room, and the copper color bled into her locks, the golden hue of her eyes chasing away the black-brown left behind by the magic.

"Is everything alright?" she asked, moving across the room with concern over her brow.

"Yes, Atlas is just hung over." Gengi sighed.

She wasn't asking Gengi, though, and her eyes remained on mine, her expression tense as she waited for my answer.

The words pressed against my resolve. I wanted to be open; I yearned for it. Every fiber of my soul reached for hers, needed to express what stirred deep within me.

But if I was being honest with myself, I knew Gengi was right. She *was* worth it to me, but the consequences of my selfishness could mean her life. Callista's. I would die with the secret etched to the surface of my heart before I allowed my own desires to get either of them killed.

"Just a headache, that's all," I said, forcing a soft smile to my lips as I ran a hand through my hair. "It was a late night. I should probably go freshen up myself."

She considered me for a moment, something lingering in the air between us before she stepped aside, folding her arms over her chest.

"Alright." She nodded. "I'll help Gengi gather our resources. There's an oil down there for head pain. Use it."

"Yes, ma'am." I winked, and the curl of her lips brought some life to my mood, the air in my lungs both feeling like a relief and a curse.

I peeled my eyes from hers and grabbed my rucksack as I moved from the room without so much as a glance back at either of them, the weight of my reality crushing my ribs with every step I took to put distance between us.

CHAPTER 21
BRENWYN

Brenwyn. Come back to me.

The voice as it floated through the abyss was familiar. It rang through my chest like a chime on the wind, the warm summer breeze a comfort to the consistent chill within my soul. The sound was the first thing I'd been able to hold on to in . . . How long had I been floating there?

Awareness came to me in slow, dragging moments as understanding dawned on me. I was one with the shadows, which wouldn't have been all together alarming, except I was unaware of how I had been trapped in this state. How long had I been there? Where was I traveling to? Which shadows had me tied to the darkness?

I pulled at my magic, called it closer, willing it to knit me back to a physical form or at least bring me to the light enough to assess my surroundings, but nothing happened. I remained one with darkness. Anxiety whirled around me, the vile emotion a torrent in my conscious mind. A dark cyclone around awareness. With no body to tether the emotion to, the abyss was wild, unmanageable.

The darkness was a good place to lose myself if I wanted to be lost. But if I could not control my emotions, they would consume me in this state. It was a dangerous game to play, and I was losing.

Brenwyn.

It was Asteria. Calling to me. I scrambled to find my core, stabilize the frenzy of my anxiety, ground myself in her voice.

Why was I trapped here? I did not remember blending myself into shadows. I could not remember the last time I had been fae.

The need to cry out overwhelmed me, but the sound remained a howl in the wind. The blackness deafened me. I focused my thoughts on Asteria, reached for her voice, her presence.

It was the hardest thing I had ever tried to do. After a grueling few minutes, I managed to grip a tendril of my power and yanked on it with all my strength to heave myself through the sludge of shadow. I pulled until I thought I might lose consciousness again, until the solid wall between my power and me began to crumble. The weight lifted ever so slightly, and I launched myself toward the weakened spot in whatever had consumed me.

Hurdling through shadows, I tumbled across time and space for what felt like an endless amount of time, until I was able to feel the edges of my physical form. I focused on that ability until my voice turned from a windblown cry to a wail torn from vocal cords.

It was only another flash of a moment before my knees hit solid ground, the heels of my hands following as an unfamiliar room spun around me.

I had no time to gather my bearings before my stomach heaved and the contents spilled themselves on to the hardwood floor.

My vision tilted and tears streamed from my eyes as I vomited again, my abdomen aching from the sudden retching.

"Tell me, wraith, why is it that you felt the need to put your nose where it did not belong?"

The voice wafting through the room was not one I expected. His words coiled through my veins and locked themselves around my bones, every one of them going rigid as I called on my memory. The hatred in his tone sent a sluice of fear through me. I heaved as I tried to remember what had happened, what he could have been talking about, but before I managed to grasp a single thought, Ragnor spoke again.

"I will give you no more than thirty seconds to gather yourself before I have you killed on the spot."

I rolled back to sit on my heels and wiped the bile from my lips as I forced myself to make eye contact with the king. I had to crane my neck to look up to him from where I sat on the ground. Asteria stood behind him, her back to the wall, her expression stoic, and Oberin sat on a desk to the side, picking at his nails with the tip of his blackened blade, a map of Celvaria on the wall behind his head.

The war room. I'd been pulled to his war room.

It took me a flash of a moment, one fractured glance in Asteria's direction for my memories to flood back to me.

Pouring over blueprints of the palace with frustration, finding nothing I had not yet explored.

Callista between the witch and Oberin as they dragged her through corridors to the dungeon.

Pushing past the ward to see into the cell they'd taken her to, finding the space empty.

Curling through shadows as they fought against me, desperate to find her.

Meeting a ward I had never seen before, hurdling myself through its barrier.

Getting lost in the magic of a protection spell.

"I'm afraid I am not entirely sure what you're talking about, Sire," I said with an innocence under my tone I was sure he would not buy.

"Check her chest," Ragnor demanded, his tone a whip against the stillness of the atmosphere.

Oberin took no less than a second to cross the room, and his blade was at the fabric of my breastbone. I tried to move, to defend myself, but my muscles moved as though they were made of stone. My arms were heavier than they had been before, the debilitating magic still locked firmly around my bones. His knife sliced through my leathers effortlessly, exposing the bare skin of my breastbone as a frantic kind of panic settled behind my heart.

Asteria's eyes flared almost imperceptibly as I met her stare. I sent a goodbye through my consciousness. He would kill me. The second he saw my unmarked chest, Oberin would drive his blade through my heart. This was it.

"Get Lazuli." Ragnor's words were not ones I had expected.

The terror froze in my chest, and I looked down to find the faint mark of a crescent moon exactly where it was supposed to be. It was a considerable effort to keep confusion from my expression, but I managed and looked to Ragnor again. Surely an illusion from Asteria. How, I could not guess, but it was the only explanation.

Oberin turned from the room to appease his king's command.

"Is there a problem, Your Highness?" I asked, keeping my tone cool.

"Only that my most trusted snake got caught slithering through the wards in the castle. Would you care to explain how that would be possible?"

The door to the room swung open and Laz walked in, their chin tilted as they assessed the scene before them. Not so much as a flicker of recognition moved across their stoic expression.

"I must have gotten lost in the shadows. The corridors act like a labyrinth if you aren't careful," I said, my breath still coming in deep heaves as I tried to steady myself.

"I want to know if she is still marked."

"I can see her mark there, Your Majesty," Lazuli replied.

"Are you questioning my motives?" Ragnor hissed.

"Not at all," they responded.

Lazuli knelt in front of me and met my eye with a tight-lipped expression. They held their palm out over my mark and a faint green glow illuminated their hand as they worked their magic.

"She is marked," Lazuli said, their tone edged with disinterest.

"Leave us. I want to speak to the wraith alone," Ragnor said after a tense beat of time.

Lazuli nodded and made eye contact with me once more before they left the room. Oberin followed, but Asteria remained immovable in the background, a statue at the edge of the nightmarish scene. I waited on bated breath, fear solidifying my muscles as I tried to focus on calming the wild beating of my heart.

"I know you have been growing restless, and it has been some time since we spoke of your motives."

I nodded, unsure of where this was going as I began to spin my ring around my index finger.

"I am here to remind you that if you step out of line, there is more than just your life at risk."

"I am aware. I wouldn't dream of it." I nodded with a slight bow.

I scrambled to follow his line of thought, understand why I

still sat here on the floor alive. And my mind quickly snapped into focus. He assumed I was still concerned about his bargain. The reason I got tricked into being tethered to him in the first place. He was satisfied enough with Laz's assessment to think my motives still lay with finding a way to cross realms. A way to find my brother.

It wasn't off my priority list, if I was being honest, but my mistakes had been rooted in that desire. People were getting hurt for it. I would play into his hand, though, anything to get me through this moment.

"Are you aware of how dangerous the chambers you were snooping around are?" he asked.

"I am now. I have still not regained confidence in my ability to stand. I am sorry for overstepping, Highness. I have been patient, but it is difficult to remain in the dark, contrary to what my nature would lead you to believe."

The words of obedience rolled off my tongue so effortlessly. A direct contrast to the vitriol I actually felt for the poisoned bastard standing in front of me.

"I assure you, wraith, you have no need to worry about my ability to uphold my end of our deal. As long as you can uphold yours. This realm will not be for you much longer."

I nodded my head in a bow.

He still needs me.

Our bargain originally consisted of his need for more than just a spy, but something else. He had made it clear from the beginning he'd need me to cooperate when the time came, with no more words than that, keeping me in the dark. But it had been enough. Even the promise of a chance at finding a piece of my past had been enough. I knew nothing of his intentions otherwise. I never had. But maybe that was where I needed to start with all of this.

I hadn't been sure of his plans then, and now, with my

mind racing and a desperate need to gather any amount of information, I felt as though my window of opportunity were closing.

"Are we any closer to reaching your goals, sire?" I asked, a weak attempt to glean anything else, hope flickering in my chest.

It was a stretch, though. He'd never answered any of my questions with anything other than vague words before, but I was so sick and fucking tired of knowing nothing from any angle. I was a trained spy and assassin for goddesses' sake. It was against the very fiber of my being to remain unknowing.

"Do not worry about the progress, wraith. Keep to your task and stay out of the shadows. I will not be so kind if I find you trapped in my wards again."

"Yes, Your Highness." I nodded a bow again.

"Leave this room, I will ask for your report on the whereabouts of the firebird at our next council meeting."

With that, I rose to my feet, stealing a glance at Asteria as I found the door. She turned her head to meet my gaze with Ragnor's back turned and a glimmer of relief shone in her eye. I tweaked a soft smile of reassurance at her as I stepped into the hall, holding on to my physical form with everything I had as I made my way to Lazuli's chambers.

"GODDESS *DAMN* YOU," Laz hissed, already pacing the room as I entered. "How could you be so foolish?"

"I am alive, aren't I?" I said, stretching my arms out to the sides to indicate my whole and unharmed body.

"For how long, yeah?" They turned on me. "I did not give

you those blueprints or risk my ass every other night to watch you murdered before my eyes."

"He is not going to kill me," I said, excitement flaring in my core. I had been itching to relay my theories to my friend the entire track across the palace. "I have suspected as much for a while, but I am sure of it now."

"What do you mean?"

"The bargain we struck. The one that got me tethered to him. He promised—"

"To help you find your brother, yes." They waived me on, eager to hear the new developments.

"I am certain he needs me for something specific." Excitement lifted my tone, my first genuine flicker of hope in ages.

"How do you know?" they asked with a cautious, raised brow.

"If he even thought I was disloyal for a moment, why would I be alive? He's done worse to others for far less."

They considered for a tense moment before replying.

"What did he say to you?"

"Nothing, really. I just have a feeling," I replied with a shrug of one shoulder.

"We cannot act on stray bits of intuition, Brenwyn."

"What else do I have? We have gotten just about nowhere on anything useful in months. We know he is trying to get to the firebird's magic as that device drains Callista. We know this realm's source is killing him. But my magic is different. It's not of this realm. What if that's the key to something important?"

"I think it's a solid theory," they said, still carefully considering.

"It just *has* to be significant to something."

It had to be. I was so desperate to be useful. To redeem my mistakes.

"I'll do some research," they assured me. "Go get some rest. You still look like half your soul has been left in the shadows."

"I want to help," I said, but they shook their head.

"You are no good to anyone sleep deprived. Come back tomorrow and we can go over anything I have found."

I nodded in thanks and turned from the room.

For the first time in what felt like my entire life, a flickering ember of hope burned deep within my chest. I had no idea where to go from there, but if there was even a chance I could be useful, a flicker of a chance that I could figure out where his power came from, to free Asteria, I was willing to take it.

I ROLL OVER, *the plush comforter tangled between my legs, and find Asteria already awake, watching me, her indigo hair fanned out over her head on the cream-colored pillow sham. The sheet has been pulled up to cover her chest, but her shoulders are bare. She smiles at me as I blink myself into awareness, and her lithe fingers brush the hair from my tired eyes.*

Warmth fills my chest. It glows like a beacon in the darkness. It cleaves the shadows around my heart open, leaves a pathway big enough for her to walk through, to remind me of the simpler things in life.

In this life. In my dreams.

A world far away from the anguish I left behind when I rendered myself unconscious.

"Good morning," she muses and curls her body closer to mine.

I will never truly understand how this place works, but I don't need to. As long as it keeps allowing me to feel her skin against mine, hear her voice without the weight of sorrow and dread, see the delicate flesh of her neck without that collar.

"Is it? Morning, I mean."

"No." She laughs. "But it doesn't matter what time it is here."

"I suppose not." I wrap an arm around her waist and savor the feeling of her chest against mine as I press a kiss to her full lips, breathing in the warmth of her.

She tangles her ankles with my legs between the sheets, and I pull away to memorize the way the glowing light of a false dawn curves over her cheek. She hums with pleasure and brushes her nose against mine.

"To what do I owe this surprise?" I ask.

"Do I need a reason to visit you?"

"No, but lately your visits have not left me in the best of moods. And I did imagine you'd have something to say about my encounter with Ragnor."

"I don't want to talk about him. I have missed you," she says, a hint of sorrow pulling at the edge of her words, her lips turning down into a frown as the light lilac of her eyes glimmer.

"Asteria, I have been right here," I say as I prop my weight on my elbow, looking down at her.

She rises into a seated position, pulling the sheet up to her collarbone. Her hair falls around her in shoulders in cascades of navy that so well compliment the sky blue of her soft skin.

"Things have been . . . difficult since he found Aurelia."

"I know." I sigh. "I want to help you, but—"

"But you can't. Brenwyn, please. Please, don't go near the chamber again."

"I thought you didn't want to talk about him," I say, my tone accusatory.

"I do not. But I do need to urge you to value your own life.

He suspected you once already. He will not hesitate to have you killed."

"He would have killed me already if that were the case," I reply irritably. "He needs me for something."

"I am not willing to gamble your life on that theory. He will just as easily find someone else."

"I am willing," I defend. "I have lived my entire life owned by someone else. I finally have a chance to do something that I have chosen, and I will not allow you to convince me otherwise."

"Bren—"

"No," I interrupt, rising from the bed to stand. "Send me back, I want to wake up."

"What?"

The hurt in her eyes almost cleaves my heart in two.

"I have work to do, Asteria. Send me back. Now."

She watches me with a sad glimmer in her eye for a moment, heavy enough to crack bone, before she waves her fingers. The illusion around me begins to dissolve, and I know I will be waking soon.

I close my eyes and wait for reality to weigh on my physical body again.

CHAPTER 22
MAGE

I sat in front of the fire with my legs crossed, my hands folded in my lap while I focused on steadying my breathing to calm the whirring of my thoughts. I'd spent the entire time it had taken me to bathe in the cold river replenishing my stores of magic, centering myself with the forest, willing the darkness that had crept into my veins away.

Despina stood behind me, carefully moving my braids about my head to spread the hibiscus oil we'd brought with us over my scalp. The gentle touch of her massaging fingers washed a sense of calm through my wiry nerves, aiding in my fight against anxiety as it pushed against the cavity of my chest.

As she finished with my hair, her nimble fingers worked the oils lower, to target the worry solidifying in my neck, then my shoulders. Each rolling pattern of her touch coiled over another knot of dread. I released a hum of pleasure as her care unwound the lingering tension along the lines of my body.

I relished the familiarity, the comfort of the gesture. Despina had always been quick to offer affection in this way.

Countless gilded memories of her tender fingers over tired muscles flashed before my mind's eye.

The glow of firelight over the smooth brown of her shoulder.

A bright laugh as her lips dust the shell of my ear.

The warm amber scent of the oils on her skin.

Gooseflesh over my back as she flutters her fingers over my spine.

The contrast of her rose-colored curls on my lush green-velvet pillowcases.

Another hum escaped my chest as my thoughts drifted through the sensations. Despina had spent plenty of time in my chambers in the palace. Before council meetings, after them, late at night when she'd had no desire to go back to her home in The Capital. My heart ached for that time, the comfort and safety my position as the palace healer had offered.

Despina and I had been together like this since before the raid. I'd never expected to find a love like the one she offered me, for anyone to care for me the way she did. Even now, after I'd spent so much time hiding this weakness from her, she worked to offer comfort, extended an open heart, a forgiving one.

I released a breath and closed my eyes as her knuckles found a sharp knot over my shoulder blade and did my best to focus on her touch, the crackle of the embers in the fire, Mila's steady breath caught in the rhythm of sleep.

She'd been asleep for a while. We'd been camped in this spot for two days while we allowed her to rest. As far as I was aware, we were still waiting on word from Safe Haven and Gengi, so there was no rush that would dignify pushing her before she had a chance to recuperate. The creation fae had been in much worse shape than I had imagined her to be. I should have been paying closer attention. I was unwell, and my blood was original. There was no telling how difficult her struggle had been. I needed to figure out how to cope with my own weaknesses enough to be there for the people that needed me.

The small creation fae looked so delicate as I measured the rise and fall of her chest. She'd been sleeping for the better part of our stay here, and I'd done my best to flush healing energy into her veins periodically while still monitoring my own weakened power. I was tired, but spending time in the forest to replenish my stores of power and resting as much as possible had helped my current condition decently enough.

"Wren's report came back today," Despina's voice chimed from behind, and I tilted my head to give her better access to the braids at the nape of my neck.

The general we'd left to monitor Safe Haven, the receiving end of Despina's message.

"And?"

"Nothing is falling apart at the seams without us. Although, the other creation fae are also reporting sudden weaknesses," she replied, her tone light, though I could still feel the hurt as it tightened her voice.

She had barely spoken to me in the past forty-eight hours, and I was anxious to get past this strain. I wanted to fix it. It killed me to see the weight left behind in the wake of my poor decisions.

"I imagined as much." I sighed, heaviness weighing down my words. Relief at knowing Safe Haven was doing well and learning other creation fae were struggling as I was tangled within my core. "Any word from anyone else?"

"Gengi, Atlas, and Reia are looking for Emrys and Avery and a way to strengthen Reia's magic. Brenwyn, I have not heard from since our last message."

Anxiety knotted behind my breastbone again. The constant worry was intense. Everyone who had volunteered to act as a scout for Safe Haven had been aware of the risks, but that didn't mean I had no fear for their lives every time they went off on their own. I was responsible for them, for their safety regardless of the risks. And learning that Emrys and Avery were missing soured my resolve.

I released a tense breath and closed my eyes as I clenched my teeth, the tension coursing through me nearly too much to bear.

"Gengi and Atlas will find them," Despina nearly whispered, her tone radiating her own pain for the missing females.

"If anyone can, it's those two," I said, trying to remain positive, but my voice wobbled as my emotions betrayed me, the sting of tears pinching my eyes.

"Hey," Despina said as she settled my hair around my shoulders again, her work finished.

She moved to sit in front of me and took my hands in hers, though I kept my eyes closed against the threatening tears.

"They are alright. I can feel it. We need to focus on ourselves. Everyone else is doing what they need to do, and they are all more than capable of handling themselves."

"I know," I breathed. "I'll never forgive myself if something happens to any of them."

"I know," she whispered, and the soft flutter of her thumb on my cheek urged me to open my eyes. "We are going to get through this. Together, we will."

The soft smile on her lips cracked a flicker of light in the din of my despair and I released a shuttering breath.

"We are going to fix this." Her tone was firm, grounded in a genuine belief.

I did not have the strength to ask her if that belief was rooted in her intuitive abilities or blind hope. Either way, it was all we had to tether ourselves to, so I nodded, unsure if I was capable of the same kind of optimism in that moment.

·· ·✦ ☽ ☀ ☾ ✦· ··

"MAGE." The whisper pulled me from the edges of sleep.

It was not difficult to wake me, as I had been teetering between slumber and consciousness for hours. I opened my eyes to find Mila knelt over me, one knee to her chest and one foot folded under her seat.

"Is everything alright?"

I sat up as a flush of fear iced my veins and scanned the camp to find that Despina still slept soundly on her bedroll next to me, her hair silk pulled down over her eyes, her mouth slightly open as her chest rose and fell in the deep rhythm of unconsciousness.

"Yes, it's just—" Mila whispered again.

She hesitated as she tucked her hair behind her ears.

"Before we travel on tomorrow morning, I need to talk. About what's been happening," she continued after a beat of silence.

I nodded with a tense jaw and pressed a finger to my lips to indicate silence as I rose from my bedroll, gesturing to the forest beyond the light of our fire to find a spot to speak freely without the risk of waking Despina.

We traveled to the river just beyond the thick of trees sheltering our camp to utilize the sound of rushing water as a cushion for our voices. The sound wouldn't carry loud enough to wake Despina from here.

Mila paced back and forth in front of me, wearing a tread in the dirt as she gnawed on the corner of a nail. I kept my shoulders back and waited patiently for her to be ready to speak, which seemed to be causing her a significant amount of distress, but I knew she needed to. It had been a long time since we had spoken in confidence about the details of this apparent deterioration.

"You're having hallucinations?" she finally asked, her words coming out in a rush.

Her tone was stronger, full of energy. Much like I was used to hearing. The reprieve of sleep had done her well.

Something near my heart seized as flashes of Mariella's nightmarish scream echoed through my mind, but I steadied a breath and nodded.

"Yes, you are too. I am sorry I didn't think to check on you before now. I should have."

She waved me off with a roll of her eyes as she continued to pace, the strain of struggling to communicate with her words etched across her expression.

"I am hearing Emile," she said, her tone stoic, devoid of emotion as she did her best to continue. "And my parents. I hear their voices like they're in the shadows. Calling to me. I didn't know what it meant, and it was driving me insane. And then the other night, I got stuck in a night terror of a scene. Like all of my worst fears had been locked around my head in a vice. I couldn't really make much sense of it, but it was awful."

I swallowed past the lump forming in my throat. Mila and Emile's parents had died in The Capitol the day of the raid. Mariella was dead. The confession did not bode well for the safety and life of Emile if she'd heard his voice in the darkness as well.

But why were we hearing the ghosts of our pasts? What could possibly be causing such widespread damage? It wasn't isolated. It was both of us, and other creation fae in Safe Haven were deteriorating as well.

"I wonder if this is affecting everyone across the realm with creation magic," I said, the words floating from my lips as I turned over my thoughts.

"When we stop in Fenbrook, we can try to get a read on the creation fae there," Mila answered, still pacing, her theories etched across her brow.

Fenbrook was a small town bordering the southern edge of the blight just off the mountain range bisecting the continent. We planned on stopping there to replenish our provisions and get a good night's rest before venturing into the blight. And digging about to see if the checkpoint had any information on Emile's party.

"Are you hearing similar things?" Mila asked.

I opened my mouth to respond but hesitated, the words getting caught behind a catch in my throat. I worried that admitting who's voice I was hearing would indicate to her that her brother was lost. She must have sensed my stress. Mila stopped pacing and met my eye, hers wide and full of emotion. She searched my expression for something, every line of her body frozen as she waited for my response.

Before I could gather myself enough to answer, her eyes flitted to a spot just beside my head and they widened as her shoulders tensed.

"What is it?" I asked, my voice hushed as my muscles stiffened.

My heart stuttered at her change in energy, the power I'd spent two days nurturing turning to a living beast as it slithered beneath my skin, ready to use it in whatever way might be necessary to protect us.

"A silver stripe," she said, her voice no louder than a breath, "but it's wrong."

I furrowed my brow at her, but her gaze did not falter, her posture remaining rigid. As slowly as I could manage, I turned over my shoulder to face the river. I found the creature Mila had descried on the other side stalking back and forth, its large feline head hung low as it watched us, its shoulders rolling with a predator's gait. Its ink black fur was scattered with glittering silver in a pattern that resembled the most brittle branches of a maple tree in the freezing months. The sight of the beast sent a shiver snaking my spine as nausea rolled through my core.

What Mila had said was true. It wasn't right. Its jaw hung open slightly, as though it had been broken and healed wrong. Its teeth, which should have been a pearlescent white, were jagged and blackened. The iridescent tusks curling in front of its maw were also blackened, as though they had been burned, and its eyes, where they would normally have also resembled liquid silver, were not reflecting moonlight as I would have expected.

The most concerning thing of all was its demeanor. Silver stripes, despite their massive size, were known to be some of the gentlest creatures in nature. They were protectors, guides for those who had lost their way. But this was a beast poisoned. It prowled along the edge of the river, marking us for prey in a way that set the very hollow of my bones on edge.

"It can't get to us from here," I said. "Let's get back to Despina and ward the camp. We'll get a move on at sunrise."

I took a step back, keeping my eyes on the silver stripe as I made my way back to camp, the thundering of my heart in my ears drowning out all coherent lines of thought.

CHAPTER 23
AURELIA

"You're sure you have the strength?" Gengi asked me, his tone hesitant and his brow raised as he clutched the hilts of the weapons he'd been working on tightly in his fists.

I took a breath and nodded as I focused on the buzzing energy of the sun as it coursed through my veins. The warmth of midday beat on my shoulders through the opening in the trees we'd found in the forest on the outskirts of the trade city. We'd ventured out to the sanctuary of the woods to test the devices Gengi had finally finished.

"I think I have enough to try," I answered, forcing a confidence under my tone I wasn't sure actually existed anywhere within me.

It had to, though. The time had come for me to do something about this tortured reality I'd put us all in. We were to breach the source chamber after sunrise the next day. I needed to find the confidence, the ability to wield my flame.

Atlas paced back and forth behind Gengi, who did his best to ignore the cat that curled around his ankles, trying to get the solar male's attention. The scene would have been comical, actually, if the circumstances hadn't been so dire. Gengi stood firm in front of me, ignoring Atlas entirely as he walked a quick line between two large trees only a few paces behind.

That was commonplace between them—Atlas acting in some ridiculous fashion while Gengi either called him on his bullshit or ignored him entirely. Based on their relationship and how the pair interacted, you might never know Atlas had almost a century on Gengi in age. The solar fae had only turned twenty-five this past year and was well into his maturity. Atlas, however, was unpredictable and temperamental.

Their dynamic brought me a kind of joy I wasn't sure I would have been able to express if I were to try.

"There's a conduit in each hilt. You should just need to ignite them and the charm in place will take care of the rest," he instructed as he held them out for me to take.

I grab them. The pommels fit in the crooks of my fists comfortably. I measured their weight and flicked my fingers to twirl them in my palms before catching them to hold them steady again.

"Oh, you're suddenly a master at sword handling, are you?" Atlas chimed from the distance.

He had stopped to watch me, the lines of his posture rigid with apparent nerves.

"There is nothing sudden about it," I said as I fought the roll of my eyes, although I could not deter the quirk of my mocking smile as I met his gaze. "I have not forgotten *everything* about my centuries-long existence."

"How many centuries are we talking about?" Atlas asked as he tilted his chin, looking down his nose.

"Too many." I sighed and broke his attention to look back to the weapons in my hands as I took a deep breath to center myself.

"Three, four, five?" he prodded. "How many?"

Gengi turned over his shoulder to shoot the lunar male a glare and I met his eye again with a quirk of my lips, my head tilted in question.

"Why?" I asked, my tone teasing as I pooled the energy I'd spent the past two weeks building in my palms.

The magic there felt wild and hot as it connected with the stones Gengi had charmed within the hilts. It felt natural to center my power there. The weight of it flushed me with a sense of strength I wanted to savor.

"Are you intimidated?" I continued to tease Atlas as I pushed my magic to spark flame.

And sure enough, with nearly no effort at all, fire speared from the once baren hilts to form arcing swords as I used them to cut through the air and rest at my sides, never taking my gaze off Atlas's.

His eyes flared and his lips parted slightly at the display of vivid magic, and the sight of his awe caused a stutter in the beat of my heart.

"Goddess bless, that was unreasonably attractive," he muttered to himself, his eyes still tracking the fire at my sides.

I could not control the somersault of my heart in my chest, nor the laugh the heady sensation brought to my lips.

"Alright." Gengi's voice snapped the tension between us, and Atlas broke his gaze to look at his friend. "A little focus from the two of you would be nice. Just so I know that we aren't in guaranteed danger of losing our lives tomorrow."

My heart seized in its cage, reality checking every one of my foolish nerves for relaxing even a fraction of an inch. I spun the blades at my sides and turned away from the pair of males to practice arcing movements, allowing the flow of magic to settle in my veins.

This was more power than I'd had touch with in months, and I was grateful for the relief the buzzing energy brought me.

"Once we are inside, I can get us to the source chamber," I said in an attempt to go over the details of our plan for the hundredth time, continuing my form work with the blades, keeping my attention pointedly off Atlas.

"Atlas, you've marked the entrance," Gengi said.

"I've also marked the guards we are going to take out in order to use them as our way in."

I thinned my lips and let out a breath at the mention of his plan.

"What?" Atlas's voice was pointedly meant for me and my apparent irritation.

I flashed him a glance as I continued to work my muscles, getting used to the feel of the blades and the heat they radiated, the life.

"I just don't love the idea of being carted into the prison as a prisoner. What if they don't buy it?" I explained.

Atlas's plan was to take out two males so that he and Gengi could use their palace clothes to mask as guards who had found a law-breaking solar fae and were bringing her into the holding cells below.

Me.

Altogether, I found the plan poorly thought out and juvenile. But I had no better ideas and my anxiety swelled at the thought of going in with no cohesive plan. I was willing to work with whatever got the three of us to cooperate.

"None of those males have an intelligence level above that of a field mouse," Atlas scoffed. "There will be nothing to 'buy.' Unless you find yourself incapable of holding your shit together long enough to accomplish anything."

"And we need to get to the holding cells first," Gengi reminded us.

I needed no reminding that someone significant to them remained compromised, missing. I felt responsible for them. For every one of the solar and lunar fae affected by this blunder in history. My blunder.

"We will," I assured Gengi as I pulled my magic back into its well.

The heat bled from my hands and a shiver snaked my spine as I allowed the chill of the air to seep into my skin again.

"Alright, so we find Emrys and Avery, bust them out of prison, then we all go to the source so you can put it in the little device, and we move on with a completely live firebird." Atlas recounted. "Assuming there are absolutely no guards in all of the chambers and we can waltz right through."

"Right." I released a sigh as I did my best to dispel the nerves I felt at the thought.

"You should test that thing next," Atlas said, motioning to Gengi.

"What thing?" Gengi asked, a hint of irritation in his tone.

"The device to harbor the source of Celvaria," Atlas elaborated with a roll of his eyes.

"Oh, we can't," Gengi answered, nonchalant, as he shrugged one shoulder.

"*What in the blistering underworld do you mean 'we can't'?*" Atlas's voice was a hiss of surprise and frustration, all of his words blending together, and I had to suppress a laugh from cracking my lips.

I made myself busy enough with hooking my hilts to my belt to redirect my gaze and avoid breaking out in outright laughter at his reaction.

"Well, how in the goddess's tit would we?" Gengi's retort was full of just as much incredulous venom. "It isn't as though we have a spare chunk lying around, do we?"

"Fabulous," Atlas grumbled as he continued his pacing, this

time more furious. "A never-practiced bauble to lead us to victory. I'm so glad."

"Oh, stop it," I said through a chuckle as I took a few steps closer, my shoulders relaxed.

I had to push through a wave of exhaustion as dizziness claimed my vision with the movement. Using my magic had such an alarming drain on my resolve. I would need to ensure I had enough viva berries to get me through tomorrow.

"Everything will be fine. I am more capable than you give me credit for," I said, and he only glared at me from the side of his eye as he continued to pace.

"Fine, stew on your own." I threw my hands up. "I am going to go soak my stores of magic in the sun and then get as much rest as possible before tomorrow."

I reached out to squeeze Gengi's arm in thanks as I passed him, and he offered me a smile.

I moved into the distance, measuring the sound of Atlas and Gengi squabbling until I could no longer make out their voices. Even their sounds of irritation were a comfort to me I had not expected.

CHAPTER 24
AURELIA

"I am altogether *livid*," I hissed, my tone laced with aggravation as I paced back and forth in the shadows of the alley Gengi and I had taken cover in.

The solar fae stood with his hands in his pockets, and his shoulders leaned against the stone wall. The shadows cast over his glamoured features made them look darker than usual, more intense.

"Well, I don't know what you expect at this point," Gengi said, his tone light despite the less-than-ideal circumstances Atlas had put us in. "He will be here. He said he will, so he will."

I had gone to the bathing chambers before sunrise to center myself for our task and take my time consuming the viva berries I'd need, and when I'd returned to the room, I'd found Gengi still asleep and a note from Atlas, who had left to accomplish the first leg of the mission on his own.

Livid did not begin to encompass the emotion coursing through me at his recklessness.

Gengi and I had been waiting in the spot his note had directed us to for nearly two hours.

"If he doesn't hurry up, we are going to miss our window of opportunity," I grumbled.

We'd chosen to attempt our breach after sunrise because the fewest number of guards seemed to be present anywhere in the city at that time. The more people in the strip over prism bridge, the heavier the patrol was. And the guards left behind to tend the strip this early seemed to be less than thrilled with doing so and were far less observant than others I had seen.

"What? The *several hours* we still have before the evening crowd blusters through?" Gengi asked with a tease under his tone. "If you don't calm yourself down, you are going to draw attention to us."

I had tried to calm down. But goddess damn, it I could not control the anxiety crawling through my veins, the dread at knowing Atlas could be in danger without anyone there to help.

I was not entirely sure how to corral the emotions clattering through my core. I spared Gengi a glance and did my best to stop pacing and shake my hands out at my sides, testing the ease with which I could pool the magic in my palms.

I was not sure how many minutes passed before anything else changed about our circumstances. Gengi remained appearing calm and collected while I struggled to contain my own living nerves.

After what felt like hours later, a figure dressed in black curled into the alley from the corner of my peripheral vision. Every one of my muscles stiffened, my magic on alert at my fingertips. My posture tensed and I turned to face the entryway to the main strip as Atlas moved into the shadows, his frame slithering like liquid over the cobblestones, the dimmed lighting washing over his glamoured features.

He flashed me a dazzling smile as his attention landed on me, and he tossed a bundle of fabric to Gengi where he still stood against the wall.

"Hope you weren't too bored without me," Atlas chimed, his tone bright.

Rage boiled under my skin, and I clenched my teeth against the simmering frustration. Most of the time, I could live with his jovial nature. Not now.

"What is it?" Gengi asked with a furrowed brow.

"Why in the bleeding realm did you go off on your own like that?" I replied with the question heated, my tone laced with heavy aggravation.

"You needed to save your strength," he said as he looked down at himself, his hands outstretched as if to indicate his appearance. "And I am already dressed appropriately with nearly no fuss involved. The males who originally owned these outfits will not be conscious again for at least forty-eight hours and neither of you had to lift a finger."

I huffed a breath but took a moment to take in his clothing. He was dressed in palace black, looking every bit the part of one of Ragnor's men. And he did seem to be entirely unharmed.

"I do think it would be irresponsible of us to split up again," Gengi said as he stepped up to my side, pulling a black tunic over his head. "We are stronger together."

"You told me it was fine." I turned on Gengi, irritation heating my resolve again.

"Yes, well, it wasn't really. I just didn't want to aid in your spiraling. Now that we are perfectly back on track, can we get a move on, please?"

I gritted my teeth and considered releasing the outburst I had simmering beneath my skin, but we'd already wasted so much time. I conceded with a curt nod.

"I have the manacles you'd normally be forced to wear. Are you going to be alright with them?" Atlas asked, his tone presenting a gentleness that had not been there before.

A spike of anxiety rushed through my veins as I turned my attention to the deadstone manacles in his hands. I knew I would have to wear them until it was time to be released, and I had been doing my best to mentally prepare for the weight of them around my wrists. But the last time I had been bound in any way, I'd struggled to hold on to my wits. I worked the inside of my cheek between my teeth as I considered, doing my best to muster the courage to push past the dread.

"It's alright." Atlas broke the stiff silence as he hooked the cuffs on his stolen belt loop. "Just keep your hands behind your back, your cloak will cover them. Easier than having to unlock you at a moment's notice anyway."

Relief coated my fear, and I circled one wrist with my fingers as I released a breath. That fluttering warmth I had grown used to in the past weeks pulsed behind my heart. Atlas was well aware of how being bound affected me. Knowing he was not willing to put me in a situation like that again twisted a knot of emotion deep within my core.

"Are we ready, then?" Gengi asked as he released a tense breath, adjusting the bow and quiver he'd pulled from his charmed, endless rucksack on his shoulders so that they were concealed beneath his cloak.

I nodded with a tight jaw, meeting Atlas's eye. I wasn't sure what I was searching for in his gaze, but something there caused a pang of comfort as he offered me a soft smile.

I rolled my shoulders and removed the glamour charm from my neck, allowing the color to bleed back into my hair and eyes to play the part of a captured fae.

Let's go to prison.

···•☽☀☾•···

GENGI'S HAND, clamped around my upper arm, jerked me forward as he acted the part of a brutish guard. It took us no time at all to get to the alley in which Atlas had marked the entrance to the tunnels and source chamber. I kept my hands folded behind my back as Gengi guided me on, although the charade seemed fruitless because there really was no one around to play the part for. The streets were just as empty as they always were at this time of day.

As we reached the stone wall, I flitted my gaze to Atlas, who raised his wrist, clad in a black bracelet with runic symbols etched into them. I couldn't help but watch in awe as he moved his arm in an intricate pattern, as though it were muscle memory, second nature. The gesture was familiar to me, as though it were something I should have been able to recall from memory myself. How had he managed to mark the guards well enough to learn and execute it with such confidence?

When he was finished, he gripped my upper arm with a gentle touch and nodded to the wall.

"Did that work?" Gengi whispered.

"Of course it bleeding worked," Atlas grumbled under his breath. "On we go."

Gengi nodded and I took a breath as the three of us made our first steps through the wall, Gengi looking over his shoulder with a fleeting glance and a tensed grip on my arm.

A flush of nerves washed over me for a fraction of a moment, but sure enough, my foot did not meet the hard surface of the stone as I moved forward. Instead, my toe met only a slight resistance, as though I had stepped through thick mud. I pushed forward and the cool sensation of magic flushed over my skin as my entire body became consumed by the disguised doorway. I held my breath as darkness overcame my senses, my ears falling deaf for a moment before the pressure around me fell away and my feet landed on the other side. Within a breath, the air around me opened up again.

I opened my eyes to find an empty tunnel, the walls and ceiling made of chiseled rock and hardened earth. Sconces every few feet lit with fae light illuminated the space as it stretched onward for what appeared to be an impossible distance. To my immense relief, we were alone, not another guard in sight.

We'd made it underground. I released a breath as my nerves skittered over my chest, spreading out enough to center my thoughts.

Atlas released his hold on my arm to turn to the tunnel wall behind us. He sealed the entrance again with a similar gesture of his wrist, guiding the bracelet over an invisible pattern.

"I am significantly impressed," Gengi said, genuine awe under his tone.

Atlas huffed in annoyance and turned to pin his stare on Gengi.

"Yes, well, we'll see if you still feel that way before the end of this day. Where to from here?" Atlas asked, turning his attention to me.

I focused my gaze on the seemingly endless tunnel and honed my ears, trying my best to listen for any sign of life within the caverns. The only sound I managed to pick out in the silence were soft drips of water on damp stone.

After a moment of focus, I felt it: the soft, familiar buzz of electric energy. The source chamber. It thickened the air, and I tightened my senses, reaching out to the feeling, an attempt to sense its direction. It wasn't much of an effort though. The magic called to me. It was a part of me. The source magic had twined with my own centuries ago. Manipulating my sunlight into flame. Twisting my power into something overwhelming, giving me abilities only one other fae in history had.

"We go on. I can feel it," I said.

"And the holding cells?" Gengi asked.

"We'll find them first. Let's hope we stumble in the right direction long enough." Atlas nodded.

I took a breath and offered a nod as Gengi and Atlas gripped my upper arms again to guide me through the tunnels. I followed that tug deep within my core, and we walked for an unimaginable amount of time, finding no forks or branching caverns, the only sounds for me to measure our own footsteps as they marked the damp earth and the humming of source magic as it encouraged me on.

Eventually, we reached a forked path, and the males stopped to wait for my silent direction.

Would the holding cells be near the source chamber? It was difficult to tell. It depended on what Ragnor's motives were for claiming the lives of the solar and lunar fae. Was his intention simply to imprison? Or was there an ulterior motive?

These were questions I had spent the past three months turning over in my mind. The creation male I had known before the raid had been intelligent, cunning. More so than most fae I had ever met. Of course, it was possible his motives were as shallow as wanting creation fae to be the predominant line of magic in Celvaria, but something deep within my core told me that wasn't the entire story. There was something else. It was on the edges of my memory, clouded in black fog, just out of reach.

I focused on the buzzing which had grown intense enough to rattle the hollow of my bones, my own magic a livewire as it flicked within its cage, begging me to be free. The pressure of it was almost overwhelming.

"This way," I whispered, nodding in the direction of the source chamber.

"Are you sure?" Gengi asked.

I nodded. Something certain rang within my core. Ragnor would have them near the chamber.

We wound through the tunnels, and I followed the buzzing, the call of the source magic until my vision spun. My anxiety crawled up my neck until my throat closed. Why had we seen no one else? Where were the guards? Were we going the right way? Was this all a trap?

Eventually, we turned into an opening much wider than the tunnels we had been travelling through. I stopped short and Gengi and Atlas hesitated with me. Some alarm deep within froze my muscles.

"Oy," an unfamiliar voice rang out from ahead before a male dressed in palace black emerged from the shadows of the tunnel.

The hairs along my neck rose, and Gengi's grip held firm, but Atlas's loosened, his posture relaxing beside me as he shifted his weight slightly to be a half step in front of me. My pulse spiked and it took every fiber of restraint I possessed to remain where I was.

"We're headed to the holding cells with this one," he said, his tone light but firm, steady with unshakable confidence.

With his hand on a blade at his hip, the guard assessed the three of us. I kept my brow down, my hood concealing a good majority of my face, only a peek of copper hair peeking out from my cloak as the braid fell over my shoulder.

"I was not informed of any scheduled prisoners," he said, his tone measuring.

I tensed, pooling the magic I had in my reserves at my

fingertips. The guard reached out, his fingers headed for my hood, and with a lightning quick swipe of his hand, Atlas had a dagger unsheathed. In the same flash of a moment, he had the blade at the male's throat. The movement was smooth and faster than my eyes had time to process. Surprise flushed my senses, and heat rushed my neck. I jerked my head back in start and the hood fell back from my face.

"I wouldn't if I were you." Atlas's tone curled with a deadly warning as he tipped the blade into the male's jaw, a low rumble at the base of his throat.

Gengi released me to unsheathe his bow, pointing it at the guard's chest with his jaw tensed. And although the male had no time to get his own weapon at the ready, his expression remained stuck with awe, his eyes pinned on me.

"The firebird," he muttered as realization dawned on him.

"See, I *told* you they'd know your face." Atlas turned to look at me over his shoulder with a lazy roll of his head and an irri-tated grimace.

I thinned my lips and huffed in annoyance. Atlas pinned his attention on the guard.

The firm demand Atlas uttered next snaked a shiver along the length of my spine, "Now, it would be within your best interest to take us to the holding cells. Immediately."

CHAPTER 25
BRENWYN

"Alright, but have you uncovered anything useful to anyone since you've jumped to this conclusion?" Callista asked, her tone bored but laced with a hint of irritation.

She sat on the ground as she moved through a series of complicated stretches to work out her surely stiff as stone muscles. Goddess, she'd been locked in this room for so long.

"Not exactly." I sighed irritably as I sunk to the floor, the wall at my back supporting my weight as I pulled my knees to my chest.

Laz had been pouring over research, trying to connect any dots. To find any semblance of a motive for Ragnor's actions. Any connection to me at all. And I was stuck slinking through the shadows, following the false king, the torture master, and the witch through corridor after corridor, desperate to gather any amount of information.

It had all been fruitless so far because I still couldn't get past the wards in the war room or into the chambers below the palace. And I was hesitant to try very hard again, for fear of getting caught a second time.

I wasn't confident enough in my theory that the false king needed me to trust he would not kill me if he found me in his wards again.

Callista changed her position to sit with her legs spread wide and reached forward to press her chest against the hardwood floor. I waited for her to finish her cycle before speaking again.

"Asteria wants me to leave. To find the firebird," I said, grave irritation weighing down my tone.

"I truly have no idea why you are still here if you are free to leave," Callista replied as she rose to a seat and folded her ankles under her.

"I can't leave you. I can't leave Asteria. And I don't know what good it would do."

"What good it would—" she began with a sputter. "You know this palace inside and out. You know where the wards are. The traps. If Elea is planning on making her way to The Capitol, you are her best chance at success. Honestly, I didn't think I would have had to explain that to you."

"I'm not stupid," I bit with a glare. "I am well aware of my skill sets. I don't know what good leaving would do. How would I know where she is? I just as well should stay here and wait for her to need help when she gets here."

And make sure Asteria doesn't get caught in any crossfire.

Callista's attention pinned mine with an intensity I had not seen there in weeks. I got caught in her stare as I watched her carefully crafted thoughts churn behind her eyes.

"What is it?" I asked.

"You're sure you have the silencing ward up on the room?" she asked, hesitation in her tone as the volume of her voice dropped.

"Yes, of course."

I would never speak so freely without the precaution in place.

"I can find her. If I have the deadstone off, I can tell you where she is."

Something cold dropped in my abdomen, sinking a stone straight through any chance at a protest I saw myself having. I wanted to stay. To be close to Asteria. To keep contact with Laz. It was safer for me here. Less opportunity to actually fuck something up. If I went out there, I would be responsible. I would have to gain their trust again.

And Asteria would be in here. Alone.

"What do you mean?"

"It's the bond. I can seek her through it. It's difficult to explain. If you can get these cuffs off of me for just less than a minute, I can tell you where she is. You could go to her. You could help them."

Callista spoke with the same color of emotion I felt rattling deep within my chest: a need to protect someone she loved. Not just the firebird, but her brother, too.

Fuck me.

"I can—" I began, but something cold washed over me, something vile moving within the borders of my magic.

Before I had time to process, the brass doorknob turned, and the door was thrown open with an alarming force. I released the lines of my fae body as quickly as I could as fear poisoned my resolve. Within a fraction of a breath, I was tangled with the shadows of the room.

Callista was on her feet, her hands balled into fists, her jaw tight and a demon in her eyes difficult to witness. The witch moved into the room, Oberin on his heels. They stormed in without so much as a moment's hesitation. Callista swung a fist at the witch, and it caught him in the jaw, but Oberin rounded on her before she had time to catch his advance. She was slower than average. Her suppressed magic and time spent in captivity had hindered her ability to react as she normally would.

She released a vicious snarl before Oberin had a needle in her neck. A cry passed her lips before her body melted into the venom he'd placed within her veins. Her eyelids fluttered and she fell limp. Her head hung between her shoulders, and the witch supported her weight under one arm while Oberin grabbed the other. The males dragged her from the room, her shoes scraping against the stone floor, and I was left with a wicked kind of dread coiled with panic as I vibrated through the darkness.

I took no more time to delay before I sent myself hurdling through the shadows of the palace in search of help.

AURELIA

"This is too easy," Gengi muttered as Atlas guided the guard ahead of him at knifepoint.

"I agree," I whispered, releasing a tense breath.

The air was alive, and not only with the thrum of the magic that lived in that place. Something was tense; the very atmosphere seemed pulled taut. The hairs along my arms raised, my intuition on alert.

I'd ditched any illusion that I would be able to mask as a prisoner the moment that male had seen my face. I'd told them this plan was juvenile. And now we walked through the corridors of the underground tunnel system with a male we would likely have to kill in hopes of stumbling upon no others.

Unlikely odds at best.

We came to a bend with a fork in the tunnel system and the guard stopped and pointed to the left. Atlas jerked him by his collar and peered into the tunnel.

"Well, I must say, it was a delight to run into an unmarked piece of shit. At least you had a mind of your own to lead us with," Atlas chimed cheerily after taking a long look into the tunnel and stepping back. "Give Ragnor my regards when you wake, will you?"

The male furrowed his brow and opened his mouth to speak but did not get the chance to utter his words before Atlas had his free hand over the skin of the guard's neck. Within a fraction of a moment, the guard's emerald eyes rolled back in his head as Atlas's hand flushed a faint glowing green. The male fell to his knees as the energy drained from him, Atlas's cyphin magic rendering him unconscious faster than I thought possible.

"Quickly now," Atlas instructed and moved into the tunnel.

A flush of anxiety warmed my chest and the freshly revived magic surged, but I took a breath to steady the sensation. Gengi nodded for me to follow next, and I gripped the hilts of my flame blades tightly at each side, curling the power through my fingertips to have it at the ready. Gengi followed me into the new branch of tunnel with his bow raised.

I was elated to find that just inside the threshold, the walls had been carved out into pockets with barred doors made of deadstone over each opening. The holding cells. Relief flooded my senses, but it was not enough to curb the buzzing magic as it thrummed deep within my core. Each step deeper strength-ened the vibrations. My bones ached from the sensation as the heat of my flame pressed against my skin. My magic raged through my veins stronger than it had in months. The feeling was exhilarating and terrifying.

We were close to the chamber.

I investigated each cell to find them empty, the prisoners there already carted off to The Capitol. The tunnel was long, but disappointment curled within my core as we reached the end, and I could almost feel the weight of Gengi's mood shift behind me. The space closed off abruptly with nowhere to go but back the way we'd come, the wall ahead made of the same packed earth we'd been consumed by since we'd entered the tunnel systems.

Atlas turned on his heel when he reached the end with a grave expression on his face, and something over his shoulder caught my eye. A symbol on the wall. It was almost imperceptible, but as I approached, it lit with a flicker of a glow before disappearing into earth again. Two birds with wings outstretched, their heads together, engulfed in flame and shadow.

The source chamber.

My heart leapt into my throat and my eyes stretched wide as a torrent of emotion coursed through me. Excitement, fear, dread, anxiety. The hurricane was difficult to keep up with and my vision spun.

"What is it?" Atlas asked, concern lining his expression.

"Why aren't there any guards?" Gengi asked, his bow still raised and pointed at the entrance of the holding cell corridor.

I kept my eyes on the wall behind Atlas, my attention fixed on the now invisible symbol, my pulse hammering through my ears.

"Reia, what's wrong?" Atlas stepped closer; his tone more urgent now.

"The wall," I whispered.

The buzzing of deafening magic clouded my ability to speak, my thoughts holding a thick fog over them as my hands heated with the embers of a raging flame as it flickered beneath my skin. The very essence of the source resting here fueled my core, consumed my senses.

Gengi dropped his guard for a tense moment as he and Atlas turned to look at the wall behind us. It was that moment that nearly cost us everything.

A snap sounded in the distance, too far away for me to

catch it in time, and something whooshed past my head, taking a chunk of hair with it as it sliced the shell of my ear. Pain sharpened my senses, but before I could assess what had caused the heated sensation, Atlas's voice boomed through the cavern and horror lanced my resolve as he curled over, in apparent pain of his own.

An arrow. Lodged in his right shoulder blade.

Visceral rage thrashed through me fast enough to ignite my blades of flame at a moment's notice. I released a scream, and Atlas turned to get eyes on the culprit. Everything seemed to be moving in slow motion. Gengi drew his bow, and his expression stretched with shock at what his eyes landed on at the mouth of the holding cell tunnel.

Atlas reached behind his back with his good hand and wrenched the arrow from his shoulder with gritted teeth and a cry of furious agony as he tossed the bloody weapon to the ground and drew his own sword, at the ready. When his eyes landed on the entrance, his expression twisted in shock and rage.

"Gengi!"

An unfamiliar voice flooded the space, piercing my ears. Everything was wrong. My muscles wouldn't move. My head swam with the thickened haze of source magic.

I needed to gather control. I couldn't afford a delay. I wound my magic tightly into its well and focused all my energy to find enough sense to turn and face our doom. No less than twenty guards waited at the end of the tunnel, two of them holding two females at the front of the crowd on their knees, their hands clasped behind their backs, blades at their throats.

The one that had cried for Gengi had tears streaking her brown cheeks, and her loose brown curls matted around her face, stuck to her temples with sweat, but her bright periwinkle eyes shone with a vicious fire I was all too familiar with. The other seemed older, her complexion pallid in the light of the cove, her short, dark hair standing out at odd, unkempt angles, but she held the same fire in her expression.

Emrys and Avery.

"They said you'd be down here sometime," the male holding Emrys called. "Took you long enough. The firebird comes with us or these two die and my archer's next arrow will land in a heart."

BRENWYN

"*Lazuli.*"

My voice entered the room first, panic echoing from the edges of the darkened shadows before I pulled myself together at their bedside.

"Lazuli, wake up."

I placed a hand on their shoulder and shook gently. Their eyes snapped open, and they reached for the dagger resting on their bedside table. Their expression twisted into one of terror mixed with rage and their breathing turned laborious as they raised a blade to my chest with lightning-fast reflexes. They snarled at me through gritted teeth, a wicked sort of anger livid in their bloodshot eyes.

I took a step back and put my hands up as my anxiety spiked.

"Whoa, it's me," I said.

Their eyes took a moment to focus, and a few minutes of heavy breathing passed between us as they steadied their frenzy, but eventually they relaxed their grip on the blade and their expression fell to one of sheer exhaustion.

"What in the goddess's name are you doing? Are you trying to get yourself killed?" they shot as they rolled their legs over the edge of the bed and pulled themselves to a stand.

"Are you expecting an assassin any time soon?" I hissed.

"No, but you know better than to sneak up on someone in the middle of the night like that. What are you doing?"

"I would hardly call that sneaking," I shot back, my voice strained, the panic creeping up. "It's Callista. They took her again."

A muscle ticked in Laz's jaw as their eyes flickered with a hatred I knew all too well. They took a breath and moved to their cabinet full of healing tonics with a stiff spine.

"It's getting more frequent," they said, their tone deadly.

"We were talking. I had a silencing ward up, but she'd just told me—" I choked on the words, tears burning in my eyes as dread consumed my thoughts.

That could have been disastrous. What if I had fucked up the ward? What if they had heard us?

What if I wasn't capable of keeping anyone safe?

"She told you what?" Laz turned their attention on me, and I released a ragged breath as I ran a hand through my hair, turning the ring on my finger over.

Laz waved a hand through the air, the skin over their palm glowing a faint green color. A silencing ward.

"What?" they asked again once the ward locked itself in place.

"She told me she can find the firebird. For me. So I can go help. And then they came in and took her."

The words came out in a rush. A visceral panic consumed me. It threatened to strangle the air from my lungs.

Laz's shoulders went stiff, their eyes unreadable as they turned over the information. After an agonizing moment of their consideration, they turned back to their cabinet.

"They won't kill her for it, even if that is the case. I'll talk to her after it's done."

They'll surely kill me.

"Okay," I breathed.

"Stick to the shadows until further notice," they instructed, their back still to me.

Sickening dread filled my lungs. With my chest tight and panic still settled deep within my bones, I nodded and allowed my body to bleed away, tangling myself with the shadows once more.

CHAPTER 28
AURELIA

"What will it be?"

The male's sneer told me he thought he'd won. And judging based on numbers alone, he had. Three of us on twenty of them. The odds didn't look good.

Though, the odds never accounted for how quickly my rage-fueled flame curled into an uncontained ability to kill.

The blades of flame at my sides surged as heat rushed my chest. I squared my feet and allowed the intoxicating flush of source magic free from my well. It took no effort at all to open that gate. It was as though the power had been pressing up against a dam, waiting for a crack. It flooded my veins, and the heat was a welcome sensation. It urged on the curling need for vengeance as it spiraled deep within my core.

"You want me over there?" I asked, doing my best to keep my tone level.

"No," Atlas's protest was urgent.

"It's alright." I turned over my shoulder with as much innocence under my words as I could muster to meet his eye. "I'll go. Stay on your toes."

A frantic kind of fear flickered over his expression. I raised a brow and tipped my head to Gengi. I wished I had my sister's ability to send messages through other means, get into someone's mind. I would have to settle for a line of trust. Hope he understood a fraction of my motives. Atlas tensed his jaw but offered a curt nod. I turned over my shoulder and coaxed the blades of flame back into their hilts, holding the energy in my palms, nurturing the building power there.

"That's the right choice," the guard said, triumph in his tone.

I released a breath and rolled my shoulders as I took a step forward.

"Promise you'll let them all go?" I asked with a swing of my hips and a coy tilt to my voice.

I spun the barren hilts in my hands at my hips, and the male holding Emrys furrowed his brow, confused at my sudden change in attitude, but I gave him no chance to consider. Allowing no more time for any of them to settle into a sense of comfort, I focused my magic in the pit of my stomach and urged my body to compress through space. That familiar pressure built around my head, threatening to crack my skull as everything went dark, my senses dropping out from under me as the air fled my lungs. It only lasted a moment, though, a fraction of a heartbeat, before I *ephemerated* to land firmly behind the guard holding Emrys.

The moment my feet hit the floor, I urged the flame back into the hilt in my right hand as I thrust my fist into his spine. The fire seared through his chest and a small gasp left his parted lips as the life bled from him. I called the fire back and he fell in a heap. A wild frenzy of emotion raged within my chest.

Rage. Guilt. Pity.

And above all, a desire to make every one of these spineless followers of that bastard pay for all they'd done to the realm.

The archers released their bows. The guards scrambled. The male on Avery swung his blade as he released his prisoner, taking his shot at me, but I was faster. I spun on my heel and allowed the other blade of flame to burn free as I arched it over head and struck him in the chest. His clothing sparked and he turned, frantically panicking as the fire engulfed him. Before he had much of a chance to suffer, an arrow struck him in the heart, and he fell in a heap.

I was able to spare a glance in Gengi's direction to find he and Atlas thundering down the tunnel, Gengi firing arrows as he ran, Atlas moving his legs as fast as he could to get to the now attacking mess of guards. I had no time to consider them, though. The thrall of guards acted fast, and Emrys and Avery were now on their feet but still had deadstone manacles binding their hands behind their backs. Both of them impressively dodged blow after blow, Avery using her forehead to break noses and Emrys scooping low to use her feet to trip males with sweeping kicks while I fended off striking swords with my blades.

The power in my veins was alive, stronger than it had been in the past ten years. The surge of strength was familiar, and I willed it on, relishing in the pulse of magic, igniting my skin.

I focused my vision, quickly scanning the guards for a key, anything to release Emrys and Avery from their deadstone, give them a fighting chance.

There. The guard Emrys tangled with. On his belt.

I struck out at another, cutting him down as I approached the tussle between the small lunar fae and the male. I focused my attack from behind, piercing his spine with my flame. He cried out, and I reached for the keys at his hip before he fell, the clothing around his cauterized wound singed.

Emrys snapped to her feet, her pale eyes meeting mine with a glimmer of surprise.

"Turn around," I instructed.

She did as I asked without hesitation, and I worked to unlock her manacles. I had them undone within a heartbeat, and she turned.

"Behind!" she shouted.

I turned on my heel and spun with a kick aimed immediately for the guard at my back. My boot connected with bone as it crunched his jaw, and he fell to the floor with his hands on his chin as I continued my momentum to face Emrys again.

"Get Avery," I instructed, tossing her the keys without hesitation.

Emrys nodded, and before I had time to blink, she phased out of existence, a blanket of invisibility concealing her from view. With Gengi's arrow fire keeping the remaining males at bay, I turned to see Avery falter in her high kick at a guard in front of her, but an invisible barrier caught her weight before the manacles fell from her wrists. Confusion flushed her expression, and she took a moment to recover as she dodged a blow and spared a glance my way before continuing her defense.

Another breath passed and a male rushed me as he got through Gengi's constant fire.

I turned on my heel and blocked the blow of his blade with mine as it crossed overhead. Atlas made his way to my side and had his shoulder in the male's ribs faster than I could keep up with. He tackled the male and had him down with his knees on either side of the guard's hips, his fist in his jaw before I had time to assess. Blood stained Atlas's back, but the wound in his shoulder did not seem to be enough to stop him from unleashing his own rage on the guard beneath him.

It took two hits and the male lay unconscious. Atlas sprung up and moved into the thrall of palace blacks with his arching blade. I moved to help Avery, who remained weaponless, struggling to hold her own against a male with dual blades swiping at her from all sides while she skillfully dodged. I managed to swing my flame blade into the male's back, and he fell to his knees before another few rounded on us.

I did my best to block each blow and took out two of them, leaving one with a sword to deal with. Gengi had taken out over a dozen with his arrows, I'd taken out a few, but Atlas moved through them like liquid death. I watched as floating weapons suck attacks on guards when they weren't expecting it, Emrys moving like a ghost to take her revenge on them. There were only a handful left. We were going to get through this.

Then what? I needed to get into the source chamber. But what if there was a greater danger in there? Atlas was injured and Gengi was out of arrows. Emrys and Avery looked as though they had been starved for weeks.

Before I had the time to figure out what my next course of action would be, an alarm sounded overhead. A blaring noise meant to split eardrums, rattle focus. I thrust my blade through the chest of the guard in front of me, and Atlas had the last on his knees as he jammed the butt of his hilt into his temple, and he fell unconscious. But the threat was far from over.

A thundering mass of footsteps and shouts sounded in the distance and panic laced my awareness. Atlas's chest heaved and he met my eye as frantic energy thundered through me. Emrys phased back into existence and ran to Gengi's side, who held a wound of his own on his ribs. The blood poured quickly through his fingers, and he winced when she reached him, a groan escaping his lips.

"There are more coming," I cautioned.

"We can handle them," Atlas said with strength under his tone.

I looked over my shoulder at the source chamber, the symbol on the wall illuminated the same, alight with a warm amber glow. The twin birds were plainly visible now.

"That's it," Atlas's stated through heaving breaths.

The alarm blared, scrambling my thoughts, and my breath left my lungs as the sound of the guards thundered closer. They'd turn into the tunnel at any moment. There had to be upwards of fifty this time. We wouldn't make it through them.

Well, I would.

The bastards needed me alive, but Atlas, Gengi, Emrys, and Avery? They wouldn't make it. I straightened my spine as a decision settled the pit in my stomach. My expression hardened as regret coated my tongue.

"I'm sorry," I breathed.

Atlas furrowed his brow and lunged to take a step toward me, but I left him no more time to consider my words. I called the power back to me, a desperate plea to the source itself as I funneled all of my strength into the action. I would need as much magic as I could muster. It took every bit of my focus to curl the living energy around all four of them. My head spun and a strangled sound ripped from my throat as I urged the power on. I felt it hook around each of them, and the second it clicked into place, I focused my mind on a spot in the woods as far away from the city as I could manage. Without another thought, I sent my remaining strength into hurdling them through the pockets between realms.

The strain caused a blinding pain in my temples, but within a fleeting moment, the air snapped, and they were gone. My magic released from the force needed to pull it off and my knees nearly buckled under me as pressure in my chest cracked only seconds before the first of the countless number of guards barreled through the entrance to the tunnel.

CHAPTER 29
CALLISTA

"*Come back to me, Moonlight,*" a voice called to me from somewhere deep within the darkness.

It claimed me. The abyss. I let it this time. I didn't want to fight anymore. I'd done so much of that. I'd spent all my training years enduring torture, compartmentalizing pain, learning how to pick and choose pieces of myself to lock away for safekeeping. To get the job done.

For what? To end up here? A personal power source for the vilest male to ever take a breath in this realm? For once I wanted to be nothing. To find that place in the recesses of my mind where my caretaker sang folk songs to me to put me to sleep as a child. That place in which I could pursue a simple life of telling those same stories with my own voice to others.

If the darkness could grant me that wish, then I wanted to stay tangled within its depths.

But someone had their hands on my face. And they said my name again.

No, not my name.

Moonlight.

Laz.

The grounding sound of their voice worked to pull my consciousness up and up and up through the black.

"Stop." My words floated from the hollow of my throat, and I turned my head as I clamped my eyes shut.

But it was too late.

Pain. Pain blistered everywhere. It barreled through my consciousness. Agony, really. My skin must have been on fire. Every inch of it.

I reared up with a cry of blistered fury on my lips as I failed to get ahead of it, and my eyes stretched open to find Laz staring at me, horrified. They placed their hands on my shoulders, their grip firm as they pushed me back to the floor.

"It's alright," they said, a panic to their tone. "You're going to be alright, just try to relax."

I gritted my teeth against the searing pain and pushed my heated breath through my nose as I pinned my widened eyes on them.

Please. Make it stop.

They uncorked a vile of black liquid and pressed a green, glowing palm to my breastbone. A flicker of relief pushed against the agony at their healing touch, but it wasn't enough to chase everything away.

"Open your mouth," they instructed, and a frigid sort of panic spiked my pulse.

I wanted no tonic, no substance I could not control. I shook my head, and they released my chest to grip my chin, and their lips thinned in aggravation.

"Open your goddess-damned mouth. *Now.*"

Their demand came with a sturdy grip of my jaw as a strong hand forced my mouth open to pour the liquid in. The tonic coated my tongue like oil, and I choked on it. Rage blinded me and I thrashed as I rolled over on my side and tried to empty the contents of my stomach. But nothing came with the heaving of my abdomen. Instead, a cool, tingling sensation flooded my veins. It chased away the pain, a quick, chilled liquid replacing the searing heat.

I took a few heaving breaths as the last of the venomous pain bled away, and I rolled back over with heaving breaths to rest on my elbows, looking up at them.

"Fight me when I am trying to save your life again and I will let you *die*," they hissed at me, venom in their tone laced with enough panic for me to call the bluff of their rage.

"You will not," I breathed. "You've grown fond of me, and you know it."

They seethed, their expression stoic as they considered me.

"That was kelpie poison. What happened?" they asked, their tone chiseled from their own stubborn resolve.

I paused a moment to sift through my memories as the haze of panicked pain lifted. The nightmarish scene began to unravel in my mind's eye.

"A draining. As usual. Then Oberin stuck me with his needle again. I assume with said kelpie poison."

"Why?" they asked with a pinched brow.

I thought it through. The way the males had spoken when they'd thought I'd been unconscious. The words were difficult to piece together because I nearly had been. But not enough to miss what they'd said.

Dread sunk like a stone in the depths of my soul. Alarm lit every one of my muscles on fire. My breathing hitched as realization dawned.

"You need to go, Laz," I breathed through a sharp pang of panic as I pulled myself to my feet.

I gripped their arms and pulled them up with me, a frenzy settling in under my breastbone. Confusion twisted their expression, and I scooped their vials and salves to place back in their bag.

"What are you doing?" they asked, their voice rushed and laced with confusion.

"You should not have come," I scrambled. "Can you *ephemerate*? Do it now. Leave the palace."

"Why?"

A strange kind of pain lanced my chest as the next words came to my tongue. Words that meant I would likely not see the healer again. That thought caused a hollow pang of sorrow I had not expected deep within my core. But if it kept them safe . . .

"They want to know if someone has been healing me. *Helping* me. Take Brenwyn and *hide*."

Their eyes stretched wide with surprise, and before I had a moment to express the regret behind my heart, the hollow ache of not getting to know them better before now, a crack sounded through the air. In a blink of my eye, I was standing alone in my room.

A hollow pang echoed deep within my core. A pain I had not expected as the silence of my chamber settled over my bones.

I had not expected the disappointment at knowing they would not fill this space with their vibrant presence again.

But it didn't matter.

They'd gotten out. They would be safe.

CHAPTER 30
AURELIA

I turned on my heels, exhaustion pulling at every inch of my awareness, and sprinted toward the wall. It took every ounce of strength I had left to push my legs to carry me on. My lungs burned but I still pushed. I needed to get to the chamber.

Shouts thundered from behind me, but they sounded muffled, a cotton-like feeling blocking my ability to hear clearly. I peered over my shoulder as I pumped my legs, desperation coating my resolve. The guards were gaining, and I had to dodge an arrow as it whizzed past my shoulder. It grazed the flesh on my upper arm and the wound burned, but I willed the pain away, ignoring it to turn my focus back to the door.

The pressure of the magic radiating from the source chamber vibrated in my bones, pulling at that string in my core as if telling me to keep going, push harder. It called to me; it needed me.

A cry of frustration mixed with adrenaline cracked my chest as I flung an arm back to release a curtain of flame. It ribboned from my gesture as the magic broke free of my skin, and the sensation left my mind reeling. But hopefully it would slow them down. Just enough for me to reach the entrance.

The symbol glowed, the light pulsing as I brought myself closer. Only a few more paces. I would make it. I had to make it.

The heat of my flame behind me cooled and I could hear the guards again. They were closer than I was comfortable with.

I had to make it.

I hooked my hilts back into their place on my belt as I made the last few steps. The second I reached the wall, I sent all my hopes up to the goddesses, if they were listening. As if they ever listened to me. If there was never a time, I hoped now would be the first. I forced the magic free of my well to bleed through my skin and covered my face with my arms as I leapt into the wall.

A slight tremor of anxiety told me I would not be allowed through. That the wall would remain solid, and I would be forced to deal with my reckless actions. But when my flesh met the stone, it did not feel like stone at all. That cool sensation washed over my skin, encasing me in the strange substance as I phased through the gate. It slowed me down, but I moved through it as a slight resistance suspended my weight. Before too long, my body fell through the other side, the wall spitting me out on solid ground in a space that remained entirely silent, untouched by the chaos on the other side of the wall.

I rolled over on the packed earth, the wound on my arm stinging as it scraped the ground. I steadied myself as quickly as I could, prepared for them to follow me through. Every one of my muscles braced for the continued attack, but the silence of this chamber remained. The gate had closed after me.

"For once, thank you," I heaved through laborious breaths to the goddesses.

It seemed I finally had their attention.

I pulled myself to a stand, groaning through the aches and pains plaguing my overworked muscles. As my eyes took in the cove around me, memories washed over my mind. A lifetime of sensations and familiarity clicked firmly into place. The space was not large, but it did not need to be. It was very similar to the cave on the island off Safe Haven, a cove where Asteria and I had originally hidden the source shards while we'd come up with our long-term plan. The magic of the source bred more crystal the longer it stayed in a place. It fused with the land, calling conduits for its energy into existence. That was what that place was. A cove made of jagged shards of charged crystal. More than there had been in the cove. The source shard had lived here longer. For centuries.

With the magic flowing freely through my veins, I remembered. I remembered placing it here, why the river above ground glittered the way it did. The effect source magic had on the land around it. I remembered sealing both the door to the tunnels and the door to the chamber so that Asteria and I were the only two able to get in. That bracelet Atlas had must have been charmed with Asteria's magic.

And I remembered the dais in which the source shard should have been suspended. It seemed as though my fear that the chamber had been compromised had come to fruition. I would not need Gengi's device to help me handle the source shard, for it no longer rested in this spot.

The crystalline dais in the center of the room was nothing more than an empty pillar.

"Where the fuck did you take it, you bastard?" I muttered angrily as I stepped over crystals to reach the empty dais.

The display still glowed with enchanted light, illuminating the spot in which the crystal should have hovered. I reached out and touched the surface of the dais with a gentle finger as I turned over my disappointment, disgust, anger.

The moment my flesh touched the cool material, a sharp sensation pierced my chest. A frenzied panic set in and I gasped for air, but the oxygen seemed sucked from the room. Within a heartbeat's time, my consciousness tumbled through darkness.

IT'S DARK, *the air is cool, and the trees around seem steeped in black. Thick briars hang from their branches, some reaching the ground to create curtains of thorns. I look down to my shaking hands.*

Blood.

Blood pools in my palms. It is my own.

I have deep cuts sliced across each hand. The ground at my feet is overturned, but something powerful radiates there. Something dark and twisted.

I turn my palms over and kneel with my heart in my throat. I turn my fingers to the earth and allow blood to spill into the soil there. As I press my hands deeper, the sting of dirt in my wounds makes me wince, but I hold steady. A rush of unfiltered power hits me squarely in the chest and I almost release my hold. I manage to keep steady and cry out as dark power radiates through me. I send my plea to the goddesses, to the dark wood, to the spirits here to guide me, to help me seal this venomous piece of the source in the ground.

The briars begin to move, and my attention snags as the forest comes to life. They curl around the space, the sounds of the wood creaking around me until thick vines surround me in a dome, blocking out any light. Anxiety crawls over my chest. Maybe the creation goddess will consume me as well.

But I don't care. People are looking for the source shards. Asteria is growing dark. I can't let anyone bring the pieces together. I know we have plans to hide the others, but this shard is more vile than the others. She cannot know it exists. She cannot know where it is hidden.

This is what it takes to seal this thing away. Keep Asteria safe. Keep the realm safe.

I scream as the source pushes back, but I can feel her. The earth. She is with me. I force as much magic as I can into the ground, and something snaps. My life, the magic, I am not sure which. It cleaves my chest in two and I am knocked backwards as the briars open and slither back to their trees, some light illuminating the space long enough for me to land sharply on my back yards away.

It takes me a moment to assess my surroundings, but the dark wood is at peace again. The overturned earth looks undisturbed once more.

It is done. This shard of the source is secure.

And I will take the secret of its location to my grave.

CHAPTER 31
MAGE

I marked the beads of sweat as they trailed along Mila's temples from where I sat yards away, working my creation magic around the wildflowers I'd coaxed into existence. Mila tended to work her energy out with physical exertion, curling her silver whip in graceful yet vicious arcs through the air while Despina offered critiques from the edge of the small break in trees we'd found deep within the forest.

I didn't often partake in the training portion of building up a military, as my duties rested elsewhere, in the lifeblood of the resistance. Despina was better suited for the intricacies of war. She had experience with the military and could offer more stability to those like Mila, who had the drive and skill to be a physical force to be reckoned with but needed support, guidance from someone more experienced and older.

In Safe Haven, I was responsible for everything else. The resources we had, the safety of the citizens, the scouting missions designed to save those at risk across the continent. Everything from how many homes we had available to what each citizen hoped to achieve after the war. That was what I used my skills for. My passion. My need to correct this horrific blunder in Celvaria's history.

Life. I used my magic and centuries-old skills to cultivate life in Safe Haven. It was what most of the people who needed me had been missing. It was what had been stolen from them.

Kimani, Lumen, Ricktor, Evany, Remy, Cantis, Damien, Gennie, Henriette, Bernard, and Ava.

Their names rolled off in my head, floating through my thoughts as a reminder of those I'd failed to protect. A vicious pain tore at my chest, and I released a breath as my hand drifted to their beads. I counted each one, taking my time to roll them between my fingers as I remembered each of their faces. Their aspirations. Their lives.

Maybe life wasn't what my skills were best suited for after all.

But if that were not my driving force, my purpose, then what? It couldn't be just the need for violence I'd marked in Mila. I could see it on her brow, in the way her muscles flexed as she moved her weapon through the air, kicked invisible foes, screamed in frustration as her muscles finally gave out. It made something in my chest lurch. She'd always been one I'd had my eye on, her magic commonly temperamental anyway, but since her brother had gone missing, her potential for vivid darkness had intensified.

It worried me. Our magic was already compromised. What could a potential like hers turn to with the kind of corruption we faced?

"You need to keep your elbow tucked closer to your side when you practice your forms," Despina instructed. "You'll lose control of your momentum if you don't."

"She looked like the perfect warrior from here," I mused from where I knelt on the soft earth.

Green-tinged magic bled through my fingertips, ribboning

around my knuckles before waterfalling to the flowers I'd already breathed life into. I pushed my buzzing energy into the soil and more flowers in vibrant hues of blues and pinks unfurled their petals to greet the late morning sun, stretching their leaves as though happy to have been given the chance to breathe.

Excitement bloomed in my core. For the first time in days, my magic felt relatively stable. I was thrilled to be able to keep the poisonous feeling of rot that had been plaguing me at bay long enough to use it in this way.

"Yes, quite the killing machine until that whip takes on its own agenda because she doesn't have enough control," Despina argued.

"Well, ideally, we won't have to use brute force at all," I said, though the thought floated out on a dying hope.

"Unlikely at best," Mila said through labored breaths as she moved near to grab her waterskin from where it rested on the ground. "If there is even a chance that the blight is more than just rotted land, then Ragnor has men there."

"Well then, should we call for backup?" I asked, my gaze flitting between the two of them.

"I have been in contact with Gengi. He plans to move them toward the blight after they finish up in Venridge."

I sharpened my attention on Despina as her words landed. I was unaware of any updates from the trio traveling in the southeast. It was unlike Des to keep information from me. She must have sensed my train of thought because her expression softened.

"I only just received his message before break of dawn today," she explained. "I was going to wait until I heard from them on the success of their current mission."

"Which is?" Mila asked with interest as she wiped her brow with the back of her arm.

I pulled myself to my feet, wiping my palms on my pants as I took a breath to steady my nerves. Despina would not normally have held information like that from me, and it set my nerves on edge. But she had good reason to feel as though some distance might be necessary. I'd kept vital information from her.

"His messages don't reveal much detail, but as far as I can tell, they are trying to get underground to find Emrys and Avery."

"So then if we have Emrys, Avery, Atlas, Gengi, and the firebird, we will have enough power to—"

Mila spoke but her words dropped, a sudden spinning of my senses stealing my ability to process them. An eerie haze coated my awareness, and I narrowed my eyes as a dizzy spell almost swept my knees out from under me. Mila kept talking, and I could see her mouth moving, but the sound of her voice dropped out until all that was left was a poignant buzzing deep within the recesses of my mind.

I narrowed my eyes and looked to Despina, but she kept her focus on Mila. Surprise flushed me as I rocked on my heels, but still neither of them seemed to notice.

Mama.

Her voice carried itself in wide circles around my head, coating my heart in that same frigid shock of dread. I whipped my attention around the small clearing in the trees and everything tilted, the branches warping in a way that only disoriented me further. I spun on my heel until I had my eyes on every inch of the forest around us, only to land firmly where I had been before. Unfiltered shock coated my resolve as I found Despina and Mila gone, vanished into thin air as though someone had plucked them into another realm.

But something was wrong. The haze had not lifted, and everything felt heavy, a foreign weight shackled to my bones.

Perhaps it was me that had been plucked to another place.

Fear coated my awareness, and my breathing came in quick bursts. It took a few moments of diligent focus, but eventually my vision relaxed, and the dizziness stilled, my senses opening back up.

I wasn't alone. I could feel it. Someone's energy prickled at the corner of my peripheral vision.

"Despina?" I called, my voice a nervous croak.

No one answered. The forest itself seemed eerily quiet in the face of my swelling panic.

A few tense beats passed, and a rustle in the brush to my left caught my attention. I shifted quickly to see a flicker of movement in the shadowed wood before whatever it had been took off. Instinct pulled at my core, and I moved after it, the shade of the trees relieving my overwarm skin from the sun.

I made it a few steps past the camp we'd set up and stopped to assess. Everything was the same here as well. No Despina, no Mila, but the bedrolls and fire remained.

Another rustle to my right launched me into action, but before I could make it too far, I was stopped short, my heels skidding on the forest floor as the image before me sucked the air from my lungs.

A silver stripe sat on its haunches with its head tilted innocently as the guide assessed me only a few yards away. Curiosity lit their eyes and their ears perked as I met their gaze. This creature was not decayed like the one I'd seen near the riverbank. The silver stripe's iridescent horns curled over their head in sweeping arcs, and the magnificent structures shone bright, the light in them only to be outmatched by its silver eyes.

A knot of anxiety loosened, and I shook my hands out at my sides.

"What are the chances I'd see two of you in just a day's time?" I asked, my voice assessing.

If I was seeing a guide of the forest, there must have been a reason. It could not have been a coincidence.

They tilted their head in the other direction, their brow almost furrowing. A sense of familiarity washed over me as a soft whine left their throat.

"Unless I have not seen two," I muttered as the possibility settled in.

A chill over my flesh raised the small hairs along my arms. The silver stripe stood and turned at a moment's notice to trot through the forest. A tug of intuition pulled me along, urged my feet forward. The forest guide peered over its shoulder and paused as its attention landed on me. I took a breath and willed my courage to the surface as I moved to follow.

We weaved through trees for an amount of time I was not able to measure. Something odd happened to my ability to ground myself. For all I knew, it could have been hours that I followed the silver stripe through the dense brush. The further I traversed, the tighter the knots of anxiety threaded within my chest.

"Where are you taking me?" I asked after I could no longer take the suspense.

They peered over their oil slick colored shoulder at me again and released a huff but kept on, stepping out of the dense cover of trees to a riverbank, the water there rushing over mossy boulders in a symphony of the peace of nature.

"Alright, I trust you." I sighed. "But I fear I will have trouble getting back after how far you've taken me."

"You don't need to find your way back," a hauntingly familiar voice chimed merrily.

The cadence of her words circled my consciousness, dizzying my senses. My blood froze in my veins at the sound.

The timber of my daughter's voice on the wind, the chilling ghost of a sound I'd grown used to as my magic decayed, was nothing in comparison to what carried to my ears this time. She sounded so real, so alive. My muscles tensed and I fixed my eyes on a boulder in the river as I turned over the possibility, trying to free the breath from the cage of my chest.

"Mariella?" I managed to whisper after an agonizing beat of time.

"I'm here, Mama."

She spoke again, the sound solid this time. Directly to my right. A pain hitched in my chest, a still bleeding wound carved out of a decade's worth of grief aching at the hope that this might be real. I'd dreamt every night of hearing my child's voice again, only after suffering the nightmare of her death. Every. Night. For a decade's time.

"Goddesses, please, if this is a trick, I fear I am no longer strong enough to handle it." I offered my words to the higher power and clamped my eyes shut, my hands shaking at my sides as I did my best to grapple with the genuine nausea rolling through my core.

"No, Mama," she almost breathed on a laugh.

Then I felt it.

A gentle touch on my upper arm. I gasped with tight lungs and forced my eyes open, a jolt of wired emotion coursing through my entire being as I turned to meet the bright emerald eyes of my daughter glittering with her own tears, her warm smile tilting her delicate expression in one of tense unease, trepidation.

"Mariella." Her name came out on a strangled sob as I covered my mouth with my trembling hands.

My knees almost buckled under me, but she caught me with an embrace I had spent every day wishing for, praying to the goddesses for. Her build was similar to mine, tall and lithe but strong, and she supported my weight well. My daughter wrapped her arms around my waist and mine swung around her neck. Despite her height, she curled her head into my chest, a little girl falling into her mama's arms at last. I held her there, one hand on the back of her neck as I released a tidal wave of grief, my chest wracking with sobs I was incapable of controlling.

She cried too. My sweet girl. Her tears stained my tunic, and I felt them. I felt the warmth of them on my skin.

How was this real? How could I feel her here in my arms? Was it a hallucination? Had I somehow passed into the veil? I felt fine, so surely death had not claimed me so suddenly.

But death *had* claimed her. Ten years ago, her life had been ripped away from her, her light snuffed out.

Every fiber of my being radiated with a wild torrent of emotion. I could not contain the raging grief, relief, joy, and agony as they all tore through my unstable foundation.

"How is this real?" I managed as I smoothed her hair, moving some of her twists over her shoulder as I peeled back enough to look at her tear-stained face. "You're just as beautiful as I remembered."

Her bright green eyes glittered with tears still clinging to her thick black lashes. Her eyes were creation in color, but they were her father's otherwise. The shape of them was. Most of her face resembled her father over me. He was in the tilt of her mouth and the strong line of her jaw. He'd passed too, of an illness none of us had seen coming, one that even my skills as a healer could not correct. Sometimes the goddesses called some to the veil for reasons unbeknownst to us. I'd used to use that as a way to cope with death. The goddesses had needed my love, her father.

That had changed when they'd taken my baby, ripped her from the world with a brutal strike, a merciless hand.

Except, she wasn't a baby at all. In my arms, I held a grown woman, a strong creation fae. I had forgotten that she had been strong enough to make her own decisions on that day, old enough to help me get those children out through the tunnels under the palace. Sometimes I still remembered her as a faeling, just like those we'd been trying to save. A small thing, delicate but wild. But no, she had been twenty-five when she'd died. Just come into her power, but full grown, nonetheless.

"Mother, we don't have much time," Mariella said as she wiped her cheeks with the pads of her fingers.

"Baby, I am not leaving you again," I vowed, my tone sure as I took her cheeks in my hands.

"You have to," she replied, and the words cracked a violent pain in my chest. "You don't belong here yet. Mama, I have been trying to warn you. We all have. The veil, it's damaged."

"What?" I asked, confusion setting in as I did my best to keep up with her words through my still whirling emotion.

Although, I knew in the back of my mind it wasn't so much confusion as it was a lack of desire to understand. In the hollow of my core, I knew. If I was not meant to be here, if she had been able to reach me even with the ghost of her voice . . .

Something was wrong with the veil between the living and the dead, between our two realms.

"The blight. He's killing everything," she continued, cold hatred settling within her eyes, but her words were quick, frantic.

"Well, what can I do from out there? Let me help from here," I asked, my own anxiety coming to an edge.

"Oh, Mama, I want you to stay. I have missed you so much, but you can't. You're needed. They need you. To fix it. To mend the blight. He won't stop. You have to stop him."

Her words were rushed, the sentences short and broken as

she stumbled over them, taking my hands in hers between us in a vicelike grip.

"Shh, baby, it's okay. Breathe," I offered in an attempt to soothe, to prolong the time we had here.

I could already feel it slipping.

Goddesses, please. More time. Just a little more time.

"It's not. I am not speaking clearly. I can't do this. I shouldn't have been the one to come to you." Mariella's eyes began to flit side to side, and her breathing quickened.

"Mariella?" Her name came out on a croak as my heart fissured.

"Mama, I have to go," she said, her voice a mangled sound from the back of her throat, and my heart seized.

I gripped her hands in mine as tightly as I could manage, an effort to hold her here with me.

"No." My voice was a plea.

"I'm sorry. I'm okay. Da's okay. Stop the blight. Stop the decay. The crystal—" she sputtered.

"What?" I asked, desperate to understand even a fraction of what she had been trying to communicate.

"The source." Her voice grew distant, sounding like an echo in my ear, and the lines of her form began to blur.

"*No,*" I shouted, my tone desperate, the sharp panic stabbing me square in the breastbone, cleaving that wound wide open again.

I would surely bleed out this time.

"The source—mama, I love you. Fix it," she sputtered, and her eyes met mine one last time for the most fleeting of moments before she vanished, her spirit slipping through my fingers.

My chest cracked, my heart shattering into shards, and a wail of agony broke my throat as I curled over my knees, folding my arms into my chest. No words could have described the grief rattling through my soul.

Tears tracked my face and blurred my vision. I clamped my eyes shut against the pain. I would never be whole again. Every wall I'd built to shield the world from the living beast that was my grief had crumbled. I wanted to stay here, in the veil, wait for my body to decay and the goddesses to allow me through to her, my baby.

It took all the energy I had in my body, but eventually I calmed my cries. I kept my arms over my chest as I sat on my knees, my eyes still closed, and a heavy presence lingering over me. A soothing aura washed over my skin, blanket-like regret laced with an attempt to extend some comfort. The very air around me had changed.

A cold, wet nose pressed to my cheek, and I opened my eyes to find the silver stripe sitting on its haunches next to me. Looking at me with tears in their silver eyes, a genuine kind of pain etched into its expression, like the creature knew what I had suffered, what I was being made to endure.

I released a heavy breath and measured its gaze for a while. A feeling of finality settled over me. It wanted me to move on. Though I did not think the guide would rush me, I nodded. I did not want them to have to wait for me for much longer.

The creature offered a bow of its great head, and I closed my eyes.

A sense of dizziness washed over me, and my head rolled, nausea crashing through my core again. I spun through darkness for a few moments, and Mila's voice began to echo in my ear again. A distant bell, something to reach for. Then, Despina's voice pulled me further. It wasn't long before the warmth of sun flushed my skin, and a solid weight settled in my muscles. I opened my eyes to find myself in the clearing again,

Mila and Despina in the same beat of the conversation they had been in before my visit to the veil.

No time had passed at all. They had no idea what I had experienced.

"Despina." My voice was a croak as it interrupted whatever she had been saying.

Des looked to me, and alarm shattered her expression as I gripped her upper arm for support, my weight suddenly too much to keep up on my own.

"Mage," she said, her tone laced with concern.

"I saw her." I did my best to keep my tone steady. "In the veil. I spoke with my daughter."

CHAPTER 32
ATLAS

It took me a full minute to process what she had done after my feet hit the soft earth of the forest. After the coiling of nausea from *ephemerating* an extreme distance worked its way through my core, a hollow ache in my chest strangled the air from my lungs and my ears felt like they were filled with water, my muscles heavy with the onset of grief.

How could she? How could she banish us at a moment's notice? My mind's eye mercilessly offered me images of the worst-case scenarios, and nausea curled through my stomach again.

I couldn't bear it. I would not survive it if anything happened to her.

When we landed, Gengi fell to the ground, lying on his side as he instructed Emrys to sift through his charmed bag. Everyone moved without a beat, without batting a single eyelash. I should have helped him; I should have been able to react.

But I felt paralyzed. My blood was stiff in my veins.

I held my sword at my side, the weapon too heavy, a burden

to carry. I released my grip and looked to the three of them as Emrys poured a vile of green liquid over the wound on Gengi's side.

Avery saw me then. She rose from her spot near Gengi and moved toward me, concern written over her serious face. Her expression was always serious, but this time she seemed scared. I was already beginning to forget how that particular emotion felt separate from the pain. I pushed it away, willed the entire nightmare to the recesses of my consciousness. I couldn't handle it.

Avery reached out, but I flinched away. The idea of being crowded while this horrific emptiness echoed through me lit a kind of rage in my core. She stepped back, surprise lifting her brow, but I couldn't find it in me to use my voice.

She spoke but I couldn't hear her. A buzzing in my ears replaced the deafening clog that had bottomed out the sound of the forest moments prior. Gengi called to me, too, from where he lay on the ground, his chest heaving. He was bleeding out and still concerned.

I couldn't have that. This was my burden to bear. Not his.

I scanned the trees around us, and the sunlight of midday was shrouded by the clouds of lingering rain. Gengi spoke again, but I had already made my decision to remove myself from the commotion. As my glance found the edge of a riverbank, I set off into the woods to drown my dismay.

An hour passed before I gathered myself enough to come back from the river. I'd spent time washing the already healing arrow wound on my shoulder and categorizing the pain threatening to suffocate me, doing my best to keep it organized and controlled before it had a chance to pull me under. When I returned to the group, Gengi sat, his back against a tree, with Emrys tucked under his arm. The wound on his side had been healed, the only evidence was the gash in his tunic. Avery worked on building a fire over a bundle of kindling. As I approached, they both froze as though I were an animal they were afraid of spooking, their eyes wide and pinned on me.

I took a moment to choose my words but decided ultimately that no arrangement of them would lessen the discomfort I'd experience after they heard what I had to say.

"I'm going back," I told them, my tone short, curt.

"You can't," Gengi protested with a quiet tone and gently slid himself out from under Emrys, who I could now see was sleeping.

He rose to his feet and looked at me with that pained expression, the one that meant pity. It lit a fire in my core and anger flared in my veins.

"Fuck all, I can't," I muttered, though the words were heated, and I bent down to claim my sword.

"How, exactly, do you expect to get there?" Gengi asked, moving closer to me.

"I don't care," I said, still refusing to look him in the eye again as I sheathed the weapon, busying myself to travel in goddess knew what direction.

I'd spent my time by the river begging the goddesses for Reia to appear in the forest, *ephemerate* immediately after us. But she had not. And I could not suppress the fear that curled through my core at the possibility that she had not been successful in her idiotic mission to handle the source shard.

It was nearly a suicide mission with all of us to help, let alone on her own.

How could she be so source-damned reckless?

"We don't know how far away we are. The nausea I felt after that trip tells me pretty fucking far. Cyphoning my magic to *ephemerate* won't get you there. We need to wait." Gengi's words were firm, the tone of someone who had decided himself in charge.

Normally I was willing to allow him to fall into that role, willing to let him play the part of the authority figure, the one to call the shots.

Not this time. Never when it came to her.

"Wait for what?" I hissed. "It's been over an hour. I'll walk there if I fucking have to. She could be hurt. She could be—" I choked on the words. "What am I supposed to do? I can't just sit here anymore."

"She's going to be fine, Atlas."

"She's not." My voice rose to a frantic shout as I ran a hand through my hair, the crawl of panic beginning to suffocate me, the pain creaking free of the organized cage I'd coaxed it into.

"She is. She's the firebird. She is capable—"

"Goddess *damn it*, Gengi." I barked the interruption. "She's not okay. She needed us. She has been on viva berries for *months*. She's not fucking okay."

Tears forced their way to my lash line, my eyes burning as my chest stretched tight. My hands took on a tremble as the possibility of her failure in those tunnels pierced my resolve.

Gengi opened his mouth to speak, confusion and pain swimming across his expression as my words landed. The moment hung in the air between us, the energy alive with the tension drawn from my admission. I'd kept that from him. I'd kept her secret to myself. I'd decided it was her secret to tell. And I hated myself for it. If I had told Gengi sooner, if I had made her give them up . . .

"Holy mothers," Avery breathed after a few uncomfortable beats of silence.

"Why didn't you tell me?" Gengi managed.

I breathed an incredulous laugh through my nose, a huff of a dark chuckle, a mockery to my own stupidity. I shrugged a shoulder as a tear traced the curve of my cheek. A cold raindrop fell from the canopy of leaves, the first to break the heaviness in the sky since we'd landed, an echo of the pain leaking from my resolve. I turned my face to the trees, unable to keep his gaze.

"The dramatics are hardly necessary."

Something in my chest fissured and my attention snapped to find the source of those words, of that voice. My eyes landed on Reia, standing with her shoulder propped against a tree, her arms folded over her chest. The intensity of her stare was for me, her gilded eyes locked on me with a ferocity in them I found difficult to read in that moment.

Not through the cracking of the dam I'd built within my core. My veins ran cold as the gnarled vines of grief and agony slithered from my resolve. Relief flushed away my fear, the sensation overwhelming.

More tears threatened my eyes, but the anger simmering deep within my bones did not burn away. It raged with the relief, the elation at seeing her alive. The two emotions danced together in a twin flame burning hot behind my heart. I released a shaking breath through my nose as I took a tense moment to take her in.

She had a bag over her shoulder, her braid had come loose in spots, and she looked exhausted, but whole. I found no sign of injury on her.

"Hi," she said, her tone still terse, her eyes still locked on mine. "Are we airing out everyone's dirty laundry, then? You go next."

I simmered as I clenched my jaw, anger flicking my ribs, but no words crossed my lips. They were all stuck behind the livid rage boiling in my blood.

"Silence from you is unsettling," she said, her tone still unnervingly level. "Say something."

"Say something?" I seethed, the words finally breaking free of their chamber. "What would you like for me to say? That I'm happy to see you? I'm glad you're alive? I wouldn't have to *say* any of those things if you had stuck to the plan. If you hadn't decided you were capable of taking on an army of men on your own. *Goddess bless,* what were you thinking? You weren't. Because of those goddess-damned viva berries. They are *killing* you."

My outburst did not leave me feeling any more in control of myself. Gengi and Avery stood by, Emrys still remarkably asleep. Reia burned her gaze into mine as she took my onslaught. She said nothing for a tense moment, the lines of her posture rigid as a muscle flexed in her jaw. I was feeling out of control, frantic, at a loss for what to do with the emotions barreling through my chest. If she didn't say something soon, I'd have to remove myself, sort my thoughts.

"I got all of us out alive, didn't I?" she asked finally as she released a breath.

"That's not the point. We could have helped you. You could have died," I said, the words launching from my lips as though triggered; my voice was a croak of pain.

"No, Atlas. *I wouldn't have.* I don't think you're under-standing the gravity of the situation. He wants me at his side like Asteria is. He wants that collar around my neck. He needs me. He doesn't need you. In fact, I am sure he wants anyone I have ever cared for *dead.* I would not have died. *You* would have. They would have."

She gestured to Gengi, Emrys, and Avery, a vivid kind of pain in her eye as her resolve finally cracked.

"Atlas, she's right. And she is fine," Gengi said.

The hurt still simmered off my shoulders. I couldn't contain the hurricane of wild emotion any longer. Gengi's voice marked the last of my ability to shoulder this weight.

I clenched my jaw and seethed against the pain pressing against my resolve. Her words tumbled through my mind faster than I could hold on to them. A curling darkness settled over my mood and my shoulders stiffened.

"I will not risk your life," she said, her tone firm. "I will save you first every time. Do not expect me to apologize for that."

Something cracked. Behind my breastbone. The pain was absolutely unbearable, and it stole the breath from my lungs. I wasn't sure if it was the betrayal tinted panic that had been coating my resolve or if it was something deeper. Something like agony at realizing she was just as willing to die for me as I was for her. I couldn't handle that. It was too much.

I considered her under the weight of my disposition for a moment with my jaw clenched, my eyes locked on hers before I turned my back on her, unable to hold her stare anymore.

"Where are you going?" she called after me, concern lifting her tone.

I passed Gengi and swiped his bow from where it rested near his bedroll, the quiver full of arrows from his charmed pack.

"To find dinner," I said without turning to look at her as I slung the bow over my shoulder.

Another drop of rain met my flesh, then another and another until the pittering sound of water on leaves offered me something to focus my racing thoughts on as I moved through the forest, a desperate attempt to escape the raging of my heart as it thrashed against the walls of my chest.

AURELIA

I'd been staring at the fire, watching the way the flames flicked over the singed wood, and listening to the crackling glow of the embers for a long time. The sound of the rain on the leaves above kept an even droning sound for me to relax my mind to as I did my best to unwind the curling pain in my core. After Emrys had woken, she had lifted a shield overhead to protect us from the rain, much like the one Callista had forged in the meadow back in Safe Haven, except this one was just a solid pane, like a floating window to catch the falling water before it soaked our bedrolls and put out our fire.

Atlas had been gone for a long time. The sun was setting, and the dim grey of the clouded skies grew darker. A creeping worry began to set in. The creatures of the night weren't as kind as the ones that spent the waking hours in the forest. Especially in the past few months. In my own travels, I had noticed my nerves setting on edge, something about the shadows of the forest not being as serene as they'd once been.

"Should someone go after him?" I asked, not taking my eyes off the flame.

Gengi turned from where he crouched, sifting through his bag, with a surprised raise of his brow.

"I planned on it," he said with a heavy sigh.

"No," Emrys protested, her voice stern.

I pulled my attention to the lunar female. She sat on her bedroll with her legs crossed under her while she worked a cream through her long curls, wet from her wash in the river. Gengi had made the salve for her with materials he'd pulled from his never-ending bag. She had insisted on washing in the storm, enjoying the feel of the rain, the energy of the shift in weather.

Her rich brown skin glistened under the warm glow of the fire, and her intense, icy lilac eyes shone brightly in contrast. She was small, a few inches shorter than me, but her frame was slight where mine held curves and muscle, hers almost delicate looking. But with the intensity in her eye and the ferocity of her expression, her posture rigid, I got the impression that her featherlight appearance was misleading in comparison to her actual internal fire.

"Someone has to." Gengi ran a hand through his hair.

"I don't want us split up," she said as she hurried to rake her fingers through her long hair and twist it into a furious knot at the base of her neck.

"I'll go."

"I'll go."

Avery and I spoke at once, our voices overlapping, and her eyes met mine. It was a cleverness I marked in her charcoal-colored eyes. Such an unusual color, and her ears were pointed like a fae's, but she had no marking to indicate which lineage she hailed from. Perhaps elven. Her hair was short, cropped to her ears, and stuck out in jagged frills, as though it had been shaved and grown out. It was a rich brown, the color complementing the taupe driftwood of her smooth skin.

In contrast to Emrys, who sat at her feet while she leaned her broad shoulder against the tree trunk to her left, Avery was large for a female. In size, she rested somewhere between Gengi and Atlas. A dominating force to be reckoned with, but a twinkle in her dark eye settled a sort of comfort within me.

"No, I want you three to stay together. I know how to handle a moody Atlas," Gengi protested again, more fire in his tone.

"So can—" I began, but Gengi stood and cut me off with a firmly pointed finger.

"You surely cannot. You two rile each other up faster than a brownie turns to a boggart. Absolutely not. And I want you here to protect them."

I huffed irritably, but Avery spoke before I had a chance to retort.

"We don't need protecting."

"Bullshit," Gengi said. "Let's lay some things out right now. You two have been held in captivity for weeks and need a significant amount of rest and magic restore, and *you*"—he turned his attention to me—"are an absolute fucking loose cannon with an attitude *and* a viva problem. None of you are leaving camp until I am certain we are all in good enough condition to travel on without killing one another."

I gritted my teeth and seethed, but I could not deny the authority Gengi held in his tone, the truth to his words. Before anyone could offer anything else to the discussion, Gengi's shoulders sagged, and he rolled his eyes.

"Is that his goddess-damned cat?"

I turned my attention over my shoulder again to look at Emrys, who had the cat I'd brought with me in her lap. His fur was sopping wet from the rain. He had refused to follow me for a while, and I'd let him go in the forest in a fit of frustration. After a significant struggle, I'd ultimately decided that allowing the cat to follow me of his own free will had been my only option. Stubborn thing must have wandered all day. If he had just come with me when I'd wanted him to, he wouldn't be sopping wet.

Emrys smiled at Gengi with a bright twinkle in her eye as she scratched behind the feline's ears.

"Did you bring his fucking cat here?" Gengi asked me with distain in his tone.

I couldn't help the curl of laughter that bubbled up in my chest at his distress over this creature. The bright feeling broke some of the dismay that had been pressing on my breastbone. The shift in Gengi's attention completely negated the authority he'd held moments prior. The corner of my lips twitched, and I shrugged one shoulder, feigning innocence as I held his stare.

"What about my cat?" Atlas's voice rang from the edge of the trees and my heart skipped at the sound.

My attention shot to find him also sopping wet, his white hair dripping in his eyes, the black tunic he still wore clinging to his frame with the weight of rainwater, highlighting his every muscle. He held a string of rabbits in one hand, Gengi's bow slung across his back.

"Archer?" Atlas's voice tilted in confusion as his eyes landed on the black-and-white feline.

The cat mewed and leapt from Emrys's lap to curl himself between Atlas's ankles. The lunar male bent down to pick him up with his free arm, curling him into his chest.

"You're all wet," he said to the animal as he moved closer to the fire to sit cross-legged across from me to warm up his little creature.

I could not help the stretch of my smile as a vivid warmth flushed my chest, nor could I tear my eyes from the male in front of me. The dimple on his cheek as the smile split his expression made the struggle of having to retrieve the cat from the inn against its will worth it.

"Did you bring him?" Atlas asked, his voice tentative as he flitted his eyes up to meet mine.

"I'll be honest, I don't care about the cat nearly as much as I care about the viva berries." Avery's voice broke the blissful trance that had washed over me, and I pulled my gaze from Atlas's to look to Avery, who moved to crouch on her heels near the fire. She warmed her hands as she narrowed her eyes on mine.

"What the underworld is that about?" she continued.

A vivid flush of panic rushed my veins as the attention shifted solely to me. All four pairs of eyes homed in as they waited for my answer. A crawl of anxiety skittered over my chest, and I pinched the inside of my cheek between my teeth.

"They help with fatigue," I managed to say.

"No, they've been helping you to avoid sleep," Atlas protested, his voice stern.

"You know what those things can do to you, right?" Avery asked.

Her tone held no judgement, and it offered a sense of comfort in the face of the slinking shame threatening to crack my resolve. Even so, that feeling of a grunge-tinted film slithering over my skin made me want to remove myself from under their attention.

"Yes, well, maybe there is a reason I have been so reluctant to sleep," I managed to answer.

I intended the words to come out softer, more kind, but they did not. They launched themselves off a platform of anger, hatred, a visceral pit of self-loathing. Those things were easier to face, to tangle myself with. They were familiar. I leaned into the heat of anger and pulled myself to my feet. Atlas set Archer down and rose as well, Avery following. Gengi moved closer to the fire, and Emrys rose from her bedroll.

Suffocation. The feeling closed my throat, threatened to steal the air from my lungs. The edges of my vision blurred as they closed me in, their very energies crowding my space, and I took a step back.

"Okay, what *is* the reason?" Atlas asked, his tone gentle, but it did little to assuage the vibrating emotions.

"Why does it matter?" I snapped.

"Maybe we could help," Gengi offered.

"If I wanted your help, I would have asked."

"That's a crock of shit and you know it," Atlas bit, his tone harsher now. "You seem much more inclined to wallow in your own misery for no apparent reason whatsoever."

Atlas's eyes flitted to the pouch on my hip, and I watched Avery measure the shift in his attention. I became aware of the weight of the berries there and an intense urge to protect them overcame me. I removed them from my hip and held the pouch tightly to my chest before she had a chance to make a move.

"Reia, don't you think that could be contributing to the struggle you've had with your magic?" Gengi asked, raising his hands in a sort of truce with pity in his eye, laced through his tone.

Disgust rolled through me, fueling my anger. I didn't want pity. Goddesses above, that was the last thing I wanted. The glimmer in his eye intensified that film, the shame as it weighed on my shoulders, pulled at the edges of my awareness.

"Struggles with magic be damned, if she's been on those things for weeks, she'll be dead before we can blink." Avery spoke to Gengi, her attention off me entirely. "Has anyone else seen the actual effects the viva berry can have?"

Fear flashed through Atlas's eyes as he moved around the fire to approach me, his steps quick as though motivated by a new flush of urgency. I stepped back, keeping the distance between us.

"Aurelia, please," Atlas choked.

All I could feel was anger, and pain, and betrayal. I hadn't asked him to keep the secret, but somewhere deep within my core, I'd thought he would. I'd trusted him enough to.

But the way he looked at me, the way his eyes pleaded with me as though he were pleading for my life . . .

Panic lashed out at my heart, seizing the very air within my chest as a flash of that nightmare realm chilled my bones, the echo of pain from that world carved into my flesh as a reminder of why I held onto them so tightly.

I needed them. I couldn't risk falling asleep.

"*I can't*," I hissed, my lashes brimming with tears, and I gripped the bag tighter.

"If you don't take them, I will. She's a danger to herself and those around her." Avery's tone was serious, a note of finality.

Atlas held up his hand to silence her but kept my stare, his own eyes shining with an intensity that stirred something uncomfortable deep within my core.

"I need them," I whispered, my bottom lip trembling slightly as the words came out like a plea.

"And we need you. Don't make me take them," Atlas said, his tone level, soft, understanding.

The anger flared again, and I considered turning on my heel, turning my back on all of them, on Atlas. But something in the way he stood there staring at me, waiting for me to make my own decision with his jaw tight, his eyes fierce made me pause. It was as though the energy of his very soul begged me to make the right choice, to trust him, to lean into the security he was there to offer.

But what was the right choice? If I gave them to him, I

would have to face that place. Nausea rolled through me, and my thoughts spun.

Another wave of anger cycled, and I released a frustrated groan. Avery lunged for me, and Atlas tensed, his posture shifting to defend. In a flash of a moment, one I had little control over, I moved to slip between them and released a cry of strangled emotion as I threw the pouch into the embers of the fire.

I gasped in surprise at my own actions as a frenzied panic flushed my senses. The rush dizzied me, and I brought a shaking hand to my lips as I watched the fire curl over the leather sack as it melted away to reveal the viva berries. For a fraction of a moment, my instinct urged me to stick my hand in the embers, to retrieve the berries. But I refrained, every one of my muscles frozen in absolute shock.

"Aurelia." Atlas's voice was gentle as his touch met my shoulder.

I shirked him off, moving quickly to avoid his hand and backing away and trying to avoid his stare as I turned to storm off into the rain-drenched forest. My efforts failed enough to catch the flash of hurt in his expression. I buried the desire to fix it, to wipe the look of pain from his face as I urged my legs to carry me away from camp.

The cold torrent of rain drenched my hair and clothes as I picked up into a run. I relished the feeling, begged for the relief it offered in the face of my raging inferno of emotion.

ATLAS

"I think you're being too hard on her." Gengi's voice pierced the thick of my daze, and I pulled my attention to his.

"Oh?" I snapped the twig I had been turning between my fingers. "Am I? Please tell me how to better handle this impossible situation, oh *wise one*."

Gengi rolled his eyes and leaned forward, resting his elbows on his knees, the glow of the fire between us illuminating his golden skin, the whisps of his hair shining brightly in the dim light.

Since our argument about the berries, Reia and I had made good work out of firmly ignoring one another. Seething in our own corners of the camp while Emrys and Avery spent the past few nights under the moon, replenishing their stores of magic, recuperating from their time in the prison cells, which they'd been held in in hopes of luring more of us from the resistance. They were both near the riverbank, soaking in the moonlight.

In our time since the holding cells, we'd learned the guards knew we were there somehow. They'd been marking us just as we'd been marking them. Our best guess was the trap was set in hopes of having a better chance at success on their part if they had us conferenced in their own prison.

The only unfortunate thing for them had been our advantage of an ancient fae whose magic had been charged by the very chamber they kept their prisoners in. Whether or not they accounted for her in their attack, we'd never know. Either way, they knew she was on the move after the incident. Ragnor would know what we were after.

Which lit an urgency under us, one that was being annoyingly ignored as Reia sulked and our companions rested.

"If you would stop moping and acting like an ass, I think you'd have an easier time on your own, actually."

He flicked his glance to Reia where she lay on her side, her back to the fire with my cloak tucked under her to support her neck, Archer curled up near her head. Relief chased away the ache I'd been fighting in my chest. I followed his gaze and the icy exterior encasing my disposition melted a touch. I measured the rise and fall of her chest and the relief that washed over me knowing she was getting some rest overwhelmed my senses.

She'd finally fallen asleep. She'd fought it for the first two nights, for reasons she had refused to share with anyone, and it had eaten at me to watch her deteriorate, watch the sunken bags under her eyes deepen, the curve of her shoulders worsen. But finally, she'd succumbed to the pressure of needing sleep. Goddess bless, she needed it. I hoped she would sleep for the next twenty-four hours.

"I am terrified for her."

My voice came out on a whisper, a croak of emotion cracking the words as a heavy kind of sorrow weighed on my chest. She stirred slightly and we both froze, waiting for her to wake. When she did not come out of her slumber, Gengi continued, his voice quieter.

"I know. You have to give her more credit, though. Did you see her in those tunnels? For source's sake, she *ephemerated* all four of us without touching any of us. I've never seen anything like it."

His words turned over in my dismay and I tried to find a way to argue, to hold only to the worry I'd kept so close to my chest, but he was right. She was a remarkable force even with the berries. I couldn't fathom her power at full strength.

She just wasn't there yet. Something was wrong and it drove me mad not knowing what it was.

"I just want her to be alright," I whispered after a moment of silence hung between us.

"I know. I just think you should—"

Whatever Gengi's next words were meant to be, I would never know because the sound of an earsplitting scream severed his voice, slicing through the air in a violence that rattled my thoughts. It spiked a visceral kind of panic in me and brought me to my feet, my hands reaching for the blade I'd left resting next to me. It took me a moment to sift through the disorienting change of events to realize that the sound had come from Reia.

To my distinct horror, she no longer lay curled on her side peacefully. Instead, she was on her back, her arms at her sides as though pinned there and her spine rod straight as her vocal cords tore through her scream. Archer leapt away and cried in surprise as he skittered off to hide in the safety of the shadows.

It was odd, unsettling to see the sudden change in her posture. She had been so relaxed only a moment prior. I hadn't noticed her move. Why hadn't I seen her move?

A sickening chill coated my veins as I tried to process the

scene before me. Despite her change in position and her rattling wails, her eyes were still closed. She was still caught somewhere, some kind of nightmare. That should have been a comfort, but something kept me from releasing the dread wound through my ribs.

I snapped into focus and found my ability to move as I dove to her side. Gengi followed suit to kneel across from me, stress and panic etched into his expression.

"Aurelia," I said, my voice stern, though it came out almost as a plea as I placed an uncertain hand on her shoulder.

A night terror. That was what this had to be. Which meant, much to my dismay, I needed to wake her. Especially if she was going to keep screaming like that. Gengi looked around, inspecting the dark wood for any sign of treacherous wildlife potentially disturbed by the sound. We needed to remain hidden, and her voice would be a beacon for trouble in the night.

A dual set of footsteps thundered through the brush and Emrys and Avery broke into camp again, concern etched into their expressions.

"What happened?" Emrys asked, her stance stable, ready for a battle.

"A nightmare, I think," Gengi responded, uncertain.

Avery's posture relaxed but her brow remained tensed, her eyes fixed on Reia as though she expected her to burst into flames at any moment. Emrys moved to retrieve Gengi's bag and knelt near him. Reia screamed again and my heart cracked, panic fluttering in my chest.

"Is there anything in here that will help?" Emrys asked, and Gengi sputtered an incoherent response as he took the bag from her.

Everyone was afraid of those berries. The hallucinations

they could cause, the damage they could do to someone if too many were consumed.

"Aurelia," I said again, more firmly as I placed a hand on her cheek.

She did not respond to my touch, my voice. Though, she stopped screaming and tears began to streak her face as she gritted her teeth, every muscle in her body tensing. My other hand fluttered around her face as I struggled with how best to help her, a knot of dread strangling the air from my lungs, my muscles frozen with fear.

"Oh, goddess, Atlas." Gengi's voice was rushed, panicked, flushed with a tinge of terror, and the urgency under his tone drew my attention to his golden eyes flared with a frenzy of anxiety.

"She's bleeding," he said, his face draining of color.

"*What?*"

A vile kind of emotion lanced my awareness. Rage mixed with hysteria blurred the edges of my vision.

I moved my gaze to where Gengi's was fixed and found a pool of blood seeping through the fabric of her tunic on her abdomen. My heart leapt into my throat, blocking my airway, my blood thundering between my ears. I swore and moved to put pressure on the wound as instinct took over, pressing my palms into her stomach.

"*Aurelia,*" I said again, my tone firmer, nearly a shout now, but the plea remained there, begging her to hear me.

She shook her head, her voice coming out in distressed whimpers, her chest heaving, and then that scream tore her throat again, her face twisting in an expression of sheer agony.

Helpless. I had never felt so helpless. What was I supposed to do? My own horror spiked in my core and my lungs felt starved for air.

To my horror, I could feel the wound under my palms

spread, the laceration stretching under the contact of my hand. My heart seized again, and something hot lashed through my veins. I lifted the hem of her tunic to get a better idea of what the fuck was happening to her, and my heart dropped from its lodged position in my throat to my feet, leaving a cavern in my chest so deep I was sure there would be a physical hole left there in its wake. That heat coursing through my veins turned to ice as my eyes traced the lines of her fresh wounds.

Dove.

The lacerations there made the word scrawled on her stomach. Not just once, not just this fresh mark, but a dozen times over, left behind in raised, angry, jagged scars. Already healed over from the goddesses knew when.

And slowly, at an agonizing pace, fresh lacerations formed over the first letter, a bloody D already finished, staring angrily up at me.

"*Fuck,*" I hissed and took no time before I scooped her into my arms.

It was him. This was more than a nightmare, more than the effects of those berries. It was that fucking bastard somehow visiting her in her source-damned dreams again. *This* was why she wasn't sleeping. Why she had been afraid of sleeping. He was fucking *torturing* her. And the evidence remained here on her body. On the soft skin of her stomach. It wasn't just a dream. It was something else, something wicked I had no time to process in that moment.

"What the shattered source is going on?" Gengi asked, gathering my change of momentum as understanding.

His voice was desperate, frantic, but I did not have the space to answer him. I did not have the time to focus on anything but her.

Reia's head lolled back in the crook of my elbow as I positioned my arm under her shoulder, and I pushed the wild hair from her face, focusing my energy on my one magical ability. If the curse of a cyphin's power was ever to be useful to me, now would be the time.

I pressed my palm to her cheek, brushing her hot stream of tears away with the pad of my thumb as I pulled from her well of magic, working to cut her off from it. I'd never worked to draw someone's energy so quickly, and the sensation was dizzying. The effort was laborious. Something held her there, kept her hovering in that in-between space, and it took most of the energy I held in my own well to bring her back to me.

You cannot have her, I called out to the aether, sending every bit of my rage, dismay, agony into the pit of darkness that held her soul. *I will fucking kill you, you spineless bastard. You will not take her. You cannot have her.*

I hoped with every fiber of my being that he heard me. That he felt my rage, feared my presence. I pulled harder and the tether to that place felt like a living thing. My vision spun and something in my core twisted viciously, but I held on. I had to hold on. She needed me to hold on.

It was so fucking hard. I'd never struggled like this to cyphin energy. Panic began to cloud my focus, and just as I thought my own exhaustion would give way to the anchor holding her there, my vision blurred, and I felt something loosen. A bright spot in the dark reaching back for me, stretching toward my tether to her magic. I held on to that, gripping with every tendril of cyphin power I could muster. And as suddenly as her nightmare had taken her, I felt the binding snap.

Her flow of magic broke, her well cut off from her soul as my power locked itself firmly in place around her essence.

The very second the blanket of my magic settled over her, her eyes snapped open, golden orbs swimming in desperate panic as she sucked in a breath so large her chest might have cracked. The hysteria in my own chest fractured, a weight lifting enough to cause a prick of tears behind my eyes.

She heaved a few breaths and tangled her fingers in the fabric of my tunic, staring up at me with wide eyes while I stroked her hair from her face, trying desperately to gather my own thoughts in the wild storm of the past few moments.

"Atlas," Reia breathed after a few earth-shattering beats of stillness.

"I'm so sorry," I said, my voice cracking under the weight of my own pain, fear, shame.

Shame at not being more willing to understand what he had been doing to her. Why she had been taking those berries.

I wasn't sure what else to say. No words could wipe this away, account for what had just happened. What had *been* happening to her.

How big of a fucking asshole had I been to her about not sleeping? About those damned berries? I wished I could take it back. I wished I had known.

Aurelia's hand fluttered to her stomach, and the moment her fingers touched the wet of her own blood, she stiffened, pulling herself to a seat. She peeled herself from my arms, leaving a cold, hollow ache behind as she moved away from me. My hands fell into my lap, but I kept my eyes on her as she recoiled, her golden eyes swimming through whatever she had just experienced.

"What happened?" Gengi asked, and it was the first time in minutes I remembered his existence, any of them, my own tortured emotions coiling me into a tunnel.

Emrys and Avery sat on either side of Gengi, their muscles tensed, their eyes fixed on Reia as she continued to recoil, to back away from us.

"I was just there," she muttered, her eyes flitting back and forth, her fingers trembling as she pulled her knees to her chest, her bloodied fingertips smudging red over the fabric of her leggings.

"Hey," I breathed, shifting my weight to move a little closer, my hands outstretched but careful not to touch her, worried about overwhelming her in this state. "You're not now. He's not here."

"Will someone fucking tell me what just happened?" Gengi asked again, his voice rising with increasing stress.

Emrys placed a hand on his arm but kept her stilled attention on Reia.

I thinned my lips and looked to Aurelia. I knew what had happened. The second I'd seen that word. That vile pet name he'd used for her. *Dove.* In Safe Haven, he'd used it. Taunted her with the name. Tried to rattle her with it.

And now it was carved into her skin.

A reminder of the claim he tried to make on her.

Fucking disgusting.

No, I didn't need her to explain. I knew where she had been. Wherever it was that he could get to her. He had been able to reach her before. That night after the festival, he'd done it. And he was still doing it.

The very thought of it made my blood boil, and my skin pulled tight with the need to peel *his* flesh from his bones.

But I could not answer Gengi. This horror was not mine to tell.

"Why am I back?" Aurelia ignored Gengi.

Actually, I wasn't sure she'd heard him. Instead, she looked to me, her eyes locked on mine, a kind of desperation shining in her golden irises.

"I pulled you out of it," I said, my tone steadier than I expected.

"How?"

"I cut off your magic."

I shrugged one shoulder, and her bottom lip trembled as she processed my admission, a tear falling from her cheek as she shifted her weight, curling farther into herself.

The need to be near her overwhelmed me. The need to curl her into my chest and soothe her pain, *take* her pain and make it my own. I would suffer it myself if it meant she did not have to relive the trauma of what he'd done to her.

"It's why you haven't been sleeping." My words did not come out as a question.

And why she had a panic attack about being bound on the bridge.

Oh, fuck me. I had been such an ass. I wanted to fix it. I needed to fix it.

She nodded and squeezed her eyes shut, more tears falling over her cheeks. Exhaustion weighted on her shoulders, and they curled in as though something in her chest had deflated slightly.

"I want to help," I whispered, "Let me help you."

"I don't know if anyone can," she said, her words cracking with desperation enough to break my resolve.

I moved to her and scooped her into my lap, giving in to the urgency fueling my need to comfort her. I paused, offering her an opportunity to move away if she needed to, but she did not. She relaxed into my embrace, twisting my tunic into her grip again to pull the fabric to her eyes as she released heartbreaking sobs. They sounded as though she had been choking on them, trying to hold them back for months, finally given the space to be free. I held her head to my chest and looked to Gengi with a tight jaw as I rocked her, allowing her tears to bleed through my tunic, soak the skin of my chest. My friend looked absolutely beside himself, horrified, still unsure of what to make of the scene.

"It's alright," I murmured into her hair. "You're safe."

My words only caused her heaving sobs to shake her harder, her shoulders trembling as she curled tighter into my arms. The sounds cracked my very soul in two. I held her tighter and swallowed my own grief as I worked to control the tears pressing against my eyes.

"I can't go back."

"You don't have to," I said. "I can keep you from it."

She said nothing but cried like that for an impossibly long while. Avery rose to move to her own bedroll again, and Emrys gripped Gengi's arm, moving him away from us as well, both females understanding the need for space. Gengi remained wide-eyed in a kind of shocked state I had no ability to deal with.

I muttered into Reia's hair over and over that she could relax, fall back to sleep, that I would keep her safe.

But she did not.

We stayed like that until the ink of night bled from the sky and the morning birds began their songs to remind us of the inescapable passing of time.

She eventually peeled herself from my arms, and I did nothing to stop her. Reia did not so much as spare a glance at me as she hiked away from camp toward the sound of the rushing river, presumably to wash off the night terror from hours prior.

Gengi did not sleep either. He sat across from the fire, staring into it, waiting patiently to be brought up to speed while Emrys held him from behind, her slight arms wrapped around his waist to offer him some comfort. Exhaustion pulled at his expression as I met his eye. He raised a brow at me, still waiting for a response, the lines of stress pulling his mouth into a frown.

I had nothing to say.

No words came even close to expressing the tumult of

emotion careening through my chest. I tried, but nothing would cover the length of what had just happened.

So, I heaved a sigh and reached into Gengi's bag and sifted around until I found my sparring gloves. I pulled them from the sack and took off into the woods at a brisk pace, desperate to find a way to work off some of the living inferno of fury building in my chest.

CHAPTER 35
AURELIA

The smell of onions and other wild herbs hit me squarely in the face before I had sight of camp. It made the hunger in my stomach curl in on itself, the pain more of an annoyance than it had been for most of the morning. The fragrance of fresh food made me pick up my pace, eager to see what was in store.

I crested the hill, my muscles feeling stronger after my time spent near the river soaking up the sun and allowing the fresh wound on my abdomen to heal over, the horrors of the previous night tucked safely away in the recesses of my mind to work through later.

Or never. Never would be fine.

Gengi stood over the fire, stirring a pot full of whatever he had been cooking. His golden brow pulled together in a way that left a crease above his nose, as though the expression had been stitched into his features for hours. His usually warm, sandy complexion had been washed to take on a sallow grey tone, and I marked the lines of exhaustion over his shoulders.

"Welcome back," Emrys chimed from her perch in a tree overhead.

I craned my neck to offer her a slight smile. She nodded back, one foot swinging under her as the branch supported her, the other leg stretched out with her back resting against the sturdy trunk. Avery sat at the bottom with one knee tucked up, a book in hand as she focused on the pages. Atlas was nowhere to be found.

"This smells incredible," I mused, my tone light as I moved for my sack for a fresh set of clothes, eager to get the evidence of last night's horrors off me.

"Are we going to pretend like you weren't nearly diced in half by an invisible blade last night, then?" Gengi asked, his tone heavy, no hint of his usual tease under his words.

My stomach flipped as dread sunk a stone in my core.

"I had hoped so," I said, turning my attention to the contents of my sack near my bedroll. My pulse quickened at the prospect of having to relive the horror after decidedly ignoring it.

"Well, that really isn't going to work for me." He sighed. "I'll work myself up into a knot of worry so tight, I'll turn into a little ball, and you'll have to roll me around everywhere we go."

He placed some lightness back into his tone, and it eased some of the itching over my chest. Avery snickered from her spot but kept her eyes on her book. I looked back to Gengi with hesitation and pulled a fresh tunic out of my sack as I rose to my feet again, eager to get the one stained with dried blood off.

"I made this for you. I found some fresh wild onion in a field nearby," the male said, gesturing to the pot of what I could now see was stew.

"Thank you," I said, my tone soft, and my stomach rolled loud enough for the sound to reach across camp to his ears.

Gengi served me a bowl of the stew he'd made from foraged carrots, potatoes, and onion, and we settled in cross-legged on the ground across from each other. I accepted his gift without any offer of an explanation for the evening's events, and he chanced another inquiry.

"That was really terrifying," he said, a weight in his tone choking the words in the back of his throat.

He focused on his stew to avoid my eye contact.

"I want to be able to help you with whatever that is. And I know it's probably difficult to talk about, but I need to know. If we are traveling together, saving the realm together, I need you both to be transparent with me. People get themselves killed being more informed than I am right now."

The knot in my core tightened and that frantic energy that always came with the memory of that vile place sent that now familiar buzzing over my thoughts. The skin over my chest stretched tight.

I wanted nothing to do with them. The memories. The scars. That place. The terrors he forced Callista to endure. But Gengi was right. I could not expect him to travel with me to the ends of the earth, trust me blindly, if I did not trust him enough to talk about this.

Although, I had expected Atlas to have done that legwork for me.

I knew Atlas had understood. I saw it in his eyes, the tremble of his bottom lip. He had pulled me from that place, saved me from the torture. I knew he'd understood why I hadn't been sleeping.

But he wasn't here.

His absence carved a hollow ache deep within the cavities of my chest. I peered around camp for any sign of his where-abouts. My brow pulled together, and anxiety flushed me.

"Atlas hasn't told you?" I asked.

"Atlas took off about thirty-six seconds after you did to beat the hell out of some trees about it and I haven't seen him since."

Something pinched at my resolve knowing Atlas had been away all day, too. A warmth spread through my chest, washed over my heart at knowing he had not shared my demons with his companion.

Our companion.

I looked Gengi in the eye, mustering all the courage I could summon from beneath the pits of my general dismay, and took a short breath.

"I do not sleep because Ragnor can reach me. He does . . . terrible things to me. To Callista."

Even the sound of her name on my voice, that admission, was strained with the dread-laced terror constricting my resolve. Panic flushed me at the thought, and I focused on stirring my stew, centering my frenzy to get my mind away from the possibility of her harm.

"How can he do that?" He gaped and set his bowl down, his eyes flitting to the spot on my stomach.

"I assume he uses Asteria," I said, and the words spoken aloud cracked something in my chest, the pain unbearable, a violent thrash of a truth.

It made the most sense. One of Asteria's lunar talents was astral projection, which included visiting others in their dreams. Somehow, Ragnor had twisted the magic, amplified it so he could inflict real-life physical harm.

The idea of even the possibility caused such violent pain and remorse for my sister. I knew how viscerally Asteria would have protested such horrors. How even the prospect of committing them would drive her into a deep sorrow that would normally take her days to recover from. She was so gentle, so kind at her core. I couldn't stomach what he was doing to her, to her magic.

And all I could think of my sister was her vacant eyes. The gutting way her soul remained nowhere near her physical body under Ragnor's control. The way he wielded her body to attack those I know she'd rather die before harming.

Was she aware of the violence she inflicted? Goddess, I hoped not. If I prayed for anything, it would be that my kind, sweet, caring, gentle sister had no recollection of the horrors that monster subjected her to. Made her responsible for.

"Why?" he asked, his eyes swimming.

"To break me." I shrugged a shoulder. "I do fear it's working."

The last bit came out weak, my voice nearly a whisper as I allowed myself one tiny flicker of vulnerability. It was almost as though I had not consented to the words, like they had slipped free of my resolve quickly, sneaking past my exterior of hard, unwavering stillness.

"It's not." The sound of Atlas's voice over my shoulder startled me and I jumped in my seat, the stew in my bowl sloshing over the edge.

I had not heard him coming, but his presence washed a warmth over my anxiety, a comfort I wasn't sure how to compartmentalize.

He tossed his sparring gloves to the ground near his bedroll and moved to us, crouching down to balance on the balls of his feet, his elbows supporting his frame on his knees.

"You are stronger than you are currently giving yourself credit for. The female in that cave, the fire goddess I watched fight off dozens of those men, the one that fearlessly saved us from that nightmare of a male's guards to sacrifice herself for the cause without a flicker of a thought? She is the very same one that fought for all our lives in Safe Haven, the one that freed Brenwyn without a second glance, who is willing to risk *everything* she has for the people she cares for. *She* is a force to be reckoned with. And I will not allow that source-damned, shit excuse for a mortal being to make you feel like any less of the goddess that you are. Fuck that. Fuck him. And fuck every single one of the lies floating through your head telling you otherwise."

I gaped at him, allowed him to speak through every one of his thoughts as he vehemently delivered his words, and they left me near a state of speechlessness. I wished I felt as strongly about my abilities as he seemed to. But I supposed it counted for something, at least it felt like it did. Some blinding sensation locked firmly into place behind my heart, a supporting weight I'd never felt before.

"That was quite a speech," I said, releasing a sigh, and the corner of my mouth twitched at the sudden lightness in my chest. The brightness had lifted with each of his words. It allowed my strength to take root, fuel my muscles, chase away my exhaustion.

"Is that what you did in the woods all day by yourself? Practice that?"

"Yes, actually, if you must know," he said, his tone light, the familiar lilt of his tease back as he reached across us for a bowl for his own stew. "It took me a very long time, so I hope you appreciated it."

I could not suppress the smile as it replaced the lines of tension that had been around my mouth. I peeled my eyes from Atlas to focus on my own food as I wrestled with the living beast of bright emotion within my chest, still very eager to chase away the hunger plaguing me.

Gengi's gaze caught mine and he smiled softly. Something about the presence of these two washed away some of the horror, the dread, the pressure of all I was expected to do. If only their confidence in me were enough to propel me into the coming days. And if it was not, at least the warmth in my chest was a comfort enough to chase away the lingering chill of hysteria at the memory of that nightmare realm.

ATLAS

Gengi and the lunar females had fallen asleep hours ago, long before the sun had dipped below the horizon. None of us had really slept after the nightmare realm incident, so I was not surprised at his eagerness to fall into the bliss of slumber with Emrys curled into his chest. To leave behind some of the pressure of the reality of our situation.

But Aurelia remained awake, staring at the fire, unblinking as she twisted the hem of her tunic between her fingers. The edge of the fabric was beginning to fray, wearing under the stress of her anxious fidgeting.

"You can sleep. I promise it will be better for you than staring at the side of my face all night," she said, her voice low so as not to wake the others.

Though she did not turn her gaze from the fire, the corner of her mouth twitched, the ghost of a smile on her lips.

"If you're awake, I'm awake," I whispered, my tone sturdy.

"I know." She sighed, but the words did not hold a hint of irritation.

Instead, I felt relief roll off her shoulders, and the thought made that tight coil within my chest release some long-strained tension.

"I can help you sleep," I offered on a hesitant hope.

She had not been willing to accept help, but maybe after everything, she'd let me do something to offer her comfort.

I had spent the day deep out in the forest, taking out my frustrations of the soft bark of the birch trees. That, and trying to work up the courage to make this offer. I was capable of taking away her troubles. I could help her sleep through the night, every night for the rest of my life if that was what she needed. If she'd let me.

She turned her gaze to mine, shifting in her seat to better meet my eye, and gestured for me to go on.

Surprise flushed me at her lack of protest. I cleared my throat, nerves crawling along my chest, scattering my thoughts.

Get it together.

"I can turn your magic off. We don't have any deadstone, but I'm not sure that would work anyway, and I don't want anything like that around your wrists. It took a decent amount of concentration for me to—" I stopped as her gaze hardened and my train of thought scrambled, and it took a beat for me to regain it. "I could help you sleep. If you're alright with me staying close to you."

I watched consideration pass through her eyes, and for a moment, I thought she might protest, offer me more of that hard exterior she had worked so hard to build, but she did not. Instead, her shoulders curled in as she released a breath as she bit down on her bottom lip, a glimmer of tears staining her lower lashes.

Something wild behind my heart drew me to her, an incessant need to wipe that gutting expression from her face, to be the stop to her pain.

"Hey." I leaned closer and could not stop my hand from

shifting the stray hair from her cheek, tucking it behind her pointed ear.

I could have sworn she leaned her face into the touch as she met my eye, but that might have been a delusional trick of my own heart.

"I didn't mean to upset you. We can sit like this in silence forever if you'd like. I don't mind. Really."

"No." She huffed through a tear-stained laugh as a few glistening streams fell over the apples of her cheeks. "I very much do not want that."

"Well, then, what do you want?"

The question was weighted. I did not intend it to be, but it held so much of my heart in it, and I knew what that cursed muscle wanted from me. I knew what it wanted to hear from her. But it would not. I was not her fated. Even that thought sparked wild guilt, pain for my sister that contradicted every desire I had ever had.

Reia could not possibly feel the capacity of what I felt. It was that simple, and I needed to keep it that way.

If only I could control my own damned emotions long enough to cage them for one bleeding minute.

"I want to sleep," she said finally, her lip trembling as her face crumpled, the weight of the tears she had been holding back breaking the dam of her forged exterior.

I nodded, the pressure of waiting for her answer cracked, and I released a tense breath. I held out my hand for her to take. She did as much, and I guided her to her feet and then to her bedroll. She said nothing as she lowered herself, and I waited for her to get comfortable before I settled in on my side next to her.

Reia stared at me with wide eyes, her head resting on her arm, the glow of the fire a backlight to her copper hair braided over her shoulder, her striking features cast in the shadow of night. The darkness did nothing to temper the gold glitter of her irises, though. Their mesmerizing glow had a tendency to wipe the thought clean from my conscious mind.

"Do you not need to be touching me?" she asked with an amused lilt in her tone after a few moments of me blankly staring at her. My entire body remained rigid as I lay merely inches from her, keeping a solid space between us.

"You're right," I said, forcing a tease under my tone.

I scooted closer, and she moved to make space for me on her bedroll. Every nerve in my body lit on fire as she raised her head and pulled my arm under her neck for support before curling into my chest. Her arm draped around my waist, and mine fell over her shoulders. The bright, citrus, and sunshine fragrance of her hair clouded my already buzzing thoughts, and I had to work incredibly hard to keep my breathing steady.

I had not necessarily meant *this* close. I only needed to be near enough to have contact, but knowing she wanted to be like this with me sent a confusing pang of soaring emotion straight through to my heart. She settled in, and I felt the lines of her muscles relax as she let go of her fear, her apprehension.

Goddess bless. I am still so fucked.

"It's easier to be them," I said low, almost a whisper.

"What?" she asked, her voice already weighed down with sleep.

"Enora and Kier," I replied, though I had to swallow the lump in my throat at the mention of our ruse to escape reality—how much it had meant to me to see her let go of even a fraction of the darkness shrouding her.

"Well, I wouldn't imagine a fisherman has many stresses to overcome from day to day." She sighed heavily.

"Oh, you'd be surprised," I murmured. "It's *your* life as a lady of the wilderness that has me yearning for peace."

"Enora's life," she whispered, some of that fear creeping into her tone as she released a tight sigh. "Not mine."

"Let's be them. For tonight. If it will make it easier to sleep. Think of how mundane our adventures would be as the fisherman and the common elven."

She took a few breaths but said nothing for a while. Anticipation coated my senses as something tight pulled behind my breastbone.

"Thank you," Reia murmured sleepily after some time.

Her muscles relaxed again, but she still clung to consciousness.

I hurried to wrap my magic around her before slumber claimed her, blanketing her in the comfort of my ability to sever her connection to her magic and keep her from that nightmare. She felt it, the way my magic pulled at her. I sensed it in the way her muscles tensed, the slight intake of air to fill her lungs. When my work was done, she released a sigh, her body releasing pent-up tension as she allowed herself to relax into my chest. Relief bled through every inch of her frame.

It was not long before her breaths came in slow, even beats, the relief of sleep finally washing over her.

"I'm sorry," I breathed into her hair as I tightened my grip around her.

The words cracked my chest. I was so fucking sorry. For not trying to understand. For being incapable of protecting her from that monster. For allowing any amount of my emotions to cloud our goals, our need to get Callista back.

But she did not respond, her chest rising and falling with the rhythm of sleep. I would not so much as move another muscle for the entirety of my life if that was what it took to keep her safe.

I lay there through the night, watching the dying embers of

the fire, tracking the beats of her heart, the rhythm of her breath until the rose-wash of sunlight bled through the trees to chase away the twinkle of stars overhead.

CHAPTER 37
AURELIA

It was not the sweet comfort of coming out of a deep slumber naturally that brought me back to life; rather, it was a sharp pain on my forehead, right between my brows, that jerked my consciousness into the land of the living again. I opened my eyes to find Gengi crouched over me, staring down with something like expectant irritation written into his expression.

"Ouch," I grumbled irritably as I blinked the haze of sleep away.

"Oh, hey," Gengi said, his face lifting with a mockery of lightness. "I was just checking to see if you were still alive. Glad to see that's the case."

I groaned and pulled myself to a seat, my muscles aching at the stiff movement. Archer mewed irritably as my sudden shift disrupted his rest. The creature had been curled up near my head. He gave a deep stretch and moved to curl himself into Atlas's lap, who chuckled from where he sat next to me. Anxiety flushed me for a brief moment as I remembered how we had fallen asleep, the serene peace and sense of security I'd felt in his arms.

When had he moved? Why had he moved?

He must have sensed the anxious skitter of my thoughts because he met my eye and spoke before I had a chance to gather myself.

"I've been right here," he assured me, "all night. You're safe."

I released a breath and nodded as the flutter in my chest eased. I looked to Gengi, who still sat on his haunches.

I rubbed at the still stinging spot between my brows.

"Did you *flick* me?"

"Yes," Gengi answered, his tone tilting with amused pride. "You've slept through to the afternoon and the rest of us have been patiently waiting for any kind of direction that might get us out of this forest. Have you had a nice rest?"

I smoothed stray curls from my face and moved my fingers to unwind the braid over my shoulders to shake my sleep-tousled hair free as I took a moment to gather my bearings.

The past few days had been absolutely exhausting, and I honestly felt as though I needed to sleep through an entire week to recover. A weight in my muscles made it difficult to shake off the veil of sleep, but I stretched my arms over my head and rose to my feet.

"Your conduit is sourceless, which would lead me to believe that the shard was not in the chamber, but that doesn't explain why you were randomly gifted with the kind of magic you wielded in those tunnels," Gengi continued as he followed suit.

"Where are Emrys and Avery?" I asked, ignoring his fluttering as I peered around camp for the two females nowhere to be found.

"Why are you deflecting?" Gengi asked.

"I'm not." I shrugged with a huff of a laugh and moved to

slide on my boots. "I haven't slept in three months, and you *flicked* me awake. Give me a second."

"I think we are all just curious as to whether or not you have your magic back, Feathers. We are all eager to get to The Capitol and get everyone home safely." Atlas's voice was weighted differently than I was used to hearing; there was a heaviness there that I had not expected.

I looked to him with a pinch in my chest. Grief lingered there. In the lines of his eyes, the tension in his shoulders. Grief for his sister. Callista. An emotion reflected in the cavity of my chest—a hollow ache carved out of desperation to stop her suffering.

We needed to get a move on.

I hadn't dared test my stores of magic since setting foot in this forest. It had taken me a wild amount of energy to get here, to *ephemerate* the distance between Venridge and these woods. I'd sent the four of them as far as I could in the direction of the Darkwood, the briars protecting that shard of the source. And I had hoped that the surge of power I'd felt in the tunnels would be enough to bring my strength back to health again.

But the second I'd landed, I'd felt the drain, what that effort had done to my well.

The essence left behind in those tunnels by the missing source shard had given me temporary strength, though I feared it was gone. All the more reason to get ahold of a shard for myself, to get to the Darkwood.

"The tunnels were charged with residual source magic, just like that cave on the island off the coast of Tenebria—Safe Haven. I had that strength in the tunnels."

"And you do not now?" Atlas asked from where he sat, one arm slung over a propped knee.

I marked the bags under his eyes, grey tinge to his usually bright skin, the sharpened hollow of his cheeks. He had not slept in the past weeks either. Worry coated my awareness as I noted just how much exhaustion had worn on him.

"Not much." I shook my head. "Will you please sleep?"

The corner of Atlas's mouth twitched, and he tilted his chin.

"If you're awake—" he began, but I cut him off.

"Yes, but you had that rule in place because I wasn't sleeping. I am now. And it doesn't look like *you* are."

"I did," he said innocently with a shrug of one shoulder, though I could see the weight of exhaustion across the very lines of his posture.

"He did not," Gengi offered in retort. "He can't sleep while he cyphins. He does need to sleep."

Atlas opened his mouth to protest, but Gengi's scolding interrupted.

"*You need sleep!*" Gengi insisted.

"I want to know what the plan is first," Atlas said, leaning his head against the tree.

"Alright, maybe we should all sit again, then." I sighed heavily and plopped back down, sitting cross-legged on my bedroll.

"Welcome back to the land of the floor people," Atlas chimed, the tease returning to his tone. "It's much more comfortable down here. No pesky standing to do."

A soft laugh broke my throat, shattered some of my anxiety, and I nudged his foot with my toe, urging a soft tilt to his lips, bringing out that dimple.

Gengi sat down, closing in our small circle, with his spine rod straight.

"Emrys and Avery?" I asked with a raised brow.

"I'll brief them later. They've been out foraging for healing herbs for a while," Gengi said, gesturing for me to continue.

The pair of males watched me expectantly as I wrestled

with my thoughts, trying to figure out where exactly to start, how to explain a millennia old secret for the first time. After a few beats of awkward silence, the pressure of Atlas's need to say something snarky threatened to break the tension, and I took a breath to speak before he could derail my train of thought again.

"Okay, well, starting off with the worst of it: Ragnor has the source shards," I said.

The words were not exactly what I had planned, and I followed them with an irritable roll of my eyes as they landed.

"Right, excellent," Atlas responded with a hint of sarcasm under his tone as he nodded in recognition.

I shot him a glare and huffed a breath, preparing myself to continue.

"Listen to me, I have, historically, been horrific with responsibility, and the more I learn about my past, the harder it is to believe I will be able to pull any of this off. So, if you could just give me a bit of grace, that would be fabulous," I defended, tension creeping into my muscles.

"It's alright," Gengi said. "We're here. You have our undivided attention. Well, mine at least. I can't speak for him."

He pointed irritably at Atlas, who scoffed and rolled his eyes.

"Just—" I snapped, frustration under my tone. "Just listen."

Atlas gestured for me to go on.

"When the source shattered, Asteria and I hid the shards in safe locations underground across the realm. Those spots are where you would find that charged crystal with residual energy. There is a chamber for one under each trade city, including The Capitol. I knew Ragnor had a piece of the source in his chest, the one that had been under the palace in The Capitol. There should have been three others under the other three trade cities in the north, south, and west. We just left the trade city in the south and the chamber held no source crystal. At this point, I do not believe that there will be any under the other trade cities either."

"What do you think he did with them?" Gengi asked.

"I have no idea, but Asteria helped me secure them in their chambers, so if he knew of the one in Venridge, it's because of her, and that means he knows about all of them. Except he *doesn't* know about *all* of them. He can't."

The words weren't flowing as freely from me as I had hoped. The explanation kept getting stuck behind some kind of barrier, a centuries-old barricade against the complex emotions it would take to unravel the pain caused by the source, the responsibility of being its guardian, the burden of failing in that task.

They both waited expectantly for me to continue. I took a breath and mustered the energy to go on.

"There is one piece no one knew about but me. It's secure, hidden deep within Darkwood Forest."

"Bleeding underworld, the Darkwood?" Atlas asked, surprise and aggravation tangled through his tone. "You could have actually said we needed to go to the real *bleeding underworld* and I would have been happier about this latest development."

"It's not ideal," I agreed, releasing a short breath.

"Not ideal?" he asked, throwing a hand up. "Goddess bless, Feathers, there's a reason no one goes near those trees."

"I know that." I shrugged and nodded. "The reason *is* the source crystal."

The Darkwood rested at the base of the mountain range, only a few miles away from where I understood the blight to be, close to the city of Fenbrook on the east side of the mountains. The Darkwood was a span of land no one dared cross. The tales of those that had were full of monsters and treacherous obstacles. Very few made it through that forest alive, and as far as I was aware, no one had even so much as tried in the past few hundred years.

"What do you mean?" Atlas asked with a narrow eye.

"I placed it there because there was something wrong with it. When the source shattered, Asteria wasn't right. Aeson hadn't been right—" I choked on my words as the violent memory flashed through my mind's eye, a frigid flush of dread lodging a lump in my throat.

"Your brother and sister?" Atlas asked, his tone gentler now.

I nodded and swallowed past the thickness coating my tongue.

"It was killing her. It *did* kill him. I couldn't let her near it. I hid it without her before we started hiding the others, before she was even aware of how many there were."

"So, there is a shard no one in The Capitol is aware of?" Gengi asked, his tone brighter, as though excitement had caught flame under his mood.

I nodded.

"I need to get to it. My magic . . . I still don't have control over it. I can get to it, and I'll be able to stop him. I'll be able to get Callista back."

A familiar pain beneath my heart brought the prickle of tears behind my eyes as I met Atlas's. I did my best to keep my agony at what happened to Callista at bay. Staying focused on what had been directly in front of me these past weeks—the small goals, the day-to-day—had helped.

Though, I could not ignore the hollow ache in my chest at the mention of The Capitol, of our greater goal, the reason we were out here in the middle of nowhere.

"I'm sorry I haven't been strong enough," I said to Atlas, the tears welling as the pain in my chest swelled.

A muscle in his jaw ticked and he released a short breath as he considered me.

"I know you want her back, too," he said, his voice a croak. "We'll get her."

I couldn't separate the torrents of grief rolling through my chest, determine where they stemmed from, or which direction I needed to point them. Seeing how pained he was, knowing how much he missed his sister was almost too much in addition to my own complicated emotions pressing against my resolve.

I had done that. It was my fault she was gone. It was my fault she was hurting, that he was hurting.

"Of course we will." Gengi's voice was lighter, surer as he tried to offer some comfort to break the tension brewing between us. "To the Darkwood we go, then. Any idea where we are now?"

"Yes." I managed to force some lightness into my tone as I offered a roll of my eyes. "If we move after Atlas gets some rest, it should take only a few days. I know where we are."

"Great," Gengi said. "We'll be ready to start first thing in the morning."

"Why not now?" Atlas asked.

"Because you look like you've already been through to the veil. Get to sleep," Gengi instructed. "Reia, would you like to join me for some foraging? See if we can't find Emrys and Avery and help with some supply restock?"

"Sure," I said, but looked to Atlas, who already had his gaze fixed on me.

That flutter deep within the chamber of my chest hitched my breath at the intensity of his stare, and for a moment I feared I'd said something wrong, done something to hurt him. I furrowed my brow, but his expression relaxed, and he moved to lie on his back, stretching out dramatically. Archer shifted from his lap to lie happily on his breastbone.

"Alright," he said through a deep yawn. "If you need me for the next five hours, don't."

I huffed a laugh as he covered his eyes with his arm and rose to my feet, turning to see Gengi had already made it a distance without me.

"Come on, Reia," he called over his shoulder.

I hesitated, feeling the need to offer some words to Atlas, though I could not find them. They were stuck somewhere behind a haze of tangled thoughts. I watched as his chest rose with a deep breath, the beginning of the influence of rest, and I turned to follow Gengi into the forest.

CHAPTER 38
AURELIA

"You spend an unusual amount of time staring at fire." Atlas's soft voice carried over the sound of him sharpening his blade.

For what felt like hours, I had been using the steady rhythm of the whetstone against steel to allow my thoughts to numb into a comforting silence. It had taken a long time for me to burn the visceral emotion flushed out by having to endure that nightmare dreamscape space to a low flicker of a flame, and then eventually float it to the recesses of my mind, to rest in a pocket of space somewhere designated for turning things over at a later date. I had willed my vision to blur around the edges, focusing so severely on the curl of flame in the hearth and the *shink, shink, shink* of Atlas's work, I wasn't sure my consciousness was tied to my mortal body any longer.

That's what I'd wanted. That trancelike space in which I could detach, remove the worry from my shoulders, stare into the flame into all hours of the night.

Not tonight, though. The familiar snark in Atlas's tone

pulled my mind back to reality, dredged it through the comforting haze.

I sucked in a breath and rolled my shoulders, tightening my arms over their grip on my knees and pulling them closer to my chest.

Gengi and Emrys had been at the riverbank for over an hour, getting some much-needed recovery time after traveling nonstop for a full day. We had moved quickly, with Avery at the front taking out brush and marking the path with a type of endurance I'd rarely seen in anyone. She rested now, the sound of her light snoring left behind in the silence to mark the passing of time.

Much to Gengi's protests, Archer made it with us as well. The stubborn thing was remarkably attached to Atlas and had clung to his shoulder the entire trip. The feline was out on his own now, too, presumably hunting field mice nearby.

"Sometimes, when we sit here like this, into the night, I fear you've gone mute," Atlas mused as he set his sword on his bedroll.

I turned over my shoulder to see a genuine line of concern across his brow, despite the light tease in his tone.

"And that would be the greatest of shames. I'm reluctant to admit this to you, but I rather like your short temper and moody jabs. I'd hate for you to lose that spark."

The corner of my mouth ticked up as something other than dismay and rage pushed against the blanket of despair weighing on my shoulders. That same flip in my core, flutter near my heart, washed away some of that all too familiar dread that tangled so significantly with my disposition.

Over and over again, no matter how heavy the darkness weighed on my thoughts, the tilt of this male's smile, the glimmer of his violet eyes, the crook in his cheek that made up that maddeningly charming dimple pulled me out of it.

He was a bright spot, a beacon in the din of all that threatened to suffocate me. As much as I tried to drown in that reality, he kept creeping in, offering me comfort even when I did not want it for myself.

And just as quickly as I had allowed the warmth to flush through me, a color of guilt tinged my mood, twisted in my abdomen, a sharp spike of reality as I shook off the train of thought.

Too close. He'd gotten too close; I'd grown to lean on him too heavily.

I was so beyond grateful to him for allowing me to sleep, staying awake so I could get the rest I needed to go on, but goddess damn it if that hadn't made it that much harder to keep the cage of my heart lodged firmly in place. I needed to be careful and that was growing increasingly more difficult to do. I should just stay awake, work to keep my eyes open, tangle my thoughts with the fire.

Though, that task seemed impossible without the viva berries. The absence of them weighed on me and I would find none in these forests; they didn't grow this close to the mountain range.

Anxiety chased away the warmth that had bloomed in my chest and my lips tipped in an involuntary frown at the turn my stomach took.

I met his eye and released a breath as I offered a soft shrug, unsure of what to say.

Atlas spent a moment staring at me from across the fire, the tension between us crackling in tandem with the glowing embers as he fixed his stare on the side of my face. I could feel his concern, his need to speak, but he did not. Instead, he rose to his feet and closed the distance between us. He stood staring down at me, expectantly waiting for something. I turned to look up at him, craning my neck from where I sat on the ground.

Atlas watched me with concern in his eyes, his brow furrowed as though he were lost in his own troublesome line of thought and concentration.

"Why are you looking at me like that?" I asked after an unusually tense pause, no longer able to take the weight of his stare.

He released a breath, his shoulders relaxing as some kind of weight bled from his posture, a decision made.

"Want to go for a walk?" Atlas asked with a raised brow, a tentative line to his expression as he waited for my response.

I gaped up at him with a blank stare and ticked my brow in question. I was not keen on traipsing around in the shadows, especially this close to the Darkwood. We were only a day's hike out now and the closer we got, the greater the risk of coming across something dangerous within those trees.

"I'm tired of sulking in my own misery." He sighed. "I think a walk under the moonlight could be a nice reprieve, especially if you're feeling too anxious to rest."

"I'm not anxious."

"Lies," he said with a twitch of his lip. "You've been working the edge of your sleeve for hours and you're sure to chew a hole in your cheek if I don't do something about it."

He flashed me a soft smile and extended his hand. That tug behind my heart pulled, the flutter of wings in my chest catching my breath. I hesitated, my better judgment telling me to remain seated here, staring at the fire. It was safer than leaning over that edge again, falling further into this feeling.

But the desperate side of me, the softer side, the one that wanted nothing more than to be Enora, someone safe for him to be so free with, *she* begged to take his hand.

Despite my internal struggle, the common sense screaming at me to decline, I found my palm in his and he hauled me to my feet with a smile. The contact of his skin against mine sent a shiver along my spine.

"Gengi will panic if we are gone when they return," I said, one last meager effort to push against the instinct driving me forward.

"He will be fine." Atlas rolled his eyes, but I narrowed mine in disbelief. "Alright, he will probably panic. We won't be gone long, and I'll deal with it when we're back."

I met his gaze and found myself caught there, the deep purple irises swimming with something urging my heart to lean into that flutter, yearning to set some of the weight on my shoulders aside and follow him into the abyss. I released a short breath as my thoughts clouded and I nodded, forcing my lips into a tight smile.

He offered my hand a squeeze, his fingers tightening around mine twice, the gesture resembling the pattern of a heartbeat, before dropping the contact and gesturing to the forest as he stepped aside.

"After you," he offered with a bright smile.

We moved through the trees for a long while in silence, neither one of us daring to break the serenity of the woods with our voices. My anxiety fled with each step as I allowed my senses to soak themselves with the sounds of the forest. The rustle of the leaves above as the crisp wind floated overhead, the distant song of the chirping insects, the croak of frogs in the distance, the rushing water of the river to our right to track our path.

I love it out here.

Some part of me would always feel grounded in that setting. It often reminded me of Aeson, how he had been before the prophecy. Always in the woods, working with the life there. He had been so kind and pure then, his drive to create life overwhelming any flicker of darkness that could have ever taken root.

Until that seer had told our fates. Everything had changed then.

My stomach turned over at the ancient memory, and I sucked in a breath as a sharp pain pierced my resolve. I crossed my arms over my chest to protect myself from both the chill of the air and my own darkened past.

"What are you thinking about?" Atlas's voice startled me out of my daze, snapping my attention to his.

I looked to him, and he pulled his eyes ahead again, giving me a clear view of his striking profile, the sharp angle of his jaw, the strong line of his nose, the way the moonlight glittered through the breaks in the leaves above to shine off his silver-toned skin, glimmer through the tresses of his white hair.

"What?" I asked with a laugh under my tone, my brow furrowed.

He moved the low-hanging branches of a tree ahead to clear a path for me, waiting for me to step through before he followed.

"You heard me." He chuckled. "I want to know what's got your mind all tangled up, keeps that tension in your shoulders. This walk is supposed to be relaxing you, not making your anxieties worse."

I thought for a moment, but something ahead caught my eye. A great weeping willow tree with half of its branches dangling over the riverbank while the rest stood sturdy on solid ground. The draping leaves rustled in the soft breeze in the most spellbinding way. My memory sparked and countless images of traveling through these woods flooded my mind's eye. It was rare I got such clear images from before, but no magic could wipe these away. I picked up my pace, excitement in my jaunt at what might lie ahead.

"Where are you going?" Atlas asked with a laugh.

"The willow!" I called over my shoulder, my tone bright and eager.

He set off at a jog after me until we reached the tree, stopping next to me and waiting with an expectant stare. I craned my neck up to get a great view of the branches as they swept over the water, reaching for the ground as though they had been weighed down with the burden of time. The tree stooped to offer some sort of protection to the water there, caressing the river with elegant arms, the very ends of which floated mindlessly in the moving stream.

I had to narrow my eyes, be certain the creatures would be there, but sure enough, they were, sitting on the leaves soaking in the moonlight just as I remembered them to be.

"Would you like to see something magnificent?" I asked, that excitement lifting my mood.

I turned on my heel to meet his eye with a smile, and the intensity of his gaze as it fixed on mine caused a startled hitch in my breath. That flittering in my chest took off with wings greater than I knew how to contain.

"I already can." The words came out on a breath, almost as though he hadn't meant to speak them. They sounded private, intimate.

My cheeks warmed and something wild itched over my breastbone. I hurried to bury the heat rising in my core at the intensity of the moment stretched between us, the emotion swimming within his eyes. I tried to bring words to my throat, offer protest, insist he stop looking at me that way, but I could not. The ability to speak left my arsenal of skills entirely.

Instead, I peeled my gaze from his and turned to the willow, deciding that if I could not get control of this moment, I would do my best to ignore it, turn his attention to something else.

I focused my energy, coiled what little magic I had reserved to the surface, and willed it to wrap around the nearest branches of the willow, the ones dusting the forest floor before us. I urged my power to pull them apart like panels in a curtain and moved to step through. I turned on my heel once under the cover of the tree and waved him on to follow. Atlas stepped through, his eyes still pointedly pinned on me, and I released my hold on my magic; the branches fell to encircle us within the willow again.

"What are we doing?" he asked, his tone quiet, a hint of nervousness I had never heard there coloring the words.

I offered him a quirk of a smile as excitement flushed my resolve again.

It had been so long since I'd seen them myself.

"Watch."

I moved to the edge of the circling, sweeping willow branches, and reached my hand out before walking along the edge of the enclosed space in the forest, dragging my fingers along to disturb the leaves in my wake.

As my touch rustled the boughs, the creatures I'd known to rest there took flight in a ripple behind it. Hundreds of willow moths sparked to life in an ethereal wave of light, a cool-toned bioluminescent glow shimmering as their wings fluttered to raise them from their perches. The moths shone brightly in silvery tones. They resembled floating flickers of moonlight, shards of the sky that had fallen to the ground to bless our lands.

I walked around to the other side, winding my fingers through the sweeping willow until I met the riverbank. Moving gingerly to the trunk of the tree, I leaned around its edge to get a clear view of his reaction. An eagerness to get a glimpse of his happiness, his awe was overwhelming, and it overshadowed the excitement I felt in finding the moths in the first place.

The sight of the gorgeous male before me stole the breath from my lungs. The space beneath the willow was swarmed with the luminous moths, their glow lighting the space in a breathtaking display of gentle, fluttering wings. They lit the lines of his face. His eyes stretched wide and welled with awe as he tilted his chin to look to the highest branches of the tree, all of which now glowed with the otherworldly creatures.

They dusted his shoulders, his hair, anywhere they could take purchase, landing there briefly before taking off again in a chaotic flight of light. He stretched his arms as he gaped at the moths that dared to flutter into landing there. He gave them a gentle shake and they took flight again, leaving a bright smile on his face that would have rivaled any natural wonder.

I hadn't seen him so genuinely happy in all my time knowing him. The lines of his worry, the dread and fear I knew he carried with him had been left behind on the other side of the willow's curtain of branches. Any trepidation I'd felt, any hesitation with my ability to wrangle my heart was all worth it to see even just a glimmer of his comfort, his bliss.

"What do you think?" I asked, a bright smile on my face as I moved closer.

He shook his head, his expression still lined with wonder as he ran a hand through his hair, looking up at the willow moths again.

"Speechless? So unusual for you." I asked with a raised brow, my tone lifted with surprise.

My feet carried me closer, the bright warmth in my chest urging me to close the distance between us, and I extended my palm in the inches I'd left there to create a space for one of the moths as it dusted by. The beautiful, winged creature landed there, fluttering its wings delicately as it offered a mesmerizing glow to light the space.

"I have never seen anything so beautiful," Atlas whispered, his voice a croak in his throat.

I looked up to meet his eye and found him staring at me in that gutting way again, though this time it was easier to ignore that voice urging me to choose sense. This time, the warmth in my chest aided by the glow of the moths and the beauty of the willow tree allowed me to relish the feeling.

"I'm so glad," I whispered, unable to sort the swelling sensation behind my breastbone.

The corner of his mouth twitched, and he reached between us to cradle my hand in his. He lifted it slightly to send the moth back up into the dancing lights above. My heart thundered in my chest as my lungs squeezed tight at the contact.

"Not everything in these woods are as gentle," I said, my voice more steady than I had expected as I pulled my hand from his. "We are getting closer to the Darkwood, and I have to warn you not to go near anything else without consulting me first."

"I haven't marked anything too dangerous," he said.

"Not yet. But the closer we get to uncharted territory, the better it will be to just stick together. Which means we should probably get back."

Something flickered in his eyes and a hollow ache clattered through my chest. I very much did not want to leave—every fiber of my being wanted to stay here with him—but again, I found myself too close to my own heart, distracted enough from our circumstances to render me dangerous. That voice of reason fluttered back to pull me from the trance.

"Well, *we* do, but what about Keir and Enora?" he asked with a cocked brow and a lilting tease to his tone. "They very much have the time to enjoy this view for a while, I would think."

"And do what?" I asked with a raised brow.

A heat low in my stomach lurched and I struggled to contain the flush of desire. I worked to bury it back down, somewhere safe where I could ignore it, keep it tucked away, keep *him* safe.

"I don't know. I'm sure we could figure something out."

He flashed me one of those dazzling, crooked smiles and a wink before turning to rustle the branches with an outstretched hand, sending moths that had settled back into the air.

"Atlas," I said, a heaviness to my tone.

"Atlas? Who is that? Sounds like a charming, unbelievably handsome male." He wiggled his brow as he moved to the trunk of the willow tree.

Before I had a chance to protest again, he launched himself upward, using the lowest branch to scale the tree. Within an impossibly quick flicker of time, he had climbed high enough into the willow that I had to crane my neck.

I shouted in surprise but released a bright laugh. The crack of my voice lifted something heavy in my chest and I could not contain the heady feeling as it swam through my senses.

"What are you doing?" I asked, my tone bright now.

He found purchase with his feet on a sturdy branch and gripped one overhead to dangle out and look down at me with a stunning smile on his face.

"Having a little fun," he called. "You could try it out, you know. It might be good for that scowl you keep on your face most of the time."

"Oh, shut it." I huffed on a laugh.

The hesitation keeping me grounded only lasted a brief flicker of time. My muscles seemed to carry me of their own accord. Before I could think twice about the choice, I was scaling the tree. That desire I'd felt only moments prior propelled me on, begging me to feel something other than dread and misery for even just a moment.

Atlas reached out and offered a hand to help me onto his branch and I took it. He hauled my weight up effortlessly and I yelped as my feet landed. I teetered off balance, but he turned me with a strong hand on my hip to press my back against the trunk.

"Careful." He laughed as he steadied me.

I reached out and tangled my hands in the fabric of his tunic, and he placed a hand on the tree near my head, closing me in with the warmth of him. The moths floating behind him provided a dazzling backlight to the intensity of his presence. I heaved a few breaths as adrenaline coursed through my veins and released a laugh as I allowed my head to fall back against the tree.

"Are you afraid of heights?" he asked with a lilting tease under his tone, the corner of his lip twitching in that maddening smile.

"No," I shot, but his grin only stretched wider.

"The big and scary firebird is afraid of heights? How is that possible? Don't you fly?"

"Well, when I'm *flying*, I am just that. A big and scary firebird. Right now, I am a small fae, and if we fall, we will likely break bones, which will hurt a lot."

"I'm not going to let you fall." He breathed a chuckle and rolled his eyes.

"You can't know that," I said, though my tone held more stress than I'd intended.

The intensity of his gaze shifted, a weight settling over him, and his shoulders tensed slightly. He met my eye with a firm gaze and moved his hand to tuck a lock of loose hair behind my ear. The gesture sent a chill along my spine, and I had difficulty containing the way my heart lodged in my throat. My stomach curled low in that blistering heat as he leaned in slightly, his warmth washing over me.

"I am never going to let you fall," he repeated, his words more weighted, heavy with the reality of our situation.

That reality waited for us just outside of this canopy of willow branches, back at camp. It had lingered with us as we traveled across the continent. Something in his tone, the fire in his eyes urged more meaning through his words, a heavier intention.

Maybe I didn't want to be Aurelia, the firebird. Not in this moment. Not with the dip of his chin as it brought his face closer to mine, the way my heart beat against the cage of my chest, caused that hitch in my breath that made it feel like I'd never be able to fill my lungs again. Maybe I wanted to be Enora. Here with him, with this male who seemed to be able to offer me a reprieve to the darkness no matter how saturated, how heavily it fell.

I tipped my chin and tightened my grip on his tunic as I sucked in a quick breath, keeping my eyes trained on his. The tension between us felt as though it would crack the very air. It was a living beast, something that seemed to pull me closer. And him too. He leaned in, though ever so slightly, as though waiting for something.

"*Atlas Borden*, get your infuriating ass down from that tree *immediately*," Gengi's voice shouted from below, the sound snapping the daze I had allowed myself to fall into.

I whipped my attention to the ground, and Atlas sighed heavily, rolling his eyes before lolling his head to pin his gaze on Gengi, who waited beyond the canopy of the willow tree.

"Oh, *Mother, please*, just five more minutes," Atlas drawled sarcastically.

"Oh, shut up, you insulant asshole," Gengi grumbled.

Emrys stood next to him, her dark hair twisted into a knot on top of her head as she peered up at us with a smile on her lips, her arms crossed over her chest.

"I thought we agreed to stick together, stay in camp," Gengi protested again.

"That was my fault." I sighed and gently untangled my fingers from Atlas's tunic before moving carefully to retrace my steps along the branches to plop down on the ground. "I couldn't sleep, and we thought a walk might help."

"A walk?" Emrys asked with a coy tilt to her lips and a wiggle of her brow.

"Yes, a walk," Atlas interjected as his feet landed firmly on the ground behind me.

"Well, *don't*," Gengi said, his tone heated.

"Don't walk?" Atlas asked, his tone lifted with teasing confrontation.

"No! We are a day out from the Darkwood we don't know what's in these trees. You had me so insanely worried. We. Stay. Together."

"Alright," I consoled and reached out to offer a gentle squeeze of Gengi's arm. "We won't do it again. You're right. We need to stick together. There are creatures out here that would try to split us up if we came across them. I'm sorry."

"Thank you." Gengi huffed. "Now kindly march your hinds back to camp."

I laughed softly and moved past him, pointedly ignoring the way Emrys still looked at me, the expectant pierce of her gaze causing an uncomfortable crawl over my chest. I walked ahead of the three of them all the way back to camp, desperately working to wrangle my heart back into the cage in which it belonged.

CHAPTER 39
MAGE

Mila and I moved through the streets of Fenbrook with a silent blanket of dread over our shoulders. It had only taken us another day or so to get to the town east of the mountain range, and although I was grateful to have a bed to rest in for a night before we moved on into the blight, my worries about the decayed stretch of land only intensified as we got our impression of the state of the town.

I was wildly familiar with this city. The tapestry of memories from years past coated my senses as I moved through the market square with Mila at my side. This was where I'd grown up, where I'd lived right up until I had been recruited as the palace healer. I'd moved to The Capitol when I'd only been seventy-five. That had been over a century ago. And though I had visited over the years on my holidays from The Capitol and seen it change slightly over time, nothing could have prepared me for what waited here after the raid, with the blight looming in the forest.

I remembered Fenbrook being vibrant, full of life. Wild

gardens and vibrant foliage on every building, bordering the alleyways. The people here used to be full of vivid energy and wild ambition. Not any longer. The green tresses of vines had decayed, turned black, and the once bright gardens of wild-flowers were dried, offering no life.

The people were worn, all of them weighed down with an air of fear, trepidation. And there were so many guards. More than I had ever seen in one spot.

"This is insane," Mila muttered, pulling her cloak tighter around her neck, as though it could block her from the dread this place instilled.

My eyes caught on her hands as they fell from her hood and alarm pulled at my awareness. Her fingers had tinged black, the clear signs of rot as her magic continued to decay within her.

"Mila." I nearly gasped, taking her hand in mine.

She pulled it away, the movement sharp, an angry expression twisting her features.

"I'm fine. It's just the blight," she said, her tone clipped.

Her words did not do much to assuage the fear coiling behind my breastbone. It was true. This town, being so close to the blight, seemed more significantly affected than the rest of the continent, but it greatly concerned me that Mila was also suffering, the evidence of her struggles now a physical mark to bear.

I could not help but think on Mariella's clipped warnings. I had tried so hard to make sense of them, to place purpose in our travels. But she'd not gotten much out outside of reflections of the fear already coating my resolve. I had not much to work with to explain Mila's deterioration. To stop it.

"We can find a healer here to speak to."

"No." She shook her head. "I just want to find Emile and go home."

I breathed a frustrated sigh but knew better than to make any attempt at forcing her to make a decision when she'd, stubbornly, already settled firmly.

The guards dressed in black littered the streets, combed through the crowd of the market on high alert. And not one of the citizens paid them a single glance. They were a permanent installation, the elven, creation, witches, and mortals all moving around them as though they meant nothing in the wake of what they had been living through so close to the blight.

The number of guards made me glad for our decision to leave Despina in the room at the inn while we went out to investigate. Of course, we could have glamoured her, but the lack of breathing magic here set an alarm off in my core. Would the glamour have even worked? There was no telling.

"We need to find someone to talk to and get on our way," I said with a stiff breath.

Mila nodded to a tavern just across the street. I responded with my own curt nod, and we moved across the square toward the building.

The ambiance inside the shotty tavern offered no reprieve from the feeling of doom coating my skin. The faelight lighting the ceiling was dim, and most of the patrons sat in the shadows with their drinks, either passed out or one of the few tables taking part in some kind of gambling game.

We made our way to the poorly lit bar top and found a spot to rest our feet. Moments after we'd taken our seats, a mortal woman busted through a set of wooden doors to the kitchen, her tattered skirts hiked up, tucked under her leather corset. Her light brown hair was knotted at the base of her neck. Her rosy cheeks were flushed, her brown eyes bloodshot from what could have been a number of things. Stress, lack of sleep, alcohol. It was impossible to determine which.

"What can we get for the travelers?" the woman asked as she pulled two glass pints out from under the counter.

Mila removed some coin from a pouch at her hip and tossed a few on the countertop.

"A couple of pints." She nodded.

"We stand out, then? As travelers?" I asked with a raised brow, keeping my tone light.

The bartender huffed a laugh as she began to fill our cups at the tap behind her.

"You still have a little of that glow in your eyes," she said over her shoulder.

"What do you mean?" Mila asked.

"Well, I'm sure you know," the bartender responded with a lifted brow. "Don't you? Creation fae and all."

A stone sunk in my stomach as my suspicions were confirmed over again. Creation magic had been affected across the realm. I knew the few in Safe Haven had been struggling, but seeing the damage done to Fenbrook, the way the creation fae here seemed drained of their very essence all but confirmed my suspicions that something had been corrupted, the very core of creation magic poisoned. And it seemed almost impossible to ignore the closer we got to the blight.

"Yes, we've noticed," I offered in response.

She placed our mugs on the countertop and swiped Mila's coin before turning to walk off around the bar again.

"Wait," I said, and she stopped short, pinning her tired gaze on me.

"Can you tell us about what's been happening here?"

"Why? Are you some kind of hero here to fix it all? I doubt that, creation fae like the two of you. I can already see the poison in your auras, at any rate."

"What is it from? Why are the people here hurting so

much?" Mila responded, her tone urgent, interrupting any thought I had to inquire about whatever she'd seen in us.

"Well, the blight, dearie," the barkeep said, confusion pulling her brow together. "The farther it spreads, the less control the creation fae have. Seems like an obvious conclusion."

"Has anyone seen it?"

"Yes, but no one that has been back to tell about it."

Fear coated my resolve as a desperate urge to turn back grated at my awareness, to gain some control over my magic, focus my energy where I knew it was best reserved, caring for those in Safe Haven. I couldn't do that if we were lost to the blight.

Fix it.

Mariella's plea flashed through my mind's eye, and I was coated in regret. I still had no idea what she'd meant, what it was she had expected me to do to correct the poisoned land, the rotting core of creation magic.

I released a tense breath and felt the flick of Mila's eyes on the side of my face.

"I gather you're traveling through for just that?" the barkeep said. "To see the blight? There's no sense. You best turn back the way you came. It's a death trip."

With that, she turned on her heel back to the kitchen, the warning in her tone light, flippant as she brushed us off to tend to her duties.

A heavy silence hung between us for a moment as I allowed the news to settle in. Mila's shoulders tensed and she released a frustrated groan.

"This is piss water," she grumbled irritably as she shoved the beer away from her and rose to a stand, anger in the lines of her posture.

"Yes, well, I'm not sure what you expected from a tavern like this." I sighed and rose to my feet. "Let's get back to Despina and figure out what we are doing."

"We need to wait," Despina said as she paced the room, the glow of the firelight illuminating the wild rose curls around her warm face. "The others are headed this way. I'll send a message signaling for help."

She held a note she'd received from Gengi earlier that day detailing that the others were headed to the Darkwood, which was altogether alarming, but we had our own issues to handle at the moment.

I fiddled with the beads in my hair, my eyes glazed over as I tracked the flickering fire in the hearth, turning over the possibility with whirling thoughts. Mila had been in the bathing chamber for almost a half hour, and Despina had done her best to wait for her to come out of the room, but Des's stress was a living thing, radiating off her shoulders, and she worked a line in the floor with her pacing.

"Tell me what you're sensing," I asked, my tone level.

This much tension from Despina was alarming and it was clear to me that she was thinking with her seer's intuition forward.

"Death," she said, the word as it rolled from her lips quick and short but full of warning, the buzz of fear lifting her tone. "It's not good, Mage. We can't go into that wood without backup."

"Alright, send the note, then," I said with a nod. "We will

hang out here until Atlas and Gengi can get Reia to us. If anyone has a chance at getting through the blight unscathed, it's her."

Despina nodded and moved to her pack to remove a piece of charmed parchment to begin scrawling her message on.

"Mila won't be pleased," I said.

The thought of having to manage Mila's disappointment in another delay in finding her brother blanketed me with exhaustion. Although, I was not eager to get to the blight to have my suspicions confirmed that Emile was in the veil, already dead and trying to reach her the way that Mariella had reached me. My stomach turned over itself as my thoughts rolled through the possibility of having to face that reality, watch Mila break down over the death of a loved one.

We had not spoken of the possibility, but I'd seen the way her shoulders tensed, and her breathing had quickened as I'd explained my visit to the veil. She was intelligent, and she knew what we were up against, what her own magic had been through.

But hope was a fickle thing, quick to destroy any solid sense or ability to reason with reality.

"She'll be fine. I'd rather her pissed off and alive than chasing a wild hope and dead," Despina said.

Despina folded the note quickly, and I watched as she raised the paper to her face. She focused her eyes on the parchment and her amulet glowed a faint amber color just before a bleeding light engulfed the note, sending it into the pockets between realms to find its mark, wherever Gengi was.

"I'll tell her." Despina sighed heavily and moved to the closed door of the bathing chamber.

Des rapped three times and called Mila's name, but there was no response. She furrowed her brow and rapped again, more urgently. Still, no one answered. Fear flushed my chest, and I pulled myself to my feet, alarm stretching my eyes.

Despina met my attention with the same emotion written in to her expression and took no time before turning the brass handle and swinging her weight into the door. It flew open and hit the wall with a clatter, revealing an empty room, the window open to let the night air in, the curtains there fluttering in the breeze.

"Fuck," Despina hissed before turning from the doorway to scoop her cloak and bag off our bed.

I followed suit with anxiety-fueled terror in my veins.

Mila had taken off into the blight on her own.

I'D NEVER RUN SO FAST in my life. Despina and I thundered through the alleyways of the town, my feet carrying me on a ghost of a memory as we made our way to the edge of the forest. The inn was not too far off from the tree line, and we made it there in only a few minutes, our packs hastily strapped to our shoulders after we gathered our things at a moment's notice.

Despina thundered past me as I stopped just before the tree line; something dark washing over me stopped my feet in my tracks. I sucked in a breath as a cold terror froze the blood in my veins.

I wasn't sure where the hesitation came from, but my thoughts spun, and a haze washed over me as the lines of my vision blurred. I released the breath as something wild tapered my ability to move. And then my eyes landed on it, prowling just past the edge of the trees. When it knew I had seen it, the creature stopped and sat on its haunches.

The silver stripe. This time decayed, the same vision I'd seen by the river with Mila. I turned my attention to Despina, who had already taken off into the forest, her form beginning to bleed into darkness. I pulled my eyes back to the silver stripe, who tilted their head at me, their broken jaw dangling at an odd angle before it backed up into the forest, swallowed by night.

CHAPTER 40
BRENWYN

The shadows had been closing in on me for days. What once had been my sanctuary, a place to release the strenuous lines of my body, had become a glimpse of what I would assume the underworld to be like.

Agony. Terrorizing panic, an inability to control any of my emotions or gain purchase for a seemingly endless amount of time.

I had been trapped there, dancing with the shadows since Laz had told me to take off into the night. I'd had to.

They'd sensed our betrayal. Our ruse had been blown.

Since Callista had been taken that day, the palace had been crawling with guards, all bent on trying to locate Laz and me, who I was unsuccessful in finding. With our cover blown, it seemed there was nothing stopping Ragnor's men from turning over every room in the palace.

I could only assume they'd either gotten out or had been compromised. I hoped with my entire soul that it had been the former.

In my time in the shadows, I had been unsuccessful in locating Ragnor himself, or his witch or torture master. All of them had been behind one of the countless wards all over the castle. Those barriers that had been designed to both keep me out and trap me in a suffocating vise.

I'd spent days avoiding them, circling the grounds, sticking to the darkness, slinking through shadows for any amount of helpful information, any way to safely get to Asteria, to Callista. And for a day or so, it had been easy to remain there, hidden in the dark, blended with the crevices of every room and corridor. But as time had gone on, those wards had increased. The ones around the war room, the tunnels under the palace the most significant.

The first place I'd realized I'd been barred from was Callista's chamber. The thick fog of magic had threatened to hurdle me back to my physical body. It had caught me off guard. I should have been expecting it, but in my panic-driven state, my thoughts had been quick, and I'd gotten too close to her room. I'd managed to gather myself quickly though. Hold only to my shadows. From then, I'd treaded carefully, testing the edges of a room before entering.

The dungeons had been safe to roam for a while, and the best place to gather information from loose-lipped guards, but not any longer. I'd been barred from them as well.

I was losing purchase. The grounds in which I could remain hidden had dwindled significantly day after day, and I'd found it increasingly more difficult to evade the grip of the magical barriers as time had passed.

I was running out of options. Surely, I'd be forced to leave eventually. And I should have. I should have left as soon as I'd found Callista's room warded. But I couldn't. Every time the flicker of a possibility crossed my mind, the image of Asteria trapped here, a prisoner of war, kept me with my tendrils locked firmly in the shadows of the castle.

Brenwyn.

It was as though my thoughts had called her voice to me, the first sign of anything able to lift my panic in days floating through the abyss to my conscious mind.

I was stuck in the darkness somewhere in the servants' corridors, trapped there to deal with the recesses of my mind, the turmoil of my failures. Maybe it had been a trick of my thoughts, my deepest desires presenting a blissful delusion.

Brenwyn, my love. Follow my voice.

Asteria called again.

No, that was real. That was her.

Something wild curled within me, a distant hope ignited by the sound of her voice. I curled my shadows, my liquid smoke ready to move me through the castle. But to where?

I had nowhere to go. Panic gripped me as quickly as hope had and I began to thrash frantically in the darkness.

And as if on cue, as if she had heard my question in the ether, I felt a pull, something tugging at my consciousness as if to guide me. I wasn't sure I would have been able to resist the draw if I'd tried. Before I had a chance to consider the sensation, I was whisked away, pulled on a torrent of magic as though I had been caught in a funnel of wind. It was a whorl, a confusing spin of moments as they flashed before me.

I had no time to gather my bearings before that pull forced my body to knit itself back together, sling me back to corporeal form until my feet landed on solid ground.

A frenzy of emotion flushed me as panic took root. I sucked in a breath as I whipped my attention around, my hands at the weapons on my hips, ready for a fight. But as quickly as the frenzy had driven my muscles, it bled away, chased off by a cloud of confusion.

My eyes landed on Callista, then Laz, and finally Asteria, who looked at me with a broken kind of relief in her eye.

We were in Callista's chamber, but why? How?

"What's going on?" I asked, my voice pouring from my lips in a rushed snap.

I looked to Laz with buzzing questions, but they met my eye with their own gaze swimming through confusion. They looked worn, dark circles under their green eyes, their usually warm-toned skin flushed with a sunken pallor with a split in their lip. A bruise rested across their high cheekbone on one side.

Wherever they had been had put them through the trials of the underworld.

Callista, however, looked calm, sure. Her shoulders were pulled back, her chin tilted in that authoritative way I remembered from her time outside of this room. Her time as a soldier, a weapon primed for war. The warrior stood before me, not the prisoner, no longer the tortured soul I'd grown used to in the past months.

"Brenwyn, we don't have much time," Asteria said, pulling my attention to hers.

Asteria was already moving from her spot near the door, crossing the room with a crease in her brow, furrowed there out of worry. She held a set of keys in her hands and another cloud of confusion wafted over me. My senses spun as my thoughts did and it took a moment to understand why, to understand what was different about her in this moment.

It wasn't until she reached Callista, who held her wrists out in front of her, that I realized why I suffered from such an extreme case of shock. Why my mouth gaped, my expression crumpled in a twisted bout of surprise and fury.

Asteria fumbled with the keys for a flicker of a moment, and then she gripped Callista's hands in her own before using the iron keys to remove the deadstone cuffs from her wrists.

She was there. Really there. Not an astral projection. A whole, full person who could move and touch.

And she'd just freed Callista, the king's most prized possession.

"*What?*" I hissed, my own voice sounding distant in my ear.

"Do it. Find her now." Asteria spoke to Callista, who nodded curtly and closed her eyes with a breath large enough to raise her chest.

"I have only seconds left." Asteria turned to me, tears brimming in her lilac eyes. "I'm sending you to Aurelia—both of you."

She flicked her gaze between Laz and me, and her words clattered through my mind as though they'd been spoken in a foreign language. I barely understood them.

"What do you mean? Both of us?" Laz spoke before I had a chance to turn over what Asteria had said.

"Callista must stay. To get her here. It's the best chance we have at taking him down," Asteria answered Laz.

"*No.*" Laz's voice came out almost as a snarl, emotion I'd never seen in their expression tearing through their resolve. "You've already freed Callista; send her. Get her out of here."

"I cannot," Asteria said quickly, turning her panicked eyes on me. "My love, you will come back to me."

"Stair, what the fuck is going on?" I asked, my voice a shaken tremble, the timbre high with frantic energy.

I was barely keeping up, as my thoughts seemed to be turning over one another at an alarming rate, though the moments moved in slow motion, pulled through the laborious sands of time.

"You cannot stay. He is after you. It is time for you to go," she said through rushed words as she approached, her hands trembling as she lifted them to my face.

The promise of her touch stopped there, hovering over my cheeks, and the tears that had been brimming on her lashes spilled over. I gaped at her, that panic a leaden thing in my veins, holding my muscles hostage. I couldn't move, couldn't think.

And then I felt her touch. The very thing I had spent years yearning for, dreaming of in this world. I sucked in a breath and my own tears spilled over my lashes. She took my face in her hands and pulled my forehead to hers. I covered her fingers with mine and sucked in a breath as my heart burst into a thousand pieces, the pain in my chest both vibrant and exhilarating.

It was as though her touch had been the thing I needed to turn my thoughts back on, to catch up to the pace at which she was moving.

"Asteria, no," I hissed and pulled my face back, gripping her hands tightly between us. "I won't go."

"You must," she urged. "You have no choice. I'm so sorry."

"Asteria." Callista's voice rang out from the other side of the room, but Asteria kept her eyes on mine. The glittering orbs there were full of a tidal wave of emotion, regret, pain, love, and devotion. I wasn't sure which was more prevalent as they displayed themselves across her expression.

Asteria nodded and her eyes went cold, her consciousness sent to the back of her mind. She offered that same blank look she got when she needed to cut an astral projection short, when she needed to go back to him.

"*Asteria!*" I shouted, but my voice felt foreign in my throat.

She pulled her hands from mine, and I tried to hold on, but she tore them away. The absence of her contact left an icy and hollow ache thundering through my chest.

Lazuli lunged for Callista, who offered them a pained look of regret.

But before they reached her, it was over. I watched them fade into a dark abyss as an intense pressure coiled itself around my head. The feeling was accompanied by a sharp tug on my navel, the sure signs of traveling through the pockets between realms through the art of *ephemeration.*

CHAPTER 41
CALLISTA

The cuffs weighed heavily on my wrists. It had taken everything in me to allow Asteria to lock them firmly in place again. The bucking flash of trauma as it had flooded my veins had urged me to fight against it, to do whatever it took to keep them off.

But I had not. We had agreed to this. The night before, when she'd visited my room as her ghostly apparition. We'd talked about the best course of action going forward.

The information she'd given me had been invaluable. It could help me end the war. And I would do whatever it took to have the opportunity to do so.

Asteria had made it out, *ephemerated* back almost immediately after she'd turned the lock on my manacles. I had no way of knowing whether or not she'd been caught, but it had been nearly an hour, and no one had been in to drag me to the pits of the underworld again, which must have been a good sign.

After everything, it was my job to wait. For what exactly, we weren't sure. But I would do so anyway. I would be the bait needed to get Elea here, to give us a decent shot at tearing that crystal from Ragnor's chest.

With every fiber of my being, I wanted to be the one to do so. I wanted to watch the life bleed from his eyes with my fingers in his flesh.

Although the fantasy of murder was heavy on my mind, it was not the only thing that had plagued my thoughts.

The image of Elea in the forest as I'd followed the bond to find her did a good job at forcing those dark wiles away. I'd almost forgotten what it felt like to follow that tunnel, to feel her at the other end. I'd only done it a few times, anyway. I'd spent most of our time in Safe Haven shutting it down, hoping to all realms she kept her own deadstone on.

I wished now I had not been so stupid, so scared.

I'd made it. Through the bond. I'd tumbled through, barreled across the edges of the realm to find her, desperate to see her, feel her, feel anything.

But I had stopped short just as her image had come into view. What I'd witnessed had made me pause, caused a hitch in my heart that had made it impossible to want to disturb her.

She'd never felt me there before, but goddess I couldn't risk it, not with the image that had been before me in plain view.

I'd found her lying on the forest floor, sound asleep, her chest rising and falling in a steady rhythm, her eyelids fluttering with the burden of dreams. But it hadn't just been her. I'd found my brother there, too. He'd held her, both his arms wrapped firmly around her while she'd curled into his chest, her arms tucked up into her breastbone.

Atlas lay awake, staring at the fire with a line of stress on his brow and he released a shuddering breath. He tipped his chin to place a gentle kiss to the top of her head.

How I'd managed to witness such a tender moment, a private one, one I surely was not welcome to, I'd never know.

Out of all the possibilities, all the times I had wished over and over again that I could find her, that had been what I'd been made to see.

A tidal wave of emotion had wracked me in that moment, but I'd had no time to assess the feelings. I'd needed to get back, to be completely aware of my own mind and body, to get Brenwyn and Laz to them, get them safe, get Asteria back to her post.

Sitting in my room after the fact, I had all the time to turn over the image. It caused a strange kind of pain near my heart. At first jealousy, or so I'd thought. But as I simmered in my own misery, my mind relaxed, opening the cage of my heart to turn over the tangle of emotions there.

It was more complicated than mere jealousy.

I knew how Atlas felt about her. From the beginning, I'd known. He was never one to keep secrets. We'd had countless arguments about it in Haven, about my reluctance to accept the bond, his frustration with me. And I'd done my best to keep the thoughts of their potential connection at bay so I wouldn't have to face the looming jealousy, rage at the possibility of losing her.

But as I'd thought about it, that possessive feeling began to ebb. She wasn't a thing to have. And when it came down to it, my feelings on the matter counted very little. The least important thing was that she loved me.

I just needed her safe, alive. Atlas would manage that.

No, it wasn't jealousy, rather a longing; a desire to be with her that I felt most. I wanted to be there in addition to, not in place of Atlas. I wanted to be near, to help in the effort to storm the castle, to be strong enough to support my end of the bond, to keep her safe, keep both of them safe.

As I sifted through my thoughts, the image of Lazuli's deep green eyes, those golden dusted freckles floated through my mind's eye and a surprising jolt of emotion lanced my chest.

I wanted to keep them safe, too.

The absence of the creation fae was one I had not enjoyed, and it pained me more than I cared to admit that they were gone. But it was another topic in which my feelings mattered little.

They're safe.

I curled over my knees, my back pressed to the wall as I willed away the spike of emotion with my eyes on the moon in the sky overhead.

Moonlight.

I huffed a soft breath as a quirk of a smile tilted my lips at the thought of the nickname on their voice.

"Goddess, help them all," I whispered.

And for the first time in all my years, I meant the prayer. With every fiber of my being.

CHAPTER 42
ATLAS

Aurelia had been asleep in my arms for hours, or at least it felt that way. I counted her breaths, measured the sounds in the forest as the creatures of the night began to give way to the looming light of day. It hadn't come yet; the sun was still a few hours off. Thank the goddesses for that. She needed more rest than we had time for.

She'd fallen asleep almost immediately after we'd returned from the willow tree. So had everyone else. They'd all been so exhausted.

Goddess bless, so was I, but that didn't matter. All that mattered was that she felt safe. At least enough to sleep through the night. I could stay awake long enough to give her that peace.

I'd managed to roll us over enough to lie on my back, get a good look at the stars peeking through the rustling leaves above. The sky was clear, the indigo a color deep enough to suggest another realm out there somewhere.

I made the mistake of allowing my muscles to relax,

believing that everything would remain serene, quiet, calm, until morning broke. Considering everything we'd been through, that assumption was rather silly, if I was being honest.

As if on cue, the moment I started to enjoy the way my back stretched out on the bedroll with Reia curled up into my chest, a wild crack split the air.

The sound of someone *ephemerating*.

My instinct spared no time in taking action against whoever had appeared through the pockets of the realm. Reia's eyes snapped awake as she jolted in shock, and I slid out from under her to grab my blade, leaping to my feet in a flash of a moment.

Gengi and Avery did the same. Gengi had his bow already in hand with an arrow at the ready, pointed at our assailants, while Avery took a sturdy fighting stance. Emrys crouched on the balls of her feet, alarm in her eyes, her posture also ready for a fight from what I knew about her battle style.

But it was not an assailant that bombarded our camp. In fact, who I saw there made me pause enough to stall my entire ability to function. My thoughts stuttered and confusion spun my awareness.

"Brenwyn?" Reia's startled voice called to the wraith, who stood in the center of camp near the dying fire with a strange creation fae I'd never seen.

Both looked disheveled, confused, anguished if I was being entirely honest. Shock pierced my chest, and I furrowed my brow as I lowered my weapon.

"What the fuck are you doing here?" I spat, my words coming out on fumes of anger quickly rolling to a head.

Brenwyn whipped around, her silver eyes landing on each of us as her own frantic energy moved her in a stumbling circle before she narrowed her sights on the creation fae she'd brought with her.

The creation fae, although initially startled, gathered themselves and rolled their neck as they released a breath.

"*No! What the fuck was that, Lazuli?*" Brenwyn's words came out shrill, a shriek landing somewhere between livid anger and desperate anguish as she reached out to shove at the fae, the heels of her hands on their shoulders.

I winced at the sound and my thoughts spun again, but they quickly rebounded, landing on my own source of terror sprung to life at the realization of what their sudden arrival could mean.

Callista. Where is Callista?

"I have no idea," Lazuli responded, their tone stern and steady as they regained their balance. "I was pulled from the dungeon *seconds* before you showed up."

"Brenwyn." Aurelia spoke again, her tone tighter, more frantic now as she stepped toward the wraith.

Reia reached out to grab Brenwyn's arm, a gentle reach to get her attention, but the wraith turned on her heel with a vibrating rage splitting her expression. Before anyone could take stock of what was about to transpire, Brenwyn's fist reared back before connecting with Aurelia's jaw.

Fury flushed my resolve as chaos ensued.

Reia released a grunt muted by the crack of bone before she was knocked off balance by the blow. She covered her mouth with one hand as she turned on her heel, though she remained standing, fire in her eyes as blood spilled through her fingers.

"*Hey!*" I shouted, my voice a booming bellow as I lunged for Brenwyn, a wild kind of rage in my core, but Gengi was closer.

He made it there first, before the wraith had a chance to pounce on Reia.

Gengi managed to drop his bow and tangle Brenwyn in a sturdy grip, pinning her arms with his hands locked on the back of her head. I pivoted to check on Reia, but she waved me off, curling away from my touch, her movements lined with her own flurry of emotions.

Brenwyn wrestled for a moment, leaning back to crack Gengi's head, but he held firm. Emrys and Avery shouted, but it was the creation fae that took control of the moment.

"Brenwyn, *stop it*." Lazuli's tone held shocking authority as they stepped forward to grip the wraith's chin with lithe fingers. "This fit will get us nowhere. Gather yourself. *Now*."

Brenwyn bared her teeth as she struggled for a moment, her anger still a wild beast as she met Lazuli's eye. Her chest rose and fell in vicious beats, and she held firm, but the creation fae did not waver. After a tense stretch of time, Brenwyn's breathing slowed, and her muscles sagged in Gengi's grip.

Her face crumpled and Lazuli released her. The expression on Brenwyn's face brought an ache to my chest I had not expected. Devastation, pain, heartbreak.

Anguish lanced my core. The worst-case scenario pierced my mind's eye, flushing my awareness with frigid terror.

"What happened to Callista?" I asked, my voice low, dangerous, revealing none of the fear pumping through my veins.

Reia's posture stilled and she stared at Brenwyn with wide eyes, her chin stained with blood from her split lip.

"She's alive." It was Lazuli that spoke, not Brenwyn.

Brenwyn was gone, somewhere else. She leaned her head back against Gengi's chest, who held her with his arms around her waist now. Tears streaked her grey cheeks.

"What happened?" Reia asked.

"Asteria sent us. We were compromised. Days ago." Lazuli turned to Reia, and their eyes flicked to the wound on her lip.

"Let me fix that," they said, still impossibly calm.

"Leave it," Reia ordered, her tone short.

Lazuli's eyes flared before they offered a curt nod, the corner of their lip twitching.

"It's nice to finally meet the so-called savior of the realm. The firebird herself," Lazuli said, their tone coy. "It seems we have a lot to catch each other up on."

CHAPTER 43
AURELIA

Chaos. That was the only word I could find in my arsenal to describe the turn the evening had taken.

Gengi released Brenwyn, who had calmed down significantly, steady tension lining her jaw as the embers in the fire stoked to a fresh flame, urged on as Avery placed more dry wood over the coals. Emrys and Avery managed to coax her away from camp into the dark forest with Gengi in tow, an attempt to calm the wraith's raging emotions.

I stood across the fire, measuring this strange fae, the throbbing in my jaw from Brenwyn's blow already ebbing as my magic worked to heal the split lip.

"Asteria sent us," Lazuli reiterated.

The creation fae had not moved from where they stood. Even after everyone had allowed the excitement to bleed away, they'd remained firm.

Atlas also refused to sit. Instead, he paced back and forth with pensive tension over the line of his shoulder. His attention piqued in Lazuli's direction when they spoke, but he kept moving, one arm crossed over his chest, the other hand working at the back of his neck, running through his hair as stress rolled off his shoulders.

"I thought she was under Ragnor's control?" I said, my brow furrowed in confusion.

I couldn't help but remember the blank expression on my sister's face, the lifelessness of her eyes as we fought that day in Safe Haven. She would never have acted that way with her own agency.

"Not entirely. She has been astral projecting to communicate. Although, this time she somehow got away from him physically. It wasn't an astral projection. She was there, in Callista's cell," Lazuli recounted, their tone drifting slightly as they turned over the memory.

"How?" Atlas asked, his tone sharp, "Why isn't Callista here, then? I mean, who *is* this?"

He turned his attention to me, gesturing wildly toward the creation fae.

"I've never seen this person in my *life*. How is it they just happen to show up in the forest in the exact spot we've taken camp?"

"I understand your reservations," Lazuli said, their tone calm. "I, too, am quite shaken by the turn of events. Neither Brenwyn nor I had any idea what Asteria and Callista had planned."

"Planned?" I asked.

They nodded, meeting my eye again.

"Asteria pulled me from the dungeons to Callista's room just before Brenwyn. Before either of us had a chance to get a solid idea of what was happening, Asteria had Callista's cuffs off. She asked Callista to find you."

My heart leapt in my chest as a thunderous beat took off through my veins.

"The bond," I muttered, surprise flushing my resolve as I

brought my fingers up to brush my breastbone, find the raised scar from a past life.

I sent my consciousness into that space reserved for her, the pocket of my soul tucked firmly behind my heart. I had tried to seek through the bond so many times with no luck, that deadstone wall around her blocking me every time. I hurried to send myself through the connection, desperate to find her there.

Please be there.

As I reached the end, I was met with that blanket of darkness again, and that stone of disappointment, frustration, sunk heavy in my core once more.

"She's not there now," I said with a slight tremble to my tone.

"She likely put the cuffs back on right after we left," Lazuli explained, a glimmer of something like regret in their eye.

"What in the fuck are you talking about?" Atlas said, turning to me, his tone desperate, a frantic plea there as he choked on his words. "You can see her? Have you been able to see her this entire time?"

I shook my head, a flush of frantic energy spinning my thoughts as I turned to meet his eye. The pain I saw there caused a lurch in my chest, my heart aching to wipe the expression from his face.

"No. I would be able to if she were free of deadstone. The bond, it allows us to seek for one another, a two-way connection. But not with the deadstone."

Something wild flashed through Atlas's eye, and I watched as he turned over his thoughts. The expression of pain did not falter as he worked through my admission. He did not speak. He simply brought a hand to cover his mouth and drag along his jaw as he tore his gaze away from mine.

An ache in my chest urged me to pull his gaze back, to mend the hollow pain in the air between us. His voice broke the tension before those emotions had time to land firmly near my heart.

"If she was free of the deadstone for long enough to find us, then why isn't she here? Why would it be *you*, a stranger I have no reason to trust, and Brenwyn, the fae that betrayed us all in the first place? Why were you in the dungeons?" Atlas turned his interrogation on Lazuli, who held their shoulders firm as they took his heat, the intensity of the accusation under his words doing nothing to shake them.

"I have spent the past weeks healing your sister's wounds in secret. And I was caught. They found out we'd been lying about Brenwyn's tether to Ragnor as well. Though, she disappeared before they found her. Brenwyn only turned back up moments before Asteria sent us."

"Healing her?" I asked, my tone a wobble as wild agony lanced my chest.

Lazuli pinned their gaze on mine and a vivid fire burned there. Their jaw ticked with strain as they measured my expression, their own nearly unreadable. But I saw it, the intensity there, their own pain at the memory of what they'd endured.

What Callista had endured.

They nodded curtly. It was all the confirmation I needed.

"What has he been doing to her?" Atlas asked, his own pain radiated through his tone.

Laz swallowed and a quick breath raised their chest before they offered a swift shake of their head.

"I don't think the details will be helpful to either of you with emotions so high. If you don't mind, I would like to check on Brenwyn. I fear she's a risk for taking off into the night on her own."

"No—" Atlas began, but I interrupted.

"Go," I said to Laz. "We need to be ready to move soon anyway."

The sky had already begun to pale, the rising sun marking the end of our ability to rest.

Atlas shot a vivid glare in my direction, and Laz nodded before moving to follow the others to the riverbank. I turned to Atlas, eager to reach out to him as my own pain bled freely, but he'd already turned away from me, moving into the trees on his own.

I watched the lines of his back fade into the shadows with a heavy chain of dread locked firmly around my heart.

CHAPTER 44

BRENWYN

"Bren, I'm worried you'll lose yourself to your shadows," Emrys said from where she stood shrouded in the dim light of dusk with her arms crossed over her chest.

She'd lit an orb of faelight overhead to illuminate our space in the forest far enough away from camp for me to be able to breathe, to not feel such an unyielding desire to throw another punch at the firebird. It was a space to reel while Emrys and Avery did their best to contain my emotional outburst with Gengi keeping watch.

"That would be better than this," I said, my tone still frantic, edged with bleeding anger.

It was fading though, as quickly as the ink sky gave way to the dawn. I wouldn't be able to hold onto the fury for long. Soon, I would be left with the hollow pain of betrayal, the lonely ache left behind in the absence of Asteria.

"No," Avery said, her tone stern. "That's bullshit and you know it. Feel your feelings here."

"*Fuck you,*" I hissed, still pacing back and forth as I did my best to work out the tension in my muscles.

"Not my type," Avery grumbled irritably, and I shot her a glare.

"What happened, Bren," Emrys asked, her tone softer.

Emrys and Avery had been some of my closest friends before I'd left for The Capitol three years ago. They knew me better than most, and I would be lying if I said I hadn't been remarkably relieved to see them there with the others.

A blessing from the goddesses maybe. A consolation in the face of what I'd just lost.

"I don't fucking know." I groaned and threw up my hands. "We blew it. We were trying to find a way to help them, to get them out, and Ragnor found out. We got sloppy and he caught us."

"Well, convenient timing considering we are about to risk our asses in the Darkwood," Avery said.

"*What?*" I hissed; my tone laced with furious disbelief.

"A treat, right?" she asked with a dark laugh.

"I'll get you caught up," Emrys assured, "on everything. For now, I need you to try to come down from this. We are going to need to leave soon."

"I'm not going anywhere with *her*," I spat.

The stubborn timber of my words did not match the lurch in my chest. I wanted my anger to be directed somewhere, to be aimed at the firebird. She was the easiest target, the reason we were all in this source-damned mess.

But in my core, I knew that wasn't what hurt; it wasn't quite where my pain needed to be.

"You know as well as I do that isn't an option. I don't know what grudge you have against the firebird, but she saved our lives once already. I've seen what she can do with even a flicker of power. I'm following her to the ends of this realm, and it sounds like the person who sent you here wants you to do the same. So, I'd consider shaping up," Avery explained, her tone weighed with seriousness.

Her stern speech did not fall on deaf ears. I just wasn't ready to hear it yet.

"Brenwyn." Laz's voice broke the silence before I could offer a retort, and I turned to them.

My heart lurched as tears pricked my eyes at the pain in their expression, the exhaustion lining their posture. My shoulders sank as some of the fight left my resolve.

I saw the same pain I felt in my core radiated in their eyes. They'd been made to leave someone they cared about, too. As much as they'd deny it, I could see it. I'd marked the way they panicked and lunged for Callista when they'd realized what was happening.

"I'm sorry," I offered, my voice sounding small in comparison to the heat of the moment.

They shrugged one shoulder and a muscle in their jaw ticked.

"Don't be, just keep yourself together long enough to live through whatever comes next."

I measured them for a moment, wanting to offer some kind of comfort but falling short. All I could manage was a curt nod.

"Whatever comes next," I said on a breath, doing my best to force a willingness to go on into my resolve.

CHAPTER 45
AURELIA

Travel the next day was tense at best. Lazuli had managed to temper Brenwyn enough to get her on the road by the time the rest of us had the camp packed up. Laz had been less than thrilled upon learning about our decision to travel into the Darkwood, but the choice was outside of their control. Especially considering it seemed to be vital to whatever Asteria and Callista had planned for them to be with us.

I tried a few times to reach out to Brenwyn, but every attempt was met with an icy exterior and a pointed effort to ignore me. Instead, she spent the trip a significant distance behind the rest of us with Emrys, who assured me she'd fill Brenwyn in on everything that had happened since Venridge.

It turned out that Emrys, Avery, and Brenwyn had been close. A coincidence I was eternally grateful for, considering I wasn't sure we would have been able to convince her to go on, to keep moving with us without their influence.

The sun began to fall over the horizon, and we found we could not risk traveling any farther. The trees were getting denser, and evidence of creatures that dared venture from the Darkwood began to appear along our path; blackened branches, poisonous flowers found nowhere else across the continent.

I wasn't willing to drag everyone through this territory in the dark when the most dangerous creatures were out to prey upon ignorant souls who traveled too close.

We'd be there within an hour, but I would not be able to safely get us to the source shard, so we'd have to wait until morning.

I worked to set my bedroll next to Atlas's. Archer already slept curled up in the male's spot. Atlas had sulked off to the river to wash up. We camped closer to the riverbank this time, and I could see him through the trees with the water up to his knees, the silver tones of him standing out against the dark forest in the light of dusk. I had demanded we all stay close enough to be within visible range; it was too dangerous to wander off here.

My gaze caught on the planes of his bare chest as he rung out his shirt, his brow focused with some intense line of thought. He had spent the day in his own head, his usual spark and snarky attitude tempered by the news that Callista was both in danger and had chosen to stay in the palace. If I was being honest, I understood; my own emotions had been signifi-cantly tangled over it.

I was in my head about it, too. My heart was a mangled mess of confusion as worst-case scenario images of potential damages to her body—what Ragnor could possibly be doing to her—plagued me.

With significant effort, I peeled my eyes from the distrac-tion of Atlas in the rising moonlight to focus on my task at camp. Lazuli sifted through Emrys and Avery's collection of healing herbs and flowers while Brenwyn sat warming her hands over the fire, her knees tucked into her chest, a blank, far-off expression on her face as the glow of the soft flames lit her chin. Gengi, Emrys, and Avery were only a few yards outside of camp in search of anything we could use to fill our bellies with before rest.

Although relieved to know everyone had taken my warnings to stay close seriously, I could not stop my mind from turning over the distance Brenwyn had placed between us, how angry she seemed. I needed to find a way to resolve some of that, get past it enough to get everyone through the next day unscathed. I could not do that without feeling secure about my ability to trust the emotions of those around me.

"I need to know if you are going to be a liability in those woods or not," I said, my words directed at the wraith as I finished arranging our belongings.

Brenwyn's sharp silver eyes snapped to mine as she stood, and I found a distant pain glimmering there, something swirling under the anger she wore on her façade. She considered me for a while before continuing, though my attention caught on Atlas again, who had returned to camp, his damp skin glistening in the fading light of the sun. He moved to Gengi's pack, and I furrowed my brow at him in question, but Brenwyn's voice pulled my attention back to her.

"Do you even care about what has been happening in The Capitol? Or are you too self-absorbed with your own quest for power to remember how to stay grounded to the people who are willing to *die* for you?'

Heated anger flicked at my ribs and the sudden rush brought a tingling to my fingertips, a clear sign that my magic was stirring. I had been hesitant to test my magic since the viva berries had been lost, but it seemed my emotions did not need a reason to bring the heat back to my core. I ticked a brow at her and leveled my gaze.

"Is that where you think my concerns lie?" I asked.

"You've done nothing to prove otherwise."

"What, in the twenty hours since you popped in to throw a hitch in our plans? You've also spent the day sulking and ignoring me, so I don't know where you get off with opinions like that." My response left a bitter taste on my tongue, my voice laced with a venom I hadn't expected, my own frustration bubbling to the surface.

"She is willing to *die* for you," Brenwyn snarled, a rage through her tone as she snapped to her feet.

As Brenwyn's words landed, Atlas moved away from Gengi's things with whatever he had forgotten before his wash and trotted away without so much as a glance in our direction. The sounds of him splashing through the water filled the background with mindless noise.

A wicked fear coiled around my heart and my eyes stretched wide at the suggestion. I instinctively reached through the bond for Callista, only to be met with that wall again. Brenwyn continued before I could gather my train of thought on the matter.

"Asteria is willing to lose her life to this goddess-forsaken prophecy and for what? Why does she have to be the one to lose it all? She's there now, alone with him."

She hadn't meant Callista. She'd been speaking of my sister. A tangle of emotions washed over me at the realization, relief and dread wracking me for a different life, a different loved one at risk.

"No, I'm sorry, not alone. With Callista, *your fated*, but you seem too busy mussing around with other people's emotions to remember that she's also got her life on the line for you."

A vile kind of anger twisted in my core; a rage pierced my resolve like a jagged blade at the suggestion.

But it wasn't just anger that lashed out at my heart. It was more complicated than that. Shame, guilt, a desperate desire to somehow remove the responsibility from my shoulders, sever the connections I had to everyone around me.

"A liability then," I said, the words low, my tone dangerous with the simmering fury raging within me. "If that is the stance you insist on, then you can't come with us. Hold onto whatever opinions of me you want, but I will not risk your life or anyone else's for a half-formed impression of who you think I am."

Brenwyn simmered, her own rage vibrating from her shoulders as she clenched her jaw and spun the ring on her finger over at her side.

The silence between us hung heavy, aiding in the thundering beat of my blood between my ears. It took me a moment to level with the quiet, allow the absence of sound to give space to my anger, but then an anxious panic settled through my core.

Silence.

I could no longer hear any sound from the river.

I snapped my eyes to the spot above her shoulder to see him, ensure that he was still there in my line of sight, but I found nothing, no evidence that he had even been in the shallow water of the river to begin with.

Fuck.

I sucked in a breath of panic and lunged for my weapons, fastening the hilts of my fire blades to my thighs as I took off in the direction of the riverbank, shouldering past a shocked-looking Brenwyn as I closed the short distance between the camp and the water's edge.

My feet carried me faster than I knew to be possible, and I made it in just a few moments. I scanned the river, my attention whipping left to right, but no sign of Atlas waited for me. Fear flooded my veins for a slicing, all-consuming moment before I caught sight of a faint blue glow in the distance in the trees across the water. I narrowed my attention and saw his silhouette as he moved closer to a bobbing light.

"Goddess damn it, Atlas, get away from that!" I shouted across the river, panic lifting my tone.

A whisp. How many times had I told him to stay away from the creatures in this forest? If I didn't get to him quickly, it would be too late. The thing would have his conscious mind spun into a delirious state and would manipulate him into harming himself.

Atlas did not hear me.

I moved my legs as fast I could, careful not to slip on the slick stones at the bottom of the shallow water. It was not as shallow as I had hoped; about halfway through, the water reached my chin, and I lost purchase. My determined gaze slipped from the silver male. I gasped as I struggled to move my body through the rushing current. It pulled me downstream slightly, but I fought to swim, pumping my arms until my toes found the bottom. Soon, I was able to move my legs again and waded through the water to get to the other shore.

As I got closer, the details became clearer. The soft glowing orb of bluish light bobbed, and he reached out to touch it, causing a fresh wave of anxiety to wash over my senses.

"Atlas, no!" I shouted, fear projecting my frantic voice as it lanced my chest.

If he touched it, he'd be gone. The wisp would have him under its control.

How had he gotten so far away? I urged my legs to carry me faster. I needed to stop him.

Atlas dropped his hand lazily, the moment slow, already displaying the effects of the wisp.

Goddess damn it.

He turned over his shoulder and the most ridiculous, drunk-spun smile stretched his expression.

"Hey, Feathers," he called, a tone of adoration in his voice. "I was hoping you'd come out to see me."

"Don't touch that," I answered as I closed the distance, doing my best to keep my focus homed in on the task at hand. If the influence of the wisp had fallen over him so quickly, I was at risk too. I worked to protect my mind, shield my senses from its magic.

He furrowed his brow at me and stuck out his full bottom lip in a pout. My chest seized at the sight, and I forced my expression into a scowl.

"Why not?" he purred.

Before I could answer, the orb swelled, its light glowing brighter, and whorls of blue and silver swirled from within it. A ringing in my ears sounded and the edges of my vision began to blur.

Fuck me.

Too late, I'd reached him too late.

"It's so sweet. Just look at it," he insisted. "I've never seen anything like it. It says it wants us to go with it. I think this feels nice and I am going to go."

The wisp chimed brightly, the ringing in my ears swelling as it bounced playfully. He reached out to touch it, but before his fingers landed, it released the most charming little chime and took off to whip between the trees. Atlas shouted in exasperation, arching his arm over his head, the gesture dramatic and playful. I was still running, hadn't quite closed the distance, but my own senses spun enough to confuse my intentions at the sound of the wisp.

A laugh bubbled up in my chest as I moved to follow, and I had to bring my hand to my lips to stifle the sound. I was already losing myself to the effects. I had to focus.

"Atlas—" I began. He whipped his attention back to me over his shoulder as he ran, but I had already forgotten what I was going to say, the sight of him running and the little orb of light bounding playfully between the trees scattering my thoughts.

"Come back!" he called to the wisp with a laugh under his voice as he turned back to run faster.

"No!" I called, but the bravado had already bled from my tone.

I lunged to move faster, meaning to sprint, to run as fast as I could, but my muscles felt slow, full of a heaviness that hadn't been there moments before. I *was* running, but it felt like there were clouds under my feet, launching me forward step after step. My head bounced as I did, the forest feeling like something out of a dream. The sensation brought another heady giggle to my lips, and I struggled to contain the bubble of bliss as it began to wash over me.

"Oh good, you're coming too," Atlas called over his shoulder as he realized I was still following. "I *love* when you come too."

"Atlas," I tried to warn, but his name came out more like an adoring sigh, the sound of it curling over my voice, making my head spin.

I knew I needed to focus my thoughts, but I didn't want to. I wanted to lean into this heady feeling. I wanted the sound of his voice to wrap itself around my mind like it always did. I wanted the feel of his presence to wash away the weight of everything else.

I shook my head in a weak attempt to focus my whirring thoughts. It was the wisp, its magic. Rationally, I knew that, but it was growing difficult to separate any good sense from the dim forest as it spun around in my softened vision.

Wisps aren't so bad if you leave them be. They only bring out feelings you've buried deep within you.

The sound of Asteria's voice from a long-forgotten memory

billowed through my mind. Something near my heart lurched as a tangle of emotions wrapped themselves around my growing confusion.

But before I could make sense of any of it, Atlas was running. *So fast.* How was I supposed to catch up to him with him running like that? His legs were *so* long. My thighs pumped against the sluggish feeling in my muscles, and I moved faster, trying to catch up to him.

I needed to catch up to him.

"Keep up, Feathers!" Atlas called, but his voice sounded distant, echoing in my ears.

Had he really gotten that far ahead?

Where panic should have swelled, that heady feeling curled, bringing a warm smile to my lips as I struggled to focus my spinning vision on his moving form.

The ringing in my ears got louder, but it was starting to sound more like the wings of a butterfly in the wind.

Feathers.

The infuriating nickname usually left a lingering heat. I could not quite understand the crawling over my skin; this time, a bubbling bliss curled under my ribs. I couldn't stop the bright laugh that cracked my chest at the sound of his voice, the freeing feeling as it soared through my soul.

I moved faster, my vision spinning further, Atlas blending in and out of focus with the passing trees. The cold night air was crisp on my skin in contrast to the fuzziness blanketing my other senses.

Before too long, Atlas stopped short and held both arms out as though he were balancing on a beam. Where were we? Why had he stopped? It was only a few more strides before I made my feet halt as well, my arms hanging limply at my sides. They were so heavy. Everything felt so heavy.

Atlas teetered for a moment and his voice broke the night

with a cackle of pure joy. He seemed so far away but somehow right in front of me. The sensation was dizzying. My eyes moved past the male and found the wisp where it bobbed ahead, whirling and glowing with that beautiful whirring sound still ringing in my ears, a bright bell accompanying the butterfly wings now. It was warm. It made me want to close my eyes and lean into the bliss. It made me want to—

They feel nice, but if you cannot control your own impulses, you need to find a way to block out their song. They feed on that fire you struggle with in your soul.

Asteria's voice rang out in my memory again, and something cold flushed away some of the drunk-spun warmth coursing through me.

I shook my head and curled my fingers into fists at my sides, the movement slow and heavy, but my sharpened nails bit into my skin, the pain enough to center my focus.

I managed to narrow my attention on Atlas, who was already halfway across a deep gorge, the sound of rushing water filling my senses. He balanced on a remarkably thin branch fallen from a nearby tree. The male still held his arms out, balancing precariously as he took another wobbling step, guided by the wisp that bobbed just in front of his face. The branch cracked and another layer of my haze bled away as I managed to focus on exactly what waited for him at the bottom of the chasm.

A raging portion of the river beat against sharp rocks and boulders more than twenty yards below. The sound of the water thundered in my eardrums, chasing away the bells and wings, and the fear that flushed me at the sound of the cracking wood centered me enough to regain some amount of control.

"Atlas!" I yelled, panic laced through my words now. I called to my well of magic, a frantic attempt to do anything to get him away from the wisp.

Goddess damn him. I'd warned him to stay close. But fuck if he ever listened to a cursed word I said.

Atlas answered me with a bright laugh and reached out for the orb again.

"Can you feel this? Reia, it's incredible."

"Atlas, *please*, stay still. I am coming for you," I cried, my voice cracking and my vision still spinning around the edges, but the frantic anxiety crawling over my chest made it easy to keep my eyes sharpened on his wobbling form, to fight against my own drunk-spun haze as it still clung to the edges of my awareness.

"Why are you so far away from me? I need you to be closer."

His tone dipped but he stuck a foot out to the side, balancing on the other while he teetered. The branch cracked again, and my panic buzzed, my vision sharpening as I sucked in a frantic breath with my heart in my throat.

I pulled at my magic, a desperate effort to stop this. It coiled to the surface faster than it had in months, and I waved an arm out to catch his weight with it. For a brief moment, relief and elation coated my resolve, but it was short-lived as my magic jolted, catching somewhere between my well and my ability to wield it.

Terror spun my vision, and the wisp seemed to jingle with amusement, as though it were the cause for my stunt. I'd have to get to him another way.

"Get away from him, you overgrown firefly," I shouted angrily as I gently stepped out on the branch. It creaked, and I jumped back as Atlas laughed.

"Atlas, turn around," I called, frantic, my thoughts still spinning, the haze of the wisp's magic still clouding my focus.

"No, you come here!"

The branch cracked, the violent sound tearing through the air.

"You're going to fall!" My voice was a shriek in the night propelled on by my horror, and my heart seized in its cage.

"Well then, it will be time for a swim, won't it?" Atlas laughed merrily.

The wisp jingled and he took a wobbling step. I gasped as his toe slipped and his arms waggled around in circles to catch his balance. I did my best to step farther out onto the branch with featherlight toes, desperation seizing the air in my throat.

Atlas wobbled again, and just as I reached him, his only stable leg buckled, and he released a shout of surprise. That terror swelled to a living beast as it tore with jagged claws at the inside of my ribs. I dove to grab at his arm and made it in time to clamp both hands around his wrist as he fell, but he was too heavy.

His weight pulled me over, and my stomach dropped out from under me as we tumbled through an abyss for a moment before my free hand found the still intact branch. I gripped with all the strength I possessed as we fell, but it would not have ever been enough. As his weight plummeted beneath me, the wood snapped in two beneath my palm.

Terror stretched my lungs taut, and I released a scream as we plummeted into the water below. I did my best to curl myself around his falling form, pulling my body below his in hopes of catching his fall with some sort of magic, but again my well stayed stuck somewhere just below the surface.

Atlas seemed utterly unfazed by the reality of our situation. With bright laughter in my ear, he wrapped his arms around my waist and pulled me into his side. He turned us midair and straightened his spine just as our feet hit the water, plunging us into the depths of the frigid currents.

ATLAS

Cold. The water was so cold—frigid really. I'd never felt anything like it. The stinging sensation flushed every inch of my skin. It whirled around me violently, spinning my consciousness as the river took my loose limbs. The pain of the sensations wiped my mind clear.

Although, I wasn't sure I had my mind in the first place. Everything felt as though it were floating, my heart buoyant in my chest as I struggled to gather my bearings.

I couldn't breathe. How long had I been under? This seemed like it would have been so much fun, but my chest hurt, my lungs burned as they starved for air. The prickling of panic began to sour my disposition, pushing against the dizzying sensation overtaking my senses.

Something yanked at me, firm hands around my upper arm, and I struggled to gain purchase over my own thoughts. Those hands found my underarms, and suddenly, I had direction; they pulled me on, ripped my body against the rushing water.

It was taking so long, though, and the current was strong. It swept us along, and something sharp impacted my hip. I would have released a groan of pain, but the water pressed against my nose. The burning stunted my ability to express discomfort.

My lungs seared with a need for air, and I struggled to keep my mouth closed, but they ached. I wasn't sure how much longer I could keep the water at bay. For the first time since my feet had hit the river, I opened my eyes and tried to focus my attention, but everything spun too violently. This was it; I was going to drown.

A moment before my chest gave in to the pressure, just as my lungs threatened to collapse, my head broke the surface, the rushing water lapping my face as I bobbed. That set of hands turned to a pair of arms that wrapped themselves around my chest.

With her lips pressed to my ear as she struggled to keep me afloat, Reia released a groan of some tangled emotions as she coughed through the overwhelming currents.

Aurelia had my weight supported as she tried to kick her legs, furiously keeping us above water as the river worked to pull us under again.

I tried to move, to be helpful to her in any way, but every-thing turned leaden. My arms and legs would not work the way I willed them to, and my head was clouded with an intense fog, my chest still full of swollen bliss from that strange bobbing light in the forest.

"Gengi!" Her voice rang out sharply in my ear, and I furrowed my brow in confusion as I tried to turn my attention.

As I rolled my head, I managed to catch a glimpse of Gengi, everyone actually. They stood at the shore with strange, panicked looks on their expressions. Why did all of them look like that?

Emrys and Gengi ran ahead and worked quickly to push a rotted tree over. How had they done that?

It landed across the water just ahead. It wasn't very big, but

Reia managed to grip one of the branches as the current pulled us past the barrier. She groaned violently and her other arm tightened its grip around my chest as I continued to sweep forward, the water almost pulling me from her hold.

"Goddess damn it, Atlas, help me out here." She groaned, her tone hot with anger.

I tried to move my arms, but I didn't have to strain for long. Somehow, Gengi was already there; he'd sprinted across the dead tree on his toes while the others held it steady on the shoreline. I looked up to him with a smile, genuinely elated to see him, and he glared down at me. He looked furious.

Gengi's expression twisted mine into one of confusion again and bubbling laughter threatened to crack my chest, the strange bliss taking root once more.

Gengi bent down and locked his hands under my arms before hauling me up to my feet, but they would not hold me steady as my knees buckled. Emrys ran out quicker than I would have thought possible to catch my wobbling weight. The lithe lunar fae moved across the brittle trunk like she was on solid ground, and she helped me balance all the way to the shore.

Reia.

Panic pierced that odd elation, shocking me back into some semblance of reality. I turned over my shoulder as worry overtook the strange cloud coating my vision, but relief washed over me when my eyes landed on Gengi hauling Reia out of the river. She kept her jaw tight as he steadied her with a hand around her waist. Her clothes clung to her curves, and her long hair hung limp with the weight of river water. Her muscles shook with the tension of cold.

That water really was so cold. I should give her my shirt.

I moved my free hand to grip the hem of my shirt, but there

was nothing to take hold of. I looked down to find I did not have a shirt on.

Oh right, I left it behind.

That bright bubbling curled around my worry again and a laugh cracked my chest as I realized how silly it seemed to have forgotten my shirt. I looked down at Emrys, pointing to my chest, expecting her to think this development was just as humorous as I had.

She furrowed her brow and glared at me with confusion, as though she had no idea what I could be laughing at, and *that* confused me.

Why did they all seem so moody?

I pulled my gaze from Emrys's to find Reia again. Her eyes were already fixed on me as Gengi helped her reach the shore. Emrys let me go, and I stumbled, losing my balance as my attention snagged on the sight of Reia. I fell, landing firmly on my behind with my elbows supporting my weight. The world spun and a furious laugh cracked my chest as that bubbling bliss overtook me again.

CHAPTER 47
BRENWYN

"What in the everloving *fuck?*" Gengi shouted.

His furious tone held more authority than I remembered from the scrawny male.

Though, he wasn't so scrawny anymore. That was how I held him in my memory: a lanky, young male barely capable enough to wield his own weapon. But no longer. He was still lean and tall, his form slender, but he was strong. And the way in which he handled himself, took control of a situation, commanded attention was impressive.

I raised my brow as I crossed my arms over my chest, my lips thinned as I tried my best to suppress laughter as it curled up in my core at the scene before me.

"Remind me again who the liability is," I said, my words placed spitefully in the firebird's direction.

Her shoulders tensed from her position on the ground, but she pointedly ignored me. It did little to stifle my amusement, though. It really had been a delight to see the firebird with less composure than I had expected. A part of me was glad to see the handful she'd had to juggle out there with Atlas's reckless nature. The part of me that miserably thought she deserved the struggle had been quite amused to see the ridiculous scene play out.

Gengi was beside himself with rage, nearly shaking with it as he stared down at the pair of them. The firebird knelt near Atlas, checking him for wounds while he rolled on the ground, laughing.

Bellowing laughter, really. The sound was so out of place in comparison to what we had all just experienced. The oddity of his disposition set my own mood off-kilter.

Atlas's voice carried through the night as he wrapped his abdomen with his arms. Emrys flicked her attention to me, her expression tense and hesitant as she assessed the events, and Avery covered her mouth as she tried to stifle her own laughter. Laz, too, had a light in their eye I hadn't seen since we'd landed in the forest.

Glad I'm not the only one.

Reia looked up to Gengi, but when her eyes landed on him, a smile cracked her own expression and she sputtered, laughing as well.

What the hell happened to you two?

"Why are you *laughing*," Gengi hissed.

"I'm so sorry," the firebird said through giggles. "I'll get ahold of myself."

She wiped her eyes as she shook out her hands, still staring up at Gengi from her seat on her knees.

"You think this is funny?" Gengi shouted.

"No."

"Yes."

The firebird and Atlas spoke together and looked at one another before sputtering through another fit of laughter, leaning on one another as they roiled. Gengi turned and looked to us with his arms outstretched, his expression terse with disbelief, seeming exasperated, as though asking for help.

I chortled with laughter as it finally cracked free, his stress wearing on my resolve. It was entirely ridiculous, and I wasn't sure where to place my thoughts on the matter. At the very least, it was a welcome distraction from the usual din of my thoughts, and I was willing to see it through.

"A wisp," Reia sputtered between chest-cracking laughs. "Can't help it."

"Oh, goddess bless." I groaned, but the sound did not come out on frustration like I'd intended. Instead, my tone betrayed exactly how much I was enjoying the entire event.

The truth of it was I was glad to have something other than complete and utter dismay clouding my mood. It had been quite entertaining to watch the entire thing play out. The firebird had taken off after Atlas, and the rest of us had followed suit. It had been as though neither of them could hear us at all as we'd shouted after them. And then they'd fallen into that cavern.

That bit had been scary, but this was worth it.

"Yes, we saw as much," Lazuli said.

They'd lived near these woods for most of their lives; if anyone were to be familiar with the creatures here, it would be them.

"They're useless for now," Laz said, offering an explanation as they gestured between Atlas and the firebird. "The effects of a wisp's magic is like that of faerie wine but more potent, with more . . . giggles. They are known for aiding blissful feelings, letting your deepest desires free, but luring people to their deaths in the process."

"Yes," the firebird sputtered as she took a breath to control herself. "Nasty, overgrown fireflies."

"Might as well be," Laz said with a twitch of their lips. "Can you walk?"

"I can." The firebird nodded and got to her feet; she nudged Atlas's side with her toe, whose laughter had since subsided.

He looked up at her with a drunk-spun expression, one that radiated that infuriating infatuation, and I rolled my eyes as irritation coated my mood once more.

"Hey," he shouted and swatted at her toe.

"Get up," she instructed.

He rolled over on his side and Gengi groaned, a mangled sound escaping him as Atlas rolled to his feet.

"What in the bleeding underworld have you done?" Gengi's words came out in a violent stream as he reached for a metal device dangling on the belt at Atlas's hip.

Atlas raised his arm as Gengi snatched it and took the thing to turn it over in his hands, another mangled sound of surprise and dismay leaving his lips.

"Oh! Yes, I got it out of your bag to keep it safe," Atlas said with a proud smile as he placed his hands on his hips like a very pleased faeling who was convinced he'd done something right.

"Why in all the realms would you think it was safer with you than it was with me?" Gengi shouted, anger lancing his tone.

Atlas furrowed his brow in confusion, and the firebird moved to take the device from Gengi. Her expression fell; a grave emotion washed over her, stamping out whatever had been twisting her mood into that false brightness.

"The wisp said—"

"Oh, the *wisp* said? I don't care what the bleeding wisp said! It's ruined," Gengi lamented, running a hand through his sandy hair.

"What is ruined?" Laz asked with concern on their brow.

"The conduit," the firebird breathed, the light in her eye tempered, reality chasing away some of the drunken stupor. "For me to handle the source safely."

"What?" Atlas asked, his own tone now laced with worry, but he still stumbled as he took a step toward Reia.

"It's fine." She sighed, catching his weight with her shoulder as he fell into her.

She handed the broken device back to Gengi and helped Atlas sling his arm around her shoulders to help him stand.

"It isn't fine," Gengi insisted.

"I broke it?" Atlas asked, his tone a tremble now.

"It *is* fine," she insisted, still speaking to Gengi. "I have handled the source before. It is what it is. I'll be fine."

"No, we need to—"

"We don't have time," the firebird bit, her tone firmer now. "What we need to do is get back to camp. Atlas needs to recover, and we need to prepare for what is in store for tomorrow."

And with that, she gently nudged Atlas until he started to walk, and they began their ridiculous hobble back to camp without giving any one of us another glance.

We all watched them for a stunned moment, stiff silence hanging between us.

"On a scale of one to ten, how fucked do you think we are?" Avery asked, her tone surprisingly light and jovial.

I managed to huff a laugh and roll my eyes before turning to follow them.

CHAPTER 48
AURELIA

There had not been time to fuss about what had happened with Gengi's conduit. At least, I'd made that the case. Atlas needed rest. Everyone did. The Darkwood was nothing to fuck around with, and this group had done an extraordinary amount of fucking around thus far.

I was entirely unhappy and not at all thrilled at the prospect of taking them all into the trenches of danger.

I came incredibly close to taking off in the middle of the night, going on without them. I did try, but Gengi saw that idea coming a mile away and he'd stayed awake to babysit me. So instead, I'd stayed up the entire night to make sure the wisp magic worked its way through Atlas, monitoring his sleep.

And when morning came, we took very little time to brief everyone about the plan, what I was going to have to do before we set off. I led the crew through the blackened trees of the Darkwood itself.

I was not sure I could have prepared myself for what it felt like to be tangled in those trees again. It had been so long since I'd been to visit the wood. The memories were a blur, a distant image under the fog of amnesia. It caused deep-rooted anxiety as I led the group through the void of never-ending blackened brush with nothing but a faelight to illuminate our path.

It was dark. It should not have been, as the sun was bright in the sky on the other side of this territory. But this forest was named the Darkwood for a reason. The canopy of trees above was tangled with thick briars, venomous tendrils of poisoned earth. They'd thickened over time, so much so that no sunlight broke through to the forest floor.

The glow of the cool-toned faelight provided an eerie atmosphere as it shone on the cracked branches, the deadly-looking briars. They were enormous, the vines much larger than I remembered, most as big around as my leg. The memory of the way they moved across the forest floor snaked a shiver along my spine.

"I want to remind you again: do not touch the briars," I called over my shoulder.

"I don't think I have ever wanted to touch anything less in my entire life," Atlas replied, the familiar snark back under his tone.

The others said nothing as they moved behind me, the only sound the soft rustle of their footsteps along the brush. The tension in the air hung heavy as we traveled into the unknown.

It was not supposed to be unknown to me. I was the one that had hidden the damned crystal in the first place, but this forest seemed foreign to me, the image of the dense brush an entirely different world in my memory from what I saw before me. Centuries of overgrowth made it impossible for me to determine where I was or where I was supposed to go.

I had to rely on that buzzing in my veins, the very same from the underground chambers in Venridge. It was there. Although so far relatively faint, I could feel it. I had been relying on the sensation to point my toes, following the tug in my core.

The farther we traveled, the tighter my anxiety wound. What if I couldn't reach it? I was relying on its power to get us out, but what if I failed to find it? My instinct pulled me on, that distant buzzing lighting my veins, but my draw to the source magic had been flickering in and out for a while.

What if the spirit in these woods had chosen to lead me astray, move me away, deemed me poisoned, unworthy of finding the crystal again?

"I need a rest," Laz's voice called from near the back of the group.

I turned over my shoulder to see them looking worn and ragged, their breathing labored and the dark circles under their deep emerald eyes intensified in the glowing light.

They moved to sit on a mossy boulder nearby and we all stopped. Gengi offered them a skin of water and they took it, swallowing the liquid in great, heaving gulps.

"If you are sick, you should turn back," I said, my tone stern.

They shook their head, a fire in their eyes.

"I will not. I'll be fine."

"What's the matter?" Gengi asked, concern on his brow.

"Nothing," they began, but Brenwyn interrupted.

"Not nothing. Something has been wrong with creation magic for months. Laz, you're too weak."

Confusion tilted my awareness at Brenwyn's words. I had heard nothing of this affliction, and the possibility was wildly concerning.

"I am not. I just needed a breath," Laz said as they stood.

"I understand the need to press on, but no one wants to see you get yourself killed," Atlas chimed in.

"It's too late," Laz insisted. "We are already out here. My

magic is fine; I am fine. We can deal with it when we are out of here. We're close anyway."

"What do you mean?" I asked, a flush of surprise coloring my tone.

"I can feel it, can't you?" they asked, confusion tilting their expression.

I focused on the energy buzzing through my veins and narrowed my attention on the pulse, a wave of heat through my soul.

"Yes, but . . . you can feel it?" I asked.

They met my eye with an intensity that instilled some kind of confidence within me. I measured them for a moment as they nodded.

"Can anyone else?" I turned my gaze to the others, who all shook their heads.

"Not unless it feels like the most irritating blister on the back of my heel, no," Atlas said.

"I have a special set of skills," Laz said with a shrug of one shoulder.

"A set of skills that maybe should have been discussed before we set off into a nightmare realm, don't you think?" Atlas asked, his tone light but lilted with frustration.

I narrowed my gaze at Laz and thought for a flicker of time that I might find them familiar if they had an ancient enough power to sense the source in that way. But nothing crossed my memory. I either never knew them or the memory of them was lost to forgotten time.

"Where is it?" I asked.

"Just that way." Laz nodded, a curious light in their eye.

I considered them for a moment, unease settling in behind my breastbone, but the alarm was quickly outweighed by my desire to get this over with. If Laz could offer help, then I was willing to take it.

"We continue," I said with a nod. "But I want to go over one last time the severity of what could happen when we get to the crystal."

"Yes, yes, big scary magic. Don't touch it. We know," Atlas said, recounting some of the things we'd already discussed before we'd set foot in the wood.

"This is serious," I snapped. "We get to the crystal, and I am the only one to touch it. No matter what. I don't care what happens to me, you let it happen. And if something goes wrong, you get out."

Atlas's jaw ticked, and he leveled with me, his expression nothing short of furious. I peeled my stare from Atlas to look at Gengi.

"Promise me you will get them out," I said, my tone firm, but a plea rested there.

"I won't leave you here," Atlas interrupted.

"Atlas," I fumed as terror lanced my chest.

"I swear it," Gengi said, his voice cutting the tension between us.

Atlas's expression twisted angrily, but I cut him off again as I turned back to Laz, already moving back to the front of the travel party. I had no time to allow my emotions to tangle. No space. The feelings needed to stay tucked neatly away in their boxes until we were out. Until *they* were out.

"Alright," I said with a nod to Laz.

"Let's go get this rock," Lazuli said with a roll of their shoulders as they pushed ahead to keep walking through the Darkwood.

CHAPTER 49

ATLAS

Terrified did not begin to encompass the feeling that had seized my heart as we followed Lazuli through the forest. I did my best to contain the emotion, to level my senses. But I could do nothing with the image of failure in my mind's eye after Reia had made Gengi swear to get us out.

Even the possibility that she would not make it out alive instilled a panic so violent within my core that I wasn't sure I'd be able to think clearly enough to act as she'd asked me to. No, I knew I wouldn't be able to. If anything happened to her, there was not a chance in all the realms I'd be capable of standing by and watching.

She would just have to forgive me for that later. I'd rather her pissed off and alive than not have the ability to experience the emotion at all.

Only minutes passed before Lazuli turned to Reia over their shoulder.

"Just ahead." They nodded.

I focused my eyes to find the density of the trees broken off slightly just in front of the creation fae, the massive vines draping through the trees higher there than in most places. Reia hurried ahead to step forward and disappeared for a moment. Panic lanced me and I jogged ahead, bolstering past Laz to follow Reia.

I moved through the line of trees to a small opening, the darkness slightly alleviated as the canopy of blackened leaves above proved to be a little thinner.

"This is it," Reia said as she turned on her heel.

The others followed behind and we stood in the clearing, scanning the space and taking it in.

"Where do you need us?" Avery asked.

"I want you back in the tree line. The source is in the center," Reia answered, her tone demanding.

"Right, spread around then," Avery instructed, authority in her tone, every bit the warrior sent out to the continent for unreasonably dangerous missions over the past ten years.

The others all split, sticking to the edge of the small circle of space within the heart of the forest. I remained standing where I was, my feet filled with lead as I swallowed a lump in my throat, my gaze pinned on Reia's.

"What are you doing?" She sighed as she met my eye, a heavy line to her shoulders.

"I don't know. I can't move my feet," I said, my voice relatively quiet as I spoke the truth through my vivid anxiety.

The corner of her mouth twitched and that spark in her gilded eye lifted her expression slightly, fading some of the din of my fear.

"It's going to be alright. Just stay back and it will be over soon."

I offered a nod, but still, my feet did not move.

"Do I need to move your feet for you?" she asked, a quirk in her brow.

"Maybe," I said with a twitch of my lips.

"Get to the trees, asshole," Brenwyn called. "No one wants to be here longer than we have to be."

I rolled my eyes, and Reia nodded in reassurance as I stepped back to take cover under the branches of a great black tree. Across the clearing, my eyes met Gengi's, who offered a nod, his own posture tense.

Reia moved to the center and took a breath as she pulled a dagger from her thigh. She closed her eyes and wrapped her fingers around the blade. Before a moment had time to pass, she tensed and pulled the weapon through her grip. Blood poured from the wound, a surprising display of crimson against the dark scene around her. I sucked in a breath and frigid emotion stopped the very blood in my veins as I watched Aurelia lower herself to the ground. The massive trees around us dwarfed her in size, but everything remained unnaturally still, as though the very forces of nature knew she was one of them.

And she was. Oh, goddess bless, she was. I'd not taken much time to think about the fact, to really consider *what* she actually was. Not with my constant worry over a thousand things at one time. But now, with her shoulders back, the strength in her posture, the very fire in her presence, it was easy to see. Her internal flame stood out against the black void of the forest behind her.

It was breathtaking.

Of course she was this strong, unmovable force before me. I knew that. I had watched her take on threat after threat, snarling in the face of danger every time. And every instance only made it easier to fall in love with her. She was the embodiment of fire, living rage, but also somehow still sturdy and kind under the burden of her solid but cracked exterior.

I understood that she needed to do this alone, and I would do my best to allow her to exercise her own strength, but for the love of the under realms, it took everything in me to keep still, watching from afar, to allow her to risk her life like that.

The source was dangerous, and without Gengi's conduit, I thought I might die of tangled dread and worry on the spot.

It was my fault she didn't have it.

A fact I had not yet allowed myself to turn over in my mind too significantly. Not until we were out safely.

Reia lowered to a crouch with her knees tucked into her chest as she pressed her wound to the ground. She twirled the fingers on her other hand to ignite a gentle flame. It came to life effortlessly, no sign she had struggled with her magic in the past months at all. The fire curled between her knuckles as though happy to see her, grateful for the life she'd breathed into it. The orange glow lit her striking, warm, bronzed features—her golden eyes blazed alight and the wisps of her auburn hair, fallen from her braid, danced in the swirl of moving power as it coursed around her. The magic was a living, breathing entity. A being only she was familiar with.

Watching her use her power was remarkable. I had never seen anyone wield magic in the way she did. The sight of her radiance stilled the breath within my lungs.

Gengi met my eye from across the clearing, and I nodded to reassure him. He returned the gesture, the line of his jaw tight with lingering tension. The others remained relatively out of my sight, all concealed in shadows at their chosen posts.

With breath held firmly in my lungs, I traced her movements as she tangled her flame-twined fingers with the blackened brush at her feet. The glow highlighting her face faded as the light doused under the blackened forest floor, and she remained utterly still for an impossibly long moment.

I held that tense breath, waiting, but not a heartbeat passed before all sound dropped from the surrounding forest. The chirping creatures of the dark ceased, and the rustling of the wind through the leaves of the trees overhead stilled. A chilled eeriness settled deep within my bones as a solid wall of power radiated from her crouched form. The force of invisible magic sent her hair dancing around her face, as though a torrent of wind caught in a violent twister immediately surrounded her spot in the clearing. Reia remained still, her expression focused as she kept her attention on her palm where it met the earth.

My stomach rolled with nausea as the deafening silence stole my ability to think. An itching in my muscles made it difficult to contain the urge to move from this spot, to rush to her side. But before I had any time to process the theft of my hearing, a frenzy of thundering fear plummeted through my core as Aurelia's attention snapped up to meet mine.

I sharpened my focus on her gaze, and the flash of panic I saw in her glittering eyes forced a frigid flush of terror through my veins. I reached for the hilt of the sword at my hip and made to take a step toward her, but my feet were frozen, immovable. Unfiltered hysteria seized my lungs. Fear quickly twisted with rage as she offered a gentle shake of her head.

Confusion flushed through me for a heartbeat's worth of time before I realized what held me still.

It was her magic. Reia kept my feet locked firmly in place.

Terror laced with anger in my core. The wild emotions quickly chased confusion away and I opened my mouth to speak, my brow furrowed with the blinding rage, but in that moment, her expression changed. Aurelia's eyes frosted over, and her face slackened as charred veins of black death snaked her wrist, keeping her arm locked in place.

The veins were familiar to me, and it took less than a breath for the image of that crystal in Ragnor's chest to flash through my mind's eye.

"No!"

The mangled word came out on a shout, but it sounded distant, carried away by an enchanted wind.

Aurelia's attention remained locked on mine, and a crushing pain radiated there before a single tear slithered from her eye to curl over the apple of her cheek. The wrath of the under realms broke loose in the surrounding forest before that tear had time to reach the line of her jaw.

Chaos. There was no other word to explain what happened as the forest took life around us. The thick briars tangled in the trees sprung to life and slithered their way toward Aurelia with a frightening pace. The sight of them forced a scream from my lips as I struggled to get to her, all promises be damned, but I found I was still unable to move my feet.

I caught sight of Gengi across the clearing as he turned to face a wicked briar as it reared over him. It thrashed out and he unsheathed his bow to defend himself. The voices of the others echoed in the distance as they faced similar fates. I couldn't separate the sounds of their struggles from my own panicked thoughts as the briars began to swallow Aurelia.

Her expression remained slackened, but a warm yellow light flushed her skin, tangled with the poisoned vines on her arm as the earth under her palm cracked. The sound of the broken ground thundered through my chest.

The briars raced for her. They slithered from every corner of the clearing, and I found myself unable to understand what exactly they were aiming for, whether they planned to kill her or aid her. And although the briars did not appear to be kind entities, she showed no sign of fear.

I had no time to consider. Only seconds passed before the briars engulfed her completely, creating a living, breathing ball of black forest around her.

How had they taken her so quickly?

Terror iced my veins, and I released another scream as I tried to lunge again. The breathing ball of black vines grew larger, curling and winding over themselves, tangling in a mass of heaving dismay, blocking Gengi from view as I struggled against Reia's magical bindings.

And then her voice split the stiff air as her violent scream tore my reality in two. My heart cleaved apart; the very fabric of my soul tore as her voice shattered my awareness. Only a few breaths passed through my lungs before all I could see was a faint glowing light through the tangle of branches and thorns.

I screamed; an echo of fury a tear in my throat as I tried to move again, but this time I was not planted firm. As another cry reached my ear, my feet were released from their magical bind. Relief flushed through my horror for the briefest moment, and I raced toward the tangle of black forest concealing her. I pumped my legs as fast as they would carry me, and I unsheathed my sword mid stride.

A wild fury fueled my movements. Damn it all, everything she'd warned us about. There was not a goddess's shot in the under realm I was going to stand by and watch this monstrous thing take her, watch the source kill her before my very eyes.

It would be my fault if it did. She would have the conduit if I'd just stayed at camp . . . .

The reality cracked at my chest so violently, it caused a line of tears to blur my vision as I approached the tangle of briars.

I needed to get to her. I would get to her.

Although, it seemed the briars would put up a decent fight first. The moment I reached them, they lashed out. I dodged, swinging my blade out to cut at the beasts as I did my best to hold my ground. Strike after strike, I cut them down as my muscles burned with the effort.

Gengi shouted something unrecognizable from the other

side of the fortress of forest, and a buzz of swelling panic grew as the sound split my attention. I tried to focus on my own battle as I swung my blade. With every stride, the light from her flame dimmed as the mess of thorns grew tighter around her. It seemed like an impossible feat, but it was one I would not allow to best me.

I hacked at them with my blade, but for every branch I severed, two more seemed to snake their way through the tangled mess. Terror and rage twined together to harden my resolve, and my veins boiled as a crack of panic and frustration tore my voice. The sounds of the others were drowned out by my blood as it thundered between my ears, and my muscles burned against the strenuous effort, but I didn't care.

I needed to get to her.

I would get to her.

Her voice split the air again with a cry of pain so vicious, the very beating of my heart stopped. I lost control over my senses, and my voice took its own life as her name fell from my lips. I screamed it, the sound tearing from my throat as panic overwhelmed me. The effort of swinging my blade trailed beads of sweat along my spine. I brought the weapon down as fast as I could for blow after blow and somewhere in my blind frenzy, a briar managed to knock my weapon from my grip. I watched with horror frozen in my veins as the vine carried my blade away to be swallowed by the thick of thorns.

Anger like I had never felt before heated my core, and I ground my teeth against the wave of nausea as it rolled through me. It took no thought at all to discard the idea of using the weapon as it was whisked away into the tangle of darkness. I buried my resolve under determination and took to the nightmarish briars with my hands.

The thorns tore at the flesh of my palms. For a few strokes,

I felt the pain, but the agony was wiped away as another scream from the inside of the bundle of briars shook my core. I called for her, but my own voice seemed distant somehow. The sound of her name ragged in my throat.

I narrowed my focus on the vines ahead, pouring every ounce of energy I had into tearing them apart, pushing what little energy I had left to coil my cyphin magic through my well. Maybe if I met them with the magic dampening ability, they'd slow.

My skin shredded with every movement, tearing as the thorns fought my efforts, but little by little, they began to ebb. Exhaustion wafted over me as I fought to move on. With gritted teeth and an otherworldly pit of determination, I found I was able to curl myself into the tangle as I pried vines away to clear a path.

I moved the monstrous things enough to push the lines of my body through the mess. The thorns were angry and vile. They sliced at my exposed skin, tore at my clothes, and did their best to force me back out with their violent thrashes, but I held firm, pushed forward, ignoring every fiery rush of pain on the way.

There was no force in all the realms that would keep me from crossing this terror to her.

The lacerations came faster than my skin could heal them, and blood stained my tattered tunic, but the hope of my progress numbed the pain enough for me to keep ripping away at the briars.

"Atlas!"

Her voice tore through the din of chaos.

My name. She'd called my name.

The sound of her voice ignited a fresh wave of vivid energy, and I doubled down, moving the vines with my tattered hands faster. Her name fell from my ragged voice again, and I begged my muscles to move with more urgency. My hands left trails of blood on as I pushed one after another out of my way.

I was suffocating. It was too dark as the branches consumed me, and I began to lose my grip on reality as pain pierced my consciousness. I found it near impossible to separate the searing agony from my own thoughts for a dizzying moment that lasted far too long for me to remain calm.

And just as frantic anxiety threatened to swallow me, stutter my magic, a glimpse of her bleeding light seeped through the briars just ahead.

I forced all my energy into pushing forward, and I screamed through gritted teeth as I tore my way through the rest of the deadly vines. After what felt like a life sentence in the underworld's worth of time, I spilled into the center of this nightmare. The vines dumped me out and I landed on my hip, the pain sharp, but I scrambled to regain my balance, propping my weight on my knees. The space was too small for me to stand.

In the center of the chaos, Aurelia knelt, unharmed, with her arms outstretched to the side, the black crystal clenched tightly in one palm. Her hand burned red as coal, those poisoned veins tangling up to her shoulder now, actively crawling over the line of her collarbone. Her expression was the same as before the forest had taken her, vision cloudy and her features lifeless.

The light of her magic radiated from every pore, but they stood out in direct contrast to the deadly magic creeping over her skin.

I sat on my knees, my chest heaving as I tried to grapple with the scene before me, my terror, panic, rage, pain. It was all so overwhelming. The flesh over my hands was torn to shreds and blood dripped from lacerations over every open surface of my body. I tried to move but my muscles were leaden, a searing poison in my veins.

The thorns, there had been something in them, some vile substance meant to disable my ability to move properly. I shouldn't have stopped. I should have barreled right through to her.

My head hung between my shoulders as I tried to find my words through shattering breaths.

"Aurelia," I choked out on a mangled breath, the fabric of my soul bare in the timber of my voice.

I hadn't expected her to react, not with her mind somewhere else like that. But the moment her name touched the air, her expression twisted into one of agony as she let out a chilling scream.

Before I had time to react, flames erupted around her knees and the blackened veins spread across her chest. The briars twisted faster and closed in around us. Panic set in again, sparking me into action, and the frantic emotion managed to push past the poison in my blood. The pain was miserable, but it didn't matter. I let out a scream of fury as I pulled my aching muscles together to rise to my feet.

With all the strength I had left, I fought against my own agony and lunged for her with what was left of my cyphin magic open and wrapped my arms around her. I carried my momentum through the movement, and we tumbled to the ground as the vines worked to close in on us. I rolled us to place her beneath me, protect her from the vines with my arms on either side of her head.

Placing one hand on her cheek, I focused to blanket her with my power, to cut off the energy from its source, to end her suffering. The strain of coiling magic caused a violent split in my head. The source magic pushed against mine in a way that made it difficult for me to ground myself, to keep breath in my lungs, but I forced my will through it.

You will not take her. You cannot have her.

I pushed one last surge of energy through with a scream tearing through my throat as I held her head against my chest, and something snapped. The tie to her magic cut as my efforts proved to be successful.

Her flame went out, but the thorns were close. I held my breath as I braced myself for the pain of the briars against my back, but none came as the chaos around us ceased, the vines completely frozen as her magic fled her veins. The silence in my ears dizzied me, and I found it difficult to gain a steady breath as I assessed the sudden change of pace.

After a still moment, the vines slithered away as quickly as they'd come, back to the trees. The dim light of the forest clearing washed over in the shocking calm, the aftermath of destruction.

It took me a moment to accept the end of it and compartmentalize the pain throbbing over every inch of my body, but I found my voice quickly after, desperate to see the life in her eyes.

"Are you okay?" I managed to croak, but Reia did not respond.

I pulled back enough to get a look at her with terror tangled through my ribs. She lay limp under me, her head lolled to the side, her eyes open and staring on, lifeless.

It was then that I realized I could no longer feel her magic pushing up against mine. My walls had relaxed.

Aurelia wasn't there at all.

The fear as it gripped me was unfathomable. I lost control of my ability to track coherent thought. I could not breathe, could not stop the agony cracking my lungs open, allowing my own life force to bleed away. Her name left my lips, but I couldn't hear my own voice. A numbness overtook my limbs as I raised my bloodied fingers to her chin to turn her face to me. She did not respond. She was not breathing.

My heart lodged in my throat, and nothing else mattered. The pain in my wounds dissipated as all my focus turned to the life-altering agony shattering my soul.

I had no control over my actions as I pulled myself to my knees, scooping her limp body into my chest. Her head lolled back with her eyes still open wide, and I brushed the sweat-dampened hair from her forehead. Hot tears stained my cheeks. I couldn't feel the sting of them in my eyes, only the cold panic as it suffocated me, trapped the air deep within the cavities of my chest. I shook her in my arms, her name falling from my lips over and over to no avail. I couldn't feel her. There was no magic buzzing over her skin, nothing for me to pull from.

No, no, no, no, no!

I wanted to burn, thrash, tear the realm apart with my bare hands. To bring her soul back from the veil. I had to; I needed to. She couldn't be gone. She couldn't be.

I had entirely forgotten the others, but soon they moved to stand around us, and I thought the dark magic had stolen the sound from the world because I could hear none of them, not their feet in the brush or their voices as they tried to speak to me. Someone placed their hands on my shoulders and tried to peel me away from Aurelia, but I curled her tighter into my chest and snarled at whoever dared try to take control of this. They could not have her. I would not allow them to take her from me. I could bring her back. I needed to bring her back.

This wasn't happening. I couldn't breathe. I couldn't see. I could only feel the agony of despair as it tore through the very hollow of my bones.

Someone knelt in front of us and tried to get my attention, but I couldn't see them; I couldn't hear them. It was as though I had been placed in a chamber to deal with my agony and horror on my own. My tears fell into her hair as I pulled her close and pressed my lips to her cold forehead. Her skin was never cold. She was fire and life, always warm. She couldn't be cold.

I wrapped my arms around her as tightly as I could, squeezing her as though I could somehow offer her my strength, offer her my own life if it meant she would come back to me. The person in front of me did not try to take her, instead they reached for her hand and pried something from her rigid fingers. The thing fell and it seemed to tumble to the brush in slow motion, the weight of this impossible moment suspending it.

The crystal. I hadn't realized it'd still been in her hand.

The source shard tumbled to the earth, and before a single second could have passed, Reia sucked in a breath deep enough to crack her chest. Her lifeless form jumped in start as though some wild, otherworldly energy coursed through her veins to bring her back to life. Warmth flooded her skin, and I could feel her panicked magic push against mine again in an angry tidal wave of energy. My chest cracked and some of the pressure of pain released as I grappled to keep her magic contained under the blanket of my own heaving magic.

She gasped with panic, and I loosened my grip enough to get my hands on her face. I could not possibly describe the relief washing over my frigid muscles as I saw life in her eyes. Dead and cold only moments ago, they searched mine with a wild kind of fear, swirling with questions, and her fingers tangled in what was left of my tattered and bloodied tunic.

She grappled for air, her chest moving in shattering breaths, and I brushed her hair back from her eyes. Tears poured over my already stained lashes, and my chest heaved as I allowed the rest of the pressure of agony free. Her cheeks were streaked with the blood from my fingers, and she held onto me as though she might fall away again if she were to let go. In that moment, I would have given my life as payment for this.

"Atlas." Her voice was less than a whisper, and I couldn't bring myself to speak, only stroke her cheek with the pad of my bloodied thumb.

It was only a heartbeat before she fell unconscious in my arms again.

AURELIA

My limbs were paralyzed. My eyelids seemed permanently closed. I expected the heat of pain to startle me awake, but a blanket of heavy comfort settled over my muscles instead.

A rustling sounded from somewhere nearby, and I gathered I was on my bedroll, the softness under my shoulders a comfort with the crisp air of night on my skin. From the heavy-footed boots I heard across brush, I gathered Atlas was with me.

He was pacing. He was always pacing.

I pricked up my ears for the others but could not find any evidence of their presence.

I couldn't quite remember what had happened; the memories tangled in a thick fog. Pain, fire, heat, poison. I tried to move, but I could bring no life to any of my muscles.

Atlas shuffled across the space, his boots rustled against the ground, and he plopped down next to me. His heat was a comfort to me as he drew nearer. I tried to stir to tell him I was awake, but still, I remained under the weight of this false unconsciousness.

Why couldn't I move? What had happened? I couldn't remember. Flashes of the dark forest, the searing pain of a fire that did not belong to me, that I could not control, the horrific anger, wrath, devastation as it cracked my chest, all rushed my mind's eye.

But it was too much. I couldn't sort it in my hazed state.

A cool, wet cloth pressed to my forehead, and the instant relief it provided against my burning skin flushed a wave of bliss through me. I hadn't realized my skin was hot.

My hand burned. The crystal. I'd retrieved it.

But why could I bring no movement to any of my muscles? The involuntary stillness caused a panicked flutter in my chest, but not even my lungs were able to suck in air any faster than they already were.

Atlas released a tense sigh. The emotion tangled within that breath sparked a lurch in my chest.

"My heart can't take much more of this. Your constant refusal to consider your own safety before you act," he muttered.

I couldn't respond. A wild, frantic energy lanced my breastbone as I tried to move, speak, breathe faster, anything.

"If you could hear me right now, I would let you have it, you know. For being so reckless." His voice was laced with a kind of pain and thickness I wasn't expecting. "But you can't hear me, so what good would that do, huh?"

He sighed again, a labored tension under the breath.

"Although, this would be the perfect opportunity to get some things off my chest, wouldn't it? I'll never get to speak of it otherwise, and I think it might kill me before all of this is over if I keep swallowing it." His words were quick, a nervous ramble, and a knot twisted in my stomach.

I wanted him to know I could hear him. He needed to know. Frustration-laced panic gripped my chest at my complete lack of control. I reached for him, pressed against the stillness, but managed to bring no life to my limbs.

He went on.

"It makes me crazy when you do stupid things like that. Honestly, insane. I lose control of my better sense. I can't . . . If anything were to happen to you, I don't know if I'd be able to go on."

The knot in my stomach twisted into a tangle of emotions difficult to sift through. I begged my strength to come back to me, to reach a hand out to offer him comfort, to stop this confession before it took root too deeply within my soul.

The effort was fruitless. My panic only swelled, my heart beating faster against my churning emotions as he continued, and I remained unmoving.

"I know I am not supposed to feel this way about you. Goddess bless, I know it. I am reminded of it every bleeding day. And even if there is a shot in the other realms that you feel similarly, I can't risk your life for it, or Callista's—especially not hers. What we are doing is too important.

"Oh, goddesses above, it's so important. You are so important to everyone. And it makes sense to me that the goddesses chose Cal for you. Of course, they did. She is your equal in every way. You're both so strong, vibrant, perfect for one another honestly. For the first time in a decade, we have hope of taking this cursed realm back from that bastard. I can't get between that.

"But if you'll forgive me for being honest, I hate it. Everything about it. It's selfish of me, but I wish I had been the one. The one with the strength, the magic, the ability to help you save this realm. Callista is the right choice, of course." He paused and I heard a shift in his weight before he moved on. "But she is *always* chosen, always the strong one, while I fall short every time. I mean, goddess bless, she didn't even want the infernal bond to you. She avoided you for so long, ignored the damned thing, and I would have . . . Well, I don't know what I would have done, exactly. But I know there isn't a fiber of my being that would have ever been able to ignore you, keep a distance from you. In any realm, in any life.

"But none of that matters. My idiotic feelings on all of it are insignificant in comparison to what we are trying to accomplish. So, I will continue to shoulder it. I will do my best to step aside. I'll get you to Callista so you can put the pieces of this realm back together."

He paused, the weight of his words landing like boulders on my chest, the beating of my heart a thunderous thing between my ears.

"I only wonder if you would have felt the same way about me as you do about her if the goddesses had chosen me instead. I wonder if I would truly stand a chance at your heart if I had been the one blessed with the strength to be your match," he said, his tone soft, laced with unfathomable pain.

That pain echoed the cracking of my heart as it splintered into pieces beneath my breastbone.

Atlas swiped the damp cloth over my burning cheeks. My heart brimmed, threatening to explode. My pulse raced in its veins like molten metal, but still, I could not move.

Goddess damn it, move.

"It's alright though. Callista's safety, your safety, your strength are all that truly matters to me. I hope you'll forgive me for all of my selfish desires. For wanting to be the one your heart chooses. But I suppose there is nothing to forgive if you never know, is there? I think it's better that way. The goddesses know what they are doing, don't they? I know your heart is hers, but I'd gladly take however much of it you can give me. Even a piece of it in the aftermath of all of this is better than not knowing you at all."

My heart fissured; the vibrant emotions impossible to bear in the wake of his confession. He set the damp cloth down next to my head and his gentle fingers brushed loose hair away from my brow. His presence loomed over me as he leaned down to press a soft kiss to my forehead. My heart cried out, screaming for him, thundering at the tenderness as the sensation left a trail of vibrant life over my skin.

Atlas let out one final sigh and rose to his feet.

"Try not to wake up before I come back," he whispered, and I listened to his heavy footsteps fall across the forest until he disappeared into the abyss.

THE MOMENT I'd found the ability to move again, I'd set out to find him. My footsteps fell in slow motion. Every one of my strides pulled me through the sands of time, through frigid tension in the air. Gengi told me he would be near the river.

I needed to get to him.

I had trouble categorizing the emotion as it worked its way through me. I'd had some time still paralyzed by the healing tonic Laz had given me to sort through some of the agonizing feelings, most of which centered around pain, regret, and guilt. I'd had time to turn over how my heart still bled for Callista. Getting to her felt more important than saving the realm. More important than saving myself. She seemed written into the fabric of my soul, the bond between us an ache in my chest, resting on the other side of that deadstone barrier.

But I could not deny the way my heart thundered for Atlas as well. The heat proved to be a twin flame to the fire of Callista's burning in my chest. I'd tried to shove it away, ignore the way my soul radiated at his confession, how desperately I needed to wrap his words around my misery, use the glowing warmth to block out my despair. But I could not ignore it. The need to see him had only grown. I wasn't sure what I planned to say, but there was no way I would be capable of pretending I hadn't heard him.

No amount of strength could have prepared me for the possibility of shouldering that burden.

The ache radiating deep within my chest was unbearable. The lurching yearning cracked me in two, my heart fissuring into equal pieces, only breaking me further with every passing moment.

I couldn't bear it anymore.

The moonlight glittered on the silver display of his bare shoulders as I crested the hill. My heart stopped. His confession clattered through my mind one word at a time, the memory of his voice both a relief to my aching soul and the very reason for the turmoil twisting through the space between my ribs. It clutched my lungs in an icy grip, making it difficult to suck in enough air to keep my head straight.

I tried to choke back the lump in my throat threatening to suffocate me, but the tears did not listen to my plea. They spilled over my already damp eyelashes, breaking my thin resolve. I struggled with my feet, stumbling over the next few steps, and Atlas turned to inspect the noise. He rang out his sopping tunic, river water dripping to the currents at his knees, and dropped his hands to his sides as relief melted the rigid lines of his worried posture. As his eyes landed on me, my dread only twisted further.

The beaming smile stretching his expression faltered as his electric gaze found mine.

"Reia," he said, his tone laced with strained worry as he

took a step forward, moving from the water to close some of the stiffened distance between us.

Concern lined his achingly beautiful features. It made me want to scream. To confess my own tangled feelings as they warred within my chest, to smooth the line between his silver brows. I wanted nothing more than to keep pretending with him—to be Enora, a woman in love with Keir, a woman with no problems other than worrying about when she would get to see her fisherman again.

But I could not. Seeing him here, acknowledging the magnitude of my feelings for this male had solidified that. It had been reckless to lean into even a glimmer of that fantasy. I had already failed. Again, I'd failed to contain my heart. It would put the realm, him, Callista, all of them in danger. The flippant, emotional thing already had once.

I placed a trembling hand on my aching stomach and stumbled a step backward as the blow of his attention knocked my resolve off-kilter. My feet ached to take me back to camp. To smile and offer him a snide remark about worrying. To pretend everything was fine.

To keep his heart whole.

But I couldn't. I could not afford to.

I'd already fallen so far. I didn't trust myself to keep on with this ruse, to resist the draw I felt to him any longer. I needed to stop this, contain the feeling before the wildfire of emotion spread too quickly. If it wasn't already too late, I had to try.

But the idea of even one more line of distress in his expression caused a roll of nausea through my core.

Fuck me, what have I done?

"What is it?" he asked, something like rising panic glittering in his eye, fluttering under his usually confident tone.

"Atlas." His name was a whisper on my lips, and my heart was already cleaved in two.

The sever of my chest only needed the pain reflected in his expression as he reeled through the possible causes for my tears.

"You can't feel that way about me. You cannot keep looking at me like that."

That vivid panic in his expression flurried to a kind of hysteria as understanding dawned on him. The lines of his shoulders pulled taut and the rise and fall of his chest froze.

"You heard me."

It wasn't a question. He released a tight breath.

"Reia, I—"

Atlas took another step closer, but I moved back, careful to keep the distance firm between us. He stilled. The slicing hurt through his eyes was a knife to my already bleeding heart.

"What am I supposed to do with this?" I cut off his plea, my voice surprisingly free of the trembling I felt in my hands.

I tried to remain firm, but the need to reach out and claim his torment warred with my determination to keep up this façade. He tossed his wet tunic to the side, the force of the motion a clear indication of his own torrent of emotion, frustration, and he took the opportunity to break our eye contact, but I could not have missed the line of brimming tears along his silvery lashes.

"With what?" he asked, a bite to his tone now.

Anger.

Good. This would be easier with him angry.

I doubted fury was the primary emotion the male wrangled with. He often covered every raw feeling with banter, or snark, or that false flush of irritation. The fact usually caused my own flare of aggravation.

But not tonight.

Tonight, I would play into it. I'd have to. Causing a fight, making him angry with me might be the only way to protect him from what I was about to do.

I called to the familiar pit of rage as it slumbered deep within my soul and urged it to roil through me.

We can be angry instead. Anger is easy. It's an external emotion, quick to cover up what actually bleeds under the surface.

"You *know* what!" I groaned through the fresh roiling heat in my core and shoved his chest with the heels of my hands. He took a step back, absorbing my blow, hurt flashing through his eyes again, but he kept his jaw tight, his shoulders locked back.

"What am I supposed to do with this?" I rapped my knuckles on my own breastbone. An attempt to beat away the cracking pain I felt there, to hammer away the coiling agony. "With you! With any of it!"

He opened his mouth, but no sound crossed his lips. I watched with flaring anger pulsing through my bleeding heart as his thoughts crossed his expression. I waited as his own frustration faded into defeat. Then, I held my breath as the weight of despair pulled at his rigid shoulders. I had to fight the instinct to reach out to comfort him with every fiber of my being. The need itched the tips of my fingers, and I had to ball my hands into fists to focus the energy as I waited for him to speak.

"I don't know what to say," he admitted finally. The softness in his tone shattered my resolve.

I would have much rather he met my anger with a shout, a demand, anything to keep the fire sizzling over my pain. But I could do nothing to keep the ache at bay with that desperate sorrow in his tone. Anything would have been better than the quiver of agony under his usually bright, vibrant voice. His eyes lined with the silver of brimming tears, and I feared I would not be able to hold onto my purpose.

I would not be strong enough. I was never strong enough.

I choked on the pain as it bubbled up in my chest. It stole some of my will as it broke my voice through a ragged sob.

Tragic, really. I had never quite felt this way. This was even different than the bond. In all of my centuries, I had never thought this magnitude of emotion would be possible. It was cruel twist of fate to find someone to make me feel so alive in the face of so much misery, yet have to sever the connection. A punishment, if I had to guess. For all of my impulsive, careless indiscretions, all of the pain and death those careless actions had caused.

I couldn't let it happen again. I could not lose him like I'd lost so many. Fabian, Callista, even Ragnor had been lost to a darkness I had not seen coming.

It had all been my fault. Every time.

I wouldn't survive it again. Not with him.

"Take it back," I nearly snarled, a sorry attempt to cover pain with the false anger I so desperately clung to.

But the words sounded empty, even to me.

Atlas's eyes glittered with an echo of the heat I felt as it clamored through my chest.

"I won't." He shook his head, his tone firm. "I will not lie to you."

I reached out to push at his chest again, begging the frustration to numb this nightmare. The tingle of my fire burned at my fingertips, my magic swirling beneath the surface, but he caught my wrists before my palms had the chance to make contact. The gentle tug of his magic pulled at mine as he bled it away, cut the connection to my core.

I let out a mangled sob at the familiar dizziness that came with his talent. I hadn't realized the heat I'd felt was the burning of my magic. It was a comfort; a cooling presence I wished I had not yearned for so desperately. He worked quickly, and the drain on my fire nearly sapped the rest of the fight out of me with it.

"Take it back," I said again through gritted teeth, forcing my gaze to meet his. "I can't take it. I can't take this, Atlas."

My words were all but a plea as they fell from my lips.

He held firm, but after a few beats of rigid silence, with nothing but the sounds of the river to drown out the thundering in my ears, his bottom lip trembled. That was all it took to whisk away the rest of my rapidly depleting strength.

My knees gave out and another sob cracked my chest as I fell to a heap on the ground at his feet. Atlas followed me, one knee at a time, all the while holding my hands closely to his broad chest.

"If I had never seen you look at me like that, I would've considered it," he said, his tone surer than I had expected.

He released a breath, his voice tight with strangling emotion. I squeezed my eyes closed, forcing the waiting fall of tears to stain my heated cheeks. I couldn't look at him. Couldn't bear to face the emotion in his gaze.

I didn't deserve it.

I'd been the cause of too much suffering to deserve that.

Atlas released a hand to brush each falling tear away with the pad of his thumb. The gesture was gentle and made something behind my breastbone twist, the pain making me wish I had been strong enough to pretend I had not heard him. I should have pretended to be asleep, allowed his confession to be a silent one.

I'm fucking things up again.

I want to take it back. I'll pretend.

I begged the goddesses, but they never listened.

Let me take it back.

No one answered. As usual, I would be left to my own

misery to clean up the messes left behind by my reckless, mangled heart.

Atlas released my other hand to take my face between his tender palms.

"Look at me," he instructed, the sternness returned to his tone surprised me.

I opened my eyes to obey and found his face inches from mine.

My breath froze within the cage of my chest, and I wasn't sure I would ever be able to release it. Not under the heat of his focused attention, those radiant eyes so close to mine.

"I will not take it back." He swallowed; his tone stable. "I will not apologize for how I feel. What I *will* do is swallow it, for the good of the realm, for you, for Callista. I never meant to hurt you, Feathers. I never wanted this to hurt you like this."

I let out another ragged sob as my heart fractured further. How could every word uttered by his voice affect me in such a way? Ruin my already mangled heart?

"I will swallow it, but not tonight. Tonight, I will be selfish because, frankly, I am not strong enough to fight this for moment longer. Tonight, I will ask you to choose me."

Oh, goddess help me.

"Atlas," I whispered, desperate to stop him.

My bottom lip trembled as his name fell from my lips. Unable to control the driving need as it took my hands, I spread my palms out over his chest. His heart raced under my touch.

Of course, he thought there would be a choice—most did. But that was never how my heart had worked. There was no choice to make. A connection like this, like what I felt for both him and Callista was not so selfish as to take up all the space in my heart. The feelings I had for him had no bearing on the feelings I held for his sister. It was not at all that I wanted to choose her over him, or the contrary.

It was not that he was not enough.

It was so much more complicated than that. It was that I really could not allow myself to love anyone like this.

I was not a safe person to love.

I wanted to explain, to express how important he was, to tell him everything that had been on my mind for the past months.

I could entertain none of it, though. The risk was too high. My heart was too dangerous. It was *because* of how fiercely I had chosen him, both of them, that I had to break his heart.

I thinned my lips and shook my head, tearing my gaze from his as the tears fell freely.

"No," he protested through gritted teeth.

Atlas let his hands flutter to my neck, brushing my hair away from my face. The sensation left a trail of tingling electricity after his touch.

"Please," he choked out.

The agonizing knife already lodged in my heart twisted, but I could not bring my voice to my lips to stop him. All my senses seemed frozen in this suspended moment in time.

"Choose me now. Because I know you must choose her. I know you *want to* choose her. Let me be what you need now because I can't be when it matters. I will never be the half of you that will help save the realm. I will never have the strength to match yours. The goddesses chose her. I will be loyal to that reality. I will forget you ever looked at me like that. Tomorrow, I will, I swear it. But tonight, I am asking you to *choose me*."

The last of my strength dissolved and tears flowed freely over my heated cheeks. My lungs deflated. If I never took another breath again, I was sure I could make do with that. The blood in my ears thundered so loudly, I could not hang on to any singular fleeting thought.

I could not control my instinct to reach up and cup his

cheek in the palm of my hand. My fingers trembled still, but I needed to touch him. The urge to offer some kind of comfort in the light of his gut-wrenching confession overwhelmed all my goals, my good sense. He leaned into the contact and gripped my wrist, holding my palm to his face, the gesture born of vivid desperation. I pinched the inside of my cheek between my teeth in an attempt to slow my whirring thoughts as he squeezed his eyes shut against his own torrent of emotion.

"I—" My lip wobbled. "Atlas, I can't."

"No," he hissed, his jaw tense enough to cut steel, and his eyes snapped opened again, a startling flame there. "Don't do that, please. Don't say my name like that."

He squeezed my wrist tighter and brought his forehead to mine, his eyes closed again against whatever pain he faced, like he couldn't bear to look at me for longer than a few moments, like he was afraid of what he might see in my gaze.

His sweet breath washed over my face and a shiver snaked my spine. A knot of guilt twisted around my rib cage. In that moment, I wanted nothing more than to lean into his touch, to give him everything he'd asked me for, to fall over that edge again. To give him more. It would be so easy to let go of this pain and give into the relief I knew waited behind the barrier of despair.

I wanted to.

Oh, *goddess*, I wanted to. I had never really wanted anything more.

But that was the whole problem. Every time I decided my desires were worth indulging, it ended with despair worse than this.

The only thing worse than breaking his heart now would be watching the light leave his eyes.

Like Aeson.

Like Fabian.

I would *not* put him at risk like that. Not Atlas.

I centered myself with the circular train of thought and swallowed a lump in my throat as I prepared the words I knew would tear him to pieces.

"What is it you expect me to do?" My tone came out strangled, my voice no longer belonging to me.

I pulled my hand free and sat back on my heels, desperately begging the goddesses to release me from this torment, to detach me from the pain pouring from my chest long enough to do what I had to do.

Atlas's hands fell to his lap, and he fixed his gaze on mine. A flicker of hope burned there. It nearly brought a scream to pass my lips instead of the carefully crafted rejection. I wasn't sure I could keep looking at him. Even the thought of his heartbreak cut across his beautiful face raised bile in my throat.

"Callista is still out there, and we've been out *here* playing house for weeks. Do you expect me to pretend with you? Like we pretend to be Enora and Keir?"

"Of course not," he replied, hurt lanced through his tone. "I want you to—"

"*What*, Atlas?" I pulled all my remaining strength together and rose to my feet.

He looked up at me, shoulders curled inward. The vile, gnarling thorns of pain tearing at the cavities of my chest almost buckled my knees again, but I managed to hold my posture firm. I willed my next words to hide under the heat of false anger.

"Whatever it is you want from me is a fantasy. Nothing more."

He measured me for a moment, searching my expression while hurt glimmered in his gaze. After a few beats of tension, the lines of his expression hardened, and he rose to his feet, rolling his shoulders back as he locked his eyes on my face. I clenched my jaw, biting down on the urge to comfort the agony written in his eyes. He hid it well though, his own anger turning the lines of his expression to stone.

"Is that what you believe?" Atlas asked, his voice low now, dangerous as it quaked through a near whisper.

I nodded; my teeth clenched as I blinked back furious tears.

"It has to be," I hissed through my teeth.

His eyes flared, and I knew I'd said the wrong thing. Even that had offered him some semblance of hope.

Goddess damn me.

"Is that what you *want*?"

He took a step closer, and I retreated one, keeping the distance between us firm despite the screaming in my muscles to fall into the embrace I knew would be waiting for me should I choose it.

I did not respond. I couldn't even if I'd wanted to. My throat seized around any attempt to speak.

"Tell me what you want." He clenched his fists at his side, a blazing inferno in his irises, "I want you to tell me, *with conviction*, that it is not me."

The knife twisted again, and I was not sure I could manage any more pressure on my chest. I swallowed the misery coating my tongue, and it took everything in me to remain stoic. I claimed a few miserable, weighted moments to find the ability to bring words to my lips.

"It is not." With considerable effort, I managed to choke out the lie.

Atlas searched my eyes for any flicker of regret for only a moment before he offered a curt nod. His face crumpled, and he turned away, bringing one hand up to cover his mouth. A shuddering breath cleaved his chest, and he ran his other hand through his hair. I was going to faint. The edges of my vision wobbled as I struggled to bring breath to my chest. My knees nearly gave out, but I focused my thoughts on the biting of my nails in my palms as I wound my fists at my sides tighter.

I stared at the lines of his back, watching his chest heave through staggering breaths. I couldn't do this. I couldn't stay out here and watch him break.

My hands trembled as I shook out my fists and I took a step back, begging my muscles to carry me away. The desire to take it back tore at me, the weight of what I had done to him suffocating.

It had to be this way; I had no other option. I turned on my heel and retreated to camp, my tail between my legs like the miserable coward I was. Passing my bedroll, my feet kept pulling me along. I passed camp, ignored Gengi's concern as he approached, shoving him out of my way to get to the safety of the dense forest.

When I was sure the others could no longer see me, I allowed my knees to give out, crumpling over them in a heap. I wrapped my arms around my torso, a sorry attempt to cage in the screeching agony that writhed behind my broken heart. It clanged against my ribs, and I let out a ragged sob, the sound an echo of a life I might have chosen for myself if given the opportunity.

BRENWYN

The series of events over the past couple days had been entirely overwhelming and proved to be difficult to keep up with, but I found I was left with little choice. I did not ask to get thrown into the depths of an impossible death mission set by the firebird herself, but there I was, nonetheless.

As much as I wanted to, I couldn't leave. After Emrys and Avery's rapid-fire recap of everything they had been through and where the group was headed, I decided I needed to find it somewhere within myself to cooperate.

It turned out the entire reason we'd risked our asses in the Darkwood had been to get the firebird enough power to give her a chance at taking on Ragnor, getting Callista back, and, with any luck, freeing Asteria.

Which meant I needed to suck up my frustration with the infuriating solar fae, work through some of the blame I'd placed on her for this entire mess and learn to play nice. At least long enough to get back to Asteria.

The thought of Asteria in that palace alone caused an ache

so fierce it urged a prick of tears in my eyes if I allowed myself to linger there too long. If my thoughts got tangled in everything that had happened, the image of Asteria at his side without support, my resolve faltered, the terror and dread consuming me. Not only was I terrified of what could happen to her alone, I felt hollow; a clanging feeling of betrayal plagued my disposition.

Asteria could touch. She had not been the apparition I had grown familiar with. How had I not known? How had I spent the past three years believing that she could only visit me in my dreams?

The questions only brought a vile, poisonous kind of rage to the surface. One I hurried to bury any time the ugly thoughts reared in my mind.

I had no time for that. Any time the emotions rose too close to the surface, I struggled to keep my own will free of the shadows. I needed to keep my attention elsewhere.

Instead, I focused my thoughts on the firebird, who was about to test her stores of magic aided by the blackened source crystal. Which had given all of us a horrific scare in trying to get ahold of the damned thing. It had taken Lazuli over two days to bring her back to the land of the living.

She held it in a glove with her fingers wrapped around the stone. It was only a little larger than her hand. Underwhelming, if I were to be honest. A shard of the shattered source itself. It looked a lot like a black rock to me.

I leaned my shoulders against the trunk of a tree with Laz standing close as I waited for the solar fae to offer any kind of display, instill any amount of confidence that she would be able to accomplish our most pressing goals.

The firebird was not doing a very good job. Standing there with her shoulders tense, doing nothing but struggling to level her breathing.

Atlas stood; his arms crossed over his chest with an unusually heavy demeanor settled over him. He'd been quiet. Neither one of them had even so much as looked at one another as we'd bustled through the morning. Something had happened between the two of them. The firebird had stormed through camp without a passing glance and disappeared into the night for hours, and Atlas hadn't returned until sunrise.

I found a bit of pity, just a kernel of it tucked away somewhere in my core for them. Regardless of circumstances, a broken heart was a heavy burden to bear. And that was what I'd sensed of the two, the heavy weight to the air between them. Someone had gotten their heart broken.

I would have considered it a shame if I hadn't been so angry with them for fucking off doing goddess knew what while we'd suffered in the palace.

In any case, I did not have much room to offer any potential condolences in light of everything ahead of us. They were grown, and we didn't have time to deal with whatever had transpired between the fae. Better they keep focused on their own two feet.

Emrys had perched herself in a tree overhead, her back against the wide trunk as she sharpened one of her daggers. Gengi sat cross-legged while he wiped his bow with delicate strokes of a cloth, and Avery crouched on her heels, sharpening her own blade. All waiting patiently for the solar fae to do *anything.*

"Hi, what's happening?" My words fluttered off the surface of my rising irritation before I had a chance to catch them.

The firebird's intense golden gaze narrowed on me, and she flashed an expression of aggravation.

"If you don't want to be here, be somewhere else," she bit, her tone laced with a venom aided by whatever storm of emotion brewed within her.

"If I had somewhere better to be, I would. We've been staring at you for ages, and you've done nothing. What is it you're waiting for?"

Her eyes flared, and she dropped her hand to her side, the crystal dangling there in her clenched fist. I might have imagined it, but I could have sworn a blanket of darkness settled over her; her expression turned hard, the whites of her eyes dimmed slightly.

"You know, I did not ask for you to be here. Any one of you. If you think, for one second, that trying to function with this burden is easier with any of you here, you are sadly mistaken. This is a goddess-damned nightmare, having to wrestle even a kernel of this poison into my well, to make it useful to me, to any of you without obliterating all of us on the spot. But none of you will leave me alone for one bleeding moment. So, I am working with the very limited, cramped amount of space that I have."

It was not anger that flicked at me as her words landed, rather it was almost a color of amusement. It was refreshing to see her release some of that hardened exterior for a moment.

"So *bitey* today," I said with a flare of my eyes, a challenge in my expression.

Her angry expression surged, and something changed. I had not imagined the darkness because it fell again. Her eyes stretched and her nostrils flared as she gritted her teeth and a curling wind took the hair around her shoulders up, the torrent swift.

"Reia." Atlas's voice rang low with a tremble of concern, a warning there.

She gripped the stone tighter, and my eyes snapped to the blackened crystal. Beneath the glove, black veins spread along her forearm, the very same as the ones on Ragnor's chest. Panic gripped my resolve, and I stood up straight, rising from my lazy lean on the tree.

"Okay, I hear you. Be careful," I said, my tone lighter, a tad frantic.

Something snapped. A violent crack through the air shook the trees and she was thrown off her feet. It was as though the magic within her had exploded, a violent crash of energy stemming from her core. She curled in on herself as her body flew through the air, that torrent of wind or magic or both hurdling her straight into the great oak tree behind her. Her head cracked against its trunk, and she slid to the ground with a wince of pain crumpling her expression.

Luckily for the rest of us, she had been far enough away from everyone to be the only one affected by the magic. Although perhaps it had just been her own internal poison reacting poorly to the source.

"*Aurelia!*"

Atlas was the first to react, rushing to her side as he gripped her to support her head. He reached for the crystal, which had rolled along the ground next to her, and she shouted something incomprehensible before waving her hand. With the flick of her wrist, Atlas lifted from the ground, some invisible force sending him hurdling back a few feet as she allowed a burst of magic free.

"*Do not touch it,*" she hissed as she pulled herself to her feet.

Atlas looked up at her from where he sat on the ground, an expression of hurt and anger lanced across his features.

"Then you should not be touching it either!" he shouted as he rolled to a stand.

"Alright, cut it the fuck out," Gengi said, his tone holding that swift authority.

He moved to the stone and snapped it up with the dead-stone box he'd had in his magical bag. We'd kept it there in the days prior and it had been relatively contained. For the most part.

Laz flicked their attention to the box with a sickly expression on their face. They could still feel it. So could the firebird. For a black rock, the thing was absolutely and so wildly dangerous.

"No one touches it, and no one gets it out of this box until I can repair the conduit. Fenbrook is only a few miles away. That display of bullshit magic was all I needed to see to make my decision for me. You need the conduit, so we will take the time to go into town so I can get what I need to fix it."

Reia shot him a glare, her expression seething as she considered for a moment. The darkness seemed to have ebbed slightly, her skin returning to its normal warm bronze color. The veins in her arm retreated again.

She did not respond. Instead, she huffed an angry breath and snatched the deadstone box from Gengi's grip before storming back in the direction of camp.

"Goddess damn it, she's the moodiest individual I have ever met in my entire life," I muttered to myself. Laz huffed, the sound coming from their spot a few inches to my right.

"Well, yes, that makes sense considering you have not had the displeasure of meeting yourself," they said, and although their words were not kind, they held a glimmer of a smile on their lips, a tease under their tone, shining in their eye.

I stared at them, contemplating whether to be hurt by the jab or commend them for their ability to crack a joke in light of all this dismay.

They reached out and shoved my shoulder playfully with a quirk of their lips as they passed, and a smile cracked my own lips as I conceded to the possibility that maybe things were complicated for everyone and we all deserved at least a small fraction of grace for having to navigate this nightmare.

CHAPTER 52
ATLAS

"I am going with you," I insisted, but my plight fell on deaf ears.

Gengi held firm as he stood with his back to the door of the bathing chamber. We'd retreated to the small room from one of the bed chambers we'd rented from Fenbrook's inn to have this little argument. Irritation only thickened over his disposition.

"I don't know why, all of a sudden, you are unwilling to be reasonable, but you need to stay where she stays. A quick cyphin might be her only chance if her struggle gets too great. And we can't take the source crystal out into the city. I don't know how it will react to the magic here."

Fenbrook had been coated in a layer of poison since I'd last visited. Everything seemed on the verge of death, and it was alarming. We hadn't spent much time exploring the streets, though. We'd traveled straight to the inn to find sanctuary so Reia could release the deadstone box holding the crystal and Gengi could find what he needed to fix the broken conduit. I wasn't sure he was going to be able to find what he needed here, but we were about out of options between here and The Capitol.

He was right, though. I was the only one with the power to cut her magic off from the source if things got out of control. If that crystal's broken magic started to take root.

It already had. Those veins on her arms, the flash of shadow over her eyes as her anger flared, they terrified me. I did need to stay.

I just would rather have plucked my own eyelashes out than sit in a silent room with her while the others traipsed around town. Not after I'd left my heart bare only to have it trampled mercilessly.

No, I needed a buffer. My roiling emotions were not stable enough to remain quiet and calm in a room with her.

"Leave Avery, then," I said, my tone bleeding with irritation.

"Oh, good goddess above, what is the matter with you? You've been acting like an ass all day."

"Well, maybe I just am *an ass*, Gengi. Is that something you ever considered?"

"You *are* an ass, but I know you better than to believe nothing is wrong. What happened?" he asked, his tone softer, a hint of understanding under his words.

"Nothing. I don't want to talk about it."

He narrowed his eyes and leveled his gaze at me.

"Is it Callista? Has something happened?"

A stabbing pain lanced my chest at the mention of my sister. The feeling was so complicated. Worry for her, dread over what we would need to do to free her, terror over what could be happening to her, and under it all, a gruesome pang of jealousy. Which was so unbelievably ridiculous. There were so many more pressing things to worry about. It frustrated me to no end that I was unable to cage the monstrous emotions raging within me.

I should have been able to. I should have been capable of setting it aside, staunching the bleeding of my heart to get to The Capitol, to get my sister back.

Maybe I needed a drink. That tavern a few blocks down seemed to be the only sign of life in town. I'd heard music. Maybe a night out releasing some tension would benefit me most. Clear my palate of the distaste of roiling misery.

"Atlas." Gengi spoke again, worry under his tone after I did not respond. "Did something happen to Cal?"

"No," I managed. "Not that I know of. I'm fine. I'll be fine. Just get your baubles so we can move on."

He assessed me for a moment, something like disbelief swirling in his gaze.

"Avery doesn't want to go, anyway. Better we split up into more even groups."

"Well, I don't know why you spent the past ten minutes lecturing me, then," I said, exasperated. "I swear on the holy mothers, twenty-five years old and you act like you're over three centuries. You aggravate me to no end."

His mouth twitched in a smile, and he clapped a hand over my arm before nodding to the door behind my back.

"Yes, and you are over a century and act twenty-five. If that weren't the case, maybe I wouldn't have to *lecture* you, you asshole."

I rolled my eyes and turned to open the door, letting Gengi into the room behind me. Avery already sat with her feet propped up on one of the beds while Reia stood with one arm over her chest, the other hand at her mouth while she gnawed on a nail, staring blankly into the fire.

"I'm going to go get the others and head into town; try not to burn the building down in the meantime," Gengi said with a hand on the door handle.

Reia flashed a glance at him and offered a soft but empty smile.

"Will do," Avery said as she stretched her arms over her head, very clearly enjoying the comfort of a bed.

Archer resigned himself to sleeping at the end near her feet. I was honestly impressed with the cat's persistence. Every time we'd left him in the woods to keep him safe, he'd managed to be waiting for us on the other side, ready to travel on as though he were determined to be a part of our strange little mixed bag of a group.

I honestly could not understand it, and I feared he would get himself killed for my attachment to the small creature, but I was grateful for his company, nonetheless.

The door snapped closed after Gengi, leaving me standing with my arms hanging at my sides to do my best with not allowing my gaze to linger on Reia.

She did the same. I might as well have not even been in the room at all.

I hated this. This tension between us pulled so taut, it threatened to take the air out of my lungs with it. It was honestly easier to be in love with her on my own, sulking internally while she remained oblivious to my feelings on everything.

I wished I could take it back. Go back to when she was willing to be near me, rely on me for help when she needed it, look at me, for goddess's sake.

This was torture. The lacerations over my heart left behind by her rejection bled freely and I wasn't sure they would ever staunch.

The urge to say something pulled at my resolve, to call her attention away from whatever plagued her.

But she'd made it very clear that it was not me she needed. So instead, I settled for taking a seat on the free bed and grabbed my blade along the way to sharpen the edge; give my hands something mindless to do while I worked to contain my out-of-control emotions.

Only a few minutes of silence passed before Avery's breathing slowed and soft snores filled the room. It had been so long since she'd had any kind of comfort, I wasn't surprised sleep overtook her so quickly. Despite my need for another's presence in the room, I was glad for it, honestly. One less pair of prying eyes on me while I sulked in my own despair.

Reia held firm in her silence. Eventually, she moved to the table set up in the corner of the room to rest her legs. I did a solid job of refraining from looking at her as she moved, though I was aware of every inch of her presence. My eyes flitted to her when she reached for her bag to pull out the deadstone box.

That pulled my attention. Fear coated my stubborn resolve as she pulled the box to the table in front of her.

"What are you doing?" I asked, my tone clipped as I set my blade down, my full attention pinned to the stone cage in her hands.

Her eyes met mine and I saw that flash of darkness again. It shouldn't be possible; the thing was encased in deadstone. It shouldn't have affected her.

But it was. With her hands on the box, her skin looked dim, the normal warm bronze tone a sickly color. Her eyes held a film of darkness, the very energy around her vibrating against her usual radiance.

"There is absolutely no reason for you to be handling that thing right now. What are you doing?" I asked again after she did not respond, my tone more firm now.

"I don't know that it's any of your concern what I choose to do with it," she said, her own voice full of bite.

"The fuck it's not," I said, rising to my feet, my eyes flitting between her hands and the aggravated expression on her face.

"There is only one person in this room who has been burdened with the title of guardian of the source, and it is not *you*," she snapped.

"Well, maybe if you could handle your own overworked well of magic, I would believe you deserved that title in the first place."

The words as they left my lips were unkind, launched off a platform of pain and rage. I hadn't really meant them, but they landed, nonetheless. The harsh accusation caused a vicious flare in her eyes as she rose to her feet, the box still clamped firmly between her hands.

She did not speak, but the emotion roiled behind her stare, and my attention drew to her hands again, where a faint bleeding of those black veins flushed with her rage.

Panic seized my heart, and I stepped forward with my hand outstretched, my movements based entirely on terror-driven instinct.

"Give it to me," I said, the demand in my tone firm.

"Excuse me?" she snarled.

"You heard me. Give it to me, it's affecting you even through the deadstone. You haven't been yourself since you got that thing in your hands."

She held it firm and shook her head, a fresh flash of emotion in her eye. Something broke the anger and the veins bled away, as though something within her soul pushed back against the darkness, but the rage settled in despite the flare of wild emotion and the veins surged again.

"Goddess damn it, Reia, give it to me or I will take it. I won't watch that thing eat you alive."

Her voice came out on a strangled shout of rage and frustration, but to my relief, she put the box down, sliding it across the table. The veins fled, and the glow of her skin flushed the dark pallor away. The binding around my heart loosened and I moved for the box, but she stepped in front of the table, blocking my reach.

"Reia, I can contain it. I can hold it for you. It won't affect me the same way it affects everyone else. My magic—"

She cut off my words with another snarl of aggravation.

"Stop trying to be the hero. Stop trying to help where it is not welcome. I don't know how many times I have to tell you I do not want your help. But you can't seem to get it through your head, can you? Goddess bless, you're so fucking stubborn. You keep pushing, keep trying to be a part of something you have no business being a part of. You said it yourself; the goddesses would have chosen you. But they didn't, did they?"

Her words landed like knives in my chest. She *had* told me. Over and over again. When I'd first found her, she'd told me she hadn't wanted me there, and in Venridge she'd reiterated she had no need for my help. Maybe I had pushed. Maybe I had ignored a boundary simply because I had not wanted it to be there.

The thought sickened me, rolled nausea through my core. I had been following my instinct, my need to protect her, and I had thought she wanted to be around me, that when she'd tried to push me away, it had been born out of her own stubborn need to martyr herself.

And on top of it all was the confirmation, again, that she wanted nothing to do with even the idea that I could be a match for her.

It was all too much to bear. The emotions rolled through me, my thoughts buzzing as I tried to sort through the din of it all. I released a shaking breath and dipped my chin once in clear understanding.

If she did not want me there, then I would give her the peace she'd so clearly demanded.

I broke my gaze from hers, unable to bear the weight of it any longer, and turned to the door, swiping the glamour amulet from the table on my way out as I stormed from the room.

CHAPTER 53
AURELIA

It was my turn to pace incessantly, to work a line over the floor with my feet as I put forth significant effort into coiling the rage of my emotions back into their cage.

Out of control. I felt out of control. The source, the darkness, the unbridled rage, the aching of my bleeding heart, it was all too much to contain.

And Atlas had taken off in the middle of the night on his own. I wanted to be angry about that, but it had been my fault. I'd used words I'd known would hurt him, keep him angry enough to forget, for even just a brief moment, the way he felt about me.

Those words had pushed him away. I'd been made to turn over the look of agony as it crossed his expression, the pain he'd experienced at my cruelty a hundred times over since he'd run off.

My feet itched to go after him. I was sure he'd be somewhere to release some tension. If I went to the pub, he'd surely be there pretending to be someone else, putting forth effort to shirk off the pain. But I couldn't. I'd placed the hurtful words on purpose, hadn't I? I needed the distance between us. I needed him angry with me. It was the quickest way to get him past this.

"If you would ask me, I would tell you you're being a blathering idiot." Avery spoke, her voice startling me out of my daze.

"I thought you were asleep," I said, my tone rushed with surprise.

"After your tantrum? No," she replied through a huff of a laugh. "Do you want to talk about what's going on between you two?"

"Absolutely not," I dismissed, my tone heavy with finality.

"Too bad, I do. If I have learned anything in my time out in the field, it's that nothing good comes from going into dangerous territory with an unnecessary burden on your heart. And to me, it seems like *you* are placing that burden, and it is for certain unnecessary."

Irritation flushed me and I shot her a scowl as I continued pacing.

"Why is it so hard for any of you to leave me to wallow in my own misery?"

"Oh, easy," she said with a teasing brightness lifting her tone. "You are our one and only hope at taking that bastard out and getting our home back. We need you at your best. That, and it seems like just about everyone cares very deeply for you, despite your miserable attitude ninety nine percent of the time, so that's significant."

"Well, they shouldn't," I bit.

"Unfortunately for you, you do not get to decide how much someone cares for you. It's not in your control. The best you can do is not abuse what they choose to give you for it. And you are not doing a very good job at that with that male."

Pain lanced my heart as her words landed. Something

heavy pierced my resolve, and my shoulders sagged as a bit of the lingering misery cracked my furious exterior.

"What do you want me to do?" I asked, exasperated, throwing my hands out at my sides.

"I think you should go after him, repair some of the damage you've caused. You're not going to win any wars tearing a path of destruction through the people here to support you."

Avery's words landed as she stretched her arms over her head.

"I don't care how you do it, just fix it," she finished as she pulled a pillow down from behind her head to bring it to her chest, rolling over on her side to snuggle back into the bed.

Anxiety crawled over me as my eyes flitted to the dead-stone box on the table.

"I'll watch the box of doom, don't worry." She sighed through a yawn. "The others shouldn't be long. You go and get him. Gengi will blow his head if Atlas is gone when he gets back anyway."

I released a short breath and considered for a moment, but it turned out my muscles did not need much convincing to go after him in the night. I grabbed my cloak and curled my own freshly woven magic to glamour my appearance as I stole out into the cold to find Atlas.

BRENWYN

"Are you sure glamour magic doesn't work on you?" Emrys asked, speaking to the shadows as she spun her dagger over the heel of her hand with her shoulders leaning against the alley wall.

Her own glamour did not change her appearance much, just the color of her eyes from a pale periwinkle to a deep brown. I released my voice from the shadows I'd bled between.

"Yes," I breathed.

It was usually a significant effort to speak without pulling my body together, the magic required often draining, but this time it did not feel quite so difficult. Something about being in this town felt different. My shadows knit together quicker, more effortlessly, a sturdy kind of strength supporting my power.

Emrys peered into the open to get a view of the apothecary Laz and Gengi had ventured into.

"Okay, well they are taking forever. It's been over an hour. Come down so we can go inside."

I pulled myself together at a moment's notice, landing in the dark corner of the alley and narrowing my eyes at her.

"We were told to stay out of sight," I said.

Her wide eyes flared, and her lips curled with a mischievous smile as she sheathed her dagger at her hip. She held out her hand.

"We will." She wiggled her brow.

I thought about protesting, but I, too, had been anxious waiting on the pair. If something had gone wrong, we needed to be there.

I took Emrys's hand, and the cool tingle of her magic bled through my veins quickly. I watched her body fade from existence as her blanket of invisibility covered us both. I would have taken more time to offer praise over the unique ability, but she pulled me on before I had a chance to settle into the strange, tingling sensation.

We moved through the crowd on the strip, careful to weave between browsing citizens without bumping them to make our way to the apothecary. We waited for someone to open the door and slipped in after to avoid unwanted attention.

To my relief, we found Gengi and Laz over a counter, sifting through various gemstones, muttering to one another as they inspected each one.

Emrys led me to their side, and as we approached, Gengi jolted in surprise, a strangled sound escaping his throat as his eyes stretched wide. Laz looked up, alarmed.

"What?" they asked, their tone rushed.

"Emrys is with us," Gengi whispered as he shook off a shiver, the apples of his cheeks flushing a bright pink.

"I hate it when you do that," he continued with a singsong voice.

She released a soft chuckle.

"I'm here, too," I muttered quiet enough for the two of them to be the only ones to hear.

Laz's eyes stretched wide as they looked around to find me, their attention landing on nothing.

"What in the realms are you doing?" Laz whispered, their tone tense.

"Emrys's specialized talent happens to be the art of invisibility. And I thought we agreed you would keep watch in the alley until we were all done."

"You're taking forever," Emrys said, her tone soft. "We needed to be sure you were not compromised."

"No, just struggling to find the right conduit stone." Gengi sighed.

A frustrated breath escaped my resolve. I wanted nothing more than to just be ready to get back to The Capitol, but every step of this journey had proved to be a struggle. I rolled my neck and peeled my eyes from the tangle of stones, my attention stretching to scan the apothecary.

Nothing stood out as an immediate threat. The shop owner sat behind the counter reading a book while two other patrons took their time looking over herbs used for various tonics across the shop. They mused on in conversation, their voices a drone in my ear.

Just as I made to relax my awareness, my attention landed on a notice behind the counter. It was small, but the image there seized my muscles with momentary shock. The hand drawn sketch pulled every fiber of my focus. As I scanned the notice from afar, I found most of the scramble of letters was unreadable at this distance.

Something near my heart jolted and I tugged on Emrys's hand, moving her to the counter on silent feet to get a better look at the poster.

The full image of the parchment stole the breath from my lungs, a vivid kind of terror lancing my heart as my mind tuned over the words there while I worked to turn over the pit of dread deep within my core.

AURELIA

It did not take me long to figure out where Atlas had likely taken off too. The tension laced through Fenbrook's air weighed heavy, and most storefronts looked as though they could have been abandoned until I came close enough to see in their windows. I followed the strip until I found the bustle of nightlife, a singular tavern drawing a slight crowd. I knew it would be there. Every town had one.

The one consistency I could always count on, no matter the year, circumstance, anything. People needed release. Especially in the darkest of times. There would always be a space for that.

I was certain he'd be there. My confidence carried me on, blanketing the twisting of my heart as I approached.

Fix it.

How? What Avery had said weighed on me more than I was willing to admit. I *was* trying to control how much he cared for me. I had firmly decided to wedge space between us. He'd gotten too close.

But having to face his pain, the devastation my words had caused had been something I could not have prepared myself for. I didn't want to be the cause for his agony, his stress. I wanted to show him beautiful things, like willow moths glowing in the night. I wanted to go back to that tree, close the curtain of the branches, and leave the rest of the world behind.

Had I made a mistake? Should I have been honest the other night by the river, instead of choosing to drive him away?

I wasn't sure what the right answer was because I was certain caring for me the way he did would get him hurt or worse, but maybe I couldn't control that. Maybe the amount in which someone cared for me was not up to me. And he wasn't the only one at risk. Even the thought of the damage I'd already caused to Callista turned my stomach.

Maybe I could fix it but keep the distance, keep his heart separate from mine. Keep both their hearts separate from mine.

Although, I'd already laid the groundwork for hatred. I couldn't very well take that back, not without revealing everything I'd already failed so miserably at concealing.

I ran out of time to consider as I moved toward the door, slinking through drunk fae both coming and going from the entrance. A solid breath inflated my lungs before I stepped through the threshold into the darkened space.

The entire room had been blanketed in soft blue faelight cutting through the darkness, illuminating a surprising crowd of people as they moved to a sensual beat. The music urged on the crowd of dancers, lifting the energy of the room on booming wings of a fast-paced melody.

There were more people here than I expected, more life. The scene set my senses off-kilter as I worked to take it in. I'd hoped for a simple tavern with gambling, drunk patrons. Instead, I was greeted with a heated dance floor, one very similar to the one we'd found in Venridge.

He'd be in here. Deep within my core, I knew that for a

fact. Although, it would be more difficult to locate him in this tangle of bodies than it would have been otherwise.

I scanned the room, my eyes straining to find any sign of Atlas. The urgent beat quickened my pulse as my gaze fell on the writhing bodies. They moved on each other indecently, and the sight caused a hitch in the flutter of my heart.

I cursed under my breath as I failed to find him. His glamour sapped away his individuality, stole the silver tone from his hair and replaced it with an average brown. Impossible to tell apart from any of the others. Especially with all of them moving like that.

I heaved a tightened breath and tried to weigh the options. I could tunnel through the dancers or just turn around to head back. I could wait for him outside or for his return to the inn. He'd come back eventually, and then I could—

Mid-thought, just as I'd resigned myself to turning around, my gaze snagged on the familiar lines of his face halfway through the crowd. In that moment, I would have sworn the goddesses mocked me. They slowed time itself, the moments stretching to an impossible length as I watched the way his face tilted to the faelight. The glow wafted over his glamoured skin, highlighting the strong line of his nose, his jaw. His smile stretched wide as he moved his body to the beat, that dimple clear from even this distance.

Happy. He looked happy. And I was surely about to ruin that.

The twisting knot in my core turned to blades of dread, urging me to turn around, leave him to this relief, the bliss that had replaced the stretch of agony I'd placed there. He'd worn that pain only an hour or so prior, and now he looked as though he had been successful in leaving that behind. I couldn't take that from him. I wouldn't.

I tried. I truly tried to put forth effort into turning around, to leave the room and wait for him outside the pub. But my gaze seemed frozen on the male, the slowed sands of time keeping my feet planted firmly in place, my attention stuck in the trance of his beauty.

The crowd parted enough for me to see a woman moving against him. The suspended time snapped and the warmth that had flooded my core shifted into something cold as I stumbled, my feet trying to decide which direction to take me. A lump rose in my throat and my lungs shrieked for air as she turned around to press her backside into him, leaning her entire frame against his chest as his hands roamed over her stomach. Her head fell back into the crook of his shoulder, and he moved with her to the beat of the gyrating music.

I should have left. Why had I lingered so long? He was doing his best to let go of some tension, put what had happened between us behind him. Good. He deserved to after all I'd said to him. I needed to leave him be, turn around, wait in the room for him to return. I could wait in the room.

All of those thoughts seemed rational, entirely something I could accomplish, but I was stuck. Standing, staring. No, gaping at the two of them. I couldn't tear my eyes away as his hands traveled to her hips. A wild longing clattered through my chest. A strained desire to be the one to feel his touch, to spread that smile across his face. It chased away the despair I had been wrestling only moments prior. I had not allowed myself to linger in my own desires in all this time, but in that moment, I could not contain the curl of heat low within my core. I would have given anything to have his hands on me like that, have him look at me with that line of lust in his eye.

Oh goddesses, I need to leave.

But again, the goddesses mocked me. Maybe they gave him the ability to sense me, read my thoughts just long enough to torture me, because just as I'd managed to stumble a step backward, his wild eyes snapped up and they landed on mine. Atlas's furious stare burned a hole in my face, his smile faltering as his body stilled, his frame standing out among the still moving crowd. A strange sense of shame slithered over my skin, my stomach knotting with dread.

I should have left. Why hadn't I left?

But still, my gaze remained caught in his attention, snared as though the very flare in his focus had the ability to keep me still.

The knot in my stomach soured as he leaned down to whisper something to the woman. She curled through the crowd to find someone else to dance against, and Atlas began moving through the bodies toward me. I sucked in a breath as the distance between us pulled tighter, and I managed to turn for the door, making a significant effort to run away from the thundering of my own heart.

How had I gotten so far away from the door? Hadn't I just stepped inside? It was impossibly far away. Anxiety crawled over my chest as I darted, desperate to be free of this heated haze, but the moving crowd corralled me closer to the wall instead as I tried to move through them.

I made it no farther than a few steps, the door still too far away, the crowd of dancers not far behind before Atlas's hand met my elbow. The touch was gentle, but it sent a flush of vivid heat coursing through my veins as my heart seized. I stilled, every muscle in my body frozen at the contact.

"You followed me." His voice cut through the heavy music, the tone level, assessing.

I turned on my heel to face him, looking up into his eyes with the wings of my heart beating furiously against my ribs.

But I said nothing. My voice had been stolen. Another cruel trick of the goddesses.

"Why?" he asked.

His brow pulled together as his tone rose, his emotions close to the surface. And still, my breath remained trapped within my lungs, and I failed to bring my voice to my lips.

"Goddess damn it, Reia," he snapped, leaning back to run a hand over his chin in clear frustration. "What do you want?"

The question seemed weighted with more meaning than just those words implied. I could feel it, the way his soul reached out to mine, begged me for an answer that would quell his own storm of desires.

My heart thundered between my ears, and I opened my mouth to speak. A surge of energy gave me life, but the words fell short, and I sputtered.

"What do you want me to say?"

"I want you to be honest with me, with yourself for one goddess-damned moment."

I sucked in a breath as heat coiled beneath my skin, my living magic breathing at the raging inferno of emotion. I leveled with him for a moment and did my best to raise my strength, bring it to the surface so I could communicate anything.

Anything would be better than nothing.

He watched me, his eyes swimming, and he released a breath as he brought a hand to his chest.

"If you have nothing to say, I'd like for you to leave," he said, his tone low, laced with pain.

A hollow ache in my chest clamored to a cavern of agony as he turned over his shoulder. Panic lanced me, and my muscles sprung to life as if on instinct. I reached out and grabbed his hand, halting him where he stood. His muscles stiffened, and he turned to look at me with surprise over his features.

"Wait," I said, my voice strained. "Dance with me."

"*What?*" he hissed, rounding on me again, but his expression surprised me. It was twisted with frustration, devastation, disbelief. "Why would you think I'd want to dance with you?"

"I just . . . I'm sorry I thought we could be them, Enora and Keir. We could—"

"Oh," he said with a disbelieving, dark laugh splitting his voice. "I see. You only want me when it's pretend, do you? I suppose that makes sense. I'm the one that encouraged that charade, aren't I? Well, I'll tell you what: fuck that. This is *killing me*, Aurelia. If you want me, then you are going to have to want *me*."

He stepped closer and I stumbled back, my shoulders hitting the wall behind me, the heat of his frustration washing over me as he thrust a finger into his chest.

"*Me*. The person who has been here to scrape you off the ground every time you have fallen far enough to break. The person whose heart you tore out and left in the river the other night. That is the male you have to face now. Not Keir. Not some fantasy that allows you to leave behind how you feel for however long before you decide to pull my heart out of the depths again."

I gaped at him, my thoughts roiling as fast as my thundering heart. A pain cleaved in my chest as each word landed, and I wasn't sure how to sort through them in the chaos of my raging emotions. My fingers heated and my breath hitched as he leaned in closer, one hand on the wall near my head as he dipped his nose in close to mine, his sweet breath washing over my face, clouding my thoughts.

"I want you to tell me again," he said, his tone a low, grumbling warning. "Tell me, *with conviction*, that it is not me that you want."

Something broke deep within my core. A barrier that had been holding too much pressure finally cracked under the weight of this. I lost control of my limbs as the intensity of his eyes burned through mine and his breath tangled with my haze.

Before I could make sense of my own actions, his lips were on mine, the violent crash of a tidal wave breaking shore as my hands tangled in his hair, pulling him as close as I could. I arched my chest into his, and he released a guttural groan as he wrapped his arms around me, dragging me into him as though my body meant restoring the life within him.

His mouth parted for mine, and the rate at which I lost myself to him was alarming. I panted as I drank him in, my hands roaming his shoulders and neck as though I had never felt anything more significant in my life. His touch slid from my back to find my hips, and with one swift jerk of strength, he had his fingers gripped tightly around my thighs as he hiked me up to press my back to the wall, his hips pinning mine in place.

I gasped as his length ground into the sensitive warmth between my legs and my magic sparked to life, a curl of vibrant energy bleeding through my veins as his mouth found the sensitive spot at the base of my jaw. I tangled my fingers in his hair and another sharp breath pulled my chest taut. I felt the cooling draw of his magic as he pulled from mine.

Before I could take stock of what he was doing, that violent tug behind my navel jerked at my physical body and that blackened pressure around my head stole my vision as he hurtled us through space, *ephemerating* us to goddess knew where.

THE SENSATION WAS DIZZYING, absolutely and utterly disorienting.

We landed in an empty room of the inn, Atlas's hands still firmly gripped around my thighs as he turned to pin my back to the nearest wall again. I gasped at the sting of the impact as he continued his exploration of my neck. His lips forced a dizzying haze to roll a violent heat low in my core. I arched into him, tipping my hips to roll against his.

He groaned, the sound born of desperation as one of his hands moved to my waist, his fingers gripping me there as though he might lose me if he released a solid hold on me.

"Kiss me," I breathed, desperate to drink him in, to lose myself in the blinding light as it poured through the jagged cavities of my chest.

He obeyed, his face snapping back up to mine within a single breath, and his lips were parting mine again, drinking from me as though I might give him life.

I laced my fingers in his dark hair, still glamoured, and I met his desperation with my own, my chest heaving as I struggled to keep up with his frantic movements, the way his lips parted, the sweep of his tongue against mine. His hand at my waist roamed higher, the touch gentle, tentative as he found my breast.

"Yes," I managed to breathe between kisses, and the word sparked a fresh wave of hunger in him.

His grip tightened, and then he moved his nimble fingers to my nipple, giving it a gentle twist as he rolled his hips against mine. A whimper escaped my lips, and my muscles weakened as that heat consumed me, the curl low in my stomach driving a need between my legs, a desperation to have him sate it. I angled my hips to press my center to him, the swelling ache in my abdomen urging me closer, needing to feel him, to bleed the lines of my body with his.

At the curl of my hips, his beautiful lips turned up into a smile against mine and he released a soft chuckle, the sound undoing any amount of self-control I had left in my arsenal. The blinding light radiating through my chest was all-consuming, a desire to drown in his presence, the light brimming from his own soul a wild terror through my core.

Atlas tilted his head slightly, just enough to capture the line of my jaw with his lips again, and I leaned my head back to rest against the wall, my vision spinning with the thrill of his touch, my chest heaving with lost breath. I gripped the fabric at his shoulders, my knuckles turning white as desire drove my strength.

"So eager," he purred.

The sound of his curling, heated voice undid me. Everything I was, everything I had ever been melted away and I moaned and closed my eyes as his teeth grazed the sensitive flesh below my jaw.

"Do you want me to touch you like this?"

He released my breast and trailed his fingers down the planes of my stomach until the tips dipped closer to my pant line. The trail of his touch left my head spinning and I sucked in a breath as he leaned his hips away from mine, the absence of his warmth shocking.

He lifted his head to level his eyes with me, and I threaded my fingers through the tangles of his hair again as he brushed the tip of his nose to mine. He slid his touch below the line of my leggings, the pads of his fingers reaching the tuft of hair there. The sensation jerked my core, warmth pooling between my legs as my lungs stretched tight, starved for air.

My heart was going to explode. Straight out of my chest. I wasn't sure I was strong enough to handle this.

"Yes," I breathed, the sound a plea on my lips.

Goddess, yes. With every fiber of my being, I wanted him to curl his touch lower, find the desire waiting for him there.

The corner of his mouth twitched, a defiant yet triumphant

flare in his eyes, and my heart flipped, a wild, living beast within the cage of my chest. He slipped his fingers lower, and I bit my bottom lip to keep from groaning through the sensation of his skin. He kept his eyes trained on me, his furious gaze on my face, tracing the lines of my expression as though he were trying to memorize it.

His fingers found my clit and I thought I might pass out. The sensation was wild enough to send my consciousness hurdling through another realm of existence. He applied just enough pressure to urge a strangled sound from my throat and my eyelids fluttered closed. He slipped his fingers through my folds and a heated, lust-driven rumble released from somewhere deep within the cavities of his chest.

"You're so wet for me already," he crooned, pressing an open-mouthed kiss to the line of my jaw.

Fuck me.

The sound of his voice, the proud curl to his tone as it wound its way through my consciousness was almost enough to bring me to completion on its own. I tilted my hips, a silent plea for him to explore further, and he tsked. The disapproving sound sliced through the whirling fantasy of my thoughts. I opened my eyes to find a light in his, the glimmer there made of pockets of starlight. Something aching but sweet burst behind my heart.

This male was going to be the end of me.

"Use your words." He leaned in to drag his nose from my collarbone up to my ear, and I could not control the shiver as it snaked my spine, the gooseflesh as it rose over my arms. "I want to know exactly how much you are enjoying this."

"Atlas." I gasped, my voice still a plea.

Without warning, he slipped one finger into me. A mangled sound escaped my throat, my heart thundering against my chest as I leaned into him, gripping the fabric at his shoulders to steady myself, but he leaned in, pinning my back to the wall again as he increased the pressure of his hand at my core. My eyes rolled back, and I writhed against him, desperate to feel more.

I needed more.

"What was that?" he asked, his tone laced with authority, a lilting tease of false innocence there.

"*Fuck*, you are going to kill me." I groaned through gritted teeth, and he pulled his fingers free, dragged his touch up to circle the bundle of nerves just once before he pulled his hand up again.

I leaned my head against the wall, disappointment cleaving my resolve as I took a moment to regain my breath. My eyes flipped to the ceiling, but my gaze did not stray far as he gripped my jaw with firm fingertips and straightened my face to look at him again.

Sharp surprise pulled a gasp free of my lungs at the intensity of the movement, and my voice froze in my throat. My eyes stretched wide, and a curl of heat moved through me. Frustration laced with an extreme and unyielding desire; it claimed my actions as I yanked back on my grip just enough to tilt his chin, his neck exposed as I took control.

He sucked in a breath. Heated desire a fire in his eyes.

"I want you to take me to that bed and fuck me until I have no control over my senses. Immediately." I forced as much authority into my shaking tone as I could manage, and a wicked smile turned up the corners of his mouth.

A challenge rested there I wasn't sure I had the strength to meet, but goddess bless, I would try.

In one swift, sturdy movement, he spun me away from the wall, both hands gripped firmly around my thighs again to support my weight. The shift was dizzying, and I gripped the fabric at his shoulders again. It took him two long strides to get to the edge of the bed. He slowed as we approached and lowered me to the mattress, leaning his weight over me with a tenderness I thought might cut my heart from its very spot in my chest. He shifted until his nose was close to mine, our breath mingling, his wild eyes pinned to my attention.

"Tell me you want this," he breathed, tipping his chin to dust his bottom lip over my parted mouth.

My breath hitched in my throat and my vision spun. The hairs on the back of my neck stood on end and a knot in my lower stomach twisted as the final word to his plea fell.

"*Me,*" he continued.

A pain twisted in my chest, and I had to fight the onslaught of tears as they burned behind my eyes. I brought my hands to his face, cradling the line of his jaw as I worked to find the strength to bring the honesty to my lips and repair some of the hurt I still saw glimmering there.

Something in his expression cracked as I struggled to find my words, and he brought his thumb up to my cheek to brush it along my jawline, his own jaw tense with visibly clenched teeth as he waited for my answer to fall.

Panic gripped me. I would not ruin this; I couldn't. I scrambled to sift through the emotions, find the words, and they fell from my lips with a desperate breath. My heart was a wild beast as it raged to be closer to him.

"I want this. I want you. Goddess bless, I want to give you more words. Prettier words. Words strong enough to explain to you how exactly I feel about you, but I can't. They don't exist. I want you. I need you, Atlas."

His eyes glimmered as he took in what I'd said, listened with bated breath. As my confession fell between us, some crushing weight lifted from his shoulders, and before I could catalogue exactly what his change in expression might mean, he leaned in to tangle his lips with mine. A feverish need drove my desire to match his pace, one more wild even than it had been moments prior.

I worked to take it in, keep up with the rushing torrent of emotions as I arched into his touch, my hands roaming the planes of his shoulders and chest. His fingers found the hem of my shirt and in one swift movement, he pulled it over my head, exposing me to cool air.

Without missing a beat, he trailed his lips from the line of my jaw to my navel, each touch sending an explosion of sensations straight through to my very soul. Before I could grapple with the loss of his weight over me, he pulled my leggings off as he rose to his feet again.

It was a swift change, and I followed him with instinct driving me through the haze of my desire as I pulled myself up to my knees, every inch of my bare skin alight with vivid need. I reached up and gripped his face in my hands, sucking his bottom lip into my mouth again as I arched my bare chest into his. He moaned and wrapped his arms around my waist, but the sound ended on a soft chuckle as he peeled his face from mine.

I furrowed my brow and offered him a pout as he took a step back, his hands slipping from my waist as he left me on my knees, bare before him, the space between us feeling too distant.

"What are you doing?" I asked, tight anxiety lifting my tone.

He offered that dazzling half smile before hooking his fingers under the hem of his own shirt, and he pulled it over his head. The sight of his carved muscle, the planes of his chest and abdomen stole my attention. That heat curled tighter, the pooling of desire between my legs difficult to ignore.

"I want to look at you," he said, his voice a low rumble, a heated breath as it curled around my desire.

His fire-stoked gaze roamed my bare flesh, his expression one of unfiltered need as he undid his belt and dropped his trousers to the floor, all the while keeping his eyes trained on mine.

I found myself utterly incapable of holding his gaze as he stood before me, every inch of him carved from marble, a godlike, statuesque picture of a male. My mouth went dry, and I lost my ability to keep clear trains of thought altogether.

I bit my lip, an exerted effort to keep my jaw from slackening, and sat back on my feet as he took a step toward the edge of the bed again. I swallowed a lump in my throat as he approached. He slipped a hand in the hair at the base of my neck, tangling his fingers at the roots, and tilted my face up to look at him with a soft jerk. A silent demand laced through the gesture and pulled a sharp gasp from my lips.

"You are a goddess," he whispered and stroked a thumb across my cheek.

I nearly choked on the swelling emotion. Too much. This was nearly too much. I couldn't think, couldn't pull an even breath. I needed him. Every inch of my body screamed a plea for his. I wanted everything, his hands, his lips, his heart, his soul. And more significantly, the desire to give just as much of myself radiated from my core.

I brought my hands up to grip his hips and steady myself, an aching desire to turn my own mouth to use at his length driving my need. But to my surprise, he moved too. Sliding my hands from his hips, he knelt on the bed in front of me. My muscles went slack but he gripped my hips to turn me with a tender touch until he was able to press my back to his chest. He positioned my legs so that I was nearly sitting on his lap. He brought one hand up to my throat to rest there, the sensation curling that wild need again, and I leaned my head back into the crook of his neck.

His breath in my ear sent pinpricks of sensation over every inch of my skin. I gripped his wrist at my throat with a gasp, and he nipped at my ear with his teeth as he positioned his length at my entrance. I yelped at the sensation and leaned back into him.

"I want you to ride me," he whispered, and my breath hitched as he tilted his hips, teasing me enough to elicit another surprised gasp.

I found it difficult to maintain control, but I did as he asked, leaning back as his hand moved to support my weight with a grip around my waist. I cried out as he split my core in two, and his other hand made its way around to the bundle of nerves between my thighs without hesitation. Another cry split my throat as his touch sent stars dazzling through my vision. I reached up to steady myself with a grip on his hair behind my head, and his fingers began slow, punishing circles while he thrust into me, the movement of his hips also deliberate, slow, meant to drive me into a coiling frenzy over time.

I whimpered, the sound mangled through desperation, and he released another one of those chuckles, lighting every nerve on my body on fire as his breath washed over my neck. He moved to graze his teeth over the shell of my ear and rolled his hips again, curling that swelling pressure tighter between my legs as his fingers moved quicker.

"I believe I gave you an instruction," he purred in my ear, and what little breath I had left coiled from my lungs. "Ride me."

The sensations of his fingers were overwhelming, and I began to move, rocking with him as he continued to coil the tension between my legs tighter.

"That's it. You like that, don't you?" His voice was a rumble low in my core, and something in my soul shattered at the sound of his approval.

I let out a strangled whine and rolled my head back to his shoulder as my pleasure came to a crest, the coiled heat ready to explode, to send me hurdling over the edge.

And just as the cry began to leave my lips, the moment my release brightened between my legs, he sat up, his hand leaving my clit, but he had a sturdy grip on my waist. Shock flushed my resolve as the crest of release flushed free, and I yelped as he tilted me forward so that I landed on my elbows, all while keeping himself buried within me.

Atlas tucked a knee between my legs and kicked them apart, leaving room to position himself behind me. He released my waist to take a firm grip on my hips and thrust into me from behind. I cried out as the sensation of him stretched me, the pleasure in my core rocking my consciousness into another realm.

I managed to turn to peer at him over my shoulder, flinging my hair out of the way to see his powerful claim on me. His eyes lit with hunger as they met mine. He reached around my thigh to take up the circling of my exploding nerves with his fingers again as his chest pressed firmly to my shoulders.

"Oh fuck, Atlas," I breathed, the tension built there still lingering, ready for him to send me over the edge.

"I asked you a question," he purred, grinding his hips against my ass.

The pressure of his length inside me sent spots dancing through my vision. The strangled sound as it escaped my throat at the way he churned against me was unlike any uttered from my voice before.

"Do you like the way this feels?" he asked again.

"Yes," I breathed, my voice a tatter in my throat.

"Do you want me to make you cum?"

He gripped my hip tighter, and I choked out another mangled *yes* in response as he continued to circle my clit with his strong fingers. He picked up his pace, rocking me with every powerful claim.

My chest heaved as that tightness curled in my lower stomach, my voice coming out in pleading pants and moans as he brought me to the edge of ecstasy. It didn't take long. I was already there, already ready to come apart for him.

And again, just as my body told him I was there, my muscles shaking and my cries strangled, he released me, pulling himself free. He hooked his hand around my stomach to bring me back up to sit in his lap, my back pressed against his chest again.

"*Fuck,*" I hissed as disappointment caved my chest in, my desire a breathing beast needing to be sated.

"Not yet," he breathed, pressing an achingly tender kiss to the nape of my neck.

Atlas hummed with pleasure as his fingers danced over my arms, and I sucked in a breath at the familiar sensation of his magic pulling at mine, a sharp pang of surprise tugging at the edges of my awareness.

"I want to be looking at *you* when you cum for me, not your glamour. Aurelia, I want to see *you*," he said, his tone soft as he released his hold on me.

My heart lurched, and I twisted in his lap. The glimmer in his eye, the adoration in his expression overwhelmed me. He leaned in to press a tender kiss to my lips, tipping my body until I lay flat on my back. He propped his weight on one elbow at the side of my head, his chest hovering over mine delicately as he dusted his fingertips over my cheek.

He kept his gaze pinned on mine, the overwhelming emotion I saw there echoing my own, and I could have wept at the sight. His touch trailed lower, the flutter of his fingers trailing the raised scar between my breastbone. I sucked in a breath as chill bumps raised the small hairs along my arms, but I held his gaze, not daring to break this moment.

And still his touch trailed lower, a curling sensation winding over my ribs until he found the evidence of my torture.

My heart lurched and I gripped his wrist on instinct, a sudden flush of fear washing my blood into a frigid stream.

"It's alright," he whispered, his muscles frozen. "Stay with me, Feathers."

My breath stretched tight, and I found it difficult to work through the sudden tangle of uncontrollable fear and anxiety. But he leaned in to brush his nose to mine, and the sweet gesture rolled a sense of comfort through my tense muscles. I closed my eyes and willed my muscles to relax, my grip still taut on his wrist.

"Aurelia," he breathed as his lips dusted my cheek, his breath a warmth over my skin. "I am here with you."

I offered a soft nod and released a breath.

"I will not move without you. Take your time. I am here."

A pressure in my chest cracked and it was an effort to keep the prick of tears at bay as his words pierced the haze of anxiety. My heart bled free of the cage of nerves and warmth flushed my veins. My breath came easier as a weight lifted from my chest.

I relaxed my grip on his wrist, keeping my eyes pinned to his. He did not touch the scars over my stomach, though. Instead, he offered a glimmer of a smile and brushed his knuckles over my cheek, a pained glimmer in his eye.

"I'm sorry. Do you need to be done?"

I shook my head, a violent crash of emotion cracking my resolve as even the kindness of those words landed on my chest. I gripped his face and curled into the lines of him as I claimed his mouth with mine. The bright beams of my heart reached out to his and every inch of my skin lit with the need to feel his again. The corners of my soul made room for his.

He tangled his fingers in my hair and leaned into the kiss, his tongue sweeping against mine as he pressed one palm to my cheek.

Just as before, the dragging sensation of his magic pulled at the contact, the dizzying torrent added to the haze of passion consuming me. The draw intensified, and the magic of my glamour bled away, the color returning to my hair, skin, and eyes.

He pulled back and his gaze swam as he took me in. A wild heat simmered in his expression; it was difficult for me to process. It stole the breath from my lungs. I met his stare, a firm intensity locked between us as I reached between us to grip his glamour amulet. Without a word, I yanked until the chain snapped and tossed the thing to the floor.

I watched as his hair faded from black back to white, his rounded ears stretched to return to their normal pointed shape, and the familiar glow of his violet eyes returned, the darkness of his glamour gone. I did not expect the gravity of the welling emotion as it clamored through my soul. A pin cracked my chest as I choked on a sob. He furrowed his brow and took my face in his hand as he brought his forehead to mine.

"Hey," he whispered, his tone gentle, "where did you go?"

I shuddered through the wracking of my chest and took in a heaving breath, doing my best to steady my breathing.

"Nowhere, I'm here. With you," I managed as I brought my hands up to smooth his hair.

"Okay. We can stop. Did I hurt you?" he asked with concern under his tone.

"Goddess, no," I breathed through a laugh and tilted my chin to claim his mouth again.

"I'm fine. I'm okay," I assured him between kisses, but he tensed.

"Are you sure?" he said as he pulled back to look at me again.

"Atlas, I am alright. I am here with you. I want you. Please. Goddess bless, I need you," I said, my words firm but clipped, my chest heaving as I did my best to describe the torrent of vivid bliss radiating within my heart.

He searched my expression for a long moment, looking for a hint of discomfort, evidence that I had been covering my truth. When he found none, he relaxed and released a breath.

"Well, it *would* be horrifically rude of me to edge you so many times and not allow you to finish. I think, if you're alright, I would at least like to let you get your release, if you are absolutely sure that's what you want," he said with a quirk of a smile, some concern bleeding from his tone as he tilted his hips into mine.

"Fuck, yes. *Please*," I panted.

A smile curled over his expression, and he moved, shifting his weight to trail kisses along the length of my neck, breastbone, stomach, and every inch until he claimed my core without warning. I cried out as the sensation sent my soul soaring through time and space, bursts of stars clouding my vision. Mangled sounds of pleasure filled the room, and I arched into his tongue as I gripped his hair in both hands, holding his face to me.

I was already there; my pleasure required no build this time. He groaned, his fingers digging into my hips as his tongue brought me over the edge, the burst of sensation sending tremors through my muscles, my entire body convulsing as I turned over on my side and released my grip on his hair.

I heaved shaking breaths and curled in on myself. My muscles shook, the ecstasy still rocking through me as he climbed back up the length of my body, his tender hands moving me to curl my frame into his chest. I melted into him as his hands stroked my hair, pulled me into his embrace, the waves of pleasure still tipping my awareness.

His chin fell to the top of my head, and he offered calming words, soothing sounds as he helped me come down. He stayed there, unmoving while he offered comfort for longer than I could have been aware of.

Eventually, I managed to tip my chin to look up to him, and he pressed a tender kiss to my forehead, his fingers tracing lines over my shoulders and back. My mind came back to me, but exhaustion had clouded my vision, and a comforting weight settled over my resolve. I reached up to run my fingers through his silvery hair and blinked slowly, sleep pulling at the edges of my resolve.

"You can sleep. This is one of our rooms. Gengi has it protected with a charm. You're safe. I've got you." he offered with a soft smile, and I tried to protest, to say anything.

But the calming draw of his magic washed over me, and my eyes fluttered closed as the warmth of his arms pulled me through the void of unconsciousness.

CHAPTER 56
BRENWYN

Gengi furiously scribbled on a piece of parchment against the stone alley wall. Every one of us had changed our course of action the moment I'd brought attention to the notice behind the counter, all desperate to close the distance between ourselves and The Capitol.

Laz stood stoic with a tense expression, an echo of terror in their emerald eyes while Emrys and I kept watch so Gengi could get the message he needed to Despina. I'd since learned the solar witch had not returned a message for over a week. The trio of females had been on their way to the blight, so ideally they were close, and we would gather as much muscle as we could before making our next move.

At the very least, having a second witch on hand would help Gengi construct a conduit strong enough to maintain that monstrosity the firebird had pulled from the earth.

"Alright," Gengi said, his tone stretched thin with anxiety, "sending now."

Emrys nodded but held her position near the mouth of the

alley firm. I curled my shadows from within my core and pulled a wall of darkness from the depths of the stone to shroud us in the black magic, an effort to conceal the solar magic Gengi would have to use to send the parchment.

I turned to watch Gengi as he held the parchment in front of his face with a focused eye. The edges of the folded paper lit with the ember glow of solar power before light bloomed and the parchment folded in on itself, sending the message through the pockets of the realm to wherever Despina waited on the other side.

"Now what?" I asked, still holding my shadows over us.

"We wait for their response. I told her we would be waiting so it should come relatively—"

Gengi began, but a burst of that same light filled the space again, except this time it was tangled with darkness, black plumes of poison curling through the space in which the note had just disappeared. The parchment snapped into existence again, its edges blackened, touched by some wicked magic in just the short few moments it had taken in its travel to Despina.

It fluttered to the ground and Gengi gaped at it, clear surprise stretching his expression.

"Was that supposed to happen?" I asked, worry under my tone.

"Absolutely not," Gengi replied as he bent down to pick up the ruined message.

Laz stepped forward to pluck the paper from Gengi's grip. They rubbed the charred edge of the parchment between their fingers and their eyes stretched wide with vivid concern, a tinge of fear slackening their jaw.

"The blight," they said, dread weighing on their voice. "Whoever this note was intended for is in the blight."

ATLAS

I had never felt so whole. The jagged, broken shards of my soul had been that way for so long, clattering around inside my chest, adding to the scars there. They had been mended, somehow pushed back together, meticulously aligned by every breath, every touch, every press of her lips to mine.

Every sound elicited from her voice as her pleasure came at my touch. Every curve of her body is it fit fluidly into the lines of mine.

Overwhelming and utterly unbelievable. Every moment spun through a golden-tinged haze as I turned them over in my mind.

The entire thing had moved so quickly, every action launched from a place of frantic desire, a need to be close to her, to memorize every flashing moment.

I tried to memorize everything. Her voice, her warmth, the way she'd said my name, the expressions her beautiful features twisted into as she lost herself. The way her body trembled, her heaving breaths after release and the way she'd curled into me, resting against my chest as though my arms would keep her own rattling pieces together. The soft flutter of her eyelids as she drifted to sleep, the heaviest of burdens lifted from the strong line of her shoulders.

Goddess bless, I would have given anything to have this moment, feel her skin against mine, measure the steady rise and fall of her breath as she rested, recovered from the earth-shattering bliss.

My heart sprouted wings somewhere in the middle of it. No longer a dark and twisted thing, bound by briars, its ability to fly clipped. No, now it soared, great feathers lifted from the aftermath of my raw connection to this female in my arms. It beat against the cage of my chest, the space there still too small for its need to fly. I felt as though I could hook my fingers under the cage of my ribs and pry it open, give my heart enough space to fly straight to hers.

A golden light seemed to have washed over the room, the very particles of dust in the air alight with the glowing embers of the fire in the hearth.

Nothing mattered. Nothing but this: her head on my chest as I traced soothing lines over her shoulders. I prayed to the goddesses that it would last. Forever, ideally. A perfect, suspended moment in time. I wanted nothing more than to stay here, away from the danger I knew lay outside that door, the despair and pain everyone had been through. The pain still to come.

At least let me have the night. I called the silent plea to the goddesses with a heavy sigh. *Just tonight.*

It was as though they heard me, and the answer was an overwhelming, resounding "no." Nearly the moment I'd sent my thoughts to the goddesses, the door swung open and it crashed against the wall. The sound sent a flush of alarm through my core.

Reia started and I pulled the blanket up to cover her as I

shifted to move her behind me with one swipe of my arm, sitting up straight to face whoever had intruded on our peace.

It took me a moment to categorize who stood before me. Confusion twisted my expression as the strained panic fled, but my face stayed lifted with alarm.

"Oh, shattered source," Gengi nearly shouted, his tone laced with frustration, edged with anxiety. He threw a hand out in frantic panic as he held up his other to shield his eyes, the gesture dramatic. "What the fuck?"

"Gengi!" Reia shouted in surprise as she moved to conceal herself behind me.

"What do you mean 'what the fuck?' What the fuck are you doing?" I asked, exasperated anger lifting my tone.

"What the fuck are *you* doing?" Gengi shouted back, still shielding his eyes but flailing the other arm dramatically. "I honestly cannot believe—oh, goddess bless."

"Why would you break in here like that! Get out!" I shouted.

"Because we've been looking for both of you for ages! We need to go. *Now.*"

"In the middle of the night?" I asked, incredulous, but Reia peeked over my shoulder.

"Why?" she added, her tone tense.

"Mage, Despina, and Mila are caught in the blight," he began, his voice rushed, and Reia interrupted as she slid from the bed to begin retrieving her clothes.

"What? How long?" she asked.

"I don't know, a week maybe, and—"

"Okay, what do we know about the blight?" I asked, following suit.

"Nothing, but—"

"I need—" Reia began, but Gengi cut her off again.

"Shut up for one bleeding second!"

Surprise flushed me and I looked to Gengi as I pulled my pants on.

The words that next fell dropped a stone straight through to the pit of my core, rattling my ability to catch any of my buzzing trains of thought. Gengi's voice cracked a terror in my chest I was sure would stay with me until my dying day.

"That's not all. We need to get to Despina and Mage, but Callista is set to be executed at week's end. We need to get to The Capitol. Immediately."

CHAPTER 58
MAGE

rip. Drip. Drip.

I could not tell if the sound was real, still a part of the physical realm, or if I had imagined it again. The water as it broke against stone was the only constant I'd had to keep my mind centered for days. The chilled darkness of the cave was all-consuming, suffocating. It had wiped all sense of time, reality.

Drip. Drip. Drip.

The sound was solid. Not a figment of my imagination. I took a breath and focused on the haze of my thoughts, reaching out to my left to see if Despina still sat next to me.

She was there. My hand met hers and she offered my fingers a squeeze. Her warmth grounded me. She was real, her stability, her love, her comfort.

That stability had been the only thing helping me hold on to my sanity—turning over golden-flecked memories from a time before.

I took a shuddering breath as I shifted my weight, my feet asleep under me from having my legs cramped for so long.

So long. So quiet.
We had to be.
Our lives depended on it.

CHAPTER 59
AURELIA

"Are you strong enough?" Atlas asked, concern lifting his tone as I secured my weapons in their spots on my leathers.

Goddess knows.

I released a tight breath as I glanced to Gengi, who worked with Laz on his knees to finish charming the conduit he'd been furiously trying to repair. The pair worked with a small, glowing faelight overhead, the sun not yet risen in the east. Emrys, Avery, Atlas, and Brenwyn stood in a circle around us keeping watch, inspecting the dark trees on the edge of Fenbrook's city line.

I worked to suppress the wild tangle of emotions curling through my core. The terror at knowing Callista was up for execution. That I'd waited too long, let myself get too distracted. We were out of time.

The surge of frantic panic at that thought made it difficult for me to think straight. I needed to center myself, focus on one task at a time.

"Gengi?" I asked, pointedly ignoring Atlas's question.

"Oh, the lack of response instills a significant amount of confidence in me, yes," Atlas griped, and although the line of concern in his tone urged me to respond, I could not.

"Almost." Gengi also chose to ignore Atlas, his tone low, weighed down with concentration.

Anxiety doused my resolve. The crawl of it chased away any space I had for comfort, for relishing in the bliss of being wrapped in Atlas's arms, the ecstasy of letting go, being so close to him, releasing the burdens shackling me if even for a few hours.

I'd give anything to have had a night to set everything aside, relish the bliss of how my heart had wrapped itself around his. But I couldn't.

My punishment for this lapse in judgement, my inability to make sound choices was this nightmare of a space in which someone I loved was at risk. This time of losing her life.

Goddess bless, how could I let this happen? I'd tried to be so careful. Gather enough strength to save her from that terror of a male. I needed to be strong enough, just this once. She needed me to be. The entire realm needed me to be.

But I'd waited too long. I'd taken too long. I'd let my heart distract me.

I needed to get to The Capitol. I'd almost taken off on my own. I would have without a second thought, but Mage and Despina. They were in danger. I couldn't very well let them rot in the blight either. The thought of losing either of them proved to be a weight too difficult to bear as well.

I worked the inside of my cheek between my teeth, a sour attempt to quell the raging fear within my chest, but I could not contain the dread, the terror as it cracked some of my carefully crafted composure.

I took a steadying breath. The execution notice had said we had days. Plenty of time to get to Mage, Despina, and Mila first.

If only Gengi would hurry the fuck up.

"I don't like how this forest feels," Brenwyn said, her eyes searching the wood, scanning the canopy of trees with a furrow over her brow.

"What do you mean?" Emrys asked.

"It's not right. Something feels . . . different," the wraith nearly murmured.

"I can't feel anything," Avery offered.

Brenwyn turned to meet my eye, a question there. I nodded. I felt it, too. A lingering presence in the trees, something pressed up against the edges of my senses, setting an alarm off in my well of magic.

"I can," I assured her.

"So can I," Atlas said, snapping my attention to his, a spike of anxiety flushing my awareness.

I had not expected anyone else to sense it. Brenwyn and Atlas's ability to detect the abnormality set my nerves on edge.

The crystal reacted to the darkness here as well, the darker tendrils of its tendency to overcome me reaching out more vividly. The shard pulsed with bleeding life as we approached the trees on the outskirts of Fenbrook, raging against something as though it did not want to be near it. I could feel it deep within the hollow of my bones. The thing had been begging me to take it away, back to the Darkwood.

"What is it?" Emrys asked.

"I don't know," Brenwyn replied. "I don't like it, though."

"Done," Gengi said, breaking the tense air lingering in the aftermath of Brenwyn's confession.

I bent over to pick up the deadstone box and Gengi rose from his place on the ground, a small metal cage made of winding circles in his hands. The garnet crystal he'd used as the conduit looked nearly black in the dark shroud of the forest.

"Is that going to work?" Atlas asked, tense fear lining his tone.

"No way to know until we know," Avery said.

I took a breath and steeled myself, prepared to move quickly before opening the box. The second the lid cracked, a raging torrent of darkness thundered through my chest, the sensation nearly taking with it the stability in my knees. The forest hissed in response, a clamoring chorus of deadly whispers and violent hisses in protest as the source broke free of the bind around it. I gritted my teeth and took the conduit from Gengi, quick to clamp the metal circles around the source crystal.

The raging sound dizzied my senses, nearly setting me off balance, but I managed to lock the mechanism in place. The second the conduit took hold of the out-of-control darkness, the pressure against my chest subsided, the howling sounds of the spirits in the wood ceasing as though they had never existed. I took the thing and turned it over in my hand.

I could feel it, the power there, but it was more controlled, the vibrant darkness trapped somewhere within the garnet. I called to my magic, gently urging it to prod at the energy radiating from the source crystal. The two twined together as though old friends and a wild flush of heat made its way in currents through my well.

"Well?" Gengi asked, his expression pinched with nervous energy.

I offered a nod and met his eye.

"It seems to be working."

Relief cracked the tension on his shoulders and a long breath passed his lips.

"Great," Avery said with a loud clap. "Let's go kick some blight monster ass."

CHAPTER 60
BRENWYN

My feet landed with an unnecessarily violent thud and the gutted sound tearing from my throat was altogether embarrassing. A vicious bout of nausea curled my stomach as that pang behind my naval wound a wicked sensation through my conscious mind.

My head hurt. Oh goddess, my head hurt.

Why would anyone ever travel this way?

"Are you alright?"

It took me a moment to gather that the firebird had spoken to me. I had my hands on my knees, heaving breaths as I tried to steady my spinning vision.

"I wish you'd just let me get here on my own, goddess damn it," I grumbled irritably.

"With what map?" Avery asked, her tone laced with irritation.

I shot her a glare from under my brow.

The firebird had used her freshly restored magic to somehow *ephemerate* all of us. Although, we were supposed to land at the base of the mountain range, and when I managed to look up from my knees, I found that we were in no such place. Instead, the sight before me illuminated by the light of dawn chilled the very hollow of my bones.

"What is this," I breathed, terror gripping my resolve.

"The blight," Emrys answered, her tone surprisingly level.

But it wasn't, not yet. We still stood with our feet on plush green grass, a span of healthy, vibrant trees at our backs. But just inches in front of my toes lay a valley of charred earth, the very stones in the ground made of a striking obsidian material. Everything was different over the line of the blight. The trees, though sparse, were twisted and mangled, charred as though burned to a crisp. The sunlight seemed to shine through the atmosphere there differently, a grey tinge to it as though a haze of darkness shrouded the space.

Something deep within my core, my very well of power, rattled, begging to be free. The beast sprung to life, reaching for the darkness there, desperate to soar across the ashen desert of ruined land. The very blood in my veins seemed to vibrate against the strange blight in front of me. It startled me, forced the breath from my lungs.

"We won't be able to use magic in there," Laz said, and all heads snapped to them.

"What?" Atlas bit, his tone vicious, laced with panicked venom.

Laz remained calm.

"The blight is just that. It is free of life. The core of magic here does not exist."

"You could have thought to mention that before we wasted time on the conduit," Gengi snapped.

"I have reason to believe Aurelia will be able to wield the source. The rest of us, though, we will be vulnerable," Laz said.

The firebird looked to Atlas, a frantic energy lifting her expression as her breathing quickened.

"I go alone then," she said, moving her eyes away to look out into the blight.

"No!"

"You can't."

"Not a fucking chance."

The voices came from Atlas, Gengi, and Avery all at once as their protests overlapped each other.

"I can't take any of you in there if you can't defend yourselves. Laz, are you sure?"

They nodded curtly, an intensity over their expression.

"How can you know that?" Atlas asked, his tone edged with accusation.

Laz looked to him; their gaze sharp.

"Either you believe me, or you do not," they said. "That's your choice. I just wanted to prepare you."

"Alright," I interjected before anyone had a chance to offer any retort. "We are still functioning under urgency, and as far as I was aware, wasting time arguing about shit like this was not on the agenda."

"She's right. We need to go. There's no telling where Mage, Despina, and Mila are." Gengi looked to the firebird, a plea in his expression.

She looked back at him, careful consideration in her eyes as her internal struggle splayed across her expression. I rolled my eyes and released a frustrated breath.

"I'm not waiting for you to finish brooding," I bit and gave in to the urge within my core, that desperate pull drawing me into the blight.

The others shouted as I stepped through, but their voices were lost as my body moved through the line of the blight. A strange pressure blocked my ears and my skin chilled, gooseflesh rising as an oddly comforting flush of darkness washed over me. My feet landed on the other side and the screaming in my bones ceased, the ache in my chest lulled.

I felt lighter, my energy somehow lifted. I turned on my heel to look to the others, tell them they had not much to fear, but confusion and anxiety settled into my core as I found an empty green forest on the other side of the line. They were gone.

I looked around, whipping my attention frantically, but found nothing. I moved toward the line again, but before I could take a step, the air there rippled and the firebird stepped through, an expression of rage twisting her features.

Within a beat, the others followed suit, one by one falling over the line of the blight.

"Goddess damn you. Could you find it within yourself to cooperate just once?" Atlas shot; his voice clipped as he moved to stand next to the firebird.

I shrugged a shoulder.

"You were taking too long."

"Oh, good goddesses," Avery heaved. "This feels fucking awful. No more bickering. I want to find them and get the fuck out of here immediately."

I furrowed my brow; my eyes meeting Laz's as Avery's words fell. I felt fine, great even. How was it possible that everyone else seemed drained of life, the pallor of sickness coating their skin, their eyes darkening under the haze of the blight?

The others stepped on, gingerly moving a few feet into the ashen land, trying to find a direction to travel, and I stayed staring at Laz.

"Whatever comes next." They nodded, and something in my chest seized.

I could not bring any words to my lips as I nodded before we moved to follow the others through this desert of darkness.

CHAPTER 61
MAGE

It had to have been days. We'd gone through what we'd had left in our water skins, and hunger had rooted itself deep within the chambers of my core. The wild beast of starvation had weakened my already worn muscles.

Despina's hand in mine moved, startling me. I jumped in surprise, but she reached over to offer comfort in placing her other hand on my breastbone. I reached back, my palm on her chest. The rhythm of her heartbeat under my touch proved to be a thunderous rapture.

Fear and dread had already begun to give way to a strange, morbid sense of acceptance. We had no way of measuring time in this cave, no ability to detect the monstrous creatures of the blight. Not until it would be too late.

We'd only barely managed to escape last time, scraping by with wounds that had still not healed entirely. Mila had suffered the greatest damage, a solid hit to her head that had crushed her cheekbone. She'd been unconscious for days, only recently waking to the darkness, startled enough to make sound.

It had drawn them closer. The terrible creatures could not see but had ears sharper than anything I'd ever seen. The skittering of their crustaceous legs sounded in the distance, over the ruined ground of the open blight.

We'd all been quiet since.

We'd surely die here if we couldn't find a way to get past them soundlessly. With no ability to use magic and no way to tell where they were or even how many there had been, we were stuck.

Despina made to move, to shift her weight, and horror struck me when she rolled to her knees and aimed her body for the entrance of the cove, the opening to the small tunnel we'd curled ourselves into. I sucked in a breath and reached out to grip her arm and stop her.

I had grown used to the theft of my vision, but in this moment, as she placed her hand over mine and slid my touch from her arm to keep moving, the pressure of the void seemed impossible to manage. Once she was far enough away, I'd have no way to know where she was.

Terror gripped me and I reached for Mila, who tensed as I touched her arm. She shifted and moved closer, pressing her shoulder to mine. I jerked her arm gently toward Despina and she resisted, a clear decline to my silent instruction.

My heart fluttered in my chest as my mind raced, my buzzing thoughts a thunder between my ears.

A beat of terror passed, and what I heard next I thought for certain was a hallucination, a trick of my mind in light of this poisoned corner of the realm.

"*Mage.*" The voice floated through the abyss, the sound far away, as though it had been carried on the wind.

I would have written it off as imaginary, for it was Brenwyn's voice calling to me, a sure impossibility, if not for the tensed reaction Mila had the second my name landed on my ears.

Had she heard it too?

I listened for the skitter of those beasts, my heart frozen behind the weight of dread, but heard nothing.

"Mage, I'm here. Come out," she called again, the sound a floating drift, a ghost of a voice.

I shook my head feverishly, iron chains of terror keeping my feet locked in place. I would not. Mila was hurt because the spirits of the veil had distracted me the last time my legs had room to stretch. The phantoms here would not fool me into betraying those I'd sworn to protect again.

"Mage." The sound came through differently this time, my name beginning in an echo but landing firm in the cavern with us, as though she had been pulled through the realm on a curled shadow.

My eyes burned as the glow of a faelight lit, illuminating the space. Mila and I both started, wincing and shielding our eyes from the intensity of the light, but we held our tongues, neither one making a sound.

"Oh, goddesses, how long have you been in here?" Brenwyn spoke clearly, a corporeal voice.

Surprise flushed me and I worked to clear my vision. The scene before me blurred, the lines of the wraith wobbling for a moment until finally the image of her rested steady before me. Despina sat on her other side, having moved over to make room for her arrival.

Des must have sensed the change and moved to make space for her arrival. Not a hallucination.

Brenwyn was here. How had she done it? Where had she come from? There was no magic here.

I strained my ears, listening for the monsters surely stirred by her sound, but they remained silent, dormant.

A tangle of relief and dread coiled through me, the contrast between the two free flowing emotions dizzying me.

"How did you—" I began, my voice strained, a croak from underuse.

"Use magic? Your guess is as good as mine. I need to get you out of here. Why are you crammed in here like this? What happened?"

"The beasts," I managed. "The beasts, they hunt with sound, move like shadows. They've been out there, so we've been trapped."

"What beasts?" Brenwyn asked, her voice laced with confusion. "There's nothing out there. The others are—"

Before Brenwyn had time to finish her explanation, something changed, the tension in the air pulled taut. Even the mindless dripping of the water in the corner of the cove seemed to cease.

She froze, and Despina's eyes stretched wide just as a blanket of gooseflesh flecked my skin, a tight coil in my chest winding its way to my throat.

And then the earth shook, the walls of the cove trembling as rubble fell from the ceiling. The sensation was immediately followed by a thunderous sound, an explosion just outside the cove's entrance.

"*Fuck*," Brenwyn hissed, spinning on her heel to find a way out of this pocket of space.

Chunks of the mountainside began to fall in the main cavern, large enough to block the small opening to our hiding space. The sound rattled my ears, vibrated in my sternum.

"We have to go. *Now*," Brenwyn instructed.

And we moved. Brenwyn shifted with her faelight to allow us out first. I pushed Mila ahead. She scrambled on, followed by Despina, and I moved next, the rough earth scraping my hands and knees as I crawled through the opening. Brenwyn followed closely behind, her faelight illuminating the larger cove.

Just as I rose to my feet, an enormous piece of earth cracked free, the sound deafening before it fell from the ceiling. It thundered to the ground, crashing violently before splintering.

"Go!" Brenwyn urged.

We ran, all of us dodging falling debris as we made our way back to the open spans of blight. The territory that had once been a lush and beautiful forest was now nothing more than a charred desert. Terror gripped me as adrenaline moved my muscles.

Despina spilled into the open first, followed by Mila, then myself, Brenwyn falling to my side.

To my surprise, the scene we entered into held no chaos, no horrifying monsters. Unease settled over my bones as I tried to categorize what lay before me and the crumbling of the cove at my back.

The others. Aurelia, Atlas, Gengi, Emrys, Avery, and an unfamiliar creation fae all stood scattered across the plane at the base of the blackened mountainside. All eyes were on us with mixed expressions, but Aurelia looked up, her neck craned with a furrowed brow on her face.

"What the fuck was that?" Brenwyn shouted as she moved toward the others.

I winced at the sound, but still, the monsters remained at bay. The lingering unknown kept the crawl of anxiety vivid over my skin.

Why? Where were they? Had I imagined the entire thing? Had the delusion of the veil splintered my reality that significantly?

I looked to Mila, whose eye had swollen shut, her face riddled with bruises, her ability to heal stunted here.

I had not imagined it, then. Her injury was real. It had been real.

"Thank the goddesses," Gengi exclaimed.

"*Hey!*" Brenwyn shouted irritably as she approached Reia. "Did you do that? That cavern almost collapsed on us!"

The firebird kept her eyes to the mountain and shook her head, a dazed and confused expression crumpling her brow as she brought a strange metal device to her chest.

"Reia, what is it?" Atlas asked.

"We need to go," she said, her tone low, a tremble of sincere terror there.

My own senses set on edge at her warning; fear a poison slithering through my veins.

The sound of skittering above launched my heart from my chest, my breath a solid weight behind it.

"Now!" Aurelia screamed, her expression cracking as her eyes stretched wide.

I turned over my shoulder in time to see them. Dozens of the enormous beasts slithered from a crack in the mountainside. They moved impossibly fast, some completely corporeal as they raced from the black hole from which they came, others seeming to slink through shadows, curling down the mountain on a spilling mist of abyss.

Terror froze my feet for a fraction of a moment as my attention remained stuck on the monsters, long enough for Despina's grip on my arm to jerk me away.

The others were running, taking off into the distance, but there was nowhere to go. I knew that. We'd have to reach the farther planes near the forest. And if we made it far enough, the spirits would disorient us, take us back to the mountainside where those things could reach us.

But we had little choice. I urged my feet to carry me on, a desperate flight to escape the scorpion-like beasts of the void.

CHAPTER 62
BRENWYN

The very hollow of my bones rattled in time with the horrific buzz of the nightmare monsters as they clamored from their hole. They were terrible. Enormous, crustaceous looking monsters with slithering bodies, serpentine heads, skittering legs, great pincher claws, and the daggerlike tail of a scorpion. The sound of their movement muted everything else—the firebird's screaming, the thunder of feet as they took off to get away. All of it was deadened as my attention narrowed on the crack in the mountain.

Something called to me there. In the depths of the dark hole. Some distant bellow to my soul. My shadows raged within me, a wild beast taking root, suffocating my shock, my terror. The surge in my well of magic nearly swept my feet from underneath me.

I stayed frozen, staring, trapped in the horrendous break of this moment for a beat too long. The sound of chaos cracked my daze. The creatures were moving too fast. They were already at the base of the mountain, curling through shadow, slithering as though made of fast-moving liquid.

My eyes snapped to the firebird, her voice piercing over the sound of the monsters, holding her ground with Atlas at her shoulder, his weapon brandished.

That break in my concentration was all it took for the creatures to overwhelm the space between us and the cliffside off the mountain. The skittering of their legs over stone overwhelmed my senses as the firebird wielded the source in her hand, a torrent of energy sending her hair up around her head as one of the creatures charged them.

I turned my attention with enough time to curl my shadows, whip them into existence as a deadly weapon, a blade to reach out to sever the head of the beast that had crawled its way toward me. The thing screeched, the timbre curling my blood before it dissipated into wisps of shadow. Two more followed while others moved past me. Panic flooded my veins, and I called to my well, curling into the shadows myself. I bled into the ether as I dodged the snapping pinchers of one to land behind it, slicing its daggerlike tail off with a whip of my blade of night.

It reared and turned to snap at me, but I curled into the shadow again, my vivid magic aiding my quicksilver movement. Within a beat, I pulled myself together to land and sever the head of both beasts on me before they had a chance to see where I'd gone.

A scream sounded in the distance, and I spun my attention, desperate to find the source of distress.

Laz lay not far behind on their back, holding each pincher of one of the creatures in their hands while they worked to keep hold, keep themselves under the beast enough to avoid its dagger tail.

I curled into the shadows and pulled myself together on top of the creature, piercing its back with my blade. Before it could fade into a mist of black, I bled through the shadows again to land near Laz's head.

"Go!" I helped them to their feet and pushed them on.

They stumbled with terror in their eyes as they fled in the other direction. I turned on my heel to find the others. To try to get control of the chaos as it rattled through me.

Mila fought near Atlas. I thought she'd run off into the distance with the others, but none of them had made it very far. I marked Emrys and Avery, still holding their own with Gengi firing arrows to keep the monsters at bay. I then turned my attention to the firebird.

The only goddess-damned person here who could do anything about this, get any of us out alive.

She flung the great scorpions back with waves of her arms, tore their heads from their bodies with seemingly nothing more than a passing thought, launched bursts of fire at beast after beast while Atlas fought them off her back with his blade.

I scrambled as another approached, my awareness on edge and prepared to fight, my muscles alight with adrenaline, but the thing moved around me, passing by as though I were not even there.

Confusion settled over me, and I turned, hearing more skittering, but the next passed me again in favor of the firebird, who was getting completely overwhelmed by the hoard of them.

Why is she fighting like that? She's going to get them all killed.

"Do something!" I screamed at the firebird, my voice a tatter in my throat as anger spiked my blood.

The sound landed across the clearing, and the firebird's attention snapped to me for a flicker of a moment, but that was all it took to ruin everything.

I saw it happen before I heard it, the explosion of her

magic, the impact to her chest as though the power of the source had taken root inside her and found the cage of her torso not big enough to contain it. She was blown off her feet, and a solid curtain of energy ricocheted off her. The force of it sent Atlas and Mila flying, then all the monsters around them to land a significant distance away.

The firebird hit the ground, her head cracking against the packed earth, and the sound dropped out of the world for a tense beat of a moment before the explosion hit my ears, thundered through my core, rattled my bones.

Everything changed. Those things shifted their targets, every single one of them turning from where they were to skitter to the firebird. A scream cracked my throat, and I watched as Atlas rose, lunging to sprint after them, to somehow protect her from the claws of death with nothing but his blade.

She managed to rise to her feet, her entire arm coated in blackened magic, the veins curling under the line of her sleeve.

My instinct carried me from there. Within a heartbeat, I was moving through the shadows, curling faster than I had ever done before. The second my feet hit the ground in front of her, my blades of shadow cut out.

Her fire lashed behind me, the heat scalding as it lit the space. She charred the ones nearest me.

"What are you doing?" she screamed.

"Helping," I hollered back.

Atlas made it to us, and one of them overcame him.

Reia screamed so viscerally I thought the sound might split the realm. I turned on my heel and split myself into shadows to pull myself back together at its side, severing its head just as its pincher meant to secure itself around Atlas's chest.

"Get the fuck out of here," I shouted.

"No!" he protested, and another scream tore the space in the distance.

Atlas turned over his shoulder as another cry rent the air, causing a pang of panic through my chest.

Someone was hurt.

Aurelia released a wild shout, and the few monsters around blew back at the force of her magic. Her frantic energy opened enough space to get a clear view of the horror before me.

A monster flung a body into the air, the frail fae flopping lifelessly, limp blonde hair dangling in her face as its pincher tossed her up higher than should have been possible. Before anyone had time to move, its tail shot forward, piercing her through the middle, taking her body to the ground with a vicious *thwack*.

Dead. Mila lay dead on the ground. Body broken, pinned to the earth like an insect caught by a predator.

Mage screamed, lunged for her, but Despina held her back, dragged her along all while keeping her eyes trained on the fallen fae. It was only moments before creatures overwhelmed her body enough to conceal her from view.

I did not have time to settle into the nausea rolling through me, the horror.

Atlas turned with an anger on his expression born straight out of the underworld as he impaled a creature I had not realized had gotten so close.

"Atlas, get them out of here!" the firebird begged, her voice a ragged plea as she worked to keep the monsters off us.

He did not reply.

"Atlas," I called. His attention turned to me, a soft flicker of surprise over his expression. "I've got her. Go, we can hold them back."

"Please!" the firebird screamed.

I turned to look at her, the agony on her expression, the darkness as it coiled through her. It was the same expression

Asteria had taken on anytime her monster had broken free of her skin.

There was no more time. The firebird screamed, her head hanging back between her shoulders as her flame rose from her feet. It raced to devour her, consumer her whole. The light of it sent the beasts nearest skittering away, and Atlas lunged for her, tears streaking his cheeks. I gripped his arm, holding him still with as much strength as I could muster.

The firebird twisted into the flame, a blinding light consuming her entirely, and the fire swelled. Bigger and bigger, the ball of flame grew. Within just a few blistering moments, the shape of a wing curled free from the inferno, then the other.

The true firebird broke out of its cage. The monstrous bird of reds, oranges, and golds stretched its enormous wings, the lengths of which were unfathomable. She unfurled them, and her talons curled into the blackened earth, the source stone still in her grip. Gengi's conduit was gone, likely obliterated with the explosion. She tipped her head, and her cry split the sky. Her bird form stood nearly thirty feet tall, a force to be reckoned with.

"She's got this, Atlas. Get out. *Get them out*," I urged, the tone of my voice nearly a plea.

I did not wait to see if he'd listened. The monsters flooded her, moved toward her faster than they had before. Every one of them attacked as if drawn to her. She cried again as the ones nearest managed to nip at her wings, but she beat them furiously and a wave of fire flowed from the feathers, the liquid heat curling through the beasts at her side, disintegrating them with ease. My muscles itched to take me with the others, to get away to safety, but something held me firm.

She was incredible, a fury of the goddesses, but still they overwhelmed her. We needed her. What if they were too much for even this version of her?

Fuck.

My feet carried me on, my legs pumping as I raced to her aid. My shadows curled left and right to get them off her, give her a chance to use her wild booms of magic to take out hoard after hoard.

I fought with all the strength I had in me. Every fiber of my being, every shaking muscle moved to kill the bastards, send them back to wherever it was they had come from.

Exhaustion pulled at my muscles, and it seemed as though no amount of fighting thinned them. They just kept coming. Over and Over. I sliced, hacked, moved through shadows. I curled myself through darkness to land closer to the firebird, trying to fend them off her feet. It seemed they were after the source, which she held cradled in one foot.

My heels hit the earth, and I moved to slice at a daggered tail before it pierced her, my movements cut short as blinding agony sliced at my back, a stabbing wound laced with a venomous, searing pain.

I screamed and swerved before the dagger tail had time to sever my spine. The slicing monster still split my side as I moved. It opened a deep, cavernous laceration at my side. Blood poured from the wound as my knees buckled under me.

The firebird screamed into the air, and I tried to move, to rise to my feet, to blend with the shadows, but a pincher caught my arm. Bone snapped and searing agony blinded me as the thing flung me through the air.

Terror gripped me and the taste of death coated my tongue. This was it; it was going to pin me to the earth just like Mila.

Asteria's image flashed before my mind's eye. How disappointed she would be.

But it was not a dagger tail that caught me as I moved through the air. Instead, it was the forceful impact of the firebird's talons as they plucked me from the momentum. The shock forced the oxygen from my lungs, and the sound of great, booming wings thundered through my ears, the air around me sent up in whirling torrents.

I rose higher, the pain in my side blinding, my broken arm dangling below me as I watched the ground move away. The creatures coiled and raged, but they had no prey. My eyes found the others below in the distance, running far way, none of the beasts after them now.

The firebird. She has me.

Relief washed over my senses, but the pain did not fade. The fire of venom only overwhelmed me. My vision spun and blurred darkness pushed against the edges of my line of sight.

I tried to hold them open, hold onto consciousness, but the effort was fruitless. The pain pulled me under, a blanketed abyss drowning my senses.

CHAPTER 63
CALLISTA

Ding.

The great bell tower struck at the break of high noon. The booming sound marked the beginning of what could possibly be my end.

Dong.

The sound reverberated through my skull, ringing out in the hollow space between my ears, deep within the chamber of my chest.

Numb. That was what it felt like to be escorted to your execution with your hands tied behind your back, a collar of deadstone around your neck.

The decoration was symbolic, surely meant to mock Elea. It was a color of what was meant to be around her neck, what was already around Asteria's.

Ding.

Asteria had known this would happen, that he'd take action once Lazuli had disappeared. We'd planned for this. We were ready for this.

Dong.

The males at my sides pushed me ahead, urging my feet to fall over one another. The sudden jerk of my muscles stung; the pain of my lingering injuries crumpled my expression.

I must not have been walking fast enough.

Ding.

I swallowed the echo of horror and lifted my chin, forcing my shoulders to remain taut, pulled back against the strain of dread.

The corridor to the courtyard was closing, the end growing too near.

Dong.

The nobles would all be there. From every trade city and the surrounding areas. He'd shown me the execution notice. I was the bastard daughter of the *false king.*

Anorin.

My father.

He had not been a kind male, but he had not deserved to be murdered like he had. He would have done something about this. He would not have allowed one of his own to be brought to slaughter like this.

The male to my right opened the door and we stepped out into the courtyard. The sun was too harsh, too bright. I couldn't see.

Ding.

And my mother had been even less warm, but she hadn't deserved to die either. Maybe this was meant to bring everything full circle.

My eyes adjusted and I saw the pyre, on top of a platform, a stage. The bundles of kindling at the base of a pole.

Execution by fire.

Symbolic.

Dong.

Ragnor stood to the side, watching with a hard expression

as the guards brought me closer. The crowd parted for us, all turning their attention to gawk at the traitor princess.

I did not meet a single one of their eyes.

Ding.

Asteria was there, too. Her expression blank, far off, unthinking as she stood at his shoulder, a weapon ready to be wielded.

She will not let me die.

Dong.

We reached the stage, and the guards hauled me to the pyre. I could hear nothing but the sound of my own blood in my ears.

I did not resist as they latched my chains behind the pole.

Asteria will not let me die.

Ding.

Ragnor spoke. I couldn't hear him. Not the words. Just the sound of his voice as it rang out over the crowd.

My heart picked up its pace as a guard reached for a torch, standing, waiting for Ragnor to finish speaking.

Asteria will not let me die.

Dong.

The sound of Ragnor's voice stopped booming and the guard turned to face me, the heat of the torch wild against my skin.

He met my eye, something cold facing me from within the depths of his soul.

The edge of the crescent moon on his chest peaked from below the dip in his tunic.

Panic lanced me, breaking the haze for the first time. My skin flushed with ice and my breathing hitched as he began to lower the torch.

Asteria will not let me die.

A whoosh of air dusted my chin, the prickling sensation of

magic pulling at the hair on my arms, and the flame on the torch went out. I must have imagined it. My mind must have protected me from what was to come.

But no, the guard looked to it with confusion in his eyes. A murmur broke out among the crowd, and Ragnor stepped forward.

Without warning, an arrow pierced the guard's chest, straight through his spine to his heart. He released a soft grunt just before the life left his eyes and he fell to the ground in a heap of death.

Screams echoed through the crowd, and my senses blazed to life. Chaos, the nobles moving, running, Ragnor shouting in panic, trying to rally them still.

Across the courtyard, my eyes found the source of the arrow. Perched on the roof of the palace with nimble feet and a dark cloak over his shoulders, he slunk back into shadows just as I spotted him.

Gengi.

They're here.

Panic poisoned my veins. Every one of my muscles tensed as I scanned the moving crowd for any sign of any of them.

Elea.

Atlas.

Brenwyn.

Laz.

I saw none of them.

Ragnor had only announced my execution at the beginning of the week. A rushed, furious retaliation against the control he'd lost with Laz and Brenwyn.

They'd gathered themselves quickly.

I hadn't been sure they'd have time.

I struggled against my bindings, and the light touch of fingers on my wrists made me shout, jerk to move them away. I turned over my shoulder and saw no one. Confusion laced my expression before my eyes marked a key floating in midair. It wedged itself into the keyhole on my manacles and they fell to the kindling at my feet.

I pulled my hands around and someone's grip held my wrist before placing they key in them.

"Get that thing off your neck," a phantom voice rang out.

No, not a phantom.

"Emrys?" I could not stop my throat from spilling her name, the excitement in my core vibrant at the realization that my friend stood with me, her magic concealing her from view.

Frantic energy fueled my muscles, and I hurried to remove the collar, fumbling with the key. It would not be long before someone realized my hands were free. Just as I got the key in its hole, my eyes landed on Oberin, who stormed from the depths of the moving crowd, thundering toward me with a look of hatred on his expression.

He climbed the pyre, and I reared my foot back, sending my full weight into the side of his face as I turned the lock at my neck.

He howled in pain as the impact cracked his cheek and his head snapped back, but my blow hadn't knocked him free. Instead, he scrambled to grip my calf, his nails digging into my flesh.

The collar snapped free, and I ripped it from my neck, keeping my grip on the thing as I threw my full weight into swinging the stone into his arm. Bone snapped and he released me.

I waited for the swell of my long dormant magic, but it did not come. Instead, it sputtered to life, a small flicker within my core, a breath of what it once was after months of my inability to restore my magic in the moonlight.

Panic curled tighter and I looked to Asteria, but she was not there.

My heartbeat stuttered in shock. I moved to mark Ragnor, but he was gone as well.

My eyes met the crowd, and I found the nobles had mostly scattered, only guards lingering, weapons brandished, most of them standing by, waiting for some direction. A few made their way to the pyre.

I braced myself, working to control the coil of magic in my veins, call my whips to existence to protect myself, but the effort was a strain.

I did not have to defend myself, though. Another arrow shot from the distance, taking a guard out with vivid aim through the skull. The other tumbled to the ground with a scream of agony as an invisible Emrys slit the back of his knees. He rolled over and a small, almost imperceptible blade sliced at his jugular.

He bled out on the ground just feet before the pyre.

More chaos. The remaining nobles scurried away, and the guards scrambled, most of which were charging toward me.

I had to move.

I rallied my focus and took off down the stairs to the court-yard, ducking under a guard, taking out his knees to send him flying overhead as I made my way toward the only exit.

The entire courtyard was closed in with fifty-foot walls. I'd have to get through the palace to leave. My magic was nowhere near strong enough to *ephemerate* myself, let alone Emrys. I knew the palace though; I would make it.

I ran, dodging guard after guard, hoping to slip out before Elea showed herself. This was a trap. He would take her if she came for me. I needed to get out.

I thundered on, my frenzy-driven determination urging me, but before I made it more than halfway, my feet stopped short as Ragnor appeared from whisps of shadow before me. My heels scraped against the earth as I halted my flight, my heart lodged in my throat as his wicked sneer captured my attention.

"Going somewhere?" he crooned, a knowing expression on his face. "Not until I get what I want out of this charade, I'm afraid."

Anxiety pricked at me.

A trap. It was a trap.

She'd come for me. He'd take her.

"And your fated has still not shown her face. I think we should raise the stakes, shall we? Mouse?" he called over his shoulder, and a crack sounded as Asteria pulled herself into existence at his side.

"Destroy her, will you? Whatever it takes to get your sister out here to fight like a grown fae."

And with that, he stepped back, giving room for Asteria to release shadows from her palms, the slithering tendrils of night looming with deadly threat.

"Asteria," I called, my tone shaking as I took a step back.

Her eyes were void, her expression slack. She wasn't there. How could she not be there?

"Asteria, can you hear me?"

She reached out with a lazy hand to wrap a tendril of night around my neck. It locked itself firmly in place and wound with vivid strength, forcing the air from my lungs, cutting off my oxygen supply.

I sputtered and gripped at the substance, trying to get my fingers under it, but they slipped through the shadow. There was nothing to hold on to.

My eyes bulged and I called to my own magic, but a only flicker of a spark danced within my well, not enough to pull from. I tried, strained with all my energy to get the magic to my fingertips, to do anything.

But my vision began to dim, the edges blurring as my head split, the pressure there immense.

A heat curled over my face, a blistering torrent of wind. The sensation was followed by a glowing light, the blaze of fire.

The flame whipped at Asteria's hand, and the shadows released. I sucked in a lung-stretching breath and sputtered for air, my knees nearly buckling, but a sturdy presence supported me with small, strong, invisible hands as Emrys steadied my weight.

She pulled me to the side, and I fell to my knees as I tried to gather my bearings, center my thoughts. I looked up from the curtain of my hair to find Asteria and Aurelia locked in a stalemate of power, fire crashing against solid walls of shadow as the two guardians raged against one another.

Elea was goddess-like, an embodiment of living fire. Her hair, longer than I remembered, swirled behind her as the hot air of her flame raged on. Dread cracked my chest as my eyes tracked veins of black along her arms, stemming from entirely blackened hands. Her expression twisted with a kind of fury I'd never seen there before.

I scrambled to make sense of it, tame the wild thundering behind my heart. I called to her, but she did not hear me. Her rage was a living beast as her magic raged, locked in battle with her sister.

Her magic.

I sucked in a breath and reached inward; the crack of the bond there bright as I hurdled myself through it. Her magic coiled on the other side, a well that was not her own resting at the end of the tunnel. Its heat encouraged me, coaxed me toward it, begged me to use it for my own.

"I need to get you out of here," Emrys's voice rang close to my ear, and I shook my head, pulling myself to my feet.

I felt her hand on my elbow, and her flush of magic washed

a cold tingle over my skin at the contact. I gasped, surprise roiling through me as my body faded into nothing, a blanket of invisibility concealing me from sight.

"Let's go," Emrys urged, tugging my arm along.

I stumbled over my feet. Everything moved so quickly. My mind struggled to keep up with the whirling chaos.

The guards focused their efforts on Elea, and I could now see Atlas and Avery at her back, both fighting furiously with their blades to keep the palace brutes at bay.

My heart lifted at the sight of my brother, alive and well. Strong.

Emrys dragged me along, and my attention spun, finding Despina and Mage on either side of the door to the palace. Despina's luminous amulet was bright at her chest as she used her glowing magic to keep a shield over the entryway, preventing more guards from spilling free. Mage used coiling vines to fend off the ones who approached, the ones trying to get to Despina to break her concentration.

I tried to spot Brenwyn or Laz, but before I found any sign of them, my attention spun as Emrys pulled me along. I jerked back, thunder in my chest, my feet resisting the escape as a desperate need to help kept me planted. Elea still raged against Asteria, explosions of fire ricocheting off the lunar guardian's magic, the sound booming, the heat blistering across the courtyard.

Movement on the wall above her caught my attention, and I froze as my focus registered the threat.

I ripped my arm free of Emrys's grip and her magic faded as my legs carried me toward the thrall, terror gripping my heart.

"*Move!*" I screamed, my throat tearing at the cut of my desperate wail.

That coil in my chest, the tunnel to her magic blazed, a warm flush of energy settling over my veins.

A pair of guards carried a weapon I recognized from my time with the army here. They hauled it up between them, the weight almost taking them with it. That frenzy, dread, and panic washed over me. None of us would be able to defend ourselves if they dropped that thing.

I was too far away to do anything; my legs would not carry me fast enough. Elea pushed back to create some distance between herself and the wall, but Atlas still fought too close. If they dropped that thing, he'd be in its direct path.

It would kill him on impact.

"Atlas!" I screamed as I reached for the magic, and the fire I knew sat at the other end of our bond waited for me to wield it.

Atlas looked up at my voice and the distraction cost him. A blade caught his ribs, I screamed, and he cried out as he curled over to thrust his sword through the chest of the assailant.

The guards activated the device, and I saw Gengi running across the roof at full speed. He leapt through the air with impressive precision and fired an arrow midflight, the weapon striking one of the guards in the chest before Gengi landed on the wall with unwavering balance.

But it was too late. They'd already activated it. The still standing male worked to push it off the wall and it tumbled just a fraction of a moment before Gengi's arrow struck him. The poisonous bomb fell, and with it went my heart, encased in a tomb of terror as it sunk into the pit of my stomach.

My legs still carried me on, closing the distance but not fast enough. I reached up, flinging an arm out as the pressure of heat broke free of its chamber. A concentrated ball of fire flew overhead, aimed immediately for the bomb. I prayed to the goddesses I'd sent it fast enough, that it would get there in time, that my fire would burn away the poison I knew would render all of us useless if it made its way to the ground.

The bomb fell halfway down the wall as my flame connected with it.

The sound was deafening. It rattled my brain, forced pressure around my head. Within just a heartbeat of time, the air shook. Atlas and Avery were blown off their feet first, along with the guards at their blades.

Elea turned at the sound just in time for the impact to send her hurdling through space as well. Then me.

The solid wall of magic from the weapon hit me squarely in the chest and I landed on my hip, bracing my fall with my arms on plush grass as a ringing in my ears spun my focus.

I heaved great breaths, a wild desperation urging me to gather my bearings. I managed to sift through the dread-weighted panic enough to lift my eyes. The scene had been leveled. Everyone who had just been standing lay on the ground. I found Atlas and Elea. Atlas's wound bled but they were both alive. Relief flushed me just before fear threatened to choke me again. My vision spun as the fragrance of anise wafted through my senses. The debilitating poison.

I wasn't fast enough.

The sound was stolen from my ears, a thick haze coating my attention as I tried to make sense of everything.

Everyone lay on the ground, disoriented, slow-moving, except Asteria.

How had the impact not rattled her? Why had the poison not stolen her ability to move?

She stood stoic, staring at the pyre, her expression no longer a façade, the life I'd seen before flickering there now.

I followed her gaze to find Ragnor and the cyphin witch. The witch wielded that terrible black magic. It plumed from

Ragnor's chest in menacing tendrils of poison as it whipped through the air around him.

I couldn't understand it. There was no device, no fae for him to drain the magic of. Just Ragnor, the witch, and the black magic.

I tried to bring myself to my feet and every one of my muscles ached, felt heavy, weighted, invisible chains keeping me slow and lagging. The pain started then, in my lungs, spreading through my chest. This magic was meant to paralyze, just long enough to get the upper hand in a battle.

And it was working. He'd won.

Hadn't he? Why was he still on that stage?

It all happened so fast. My mind could not categorize the odd, slowed tresses of time. Something strange twisted the air near the pyre, a black whirl of void as it seemed to crawl through the pockets of the realm. The witch screamed, and Ragnor echoed the sound, though not much of it reached my ears. The hole stretched faster than I could keep track of.

Confusion colored my focus; I couldn't make sense of what I was seeing.

It was only moments before something pushed through, the claw of a great beast stretching the space of the realm. It curled through until it tore through the air, falling into existence. A great scorpion-like monster skittered over the spans of the pyre and Ragnor released a cry, his expression lifting with something like victory as he turned to the creature.

Somehow, it was tethered to him. It seemed to level with him, listen to what he had to say. I could feel it.

And without warning, the thing turned its attention, moving like liquid night across the courtyard, closing the distance to me faster than I could have possibly imagined.

CHAPTER 64
ASTERIA

It had taken everything I had reserved deep within the well of my endurance to resist his demands, to ignore his call to make me shift to my raven. It had hurt and nearly rendered me unconscious, but I had done it. Though, I could not stop using my magic at his command, and watching my sister struggle against my well-practiced power severed my heart in two. But I had not shifted.

I pushed against every demand, blocked out his voice, held firm against the pain of denying him his monster.

I would not shift.

It was agony, but that was fine. I would let it kill me if I had to. It would be better if it killed me.

But then that weapon exploded, the impact meant to disorient those around, knock them off-kilter, then fill their lungs with a poison that would steal their magic, leave them unable to move.

I was immune. Years of training with the poison at Ragnor's will, to keep me strong in the face of the weapon's effects had primed me for that.

480

After everyone remained incapacitated, I stayed where I was, unmoving. Ragnor called me, tried to pull me to stand behind him, but he could not.

I'd trained for that moment, too. I would not fall victim to his whims today.

And as he tried to split the fabric of worlds, wielded the witch's magic with the poisoned source to get to that nightmare realm, pull power from that place, absolute shock coated my disposition.

He hadn't tried since he'd failed so miserably in the mountain. That rift in the realm still bled freely. He'd been in over his head then, with no way to repair the damage there. The nightmare world poisoned our land, the creatures there sucking the life from our forest. He'd left it like that, afraid of anything he couldn't control.

But now he managed it, called to the void with determination, a precision I had not expected.

I did not think he'd have the strength to try.

But he'd drained Callista nearly dry.

I should have known not to underestimate the black void of vengeance, greed.

I scanned the aftermath of the bomb. I had not seen Brenwyn. Or Laz. My heart fissured, out of relief or fear, I was not sure.

Either they were dead or left behind for some reason.

I prayed to the goddesses it had been the latter. I would not survive a realm without Brenwyn in it.

Aurelia tried to stand. Determination gritted her expression, and she managed to fight against the agony I knew she felt in the face of the poison.

Always such a fighter.

She moved for Ragnor, and I saw then in her hand what I'd felt the moment she'd arrived.

A shard of the source.

Where she had retrieved it from, I could not guess. The other shards were accounted for, actively being used as weapons to aid in his goal of breaking through to that realm.

Aurelia had one though. A blackened crystal strengthening her stores of magic. She could level him with it if she had the control. If she weren't near incapacitated. I was tempted to let her try. But before she could make it a few laborious steps, a horrific snapping sound focused my attention back to the pyre.

The realm split. He'd done it. Another rift. The beginning of another blight. And the monster that poured from the darkness was just as horrific as it had been in my memory.

Terror lit my core, instinct gripping me as he used his tether, somehow already connected to the beast to give it direction.

It moved for Callista, who lay on the ground, scrambling to get her muscles to move enough to defend herself.

She would not make it.

I will not let you die.

The promise I'd offered her in her cell moments before they'd come to take her rang out in my memory and instinct gripped me.

One last push against his hold, the last of the energy I had in my stores. That was all it would take. I could do it.

I struggled, stretched my endurance as far is it would go, pressed my resolve against the tether he held on me. It almost suffocated me, my consciousness fading, my will slipping, until it cracked.

A breath of fresh air, the first true flicker of relief I'd felt in ten years.

I'd done it.

If only for a moment.

I released a cry of desperation and coiled all the magic I

could muster with my free will and marked every one of the rebels within a moment. I sent the energy coiling for them, pulling from the magic of the collar around my neck.

The *source crystal* around my neck. The very lifeblood of the realm that kept me tethered to him, kept him alive with a tether to my store of magic.

I used it now, begged it to aid me, to support me just once. Just long enough to help them. I drew from it with as much force as I could. It recoiled, pushed against my efforts, but I forced it on.

I wrapped tendrils of the vibrant, raging energy around each of them and without another thought, another moment for the magic to change its mind, I sent each of them hurdling across the realm, the cracks of each of their disappearances deafening as I *ephemerated* them through space.

Callista disappeared with just a fragment of time left before the beast's pincher would have snapped around her middle.

There would be hell to pay. He'd not yet known I had any free will, any ability to push back against his hold.

He was afraid of anything he could not control. Fear pushed people to do the most horrific things, brought out the more blackened corners of their souls.

Good. Maybe he'd kill me for it.

Maybe with my death, the tether he had to my magic would snap. Maybe the rift in the realm would sew itself back together.

And maybe, if the goddesses were at all listening, that would kill him, too.

I turned my head, my energy spent as I looked to the pyre, my attention forced as his tether snapped back in place.

I felt it lock tight, the iron-clad connection a prison in which my mind had no reprieve.

The rage, betrayal, and furious disbelief I saw radiated in the pits of his black eyes rivaled even that of the very spirit of death.

Good.

Let him kill me for it.

BOOK THREE AWAITS

The Shattered Source Series Continues with

The Fated & Fallen - Pre-Order Now

Releasing 6.10.25

ALSO BY HANNAH DANIELLE

Figure You Out - Pre-Order Now

Releasing 12.3.24

STAY UP TO DATE

Scan the QR code to stay up to date on the works of Hannah Danielle through her newsletter.

ACKNOWLEDGMENTS

Where to begin? I cannot express to all my amazing, beautiful, wonderful readers how grateful I am for you. It took me two years to write this book. I hope it was worth the wait, and I hope I did the characters justice. Their story has only just begun, and I cannot wait for you to get through to the end.

That being said, I want to thank my mother. I have always had a place to be myself with you. In my adult life knowing how rare that is, how uncommon it is to find a best friend in your mother solidifies how fortunate I am to have you. Thank you for reading everything, hyping me up, and being my greatest supporter.

Thank you to my amazing partner, K.F. Starfell. I am SO lucky to have a partner who shares my passion for writing. Not only that, but your skills as an editor really helped me to make this book shine. I love you with my whole soul. Thank you for finding me.

Thank you to Norma Gambini. Your editing skills saved me in a pinch. Your edits are always top-notch, and I love working with you. Thank you for hyping me up in my hour of need and polishing up this book before the world got their hands on it.

Thank you to Jamecia Bellamy for sensitivity reading this project for me. Your insight moved me to tears, and I could not have done this without you.

Thank you to Lily, my best friend. You've been here since the beginning, and I love and value you so much. I can't wait to see what you do with your own author career.

Thank you to my amazing beta readers, arc readers, and street team supporters for helping me spread this story to the readers who need it most.

ABOUT THE AUTHOR

Hannah began her professional career as a music major at Westminster College. She observed one middle school choir class and quickly learned that a life as a choir teacher wasn't the path for her. She graduated from Westminster College with a bachelor's degree in sociology. After undergraduate school, she spent four years working as a salesperson at AT&T and working on her master's degree in psychology of leadership at Pennsylvania State University World Campus. Hannah received her master's just in time for the worldwide pandemic, which left her open to explore what it was she wanted out of her career and, well, life.

Like many readers who loved young adult fantasy in middle and high school who took a years-long break, the pandemic threw her back into her love of reading and writing again full force. Since then, she has taken the chance to pursue something she truly loves. She gave up on the idea of making a living out of singing or literature when she was a child, and now, as an adult, she sees that the only thing between her and success in the things that she loves is her own self-doubt, and there is no longer space in her life for that kind of negativity.

Hannah lives in Kentucky with her incredible partner, where they co-author romance stories together, parent a wonderful child, and enjoy the company of the most loving and cuddly cat in the world. She has goals of sharing her stories and art with people who need those things most in their lives.

For more information on the works of Hannah Danielle, visit hannahdanielle.com or any of the socials below!

www.ingramcontent.com/pod-product-compliance
Lightning Source LLC
Chambersburg PA
CBHW060601300726
48975CB00005B/1410